Advance Praise for *The Bookseller's Secret*

"*The Bookseller's Secret* is a delight from start to finish. Michelle Gable skillfully twines the narratives of two effervescent heroines, a modern-day author with writer's block and her literary icon, Nancy Mitford, who is struggling to pen a bestseller in the middle of the London Blitz. The result is a literary feast any booklover will savor!"

—Kate Quinn, *New York Times* bestselling author of *The Alice Network* and *The Rose Code*

"A thoroughly entertaining tale based on the life of a legendary author. With a vivid real-and-imagined cast of unforgettable characters, Gable expertly and cleverly delivers wit, humor, and intrigue in full measure on every page. What a delightful escape."

—Susan Meissner, bestselling author of *The Nature of Fragile Things*

"Michelle Gable delivers a triumphant tale that highlights the magic of bookshops and literature to carry people through even the darkest days of war. Featuring a colorful, witty, tenacious cast of characters, *The Bookseller's Secret* deftly connects two authors separated by generations while unraveling a mystery that keeps the pages turning. A delightful tribute to an intriguing historical legend."

—Kristina McMorris, *New York Times* bestselling author of *Sold on a Monday*

Also by Michelle Gable

A Paris Apartment
I'll See You in Paris
The Book of Summer
The Summer I Met Jack

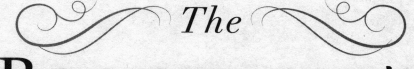

The
BOOKSELLER'S
SECRET

A Novel

MICHELLE GABLE

GRAYDON
HOUSE

GRAYDON
HOUSE®

ISBN-13: 978-1-525-81155-5

The Bookseller's Secret

This edition published by arrangement with Harlequin Books S.A.

Graydon House
22 Adelaide St. West, 40th Floor
Toronto, Ontario M5H 4E3, Canada
www.GraydonHouseBooks.com
www.BookClubbish.com

Printed in U.S.A.

Recycling programs
for this product may
not exist in your area.

For my agent, Barbara
Without you, none of this

The
BOOKSELLER'S
SECRET

THE MITFORD FAMILY

THE PARENTS

Lord Redesdale:
David Freeman-Mitford, 2nd Baron Redesdale, "Farve"

Lady Redesdale:
Sydney Bowles, "Muv"

THE SISTERS

The Novelist:
Nancy Freeman-Mitford (born 1904)

The Countrywoman:
Pamela Freeman-Mitford (born 1907)

The Fascist:
Diana, Lady Mosley (born 1910)

The Hitler Confidante:
Unity Valkyrie Freeman-Mitford (born 1914)

The Communist:
Jessica Lucy "Decca" Freeman-Mitford (born 1917)

The Duchess:
Deborah "Debo" Cavendish, Duchess of Devonshire
(born 1920)

The Lone Brother:
Thomas "Tom" David Freeman-Mitford (born 1909)

April 1946

Hôtel de Bourgogne, Paris VII

> There they are, held like flies in the amber of that moment—
> click goes the camera and on goes life; the minutes, the days,
> the years, the decades, taking them further and further from
> that happiness and promise of youth, from the hopes...and
> from the dreams they dreamed for themselves.
>
> —Nancy Mitford,
> *The Pursuit of Love*

"Alors, racontez!" the Colonel said, and spun her beneath his arm.

Nancy had to duck, of course. The man was frightfully short.

"Racontez! Racontez!"

She laughed, thinking of all the times the Colonel made this demand. *Racontez! Tell me!*

"Allô—allô," he'd say across some crackling line. *"Were you asleep?"*

He might be in Paris, or Algiers, or another place he could not name. Weeks or months would pass and then the phone would ring in London and set Nancy Mitford's world straight again.

"Alors, racontez! Tell me everything!"

And she did.

The Colonel found Nancy's stories comical, outrageous, unlike anything he'd ever known, his delight beginning first and foremost with the six Mitford girls, and their secret society. Nancy also had a brother, but he hardly counted at all.

"*C'est pas vrai!*" the Colonel would cry with each new tale. "*That cannot be true!*"

"It all happened," Nancy told him. "Every word. What do you expect with a Nazi, a Communist, and several Fascists in one family tree?"

"*C'est incroyable!*"

But her sisters and the Hon Society were the past, and this gilded Parisian hotel room was the present, likewise Nancy's beloved Colonel, currently reaching into the bucket of champagne. How had she gotten to this place? It was the impossible dream.

"Promise we can stay here forever," Nancy said.

"Here or somewhere like it," he answered with a grin.

Nancy's heart bounced. Heavens, he was ever so ugly with his pockmarked face and receding hairline, the precise opposite of her strapping husband, a man so wholesome he might've leapt from the pages of a seedsman catalogue. But Nancy loved her Colonel with every part of herself, in particular the female, which represented another chief difference between the two men.

"You know, my friends are desperate to take a French lover," Nancy said, and she tossed her gloves onto the bed. "All thanks to a fictional character from a book. Everyone is positively in love with Fabrice!"

"*Bien sûr*, as in real life," the Colonel said as he popped the cork.

The champagne bubbled up the bottle's neck and dribbled onto his stubby hands.

"You're such a wolf!" Nancy said. She heaved open the shutters and scanned the square below. "At last! A hotel with a view."

Their room overlooked the Palais Bourbon, home to the *Assemblée nationale*, the two-hundred-year seat of the French government, minus the interlude during which it was occupied by the Luftwaffe. Mere months ago, German propaganda had hung from the building: *DEUTSCHLAND SIEGT AN ALLEN FRONTEN*. Germany is victorious on all fronts. But the banners were gone now, and France had been freed. Nancy was in Paris, just as she'd planned.

"This is heaven!" Nancy said. She peered over her shoulder and coquettishly kicked up a heel. "A luncheon party tomorrow? What do you think?"

"Okay, *ma chérie, quoi que tu en dises*," the Colonel said as she sauntered toward him.

"Whatever I want?" Nancy said. "I've been dying to hear those words! What about snails, chicken, and Port Salut? No more eating from tins for you. On that note, darling, you mustn't worry about your job prospects. I know you'll miss governing France but, goodness, we'll have so much more free time!"

Nancy was proud of the work the Colonel had done as General de Gaulle's *chef du cabinet*, but his resignation made life far more convenient. No longer would she have to wait around, or brook his maddeningly specific requests. *I've got a heavy political day. LET ME SEE—can you come at two minutes to six?*

"It's really one of the best things that could've happened to us," Nancy said. "Oh, darling, life will be pure bliss!"

Nancy leaned forward and planted a kiss on the Colonel's nose.

"*On trinque?*" he said, and lifted a glass.

Nancy raised hers to meet it.

"*Santé!*" he cheered.

Nancy rolled her eyes. "The French are so dull with their toasts. Who cares about my health? It's wretched, most of the time. Cheers to novels, I'd say! Cheers to readers the world over!"

"*À la femme auteur Nancy Mitford!*" The Colonel clinked her glass. "*Vive la littérature!*"

Thanksgiving Night

Arlington, Virginia

Katie wakes up, disoriented. She doesn't know where she is, other than in the back of a car. Her phone is missing. She can't find her purse. There is a white crust on her jeans.

Cautiously, Katie wiggles into a seated position. They are on the George Washington Parkway going fifty, at least. If she's being abducted, Katie is neither nimble nor fit enough to launch herself out of the car. Her gaze darts toward the front seat, and the panic dissolves when she spots her nieces' long and glorious hair.

"Hello, friends," she says.

"Welcome back," Danielle answers. She is the older of the two sisters, by sixteen months, and the driver of the car. "Did you have a nice nap?"

"See?" says Dani's little sister, Clementine. "I told you we didn't need to have her stomach pumped."

"Aren't you a bit young to know about stomach pumping?" Katie says. At fifteen, Clem is pretty, long-lashed and freckle-nosed, but Katie still sees the snaggletoothed, Muppet-voiced kid. "Anyway, I didn't drink that much," she adds, as her stomach roils in disagreement and the night's events flash like photographs through her mind.

Thanksgiving dinner. Three tables. The forty-some people invited to feast. Katie's mother, her stepbrothers, the cavalcade of uncles and aunts. There are strangers, too. Neighbors, maybe, or distant relatives of her stepfather, Charles.

"You didn't drink that much?" Clem says, her voice high and alarmed. "What do you consider 'a lot'?"

"It was a lot," Katie admits. She's supposed to be a role model. Well, so much for that. "Listen, girls," she says, "nothing good comes from binging alcohol. You'll just end up sick, and embarrassed, and spending way too many hours obsessing over what you did."

"Okay, thanks. Good tip."

"The regret is *not* worth the brief window of fun," Katie says.

"There was a window?" asks Dani.

"We must have missed the part where you were having fun," Clem says.

Katie catches them exchanging smirks.

"Alcohol's a depressant," Clem says. "You shouldn't drink when you're sad."

"I'm not sad!" Katie insists, though she has to wonder if this is true. "More tired, than anything. But you're right, about it being a depressant."

They motor along in silence, past dark office buildings and the Arlington Cemetery. Katie squeezes her eyes shut and attempts to replay how it all went to hell. Downing two flutes of Veuve Clicquot, straight from the jump, was probably the first wrong turn.

Katie tries to remember. She sees everyone taking their seats. Katie places herself between her grandmother and Jill (Jillian?), her stepbrother's new girlfriend. An uncle poses a question. An aunt. Hackles rise. Jill or Jillian repeats a query Katie's already sidestepped two or three times. Words are exchanged.

"Shit," Katie mutters. "Did I yell at Chuck's new girlfriend?"

"You did," Dani confirms.

"It was more of a bark," Clem says. "You also told Gam-Gam to 'eff off.' Though you did not say 'eff.'"

"Oh, God," Katie groans. Her heart drops into her gut. Funny that a person can be thirty-nine and still get in trouble with their mom. "Hey, mind slowing down? You seem to be going a tad fast."

"Actually, we're going the speed limit," Dani says, and Katie can practically hear the roll of her eyes.

"Don't stress," Clem says. "Everyone understands that you're going through some crap. Plus, people always mouth off during holidays. That's what happens."

Dani nods vigorously. "It's the best reason to see extended family, T-B-H," she says.

"Yeah. And Gam-Gam didn't even seem all that upset."

"I'm sure she didn't *seem* that way, no," Katie says.

"Everyone was way more freaked out about the crying," adds Clem.

"I cried?" Katie touches her puffy, salty eyes. "There were tears?"

"Wow, you *are* drunker than you seem."

Clem smacks her sister's arm and, in a hiss, tells her to be nice.

"It was just a surprise," Clem says, and glances over her shoulder. "I mean, Gam-Gam always thinks you use your, quote, unquote, *creative license* to make things seem more dramatic than they really are."

"Your grandmother only says that when the story paints her in an unflattering light."

"But you don't seem that dramatic," Clem continues. "Far as we can tell, you're happy, like, ninety percent of the time."

"Bubbly," Dani offers.

Katie narrows her eyes. "*Bubbly.* What a horrible word. It's just a way to tell someone they're trivial, unimportant."

"Paranoid," Dani sings.

"You two have never been called 'bubbly,' am I right?" Katie says. "And do you know why?"

"Because we're shy?" Dani guesses.

"We have anxiety?" Clem tries.

"Why does all of Gen Z think they have anxiety?"

"Our formative years got a little messed up," Dani says. "As you might recall, I didn't see anyone other than Clem and my parents for almost a year."

"You guys also destroyed the environment," Clem says. "And the economy. Now we're supposed to fix it. Some might find that anxiety-inducing. God, I can't wait until normal people are old enough to vote."

"Yeah," Dani agrees. "Imagine being born in the 1900s."

"Fine," Katie says. "You might have anxiety—on some level—but the reason you've never been called bubbly is because you're both five foot nine."

"Um, okay," Dani says, and her eyes flick toward her sister.

"I'm actually five-ten," says Clem.

Katie sighs and swallows, hard. The whooshing landscape makes her sick and she sinks farther into her seat. With each passing minute, and each passing mile, the night becomes clearer, the knot of regret heavier inside. They've seen her now—each and every one of them. Yes, Katie told her mom to "fuck off," but she's also done something far worse. Katie Cabot told the truth.

Earlier that night...

McLean, Virginia

"At last! You've arrived!" her mother says. "Better late than never."

Family and friends have gathered for Thanksgiving at Little Falls Farm, Katie's mom and stepfather's wearying estate.

"It's so good to see you, darling! You look tired, though. Too thin."

Little Falls Farm isn't little. It's also not a farm but a Palladian brick monstrosity whose only "fall" is part of the zero-edge pool. On the plus side, it overlooks the Potomac, in the toniest part of the already tony McLean, and sits doors from Jackie Kennedy's childhood home.

"That woman was a saint," says Judy Cabot-Swift whenever it comes up.

Judy and Charles's guests are spread across three tables in the so-called public room, a former ballroom now outfitted with lacquered reddish-brown furniture and blue monkey wallpaper made by Hermès. Everyone is happy to be part of a large group, and the alcohol flows liberally.

Upon arriving, Katie flits from person to person, stopping no longer than the ninety seconds it takes to say hello. She is lively, and buoyant, and using every inch of her middling charm. No one asks about Armie because Katie prepared her mother weeks ago.

"He's going to visit his grandmother," Katie warned.

"WHAT!?" Judy said, eyes wide with hurt. "Doesn't he want to spend Thanksgiving with family?"

"He does and that's why he's going to Puerto Rico."

Judy accepted the news, eventually, but the lie solved only one problem and Katie can't exactly dispatch her career to a US territory. About this, she should've come up with something, and now the questions are flying at her, the very ones she'd known to expect.

"When's your next book coming out?" someone asks.

Katie smiles meekly, lifts her shoulders, and pours herself more champagne.

"What are you working on?"

Another shrug. More Veuve Clicquot. Suddenly, Katie's missing Armie in more ways than one. He's a good barrier, always quick to redirect.

"We can't wait to read what's next!"

When cocktail hour ends and dinner is served, Katie seats herself between her grandmother and her stepbrother's new girlfriend, whose name, she thinks, might be Jill. Nanny Carol is hunched over her phone, too concerned with fantasy football to worry about Katie's career prospects.

"You must have something coming out soon! It's been so long!"

Like a batter with pitches she doesn't like, Katie fouls off questions, left and right. She's skilled at this by now. After all, she's a *bestselling* author—or so her book jackets proclaim—who's not had a book out in three years.

"Come on, Katie! Spill the news!"

This, she understands, is done out of love, and the mistaken belief that "novelist" is more interesting than other jobs. No one asks her brother-in-law about being a patent attorney, that's for damned sure.

"You should do a sequel to *A Paris Affair!*"

"Oh, yes!" someone else agrees. "*A Paris Affair* is one of my all-time favorites! My book club is reading it. Again."

By the time someone presents the platter of turkey, Katie's polished off the champagne Charles left on the table.

"I'm sorry," says Chuck's lady friend. "Did you say you're a writer?"

"I've written a few things, yes," Katie mumbles. "I love your earrings. Are they real turquoise?"

Charles sidles up, just in time, a freshly opened bottle of wine in each hand. After he describes the white as "shy in aroma," and the red as earthy, or beefy, or some such, Katie gestures toward the Pinot Gris and asks for a heavy pour.

"I think they're real," Jill(ian) says, touching her earrings. "I'm an aspiring writer myself."

Great, Katie thinks, though it's possible she's said this out loud.

Katie angles herself toward Nanny Carol. "Rodgers doing all right by you today, NC?" she asks, though she doesn't really want to discuss fantasy football, especially not with her grandmother, who's been nothing but a hassle since joining her league. Incessant smack talk has turned Nanny Carol into the least popular member of the league, made worse by her first place standing and team name. No one appreciates seeing "Pussies" mocking them from atop the leaderboard, and Katie is constantly reminding them the woman is ninety-five years old. She lost her husband twenty years ago, and her only son—Katie's father— fifteen years before that. All she's left with is her daughter-in-law's family and the strangers in a fantasy football group text.

"Rodgers is *not* doing right by me," Nanny Carol gripes, jabbing at her phone. "He's not doing a G-D thing."

"You're such a screenager," Clem jokes.

"Yeah, Nanny Carol, put away the phone," Dani says.

"If I lose to Sacks in the City this week," she goes on, "then y'all can cut the lights and pull up the hearse. It'll be *goodbye, sweet world!* Over and out."

"Nanny Carol!"

"Glad to know you're not taking it too seriously," Katie says.

"I'm sorry," says Jill(ian). "I'm not trying to be a pest, but I have *so* many questions! Is there some reason you don't want to talk to me?"

Katie closes her eyes, awash in regret. What does this new girlfriend need with some failed writer giving her a hard time? The poor thing has enough problems if she's dating Chuck Swift.

"I'm sorry," Katie says. She straightens her back and throws on a smile. "I'm distracted tonight. Long week. You're Jillian, right? Or is it Jill?"

"Gillian with a hard G. Like *go*."

"Nice to meet you. Would you like bread?" Katie drops a sourdough roll onto Gillian's plate.

"I apologize if you thought I was interrupting," Gillian says, "but I'd love to pick your brain. You're a novelist?"

Katie bobs her head. "That's what they say."

"What do you write, specifically?"

"Oh, fiction. This and that. Does anyone need more wine? I'll find Charles!"

"He left six bottles on the table," Katie's sister, Britt, says.

Gillian asks what *kind* of fiction. Katie wipes her brow and pushes up her sleeves.

"Historical?" Gillian presses. "Contemporary? Domestic suspense? I'm a huge reader! All genres, really. I just enjoy a good story."

"She writes historical *and* contemporary fiction," Britt pipes in, and Katie cuts her with a glare. "What? It's true."

"Katharine, what is going on with you?" says a voice.

Half the table jumps. It's the inestimable Judy Cabot-Swift, appearing out of nowhere in her one-size-too-small zebra-print dress. "Believe me, Gillian," she says. "It's *not* just you. Katharine likes to be difficult these days, so I'll tell you myself. My daughter has written *three* novels, one of which was a *New York Times* bestseller."

Gillian's eyes swell. "That's incredible! Congratulations!"

Katie murmurs a thanks and takes several gulps of wine. She pours more and braces for what will come next.

"Three books," Gillian says, and nods approvingly. "Anything I've heard of?"

Katie slams both hands on the table. "There it is!" she says, hot with rage, despite having heard this question a thousand times, at least. "Listen, Gillian with a hard G, I just learned your name. How the hell would I know what books you've read?" For the slimmest of moments, Katie feels a lightness from having spoken the words she's repeated so many times in her head.

"For Pete's sake, Katharine," Judy says with a huff. "Gillian, I'm sure you've heard of Katie's first book. *A Paris Affair.* It's very famous."

"I'm sorry," Gillian says with a small wince. "It's not ringing any bells, but I've had quite a bit of wine!"

"You're not the only one," Dani stage-whispers to Clem.

Gillian reaches for her phone. "Maybe if I saw the cover. I'll look right now! Katie…what's your last name?" she says, and slides her thumb across the screen.

"Cabot," Judy says. "*Katharine* Cabot. Katharine with two *A*'s, like Katharine Graham."

Gillian glances up. "Do you mean Hepburn?"

"Honey," Judy says. "You live in Washington and you don't know who Katharine Graham is? You're not that young."

"Mom!" Britt yelps. "Jesus, what is wrong with everyone?"

"I'm sorry." Judy shakes her head and flails around her hands. "I forget that the *Post* hasn't been an integral part of everyone's lives. Katharine Graham was its publisher and chairwoman. She presided over it during Watergate. My late husband, Dan, insisted we name Katie after her." At mention of her son, Nanny Carol lifts her head. "He was a reporter at the *Post* during Graham's heyday," Judy continues. "Part of it, anyhow. Her heyday was pretty long. Longer than his life, in any case."

"Oh. Neat." Gillian looks down at her phone, face flushed. "Here it is! I found it! Four stars. That's pretty good."

Katie snorts. If Gillian has a drop of intellectual curiosity, she's filtering for one-star reviews.

Absolutely hated the protagonist.

Pretty sure English is not the author's first language.

This is not high literature.

The funny thing is Katie doesn't necessarily disagree.

"I'm downloading it right now!" Gillian sings. "I'll crack it open the *minute* I get home."

"You will love it," Judy says, and arches over the table. "But I must warn you…"

Katie stiffens, watching as the candlelight beats against her mother's skin, highlighting in unflattering detail the sixty-nine years she's lived.

"The book starts slowly. *Very* slowly. Everyone agrees."

"Really, Judy?" Katie says. "Do they? Everyone?"

"Ha!" Gillian chirps. "Who's to judge what's slow? Most of my favorite novels start that way! I don't need the proverbial gun in the first act. I prefer easing into books!"

For a second, Katie softens. God bless the poor girl; she's working like the devil tonight. "You're doing a great job," Katie says, and gently squeezes Gillian's hand. "Good on you. You'll need that relentless cheer if you're going to make it work with Chuck."

"Hey!" Chuck says, followed by Britt, speaking of people who are working hard that night.

"You haven't told us?" shouts a voice from two tables away. "When is your fourth book coming out?"

Katie's eyes skip around the room and she sees that, for the first time in the history of Thanksgivings, they're all part of the same conversation.

"You must have something in the works," a cousin says, "and it must be big, since you're so tight-lipped about it."

"That's truly not the case."

"Give us the scoop!"

Voices bubble, frothing to the surface in a collection of *what* and *where* and *when*. Tears prickle Katie's eyes. Someone says that his dentist has a compelling background, and she should write about him. Judy makes another mention of the book's "slow start" and Katie hops to her feet.

"Please, Mom!" she cries. "Stop! Just stop asking about my damned books! I didn't have one out this year, as everyone's rightly pointed out, and it's already too late for next year, and probably the year after that. I've tried a dozen things, and they've all failed. I think I'm done with this novel-writing experiment."

Though the admission is bleak, Katie has no compulsion to take it back, and why should she? It's the truth.

"Write a sequel to *A Paris Affair*," Judy says, predictably.

"Thank you, Mother, for that innovative idea," Katie says. "It's a miracle no one's thought of it before."

In fact, Katie would *love* to write a sequel. It'd solve ten problems, but that skill belongs to a type of writer that Katie is not.

"What will you do for money?" someone wants to know.

"Go back to my day job, I guess," Katie says.

"Grant writing?" Britt says. "That's so…dull."

"I liked it, and my goal was always to work my way up at a large not-for-profit. We're in the right city for it. I just got sidetracked by other things."

"Other things," Judy grouses. "Like your *real* dream. You loved your old job, and it paid well, yet you willingly gave it up because writing is your destiny. Honestly, Katie! What would your father think?"

"I have no idea because I last saw him when I was four." Katie exhales. "I do need to figure out some way to make money, unless you want me moving in here."

"You're always welcome!" Charles trills.

"No. She's not," Judy says. "This is hogwash. You *need* to be a writer, and Armie is perfectly capable of supporting you both. I doubt he'd even let you send out a résumé, much less buy a pair of nylons."

"Let me?"

"Nylons?" says Britt.

"I'm not sure what Armie has to do with this," Katie says as her nose tightens, and a hiccup builds in her throat. "This is my problem, not his."

"Darling, now that you're engaged, you have to agree on major life decisions. You're in this together, and for the rest of your lives. I know you like to play the lone wolf—"

"Do I?"

"Listen to your old mother. I've had two very successful marriages. I understand relationships." Without warning, Judy produces a phone, seemingly out of thin air. "That's it," she says. "I'm calling Armie. He's the only person who can talk sense into you."

Judy puts the phone to her ear and Katie lunges up onto the table. As she stretches toward her mom, something clatters. Two people scream.

"Watch out!" a guest yells.

"Oh my God!"

"The candles!"

Katie freezes, one knee in the mashed potatoes. Though she's saved herself, and the food, from a flaming candelabra, Katie's not getting away clean, not after toppling gravy across the gold-hued tablecloth. Meanwhile, the guests gawk, unblinking. They'll be telling this story for years.

"Sorry," Katie says, and slumps back into her chair. She deftly scoops the potatoes with a napkin, as if picking up dog poop.

"I'm calling Armie," Judy threatens again. "I'm calling him right now."

"You can't," Katie whispers. "We broke up."

She holds her breath, expecting a sad and respectful hush to fall across the room. Instead everyone looks at each other blankly, waiting for someone to speak. Finally, Britt tosses her hands into the sky.

"Uggggghhhh," she moans. "Not again. Don't worry, people, it'll be better by tomorrow. Can we eat now? What are we going to do about the potatoes?"

"It's different this time," Katie says. "The engagement is off. Armie moved out."

"He'll be back."

"I bought out his portion of the house."

This gets Britt's attention. "With *what*?" she says.

"You're wearing your ring," Judy notes.

Katie glances down. "You're right. All part of the costume, apparently. Ha!"

"This is hardly something to laugh about," Judy says.

"It's *fine*, Mom. All very amicable. We still talk."

"You'll be back together by Christmas," Britt says. "Anyone care to make a wager?"

Nanny Carol's hand flies into the air.

"He has a new girlfriend," Katie says. "I think they're living together. She seems very nice!"

"They're living together?" Britt says. "Jesus, when did this so-called breakup happen?"

"Six months ago."

"My, my." Judy makes a sour lemon face. "That was fast."

"Don't get any ideas, Mom. She just moved here from Chicago, and they didn't even meet until after the fact. For the record, I think it's great. Everyone needs to get on with their lives."

"Good God, Katharine," Judy clucks. "What did you do?"

"I didn't *do* anything," Katie says as tears trickle down her cheeks. "And neither did he. Sometimes things just run their course."

"Damned long course," Britt says.

"You must've done something," Judy insists. "Armie is the nicest guy in the world! Don't get mad at *me*, sweetheart. You have to admit that you can be dramatic and Armie's always so levelheaded. I can only assume you had some sort of fit, and he was good and fed up."

"That's it." Katie stands again, and tosses her napkin onto the chair. "I'm leaving. I can't do this right now. Thanks, Judy, you really know how to make a gal feel swell."

"Just speaking my truth."

"Always," Katie seethes, winded by how quickly she's switched from sadness to burning red heat. "Perhaps a touch less truth-speaking in the future. What do you think?"

"Here we go." Judy rolls her eyes. "Histrionics."

"With all due respect, Mother, I'd appreciate it if you'd…"

"Be quiet? I'm sorry, I can't."

"Fine. If you can't be quiet, maybe you should go ahead and *fuck off*."

Black Friday

Arlington, Virginia

Katie wakes up the next morning in her potato-caked jeans. On the side table is a note signed by Dani and Clem.

Call us if you need anything, they wrote. *Feel better!*

Millie the dog eagerly wags her tail at the side of the bed.

"There's my morning girl," Katie says, and scratches the dog's head, grateful to have another creature in this house.

Millie—full name Millicent—was a rescue from Thailand's dog meat trade, which explains the scars on her nose and stomach, and her missing eye. With her floppy ears and ropy, forty-pound frame, she's usually mistaken for a young yellow Lab, but her curly tail and DNA workup indicate seventy-five percent Jindo, or "Asian Village Dog." That Katie paid two hundred bucks to genetically test her dog is yet another sad fact of her life.

During the fifteen years (on and off) they were together, Armie performed a great many deeds but saved his largest generosities for the end. He let Katie buy him out of their house at a below-market price and, more importantly, she got to keep the dog.

Millie is whining now, and pawing impatiently at the bed. Katie staggers to her feet. As she swipes a sweatshirt from the floor, something glints on the dresser. Her engagement ring. She shoves it under an empty CVS bag. As Millie shimmies under the bed to retrieve her crusty, tattered toy crow, Katie tries to remember if she let her out last night. There might be a puddle—or worse—in the dining room.

"I'm sorry, Mills," she says. "Bad mom."

Katie trudges toward the kitchen, her stomach a mess. She's hungover, sure, but also afraid to see her messages, unchecked since yesterday afternoon. "God help me," she says, grabbing her phone and coat. She steps into her sheepskin boots and clips on Millie's leash. After choosing *You're Wrong About* from the list of podcasts, Katie pops in her earbuds and they venture out into the sharp, cool air.

"Can't put it off forever," Katie says, pulling up her messages.

Or can she? Who would really know?

Right away, Katie sees she's missed some forty-odd calls and texts. Everyone is predictably concerned. Did she get home okay? Does she need something to eat? It will be fine, Katie. Life has its ups and downs.

Katie opens a five-day-old message. Armie's new girlfriend is out of town, so can he come by and see Millie, maybe have her for a night? Unless she thinks it'd be too traumatic.

"Traumatic for someone," Katie says, and swallows the emotions crawling up her throat. She'd nearly convinced herself he really was in Puerto Rico.

Katie's phone buzzes with an incoming message. It's her best friend, texting from London. Although only monsters call instead of text, Katie presses the phone icon and waits for the telltale double ring.

"Oh my God!" Jojo says. "I was just thinking about you. I sent you a message!"

"That's why I called." Katie tries to smile, but the tears percolate. "I really wanted to hear your voice."

"Aw, that's sweet. What's up?"

"Not much," Katie says, and it's both a lie and the truth. "What's going on with you?"

"Almost done with the move," Jojo says. "It was barely across town but might as well have been overseas. Absolute torture. Nigel made turkey last night, the darling man. He knows how nostalgic I get for Thanksgiving even though, for the most part, my family drives me nuts."

"You're welcome to borrow mine," Katie says as Millie follows her sniffer deep into someone's boxwood. "Anytime you need them. But I get to keep Charles."

She yanks on the leash and Millie resurfaces covered in dirt and dead leaves. Katie squats to brush off her head and snout.

"Judy's a little much for me," Jojo says. "But thanks. Sounds as though your Thanksgiving was maybe not so great?"

"Judy and I got into a tête-à-tête." Katie pauses. It feels slightly barbaric to complain. Judy can be aggravating, but so can everyone else, and, really, Katie was the villain last night. "Long story short," she says, "Judy was needling and I kind of snapped."

"Needling about what? Your next book? No sympathy, girl. You know what I'm going to say."

"Yeah, I know, and it wasn't just the book. I was forced to confess that Armie and I broke up. Granted, I probably should've tipped her off before."

"Whaddya mean *broke up*?" Jojo says. "Again? Do y'all have a punch card or something?"

"It's not *again*. It's the same one. As before."

"Wasn't that like…?"

"Six months ago," Katie says. "What made you think we'd gotten back together?"

"You always get back together," Jojo points out.

Millie leaps after a bird, yanking Katie around a corner. A forty-pound dog is heavier than a person might think, and the two nearly pummel an old man and his grocery cart.

"Sorry!" Katie calls out.

"Phew," Jojo says. "You had me panicked there. I'm glad you've managed to stay away. Keep up the good work."

Katie glowers. "Even though we're broken up," she says, keeping a steady voice, "Armie is still a great guy. You don't always have to be so harsh. Not all lobbyists shill for oil drilling and assault rifles."

"Armie's fine. It's your relationship that I've never been thrilled about. All that competition and one-upmanship. Exhausting. So, you just told your mom *now*? When there were new girlfriends and real estate transactions involved?"

"I just told *everyone* now," Katie says. "I didn't hide it on purpose. People are busy, and it's taken me a while to come to terms. Plus, I knew they'd take it hard. Judy adores Armie, maybe even more than she does me." Katie's tears return. It's the hangover, she reasons, because she's fine with the breakup. It was her idea and, anyway, a lot of time has passed.

"I wouldn't go that far," Jojo says. "But I have witnessed Judy take his side more than once. How is she handling the news?"

"She's offered to—get this—*move in with me*. To nurse me back to health. Talk about the cure being worse than the problem."

Jojo cackles. "Great plan, Judy. Why hasn't she invited you to stay at Little Falls Farm?"

"Maybe because Charles turned my room into a Pilates studio?"

"You could stay in the gun room!"

Katie is about to laugh when she remembers that, with the state of things, there's a decent possibility she will have to move into the gun room. Why didn't she let Armie buy *her* out, instead of the other way around? She wanted to "win," most likely. She wanted to one-up.

"Maybe a change of scenery will give you some clarity," Jojo says. "And kick your writing ass into gear. Why don't you come stay with us?"

"What do you mean? Like a vacation?"

"Yes, of course a vacation. You think I'd invite you to live with us? Yikes. No, thank you. Four kids and Nigel is enough for one house. You need a breather, a mental refresh. And you haven't even met Bryonie and she's nearly one!"

"I'd love to see you guys," Katie says. "But don't you have a book due in a few weeks?"

"Two, actually!" Jojo says. "I'm ghostwriting another celebrity memoir, if you can believe it. I'm such an idiot for agreeing to do it during a move and the holidays."

"What do you mean *another* memoir?" Katie says, as she fights a rising irritation.

It always seems so easy for her friend. While Katie's agent was on submission with her first novel, which had taken the better part of five years to write, Jojo was pregnant and confined to bed rest with her son, Clive. On a whim, Jojo scribbled out a book, which sold immediately. One novel turned into a dozen-plus, all of them pink-jacketed, breezy reads. Meanwhile, it took Katie three tries to write something that would sell.

"You've done this before?" Katie says. "Ghostwriting?"

How perfectly appropriate that Jojo has the capacity to write other people's books in addition to her own.

"A few times," she says. "Before you ask, I'm not allowed to talk about it."

"You're very sweet," Katie says. "But you can't entertain a houseguest when you have two books to write. Thank you, but this sounds like a bad idea."

"You're not an ordinary guest, though," Jojo says. "You like alone time and can take care of yourself. I have a feeling London will inspire you, and soon you'll be busy, too. If nothing else, the city is beautiful this time of year."

Katie sighs. "It does sound nice," she says. "But I can't afford it."

"That's fine. It's on me," Jojo says, and Katie hears the click of keys. "Ah, see? Tons of availability!"

"You can't buy my ticket!"

"Why not? I want to see you, and the fares are dirt cheap. Plus, you can ignore Judy all you want, but eventually she'll show up with a suitcase and a bottle of Chard."

Katie grimaces because this is a very likely outcome.

"How soon can you be ready?" Jojo asks. "Is there someone who can look after the dog?"

Katie thinks of Armie's text. He can watch Millie, he *wants* to watch Millie, but that means Katie will have to reach out. She's been so scrupulous in staying away, in giving his new life a chance to launch.

"There's someone who can take Millie," Katie says.

"Perfect. Problem solved. Dulles, yes? That's a direct flight."

"How can you book a ticket without my personal information?"

"I have your personal information," Jojo says, and Katie blushes, having forgotten this wouldn't be the first time she's traveled on Jojo's dime. "Don't worry. I promise not to commit identity theft."

"If you're going to steal identities, you should pick somebody else."

"Okay, I'm doing it. Are you ready?"

Katie closes her eyes and sucks in her breath. She should decline, but there's no stopping Jojo once her mind has been made. "Yes," she says at last.

By the time Katie hangs up, an airline confirmation sits in her email, all plans arranged. She's going to London for one week, leaving on the red-eye tonight.

February 1942

West Wycombe, Buckinghamshire

Nancy Mitford stood on the gravel drive, luggage piled at her feet, her pug, Milly, tucked beneath her arm. Her friends had assembled to wish her bon voyage—Eddy Sackville-West and Jim Lees-Milne and Helen Dashwood, all in a perfect row.

"This is a bit of a to-do, isn't it?" Nancy said. "Either you think I'm off on a grand adventure, or destined for an unfortunate fate."

"Aw, Nance," Helen said, and stepped forward. "All good things must end, but I see brighter skies ahead."

Nancy regarded her friend with deep fondness. Helen was so lovely out here, in the morning's gray cast, this woman once considered London's prettiest brunette. Though her features had hardened in the intervening decades, she was more alluring now, her beauty more trenchant and intense.

"Brighter skies?" Jim said with a frown, otherwise known as his regular face. "We are in the middle of a war."

"Thanks for the refresher," Nancy said. Jim could bring down the mood of any room, as well as the great outdoors.

"We'll miss you," Helen said, rubbing Nancy's arm. "But you know where to find me, if everything turns to shit."

"Oh, Hellbags." A tear dribbled down Nancy's cheek. "You're the kindest, the funniest, the absolute best."

Helen flashed an impish grin. "No one's ever been able to prove otherwise."

"Be careful," Nancy warned. "You don't want to be stripped of your nickname, or asked to host a charity ball!"

"I'd rather die," Helen said.

Heir to a Canadian cereal fortune, Lady Helen Dashwood was as famous for her eighteenth-century Palladian pleasure palace as she was the pre-war sex orgies and shooting affrays once held on its grounds. Since taking over West Wycombe, she'd injected life into the monstrous old place with hunts in the winter, Ascot and polo in the summer, and year-round weekend house parties attended by the likes of Queen Mary and the Duke and Duchess of York.

Hellbags did what she wanted, husband and social mores be damned, and her version of wartime sacrifice was to host "evac-uees," which was to say her London friends. The Wallace Collection was also currently in residence, alongside a maternity hospital and Jim's colleagues from the National Trust.

"I can't thank you enough," Nancy said. "The time passed in a blink."

"Sorry the accommodations are less than grand," Hellbags said.

Nancy smiled and peered over her shoulder toward the home's yellow, fractured façade. Inside, wooden planks were scattered across broken marble floors. Holes marred the carpets and brown paint covered nineteenth-century frescoes. Water poured down the walls whenever it rained, and the preponderance of broken windows meant three bathrooms were currently buried beneath snowdrifts.

"Off to explore the Beardmore Glacier!" Nancy would say whenever she used the lav. "If I don't make it back, tell my family I loved them!"

How vacant Nancy's life would seem without this group of friends, without gathering each night to dine on whatever Hell-bags shot at the lake (swan, usually). Jim, ever the cracking bore, would appear first, with fluttery, pale Eddy arriving last, always in his blue velvet cape. Upon sitting down, he'd brandish a jeweled pillbox and select ten to twelve, depending on what plagued him that week.

"I'm on a new diet," he might say. "Only red and white foods."

With Eddy, there was always some new eating or exercise regime, typical for a man who viewed his body as a glass hive of swarming bees. He was constantly tweaking his medications, with no real basis, and worrying whether he had the right pills to take when the Germans came. After directing the servants—Helen somehow had a full staff—to remove this foodstuff or add that, Eddy would then treat the table to a compendium on the downsides of clay soil. "In point of fact, the drinking water here is madly binding," he'd say as Helen rolled her eyes. Hellbags so despised hearing about other people's ailments that she considered converting to Christian Science, until she remembered she loathed other people's religions even more.

Following the meal, the group usually moved to the small Tapestry Room to discuss the latest news: the bombing of Pearl Harbor, Virginia Woolf's suicide, Nancy's brother-in-law who was missing in action. After thoroughly covering the topics of the day, they'd turn to savagely reviewing books and friends. The nights ended with Eddy and Helen playing piano in the long, draughty hallway, after which they'd all retire to bed.

"I hadn't wanted to come," Nancy said, looking back toward her friends. "But leaving makes me want to cry buckets." Three months before, Nancy had been at her lowest, yet this rickety manse was the perfect salve.

"But leave you must," said Jim. "Heywood is waiting for you in London. If you tarry, he's apt to give the job to somebody else."

"Then I'd really be up a tree!" Nancy said. "You know how desperately I need the money."

"He's not going to give it to anyone else," Helen said, and motioned for her butler to ferry Nancy's things to the car. "No one could be better for that ratty bookshop than a bona fide writer who's read practically everything!"

"Bona fide feels a stitch strong, given my recent failures," Nancy said. "Though I'm thrilled to prove my father wrong. There is *some* use for a girl who's well-read, especially in the face of financial ruin."

"I'll never understand," Jim said, "how you can be so perpetually broke."

"I'm broke because my father is, too," Nancy reminded him. Though they'd explained it repeatedly, Jim Lees-Milne remained stymied by the idea of a baron who maintained several homes and innumerable acres of land, but could not provide a proper income to his seven adult children. "He cut my allowance again last month, in addition to the two times he sliced it before. Poor Farve was born without a lick of financial sense."

"He does have a chilling predisposition toward pecuniary calamity," Eddy agreed.

Jim shook his head, mystified. A self-described member of the "lower-upper class," he was the only one of them not born into a titled family and was thus unable to comprehend that gentry and wealth were not synonymous.

"Peter gets nothing from his family," Nancy added. "And I never see a shilling of his Army pay."

"Can we please stop talking about money?" Eddy begged. He gave a shiver worthy of the stage. "Also, why are we still outside? There is a *very* bracing wind. Hellbags, how quickly can you reach a doctor, should I catch pneumonia?"

"What about you?" said Hellbags as she pushed a dark curl from Nancy's brow. "Are you feeling all right, physically?"

"I'M FINE!" Eddy cried as the butler slammed the boot of the car.

"Oh, for goodness' sake," Nancy said as her eyes sprang away. "I'm perfectly well. My body's had ample time to recover. As much as it can, given its advanced state of decay."

"My throat tickles!" Eddy said. "In case anyone's curious!"

Nancy glanced behind her as the Daimler revved. "It feels like the end of an era," she said.

"The end, yes," Hellbags said, "but also the start of something new."

"Pray to God."

"Nothing is ever new, though, is it?" Jim mused. "All that's good is fleeting, and the bad lingers around."

"He's right," said Eddy, miserably.

"I really came to the right place," Nancy said with a chuckle. "You are all perfect demons of joie de vivre." She sighed. "Well, friends, it's back to London for me."

Back to the chaos of real life. Back to unfilled bomb craters, boarded-up windows, and loos that dangled from exposed second floors. The trip was thirty minutes by automobile, but London was another world away.

"Farewell, my darlings," Nancy said as her chest tightened. "Thank you for three memorable months. With any luck, this war will end soon, and we'll be together again, enjoying our lives as we once did."

Saturday Morning

Mayfair, London

Katie arrives at Heathrow sticky-eyed and blurry-brained from her overnight flight.

After lumbering through the airport like she has a twenty-pound weight on her back, Katie exits customs and immediately spots her curly-haired, six-foot-two friend towering over family members and drivers with signs. One flash of Jojo's high-wattage grin and Katie nearly buckles in relief.

"Welcome to London," Jojo says. "Everything will be better, starting now."

A driver is at the curb, with mimosas waiting on the console in the back seat. When Jojo lifts a glass to cheer, Katie gives a watery smile. The thought of champagne makes her queasy, but she can't very well refuse. They clink glasses and Katie takes a sip.

It's drizzling as they merge onto the M4 and, like the good friend she is, Jojo begins with a soft toss. How was the flight? Fine. How is the dog? Perfect.

"And Britt and the girls?" Jojo asks as they motor past office buildings, graffitied walls, and middle-class neighborhoods butting up against roads. "What's she up to?"

"The usual," Katie says. "Britt is like the weather in San

Diego. Sunny and seventy-five. It's the same with Dani and Clem. You've never met a nicer pair of teenagers. Where is the cunning, the bitchiness? I make one mildly snarky comment and they accuse me of having 'no chill.'"

"In fairness, you don't have a lot of it," Jojo says, and Katie shoots her a glare. "Don't worry, I'm sure they're up to some shit. They're probably good actresses."

"I don't think so. They stayed with us a lot, and Armie and I had this competition—"

"Ya don't say. A competition." Jojo rolls her eyes. "That sums up your relationship."

"ANYHOW," Katie says, glaring again. "We'd put out alcohol, twenty-dollar bills, edibles Armie's brother left at our house, but the girls never fell into our traps. Not one time."

"What happened to the edibles?" Jojo asks.

"Armie and I ate them," Katie answers with a blush.

"Atta girl. Remember when you and Britt got into that huge fight because you said her daughters looked like homicide victims?"

Katie thwacks Jojo's leg. "That's not true! I said that they were dangerously wholesome, *too* pretty, the kind of girls Ted Bundy liked."

"Exactly. Homicide victims." Jojo laughs through her nose. "I can't fathom why your sister was so aggrieved."

They approach the city, and the streets and sidewalks become more jammed. There are hostels, and hotels, and quintessentially British brick pubs. Mawson Arms. The Fox and Hounds. When Katie sees signs for Chiswick, and Hammersmith, she knows they're getting close. Everything becomes grander, more ornate.

Katie watches people push strollers and swing shopping bags, wondering if they ever marvel that they live here, in a city as great as London. Katie thinks this about DC during certain times of year, like when the Tidal Basin is pink with cherry blossoms, and tourist buses line the streets, but that's Washington, which isn't nearly the same. Katie knows she's supposed to say Paris is her favorite city but, really, London beats it every time.

As they enter Kensington, passing first the Victoria and Albert Museum, and a McLaren showroom, Katie thinks about how far Jojo has traveled from the girl she once was: Jodi Boyers of Boones Mill, Virginia, "Moonshine Capital of the World," population 285. Jojo claims she's from Appalachia, which is true but said mostly for effect.

Alas, Boones Mill never really agreed with Jodi Boyers, and so she used her basketball prowess to catapult herself out and up to Cornell University, where she and Katie met on move-in day. They became such fast and conjoined friends that the men's basketball team called them "Muggsy and Manute," a reference to their stunning height discrepancy.

After graduation, they lived in New York, though Jojo soon traded the drudgery of investment banking for the London School of Economics, where she met Nigel Hawkins-Whitshed, London born and bred. They were engaged within months and now she is a mother of four and author of twelve living in one of the swankiest places on earth.

"The Queen's childhood home used to be there," Jojo says, pointing to the InterContinental Park Lane. "The family moved out in 1936, when King Edward abdicated, and her father assumed the throne. It was bombed four years later, during the Blitz."

"Look at you! A history nerd!"

"Hardly. I know you like that sort of crap. Beyond that line of trees—" she gestures "—is Buckingham Palace. We're almost home."

Jojo lives in Mayfair, which boasts the city's greatest concentration of Michelin-starred restaurants and five-star hotels. It's home to Bond Street, and Savile Row, and brands like Tiffany, Dior, Gucci, and Chanel. All day long, Bentleys and Maseratis sit in front of the shops, drivers loitering around in earpieces and sharp suits, waiting for their bosses to emerge.

They turn left at a vape shop and, after passing several blocks of charming cafés and boutique hotels, the driver stops halfway onto a curb in front of a bow-fronted, multistory white Georgian townhouse.

"Welcome to Mayfair," Jojo says.

Katie peers through the window, taking it all in, as the driver sweeps up her bags and disappears into the house.

"I'll give you the full tour when the littles are up from their naps," Jojo says.

They walk inside and Katie ogles the high ceilings and polished wood floors, likewise every incredible room: his-and-hers libraries, a twenty-person cinema, the drawing room (there is a *drawing room*), which is dominated by a green marble fireplace. At the end of it all, Jojo presses a button to summon the elevator. The guest suite is downstairs.

Katie heart warms to see how Jojo's life has panned out. She can't hate her for it, even though she's competitive, even though she's tried, because Katie understands how hard Jojo worked to get to a place where things come easily. Growing up, Jojo's weekends were basketball tournaments, her weeknights devoted to homework and practice and free throws in the driveway after everyone went to bed. She can recall attending only three birthday parties after age twelve, her own celebrated by wolfing down store-bought cupcakes with her teammates after a game. Everyone in Jojo's small town was impressed that she'd be playing basketball at Cornell, but what was truly impressive was all she'd done before.

"Your home is beautiful," Katie says. "Your family. All of it. I'm so happy for you."

"Thanks," Jojo says, and they walk into the guest suite, where Katie's things sit on a luggage rack. "We were lucky to get this house."

"I didn't just mean the house."

As Katie flips open her suitcase, Jojo plonks onto the bed. She tucks one broomstick leg under her butt and scrunches her wild mane of hair. "All right," she says. "Spill it. What's happening with the writing? When we spoke a couple of weeks ago, you seemed super into the manuscript you were working on."

"I *was* into it," Katie says. "And my editor liked it well enough, but she insists no one wants to read a book that takes place in an Old West whorehouse."

"I'd read it, and I don't even like historical fiction. What does your agent think?"

Sighing, Katie extracts a handful of lingerie from her suitcase. "Bianca would never tell me what to write," she says. "But she sees two options. Either we keep pushing this rock up a hill… or we play ball."

"And by 'play ball,' I assume she means Paris?"

"Or something like it."

Katie turns toward the dresser, which is adorned with pictures of her and Jojo. There must be a vault of framed photographs that Jojo trades in and out, depending on the guest.

"Just write the damned sequel," Jojo says. "And be done with it."

Katie drops her lingerie into a drawer and spins around. "First of all, I have no desire to write a sequel. Second, I have no faith I even *could*. Nothing's working for me. Either the setting isn't right, or the story, or some other thing. Maybe I should just accept that I'm a shit writer and go back to what I do best."

"Give me a friggin' break," Jojo says. "You're not a shit writer. You're acting like a *shithead* writer, but your writing isn't shit."

"I dunno. Every single publisher rejected *A Paris Affair* when Bianca shopped it. The only editor who was willing to take me on has since left the industry and is currently residing in a commune in Aruba."

"Fun!"

"Meanwhile, two editors later…" Katie blubbers her lips. "I've blown past my deadline, and lapped that deadline, and am about to lap it again. My publisher is anxious to see something."

"Uh, yeah. Because you promised 'something' in a contract."

"But it's like no one believes I can write more than one thing! I really think it's less about *A Paris Affair* and more about its sales."

"Of course it's about the sales," Jojo says. "It's called a business. Has it ever occurred to you that it sells well because it's good?"

Katie shrugs. More than once she's thought of paying someone—a book reviewer, a professor, an eager undergrad—to dissect all three of her books. Maybe this fictional person can clue her in on why *A Paris Affair* connects with people to a degree her other two books do not.

"You can't predict what people are going to latch onto," Jojo says, as if reading her mind. "There's really no point in trying, and I don't know what to tell you beyond what I've already said. What does Bianca want you to do?"

"Reassess over the Thanksgiving holiday. Oh. Get this." Katie clips two skirts onto a hanger, which are two more skirts than she's worn in years. Also, it's freezing in London, and Katie doesn't know what she was thinking in packing them. "Bianca told me to have *fun*," Katie says. "Can you believe the nerve? Fun. Of all things."

Jojo snickers. "Wow. That's just mean," she says. "Has Bianca met a writer before?"

"Then she told me to stop being a baby and act like a damned professional."

"True enough," Jojo says, and shakes her head. She'll say nothing more on the subject. For all her success, Jojo recognizes when another writer doesn't want to talk about their work. "So, who's watching Millie?" she asks. "I still can't believe you left her. Remember when Armie had that trip to the Dominican Republic, and you wouldn't go because of the dog?"

"The trip was ten days long, and we'd only had her a few months," Katie says, and ducks into her suitcase for a stack of jeans. "She's staying with Armie now."

"Oh, Lord. Here we go."

"No. Not *here we go*." Katie whirls around and drops her jeans into a drawer. "He picked her up *after* I left, so no conspiracy theories, please. It was actually good timing. He'd been wanting to see her, but we hadn't arranged anything because I've been trying to give him space."

"Yet you appear to be in some kind of dog share?"

"We're not sharing dogs."

"Are you still in love with the guy?"

"You're a real ballbuster," Katie says.

"You haven't answered the question," Jojo says as one eyebrow spikes.

"It's not a matter of loving him or not. I've known him since I was five. How I feel about him is not something I sit around and contemplate. It's just…there. Like how you love a sibling."

"Ew. Gross."

"You know what I mean."

In many ways, Katie is closer to Armie than she's ever been to Britt. He was her best friend from the moment he moved in next door, a few months after her father died. Together they started kindergarten and learned to ride bikes. They joined Little League and partnered on ninety percent of school projects. Meanwhile, Britt was in her room, trying on makeup and prank calling boys. Because of the six-year gap, the sisters weren't close until they were adults, and competitiveness never factored in.

Armie and Katie, on the other hand, acted like siblings on their worst behavior, vying for grades, athletic awards, and really anything that could be commemorated with a trophy or plaque. Once, Armie wrote a letter to the president of the McLean Little League, insisting that Katie should play softball instead of baseball, since she was a girl. The real problem wasn't Katie's gen-der but her higher batting average, which was four-four-two, compared to Armie's three-eighty-nine, not that she remembers the specifics.

The rivalry didn't let up when Britt left for college, or after Judy married Charles and Katie moved into Little Falls Farm. They applied to the same colleges, but Armie was wait-listed at Cornell, which felt pretty great. Although he was eventually accepted, he chose Georgetown instead. They hooked up for the first time between sophomore and junior year, which people viewed as inevitable or ruinous, depending on who was asked. Only in hindsight did Katie realize the tension was there all along, waiting to break. All it needed was for both of them to consume an indecorous amount of tequila on the same night. Finally, after several years of flings, Katie moved back to DC, and their real relationship began.

"You're really done?" Jojo says, twisting her hair into a knot on top of her head. "Done, done? As opposed to the previous fifty times you broke up?"

"It wasn't fifty. Five, maybe," Katie says. She removes several magazines from her carry-on and pitches them onto the desk. "Things have changed, and we're older. Shit or get off the pot, and all that."

"Hmm," Jojo says. She picks up *Architectural Digest*. "Why so many magazines? Where are the books? What are you reading lately?"

"You're looking at it," Katie says. "It's not merely a writing funk, but a reading one, too. I don't like anything, and I can't concentrate for more than five minutes. Sometimes fiction seems...absurd? It's like, how many hours have I spent on people who don't exist?"

Jojo looks at Katie like she's just announced plans to move in, or become a Scientologist. "I can't believe I have to say this to a novelist," she says. "But fiction is important. Books teach us about ourselves. They teach us about humanity."

"Yeah, maybe," Katie says, and tucks a strand of hair behind her ear. "Anyway, I haven't been in the mood. Hence, the magazines."

"Bloody fine time to get into print journalism," Jojo scoffs.

There's a knock and Jojo's husband appears. Nigel Hawkins-Whitshed can be stuffy, and he's pale, and skinny, and none too appealing, yet he's utterly charismatic all the same. Katie adores the man.

"Sorry to be a bother," Nigel says, after hugs are exchanged. "Felix just called and I'm going to buzz over to Heywood Hill. They've got in *Casino Royale*."

Jojo's face perks up. "You've been waiting for months! Don't tell me the price, though. I don't want to know."

"Understood," he says, grinning. "Bryonie is up from her nap and Imogen is getting her dressed. She's already darling but, in five minutes, should be ready for full display."

"Goodness, that fourth child might pay off, after all."

"Would've been cheaper to get a show dog," Nigel jokes. "All right, cheers, you two. See you soon." He blows his wife a kiss.

"That's who I'm taking you to see," Jojo says as her husband's footsteps retreat.

"Imogen? The nanny? That's okay, I'm good."

"Felix Assan. He works at the divine little bookshop around the corner. He's Head of Libraries, I think?" She chuckles. "Doesn't matter. We go to him for everything. The shop is called Heywood Hill. You've heard of it, yes? They curated our collection, matter of fact."

"Curated?" Katie says, and wrinkles her nose.

"Trust me, it's a *thing*," Jojo says. "They're literary geniuses who can find any book, for any person, guaranteed. Heywood Hill specializes in bespoke collections, but—"

"I hate you for having said that word."

"It means customized," Jojo says. "They put together libraries for hotels and offices, and wealthy people's vacation homes, but their subscription service is just as specialized. According to Felix, the team will spend *hours* debating the perfect book to send to a specific client. I'm going to write it down."

From the bedside table, Jojo swipes a pen and a notepad adorned with a sketch of her new house. "Lionel has a birthday party this afternoon," she says, and tears off a sheet. "Teddy bear picnic, for God's sake. While I'm there, you must visit the shop. It's on Curzon. Less than a five-minute walk." She extends the paper toward Katie, who eyes it, skeptically. "Look for the blue awning," she says. "A blue plaque next to a black door. Whatever your state of mind, however confused… I promise, the minute you step inside, things will start to make sense."

Saturday Afternoon

G. Heywood Hill Ltd.

Katie stands in front of a narrow Georgian townhouse—four-story and brick, with a charcoal-painted ground floor façade. A bike is latched onto a black wrought iron fence, and the awning reads "G. Heywood Hill Ltd."

As she approaches the entrance, Katie reads the round, blue sign posted beside the door. Heritage plaques are a common sight in London, meant to honor a noteworthy person who lived or worked inside a particular building. Usually it's some unknown actor, composer, or field marshal, but this name is familiar, and it feels like a hug.

NANCY MITFORD

1904–1973
Writer
worked here
1942–1945

Before walking inside, Katie brushes her fingers across the letters for good luck.

A bell tinkles when she enters the shop. Stopping to let an older gentleman hurry past, Katie takes in the maze of blue-carpeted interlocking rooms. Books are piled everywhere—on tables, in shelves, on the floor—and the effect is more cozy, chaotic home than commercial enterprise.

Wending through circular tables and curios filled with knick-knacks, Katie scans the shelves. Between A.S. Byatt and Truman Capote, she spies a familiar white spine and her name in blue letters. KATHARINE CABOT. One copy of *A Paris Affair*, bien sûr.

Katie rotates back toward the empty rooms and creeps further into the shop, her eyes sweeping the books, the dusty chandeliers, the cobweb-tinged corners and nooks. She hesitates in front of a mountain of gifts wrapped in tan paper and bound by blue ribbons.

Someone clears their throat. "Can I help you?" the voice says, and Katie jumps.

"Hello!" she yelps. "I didn't see you there."

The man rises to his feet. When he re-caps his pen and drops it onto the desk, Katie realizes she's stumbled into an office. She blushes—hard—but, in Katie's defense, there are books everywhere, and this very much feels like part of the shop.

"I'm so sorry!" Katie says. "I didn't mean to interrupt. Or trespass. I wasn't paying attention."

"I do appreciate you stopping in," the man says. "But we are technically closed on Saturdays. The only reason I'm here is to catch up on work. I hadn't meant to leave the door unlocked."

"Oh! Oh shit!" Katie flies into a panic. "I'm really sorry!"

"It's fine," the man says with a warm smile. "You're welcome to browse for a few minutes. Did you have something specific you were looking for, or a question, perhaps?"

"I do have a question," Katie says. "Though it's not why I came in. I saw the plaque." She gestures toward the front of the shop. "Nancy Mitford. I'm surprised she worked here. I thought she published several books before the war broke out."

"Four, to be precise."

"Weird," Katie says, with a squint. "I know she didn't really hit her stride until *The Pursuit of Love*, but wasn't her father a peer? Was she just killing time during the war or something? She must not have needed the money." Katie's pink cheeks turn to red. "Sorry if I'm being gauche."

The man gives a quick laugh. "Her father was indeed the 2nd Baron Redesdale. Alas, theirs was more of a crumbling gentry, an upper-class poverty, if you will. Nancy's first four books never earned any royalties. Poor girl had to find some way to pay the bills. Luckily, her friends Anne and Heywood Hill were desperate for help."

Katie frowns, wishing bookshop assistant was a way to solve her own financial mess.

"So, you're a Nancy Mitford fan, are you?" the man says. "Unusual for an American, I've found."

"No kidding!" Katie says. "When I picked *Love in a Cold Climate* for book club, eight out of the ten people accidentally read *Cold Comfort Farm* instead. Personally, I think Nancy Mitford is one of the most underrated novelists of the twentieth century. In fact, she was the subject of my senior thesis in college."

"Now, that is something," the man says. "What was the topic?"

"Broadly speaking, how she 'normalized' relationships that were at the time considered 'other'—extramarital, same-sex, age differences, et cetera." Katie's cheeks flame again. "It's cringe-worthy and dated now, but I stand by Nancy Mitford being bold for her time, especially for a female writer."

"I agree." He bobs his head. "I'm curious, if you didn't know Nancy Mitford worked here, what brought you into our shop?"

"I'm staying with friends nearby. Jojo and Nigel Hawkins-Whitshed?"

The man's face brightens, and he walks around the desk. Jojo's name has eliminated the last remaining barrier, literal and figurative.

"Good people, the Hawkins-Whitsheds," the man says. "I enjoyed curating Jojo's library. Predilection toward books about the moon landing and economic disasters. She also wanted an entire set of *The Baby-Sitters Club*? That was a first."

"Well, it's not 1992," Katie says, "and you're not a twelve-year-old girl. Basketball must've been a theme."

"Special emphasis on Scottie Pippen."

"How many titles does Jordan win without him, I ask you?" Katie says, shaking her fists at the sky.

Laughing, the man extends a hand. "Felix Assan. Head of Libraries."

"Yes! Felix! Jojo told me to find you. I'm Katharine Cabot. Katie."

"Wonderful to meet you, Katharine," Felix says. "I'd love to help you with your bookish needs. Alas, if you're interested in our Year in Books consultation, your best bet would be to return Monday, when our subscription team is in. They read five hundred titles per year, so their expertise is far greater than mine. If you're in the market for curation, we'd need to schedule an appointment."

"As much as I'd love a curated library," Katie says, "that seems a bit out of reach. How much would it cost, if you don't mind my asking?"

"So many questions about sums," Felix teases. "It really varies. A project can run anywhere from fifty to fifty thousand volumes. In terms of price, it's usually in the six figures. Pounds, of course."

"Jesus," Katie mutters.

"We have plenty of less expensive services, of course, all the way down to advisement on a single book. I have enough knowledge to assist you with that if you'd like."

"I do need a book…" Katie says. "But I don't want to infringe. You said you were only here to catch up on work?"

"I have time for a break," he says. "Especially for a friend of the Hawkins-Whitsheds."

"Don't get excited. I don't have their budget. Not even close."

Felix laughs again. "Most people do not," he says. "How about a tour instead?"

They start downstairs, in the children's room. Although the room is empty, Katie can picture a gaggle of little ones lolling about beside the fireplace, and in the small wooden chairs, reading their Matildas and Wild Things and Hungry Caterpillars.

"We serve individuals and businesses," Felix explains as he rescues a copy of *Busy Bookshop* from the blue rug. "As well as Her Majesty, the Queen." He pushes the colorful book back into place. "When we take on a new client, the initial interview takes hours. Days. Weeks. Possibly months. It's crucial to be precise. Books are supposed to be a pleasure, and libraries should remind people of what they love. All that to say, only serious readers need apply."

Felix leads her into a basement office, a wide room with several desks that seem better suited to architects than literary types. On each table is a large ream of butcher paper, and ever more piles of books.

"This is where the booksellers hash things out," Felix says. "If it were a weekday, we would've interrupted a heated debate about which would be the optimum book to send to Franny de Worms next February."

Soon they are moving through a tight, musty corridor with ceilings so low Felix must duck. Katie has plenty of clearance, on account of being a shrimp.

"How long has the shop been here?" Katie asks as they pass a set of metal racks—the keep shelf—which holds orders ready to go out.

"Since 1936," Felix says, and throws open another door.

"That's…"

He grins over his shoulder. "Eighty-five years, yes."

"Wow." Katie shakes her head, amazed. "Just trying to *imagine* what this shop has been through… A World War. The invention of the internet. A pandemic."

"Thankfully, we do more than peddle books," Felix says. "We've changed along with people's needs. The opposite of a computer algorithm."

They've returned to the main jumble of rooms. To Katie's left is a white-and-gold-painted fireplace, surrounded by a wooden sales counter, which is itself encased in plexiglass.

"How many libraries are you all curating now?" Katie asks.

"Why, Katharine, I can't divulge such top secret information about the shop," Felix says, and wiggles his brows. "As for myself, I have eight in progress."

"All right." Katie leans toward him, conspiratorially. "I have to ask. What's your most annoying request?"

"I do endeavor to avoid viewing my clients as 'annoying.'"

"Yeah, but there has to be somebody who's giving you a hard time," Katie insists.

Felix crosses his arms and bites his bottom lip. He appraises her for a moment before admitting, "One person does come to mind. He's not a client but qualifies as a difficult individual with whom I'm presently dealing. Speaking of Nancy Mitford, the man is an avid collector. He's trying to locate a lost manuscript—a *memoir*, no less."

"And he wants you to find it?"

"He thinks we *have* it." Felix rolls his eyes. "According to him, it was written while Nancy was employed at Heywood Hill."

"So right before she wrote *The Pursuit of Love*?" Katie says.

Felix nods, and Katie thinks she'd like to see this memoir for herself. If it was the last thing Nancy Mitford wrote before the book that made her famous, she could use a few tips.

"There is no basis for this, by the way," Felix says, and Katie feels a quick pang of disappointment. "The gentleman claims to have inside knowledge, but all he could point to was the fact Nancy's less writerly sisters penned memoirs, so why not she?"

"Because Nancy Mitford's novels were famously autobiographical," Katie says. "What did she need with a memoir?"

"Precisely," Felix agrees.

"I hadn't known her sisters were writers, too," Katie says. "Aside from Decca, of course. I wonder if I can remember the others."

She pauses to think this through. The Mitford girls were so provocative, so outrageously unique, it's almost harder to recall each on her own, like trying to remember individual fireworks in a lengthy and vibrant show.

"Deborah the Duchess," Katie says. "Diana the Fascist, and Unity the Hitler chum. Pamela was...a farmer? A dabbler in Fascism?"

"A bit of both. A countrywoman, mostly."

"And the great Jessica Mitford, otherwise known as Decca, the Leftist. She's my favorite, aside from Nancy."

"Really." Felix cocks his head. "What is it about her you enjoy? The muckraking, or are you a budding Communist?"

"Hey!" Katie barks. "She denounced Communism, eventually, and I'm more interested in her civil rights work. Funny story. I have a picture of us together, from when I was little."

Felix lifts his forehead. "How'd that come about?" he asks.

"My father was a journalist with the *Washington Post*."

"Ah! Decca was great friends with its publisher Katharine Graham."

"That she was," Katie says with a sideways smile. "And she's the Katharine I was named after. Don't be too impressed by the connection, though. I'd never remember if I didn't have the photograph." The same could be said about most things associated with her dad. "Did all of the Mitford sisters publish memoirs? Even Unity?"

"All but Pamela," Felix says. "Unity wrote one, after her injury. It was never published, though you can find it online, and it's as awful as you might guess. I'm surprised some creep hasn't turned it into a manifesto."

In truth, Katie doesn't know much about this Mitford sister, other than the tragedy that made her famous. Unity was a confidante and rumored lover of Hitler's who shot herself in the head when war broke out. She survived the accident but was mentally impaired for the rest of her short and devastating life.

"Diana also had a memoir," Felix says, "and Debo wrote several. She was technically the most prolific of the six."

"Debo? Really?" Katie scrunches her face. "I never got the idea she was all that intelligent, or had much to say."

Felix flares his eyes.

"That didn't come out right!" Katie says. "I just meant… didn't she write about gardens and tending her castle? Real relatable stuff."

"Goodness," Felix says, and lets out a long whistle. "You must like your duchesses well-done." When Katie looks at him crookedly, he adds, "You've just thoroughly roasted the woman."

"You sound like my nieces, who are teenage girls."

"Thank you," he says. "I'm rather a fan of Gen Z. Let me ask you a question. When you came into the shop, did you happen to encounter an older gentleman? Distinguished-looking, medium height, mostly bald?"

"We practically ran into each other in the doorway," Katie says.

"That was Peregrine, otherwise known as Stoker, otherwise known as the 12th Duke of Devonshire. Debo's son. When his mother passed a few years back, he became executor of Nancy's literary estate. He also owns the shop."

"Oh, geez," Katie groans. "Good thing I waited until he left before 'thoroughly roasting' his mom. Scratch what I said before. I'm sure she was brilliant, and had a million things to write about, all of which were very accessible to the average person."

"So convincing!" Felix says with a laugh. "Gosh, that was fun! Now that we've gotten the faux pas out of the way, let's find something for you to read. What are you in the mood for?"

"If only I knew," Katie says. "I've been in a slump."

"Not a problem." Hands on hips, Felix studies the recent releases. "Who are your favorite authors?"

"John Irving," Katie says. "*A Prayer for Owen Meany* is my all-time favorite. *A Tree Grows in Brooklyn* is up there, too. *Little Women*. I love Toni Morrison and James Baldwin. Hemingway, at the risk of sounding grossly anti-feminist."

Felix chuckles as he glides from shelf to shelf.

"Nancy Mitford, obviously," she goes on. "Though I never really cared for her buddy Evelyn Waugh."

"Most who knew him would agree."

Katie prattles on, flaunting her predictable English major tastes: Jane Austen, the Brontë sisters, Daphne du Maurier. *Anna Karenina*. *The Count of Monte Cristo*. She also appreciates a juicy or thought-provoking memoir. "As for more contemporary work," she says, "anything by Ann Patchett or Anne Tyler. *Father of the Rain* by Lily King is in my top five. Octavia Butler, Emily St. John Mandel. T. Greenwood, though I'm not sure how well-known she is here. Shirley Jackson. Donna Tartt. For historical fiction, Kate Quinn, Kristina McMorris, Susan Meissner. Beatriz Williams and Paula McLain."

"Slow down," Felix says as something catches his eye. He abandons the shelves and pulls something from a nearby glass case. "Ah! The answer!" He spins around, book in hand. "I'm sure you've read it, but might be time for a revisit."

As Katie takes the book, she scans the cover, and a small gasp escapes her mouth. She turns to the title page.

FRANKENSTEIN;
OR,
THE MODERN PROMETHEUS
IN TWO VOLUMES

"Your taste demonstrates a predilection toward the gothic," Felix says. "That tremor of terror tinged with romance, the beasts who seem human, and the humans who do not. Things thought dead rising up again."

Felix glances at Katie, who stands gaping and pale.

"Uh, *Frankenstein* has all the hallmarks of the genre," he says, flustered. "But it also explores more classic themes—birth and creation, fallibility, ambition. It brought to the forefront the concept of the double, the idea of man pursued by himself. Are you all right? Do you need water? To sit down?"

"No. Uh, I'm fine."

"Are you, though?" he says.

"Ha!" Katie says, and fans her face. "That's the question, isn't it? It's just… I'm a writer. Was a writer? I'm not sure. You actually have one of my books on your shelves."

Felix screws up his face. "Why, then, are you questioning whether or not you're a writer?"

"I haven't had a book out in three years," Katie says. "Despite my best efforts. None of my ideas have panned out, including this." She holds up the book. "It was a story about the writing of *Frankenstein*. My agent and editor both thought it was too dark."

"Isn't that rather the point? It was the Year Without Summer, after all. The darkness, the eerie house. The Shelleys and Lord Byron. A fantastic setting, in my estimation."

"Yeah," Katie says. "It was fun."

"But not *that* fun, so let's find something lighter." Felix locks *Frankenstein* back in its case. "When was the last time you read Nancy Mitford?" he asks.

"So long I can't remember."

"There's the answer," Felix says, and leads her into a different room. "That was so easy, I don't know why our sub team is always working so much." He stops in front of a shelf packed with NANCY MITFORD spines. "Which is your favorite?"

"*The Pursuit of Love*, obviously."

"I've heard sometimes people have alternate opinions."

"Well, they're wrong," Katie says. "Speaking of human monsters, Uncle Matthew is one of the greatest in all of literature."

"That he is," Felix says. "Wretched Uncle Matthew, the alter ego of Nancy's father, the famous 'Farve.' A looming specter of a man."

As Felix says the words, Katie realizes she knows a little something about spectral father figures. Danny Cabot wasn't a monster, not even close, but he remains an ever-present, slightly haunting force.

"I agree with your thesis," Felix says.

Katie blinks, and it takes her a second to come back into the room. When she looks up, Felix is holding out a copy of *Pursuit*. He hands it to her, and she fans the pages beneath her nose.

"Along the lines of what you were saying earlier, the way in which Nancy Mitford debunks the idea of marriage is unique for such a deeply British author," Felix says. "It's more in line with the French literary tradition. Then again, the great romance of her life was French, too."

"That's right!" Katie says as a thick knot of previously buried knowledge works its way out. "Her Colonel, the inspiration for Fabrice."

Felix nods and something tugs at Katie, a feeling close to sadness. Her gaze drifts back toward the shelf. "I'm hazy on her earlier work," she says. "Was *Pigeon Pie* her debut?"

"*Pigeon Pie* was her fourth," Felix says. "It came out at the start of the war, *Pursuit* at the end. One was a massive failure, the other made her famous." Felix jimmies *Pigeon Pie* from its spot. "Alas, what's a girl to do when her lighthearted novel about the upper crust publishes during the fall of France? Here, have a look."

Felix pitches the novel at Katie. She ducks, and the book thumps onto the floor. They both stare for a second, before Felix leans down to rescue it.

"That was…unexpected," he says. "I didn't even throw it that hard."

Katie remains crouched, and partially covering her head. "No, I know," she says, and finally stands.

When Felix offers it again, Katie recoils.

"Are you afraid of a *book*?" He is, quite simply, agog.

"I told you. I'm having some…struggles…with my career. I don't need to be—" Katie wiggles her fingers "—touching another writer's bad sales mojo."

"*Pigeon Pie* was published eighty years ago!"

"Mojo's not really supposed to make sense, so…"

"Let me ask you something." Felix tucks the book beneath his arm. "When did your first novel come out?"

"In 2015?"

"Six years ago." Felix crooks a brow. "Is that all? *Pursuit* was published in December of 1945, so Nancy Mitford didn't really hit her stride until 1946. Fifteen years from when she began."

"That really doesn't make me feel better," Katie says. "Plus, a lot was going on during that time. Governments were collapsing, tyrants were coming into power. The world was in shambles!"

"As opposed to the current environment, in which nothing ever really happens. The point I'm trying to make is that it took Nancy Mitford fifteen years to experience a meaningful step forward in her career."

"Again. Not helping."

"She even resorted to translation work," Felix says. "Because, in her words, it involved the pleasure of writing without the misery of inventing."

"My mom was right. I should've studied a language in college," Katie says.

Felix cannot stop from rolling his eyes. "You can't have the highs without the lows," he says. "Everyone fails, and everyone gets writer's block, even the inestimable Nancy Mitford."

"I don't believe in writer's block," Katie says. "It's like saying you have workout block, or emptying-the-dishwasher block. It's all putting off shit you don't want to do."

"Writing is comparable to doing the dishes, then, in your world?"

Katie shrugs. "Sometimes. What I'm going through, it's not a block. More like a lack of confidence. A slump. A batter in the three-hole who keeps striking out."

"Are we talking about baseball now? And you're the hitter in this scenario?"

"Yes." She puts up a finger. "Just to be clear, I've *never* been in a hitting slump. My career batting average was four-four-two and my slugging—"

"I really do not care at all."

"WELL, I NEED TO HAVE SOMETHING GOING FOR ME!"

Felix throws back his head. He *guffaws*.

"Please, Katie," Felix says, when he's regained control of himself. "Take whichever Nancy Mitford books you want. She might give you some inspiration, jinxes be damned. That's the best thing about rereading a much-loved book. You get a different insight every time, and you can keep learning new things about yourself."

"Fantastic," Katie mutters. Learning more about herself is probably not the incentive he assumes.

"We have some of Nancy's personal papers in the shop," Felix adds. "If you're good, I might let you peck around."

"Personal papers?" Katie's face snaps back into a smile. It might not be an autobiography, or the secret ingredient to writing a decent book, but it's something, at least. And, as every writer knows, research is the best distraction. "I accept! I'd love to read the missing memoir, too, if and when you find it."

"You'll be the first to know," Felix says. "Well, Katharine Cabot, it was nice to meet you, but I really must get back to work. Consider those—" he waves a hand "—on the house."

"You feel sorry for me, don't you?"

Felix pinches his fingers together. "Little bit," he says. He pats her arm and disappears. Katie can't wait, and she begins reading *The Pursuit of Love* as she makes her way out of the shop.

Without looking up, Katie pulls open the heavy front door but stops when she realizes that something—or *someone*—is blocking her path. This object is massive, immovable, lending the general air of a redwood tree.

"Excuse me," Katie says, eyes fixed on the black-and-white-checked floor. "I'm trying to get out."

"Don't let me stop you."

"Well, you are stopping me, so…" With a huff, Katie pushes the hair out of her face, gazing up and directly into the face of an alarmingly attractive man. "Huh," she says, or makes some other sound.

"Please, let me hold the door," he says, and Katie responds with a brief "Thanks."

When she trips on the front step, the man laughs and suggests that maybe she shouldn't read and run at the same time. Katie mumbles something about the store being closed, but the door smacks shut. She whips around, middle finger raised, but it's too late. He's already vanished into the shop.

February 1942

G. Heywood Hill Ltd.

Nancy strode into Heywood Hill and, in one sweep, performed a quick but thorough examination of the room. The shop was just how she remembered, which was to say a fright: cluttered shelves, cobwebbed corners, and teetering stacks of books. The music boxes needed dusting, the snake vase was a horror, and fifteen quid was far too steep a price for a painting of deformed Victorian girls.

Nancy sighed and released her dog to the floor. "Please stay off the furniture," she said. Milly was a good pup but also a bit of a tart, and it was impossible to guess when she was pregnant, and might drop a litter on somebody's recently reupholstered chaise.

"Nancy!" called a voice. "You're here!"

She looked up to see the shop's owner, the eponymous Heywood Hill, bustling toward her, his swoopy hair bouncing up and down.

"Heywood! Darling!" she said as they embraced. "Look at you! Filled as ever with that lively, boyish charm. I thought they'd shipped out all the young men, but here you stand before me."

Heywood cackled. "Unfortunately, they've resorted to calling up even us feeble types. No official news yet, but I'm sure it will happen anytime. As for you…"

Nancy wouldn't let him finish. "I know, I know," she said, and yanked off her gloves. "My exterior has caught up with my inner tragedies. The shop front is in late-stage dishabille."

"I was going to say you're lovely as always, if not skinny."

"Don't forget pale. Visibly anemic. My low stamina strikes again."

"One day you'll let someone call you beautiful. Lady Dashwood tells me you've been feeling poorly. Is this true?"

"Hellbags is such a gossip. Not to worry. Just a minor spell." Nancy's eyes jumped away. "All is fine now. Thank you for asking. You're a dear."

"Make sure to see a proper doctor," Heywood said, "now that you're back in the city. No more of those country rubes."

"Proper doctors are half the problem!" Nancy said. "When a woman nears forty, a fella like that takes one look at her, declares cancer, and removes one or two key parts."

Heywood laughed again and squeezed Nancy's shoulder. "Tell me everything. I hear West Wycombe is packed to the rafters with refugees."

"Only if you count suits of armor, gilded snuffboxes, and the odd Rembrandt," Nancy said. "Aside from the entirety of the Wallace Collection, Hellbags is also billeting a number of friends, as well as the National Trust staff."

"National Trust?" Heywood made a face. "Jim Lees-Milne must be mucking about, trying to weasel the Dashwoods into donating their estate."

"Always! He does cut a *most* convincing argument." Nancy smirked. "West Wycombe is falling apart and the Dashwoods cannot afford to refurbish it. The National Trust will take up the mantle and 'preserve for the benefit of England this estate of great beauty and historical interest.'"

"Exactly the scam one might expect," Heywood grouched.

His wife was once engaged to Jim, and Heywood had a jealous streak a mile long.

"Jim has his uses," Nancy said. "To wit: he tells me you're shorthanded, which is why you find me standing in your shop."

"Is it true?" Heywood said, his face transforming from dismay into joy. "You're willing to work for me? Anne said something about it last week. She's been talking to Jim, apparently." Again, his brow darkened. "But I didn't want to get my hopes up."

"Feel free to hope away." Nancy grinned. "I am at your disposal."

Heywood clasped together his hands. "Oh, Nancy," he said. "You're about to save my life. We're fiendishly busy and we've just lost the book packer, and both delivery boys. Any day, it'll be my turn to go, and I already hate how much Anne works. She's running an errand right now—the very thing I swore I'd never have her do."

"You'll be helping me far more than I'll be helping you," Nancy said. "I had no idea a bookshop would be so busy during a war."

"Tremendously so," Heywood said. "Everyone is frantic for intellectual stimulation, and a bookseller's is one of the only places where a person doesn't need coupons. With the paper scarcity, books are shorter, and therefore people buy more. I can't decide if it's a vicious cycle or a virtuous one."

"Sounds like I came at the right time," Nancy said, and she almost believed this was true. She didn't want to work at a bookshop, not really, but what was a failed novelist to do when her allowance was cut, and the war they all thought would be fast dragged on and on?

"Anne will be so thrilled!" Heywood said. "I'll put news of your employment in all of our advertisements. The Heywood Hill bookshop boasts its very own in-house novelist!"

"Hmm. Well. The three people who read *Pigeon Pie* might quibble with my being deemed a 'novelist,' but I do know my way around a book. Jim teases me for having the *Sunday Times* reviews memorized."

"Well, dear Nancy, the position is yours, if you'll take it," Heywood said. "Why don't I show you around? Anne should be back any minute, but I'll introduce you to Mollie while we wait. We hired her last week to help with the accounts."

As they walked, the floorboards moaning beneath their feet, Nancy glanced around. This place, she thought, might actually be too much work.

"How is Peter?" Heywood asked. "Welsh Guards, is that right?"

Nancy bobbed her head. "He's well, as far as I know. It's been a while since I've heard from him."

About her husband's absence, Nancy's feelings were mixed. On the one hand, it was difficult to long for such a petty, imperious man, not to mention the sleep-inducing lectures he mistook for repartee. Prod was a self-professed expert on everything, and it was his feverish passion for eighteenth-century tollgate systems that earned him the nickname "the Tollgater" among family and friends.

But Nancy did sometimes miss having him around the house, and knowing one person would notice if she disappeared. Add to that Prod's smattering of positive traits: he was handsome, and tall, and his cold heart occasionally warmed, especially toward the displaced, which Nancy attributed to his standing as least favorite child. Prod was as emotionally homeless as some people were homeless in fact.

"Are you worried?" Heywood asked.

Nancy blinked. "About what? Prod? Never. He's very good at not getting shot."

"A handy skill," Heywood said, and swiped a set of papers from beside the register. "How is the rest of your family? Your esteemed siblings? I hear Diana is still at Holloway?"

"Lest anyone suggest Reg 18B isn't being put to use, we have my sister, jailed for Fascism, without charges or trial." Nancy shook her head. "It really says something that Diana is locked up for being an enemy of the state and Muv doesn't even consider her the most troublesome child."

Heywood chortled. "Rather the stiff competition with a Nazi and a Communist."

"Nazis are mostly fine by Muv," Nancy grumbled.

"And your brother?"

"In Libya, maintaining his status as most beloved child." Everybody adored the beautiful, shiny Tom, family and beyond, and he had a string of broken hearts from London to the Far East. Tom could get anyone to fall in love with him, as both Heywood and Anne Hill could attest, as well as Jim Lees-Milne.

"Here we are," Heywood said, and flung open a door. "The storage room. Could also be used as a refrigeration locker, in a pinch." Nancy shivered as Heywood looked around. "That's odd," he said. "Mollie's supposed to be working on the sums..."

They heard a shriek, and the stomp of feet, and soon Anne erupted into the room. "Heywood! It's a complete *nightmare!*" she cried, red-faced, frizzy-haired, and seemingly blind to Nancy's presence. "I just endured the worst hour of my life. Hatchard gave me a dickens of a time about that book. Whatever it's called. *Duck Staircase.*"

Heywood took a moment to decode his wife's words.

"*Swan Steps?*" she tried.

"Do you mean *Du côté de chez Swann*?" Heywood asked.

"Sure." Anne shrugged. "The point is the man ran me 'round and 'round and I sold it to him for practically nothing just to get out of there. Oh, Heywood. You *cannot* leave. I am too hopeless. It will all be a disaster! Also—" Anne halted, and her weepy brown eyes locked onto Nancy's face. After ten seconds of perfect stillness, she squealed and thrust herself into Nancy's arms. "Oh my God! Jim promised you'd come. Now you're here. He's my hero!"

"Maybe your hero should be Nancy," Heywood mumbled.

"I've missed you so!" Anne said. After a properly crushing embrace, she stepped back and flattened her dress. "Here I go again, embarrassing myself."

Anne was an unusual creature, even as unusual creatures went, and Nancy hadn't known what to make of her when they first met. Jim, her boyfriend at the time, had described her as "intelligent, male-minded, and deliciously humorous," but Nancy found her anxious and unsure. Though Nancy would come to cherish Lady Anne Gathorne-Hardy-turned-Hill, she never understood how the astonishingly progressive woman ever matched up with Jim, who was happiest in a Victorian library, dreaming of nineteenth-century stability.

"Embarrassing yourself?" Nancy scoffed. "You're mad! If anyone's embarrassed, it's me. From what Heywood says, I should've come weeks ago."

"We are dreadfully busy," Anne agreed. "Oh, Nancy, I'm so tired of this war. It's such a ghastly mix of depressing and frightful." She sighed and put a hand on Nancy's arm. "Do you hate us? I'm so passionately sorry we didn't sell more copies of *Pigeon Pie*."

"Neither did anyone else," Nancy said with a throaty laugh.

"It was just bad timing!"

"Absolutely dreadful," Heywood concurred.

"Or was it incredibly precise?" Nancy said. "It's almost as though I *planned* to release a book about the Phoney War to coincide with the fall of France."

"It should be just what people are in the mood for," her publisher had said, *"if we are quick."*

They weren't quick enough, or no one was in the mood, or some combination of these and other things. Whatever the case, Nancy Mitford's fourth book was a flop, one of the earliest casualties of the war.

"It'll be better next time," Anne said, and Nancy smiled thinly, willing this to truth.

"Never mind all that," Heywood said. "Darling, our problems are solved. Nancy has agreed to take the open position. Isn't that splendid?"

"Splendid?" Anne said. "It's wonderful, magnificent, entirely top-hole!"

Anne flew into Nancy's arms, and smothered her in kisses and good cheer. Nancy returned her hug, despite feeling oddly numbed. So, this was it. This was her new life. Nancy prayed she was starting in the right spot.

Saturday Night

Half Moon Street

"Did you have a chance to see much of the neighborhood?" Nigel asks.

They're in the dining room, gathered around a large mahogany table. Katie sits beside Cordelia, across from Lionel and Clive, with Jojo and Nigel presiding from either end. In the middle is a tangle of feathers, tree branches, and leather-wrapped goat horns, a centerpiece Jojo swaps out every two weeks.

"Mayfair is so unthinkably quaint," Katie says, picturing the curved streets and terraced townhomes, the patisseries, and bookbinders, and multicolored shop fronts. "The perfect blend of elegance and charm. Not too pretentious, not too precious. I can understand why you moved here."

"Oh, it can be pretentious," Jojo says with a snort. "You haven't visited New Bond Street yet. Bit less charm over there."

"The area's getting awfully posh," Nigel says, "but there's a good mix. You can have your Chanel and Cartier and Harry Winston, but other parts still bear the hint of Virginia Woolf's Mayfair."

"Like Curzon Street," Katie says.

She glances up to see the porcelain-skinned, rashy-cheeked

Clive peering at her from around the feathers. Although there is nothing inherently wrong with the kid, Katie finds him off-putting, which probably says more about her than it does about him.

"You went to Heywood Hill?" Jojo says. "I'm so glad! Didn't you love it?"

"I did love it," Katie says, then narrows her eyes. "By the by, they're not technically open on weekends, so maybe don't recommend visiting on Saturdays to future houseguests."

"Oops," Jojo says with a half shrug. "Oh, well. No harm, no foul."

"Other than trespassing." Katie stops to throw back a thimble of brie and crab soup because family dinners at the Hawkins-Whitsheds' include an amuse-bouche. "You also failed to mention Nancy Mitford worked at the store."

"Didn't know that was relevant, but okay."

"Shop," Clive says.

Katie shakes her head. "Uh, what now?" she says.

"You called it a store," he says. "But it's a shop. A store is where you buy milk, like a Tesco or something."

"Oh. Okay. Heywood Hill is a shop," Katie says. "Gosh. Thanks. That is very helpful!" She smiles brightly and Clive scowls in return. A small dash forms between his dark caterpillar brows. "I don't know if you recall," she continues, speaking to Jojo but with one eye trained on Clive. "But Nancy Mitford was the topic of my senior thesis."

Jojo tilts her head, mouth puckering in contemplation. "I think I remember something about that?" she says.

A chef enters with the salad course. This man is not a regular member of the household staff, but an employee of the family's personal concierge service. *Honestly!* Jojo would say. *It's not that big of a deal!* If anything, the arrangement *saves* them money, what with travel discounts, and the coordination of logistics. You really can't put a price on time! And how else would a person know whether it's more economical to hire fifteen kinkajous for your child's birthday party, or twenty, after negotiating bulk kinkajou discounts?

"Didn't Nancy Mitford have a bunch of infamous sisters?" Jojo asks as the chef leans over her shoulder with a pepper grinder. "Nazis or something?"

"One was a Nazi," Katie says. "A few were Fascists, and there was a Communist, too. You have to hand it to those Mitford girls—they didn't do anything half-assed."

"Those poor parents," Jojo says.

"Is she allowed to speak like that?" Clive wants to know. "She said *ass*." Nigel waves him off.

"Sorry, everyone," Katie says. "Anyway, Nancy Mitford was very prolific, and some of her letters are stored at the shop. There might even be an unpublished manuscript. I'm going back Monday. Felix said I could rummage around."

"Monday?" Jojo says, noodling on this before passing Nigel a look. "Ah. I see." She clears her throat. "Listen, Katie. Felix is a great guy. He's also hot as breakfast. But don't get any ideas."

"What do you mean, ideas?" Katie says. "Like, for a book?"

"Well, yeah. That'd be great," Jojo says. "But I'm referring to the fact Felix is married, and also gay."

"Cool. But I'm going back for Nancy Mitford's letters, not to hook up. Not sure why you thought…"

"Don't get me wrong," Jojo says. "I wish you'd find *someone* to hook up with, but, like I said, wrong tree."

"What do you mean, 'hook up'?" Lionel asks.

"She means snog," says Clive.

"Kids…" Nigel warns.

"I'm not in the market for a tree," Katie says, feeling suddenly sweaty beneath her cashmere. "It's probably best I stay out of the forest for a while."

"What if you made a big discovery?" Nigel says. "That'd really be something."

"Even a small discovery would be nice," Katie says. "I'd love to know what Nancy's life was like while she was working at the store—I mean, the shop." Her gaze flicks toward Clive.

"Maybe that's something to write about?" Jojo says.

"Did you know the BBC just did an adaptation of *The Pursuit of Love*?" Nigel says, and wipes his mouth. "It was Emily Mortimer's directorial debut, with Lily James starring as Linda."

Katie smiles, impressed that a finance bro—or whatever they're called on this side of the pond—has so handily referenced Linda Radlett. "I read about that," she says. "And I definitely plan to watch."

Nigel turns to his wife. "We should read the book," he says. "And then watch the program together."

"That seems like a lot of work," Jojo says.

"You'd finish it in an afternoon," Katie says. "The book is genius. I can't believe she wrote it in three months. It's completely unfair."

"Wasn't Nancy Mitford a spy?" Nigel asks as Jojo barks at Lionel to get his napkin off the floor.

"Not that I know of," Katie says.

"No, I think she was." Nigel stares into the near distance as he thoughtfully chews his salad.

"Auntie Katie," Cordelia chimes in, "did Mummy tell you? My birthday is on Christmas and Mister Assan is building *me* a library!"

"Wow!" Katie widens her eyes as far as they will go. "What an amazing present!"

"For my birthday, I plan on turning four."

"That is an excellent plan. Do you think your parents might get *me* a library for my next birthday? Maybe if my behavior improves."

"Maybe…" Cordelia says. "Mum says you are messy right now. That's why we have to be nice to you."

"Cordelia!" Jojo snips.

"Felix is *curating* you a library," Nigel says. "The library is built. You might recognize it as the ledge in your bedroom." He looks at Katie. "It's not as big a production as it sounds."

"Well, however big or small your bespoke library," Katie says, "I cannot wait to see it! You'll probably need more than one shelf, though. My guess is that a clever, non-messy girl like you can go through ten, twelve books a week."

"Yes, that is true!"

"Settle down," Jojo warns.

"You'll need a whole new library by the time you're five!"

Cordelia beams. "That is an excellent point!"

Katie laughs, wondering if these kids are hilarious, or insufferable, or some other thing. As Katie watches Cordelia refill her water glass using a crystal pitcher the size of her head, her brain swirls with possibility. Whatever she's looking for, whatever hole she's trying to plug, she might actually find her answers at Heywood Hill.

June 1942

G. Heywood Hill Ltd.

Every day, Nancy walked the two-plus miles to the shop. This was in spite of London's perpetually dismal climate, and the inevitability of encountering lorries filled with undersexed soldiers who hollered lewd things.

"I'm almost forty, you monsters!" she'd screech.

Because of this, Nancy was often harried, and always late, but patriotism was more admirable than punctuality, especially at a salary of three pounds per week.

That morning, as she had so many in the past four months, Nancy pushed against the drizzle and wind, teeth clattering as she kept a swift pace, leaping over piles of stone and blackened wood, and dodging craters left by bombs. All around, children frolicked in the ruins, dashing into and out of new hiding places.

As Nancy crossed Oxford Street at the Marble Arch, she got the sense of being observed. She glanced behind her but saw only an endless stream of gray people in gray clothes. The propaganda posters were getting to her, no doubt.

'WARE SPIES!

HE'S WATCHING YOU!

In London, a person couldn't forget the war for long.

After skirting the boundary of Hyde Park, Nancy reached Curzon Street, which, in its untouched state, felt like a fairy tale come to life. At number ten, Nancy stopped before the cozy window and studied the customers bustling inside. It cheered her to think that, even in the worst of times, people loved a good tale.

As she was about to duck into the shop, Nancy's eyes caught on the display, and her high spirits were at once killed. Perched in the window were a dozen copies of Evelyn's new book. Nancy fought the urge to put a foot through the glass.

"Damn you," she muttered, and pushed through the door to enter the shop. How was that the most miserable people seemed to have the most success?

❧

"Where have you been?" Mollie demanded. "You were supposed to arrive forty minutes ago!"

"Believe me, I'm frustrated, too," Nancy said. "Unfortunately, I got tied up marinating a side of beef. Add to that the atrocious weather, and the long walk to work. I know you rather like the bus, but we should save fuel for the boys. Now, would you mind stepping aside? You're trapping me here in the doorway."

"Don't repaint your tardiness as sacrifice," Mollie said, glowering.

"Keep your wig on, ducky," Nancy said. She darted around Mollie and onto the shop floor. "Nothing is ever as bad as you make it out to be. All I see are happy customers, plus endless heaps of books." Nancy sighed. "There has to be a better way of organizing this shop than to throw everything onto tables, don't you think?"

"They're arranged by genre. Do you see that man over there?" Mollie said, and pointed toward a large, bearded fellow in a brown Fustian coat. "He's the claimant to the throne of Poland. He tried

to get my attention for fifteen minutes, to no avail. Now he's waiting for Heywood to come back so he can have me fired!"

"There hasn't been a throne in Poland since the eighteenth
century."

"That's probably why he's trying to claim it!" Mollie wailed.

"Where are Heywood and Anne, anyhow?"

"Buying books from a dead man," Mollie said. "Worse than
all of this is that your friends have been hanging around for
hours, driving me mad. I don't think there's ever been a single
book bought between them!"

"My friends?" Nancy said, at once bounding back to life. "Oh,
thank God, someone to talk to. Well, don't hold back. Which
friends are these?"

"The usual group of insufferable literary prigs," Mollie said.

"That hardly narrows things down." Nancy stretched to see.

"The one Heywood despises," Mollie said. "With the dour
face."

"Jim Lees-Milne. He was once engaged to Anne, which is
Heywood's chief problem with the man."

"Didn't she ever dodge a bullet. There's also the persnickety
chap who always needs blankets despite the fact of his wearing a cape."

"That would be Eddy Sackville-West," Nancy said. "A slight
hypochondriac."

"The woman is also here. Hellbags? And, of course, Evelyn
Waugh." Mollie spit out his name like a curse.

"Don't worry," Nancy said. "I feel rather the same."

"Why is he always in the shop? Doesn't he have anywhere
else to go?"

"Sadly, no. We've been forced to establish the Evelyn Tolerance Charity because we're the only ones who can stand the
man." Nancy reached out and playfully joggled Mollie's shoulder. "Don't fret, he'll be shipping out soon. While we're on the

topic, don't feel compelled to put so many copies of his book on display. How's it selling? Miserably, I pray."

Mollie shrugged. "All right, I guess."

"All right" was better than Nancy had hoped, but rather less than she'd feared. *Put Out More Flags* was earning high praise, with critics applauding Waugh for being the first writer to address the upper class's contribution to the war. Namely, that they failed to deal with Hitler back when he was merely a middle-class pest. The novel had its points, but Nancy found its characters one-dimensional, and a bit unfair, and she was beyond tired of newspapers treating Evelyn as though he were some kind of savant. He might've gone to Oxford, and been part of the Bright Young Things, but, at the end of the day, Evelyn Waugh was just your workaday bloated drunk in a bowler hat.

"Thanks for keeping me apprised," Nancy said, and clapped Mollie on the back. "If you'll excuse me, I must check on my friends. Let me know if you need anything!"

Nancy pranced off to the middle room, where her literary prigs were assembled in oversized club chairs, sniggering like witches beside a snapping fire. "The reports are true!" Nancy said. "Miss Frieze-Green warned me that reprobates had infiltrated the shop. Tell me, what did I miss?"

"Absolutely nothing," Evelyn said.

"Evelyn has for the last hour been bragging about his book," said Jim.

"The term *literary phenomenon* is being used," Evelyn said. "Nancy, we must have a conversation about the window display. I have some notes."

"That's something to raise with Heywood," Nancy said, and turned away from the men. She grasped Lady Dashwood's hands and gave her a kiss. "Darling Hellbags! I've missed you desperately! I never expected to be this lonely in London, with so many people around."

"The city is awful," Helen said as the group rolled their eyes.

"Not sure if you've heard," said Eddy, "but everyone in London abhors Lady Dashwood. Grab a tissue, it's the saddest tale ever told."

"It's not funny! People are spurning me, left and right. I must be on a list at the Dorch. Nancy, do you know anything about this?"

"I do not," Nancy said as she scooted up onto a counter. "I can't keep up with these things."

"I doubt they'd even let me into the bomb shelter. Being married to Johnny has given me the *worst* reputation."

"That's how these things usually go," Nancy said, though the blame could not be placed entirely on him, given Lady Dashwood had a personality at best described as "invigorating."

"Helen, your preoccupation with your reputation," Jim said, "and who thinks what, is not only tiresome, but childish."

"Easy for you to say! You have no social standing whatever. If you disappeared, no one would notice for years. Well, I would notice, because it'd be the best day of my life. You'd finally be out of my house!"

"Poor Hellbags," Nancy clucked, and crossed one leg over the other. She brushed an errant fuzz from her black wool pencil skirt.

"Did you walk to work?" Jim said as he appraised her through one squinched eye. "Your attitude about the war is confusing, your sudden seriousness perverse."

"Even we frivolous, uneducated girls can appreciate the gravity of war," Nancy said.

"*Flags* is sweeping America," Evelyn said, though precisely no one asked. "My agent predicts it will be a worldwide hit. Meanwhile, it was nothing to write—a minor work dashed off on a tedious voyage."

"Was this before or after you and your comrades bungled things in Dakar?" Hellbags asked.

"Now that I think about it," Evelyn said, lifting one scurrilous brow. "Nancy, I reached out several times asking what you made of the subplot involving Basil Seal's incestuous relationship with his sister. You never responded."

"It was my least favorite aspect of the book," Nancy said. "Though I assume that's why you wrote it."

Basil Seal was one of Evelyn's recurring characters, a shiftless ne'er-do-well modeled after Prod. In this book, Basil was a billeting officer who conned the wealthy into paying him *not* to bring displaced urchins into their homes. It was an appalling abuse of character as just about the only thing Prod cared about was refugees.

"I'm sorry if the reappearance of Seal upset you," Evelyn said. "But readers love him, and I can understand why. It's really quite remarkable to find such dullness and depravity in one person." He put up a hand. "Before you protest, remember that I've known Prod much longer than you have."

"Is this where you remind me that you punched him at Balliol?" Nancy said. "Your one act of bravery. Speaking of books, did Laura receive my gift?" Evelyn's second wife had given birth to their fourth child, and Nancy aimed to start the little one's library with first editions of *Peter and Wendy* and *The Boy Castaways of Black Lake Island.*

"Yes, she did," Evelyn said. "Honestly, Nancy. Barrie? Most people regard his books and plays as among the most insidiously unmoral forms of children's literature. But thank you for the thought."

"You really suck the pleasure out of giving gifts," Nancy said.

"Sucks the pleasure out of most things," Hellbags said. "And not in the good way."

Nancy snickered and looked up to see a flash of gray. A customer, maybe? Or was it the apparition from earlier?

"Spare me, Hellbags," Evelyn said. "If Nancy insists on working in a bookshop, she should know the difference between good literature and bad."

"You're such a worm!"

"I *thanked* her, Hellbags. Calm down."

"Poor Laura," she said. Cursing under her breath, Hellbags flipped to the first page of her book. It was Agatha Christie's latest, a surprise, for Nancy hadn't known her to read.

"What are you working on, Nancy?" Evelyn asked. "*Pigeon Pie* came out two years ago. Surely you've made progress on something new."

"I've been busy," Nancy said, chin lifted. "With wartime duties and a full-time job. Now that life is settling down, I just need to find the right topic."

"You'd better find one soon," Evelyn said. "If much more time passes, you won't be able to call yourself a writer anymore."

"Nancy's almost forty years old!" Hellbags said. "And she's written four books! What else would she be, if not a writer?"

"A book hawker? Nancy, you'll never be happy selling other people's work."

"This is temporary," Nancy said, as Mollie's narrow little face poked out from behind a gold-painted pillar. Sighing, Nancy popped off the counter to collect the muckle of books at Eddy's feet. "I like working at the shop, and I need the money. My last book didn't sell, and Peter *never* gets paid. It's a very delicate dance."

"I'm sure Prod gets paid," said Evelyn, practically. "He probably keeps it for himself. As for your next book, I have some ideas."

"No, thank you," Nancy said, cramming Eddy's books into the nearest available shelf. "By the way, it would be absolute *heaven* if one of you could purchase something, now and again. We are trying to run a business, not a salon."

"Salon," Eddy mused. "That's a hell of an idea."

"Your strongest novel is *Wigs on the Green*," Evelyn said. "You shine when you write about things that have really happened. Specifically, your family."

"Actually, I was considering writing about you," Nancy said. "The book would be called *The Perpetual Agitation of a Million Tiny Things*."

"Very droll. Save the humor for your work."

"I didn't like *Wigs*," Eddy said. "It was silly."

"Thank you, Edward. When I woke up this morning, I hoped somebody might critique me for a book that came out seven years ago."

"That line about Hitler being a splendid fellow?" He made a face. "It was upsetting."

"A splendid fellow who carried things a 'shade too far,'" Nancy reminded him. "It was a parody. Obviously, I don't think Hitler has any redeeming qualities!"

Eddy pondered this as he fiddled with his ring. It was a gold, gaudy affair dominated on this day by a five-carat pink sapphire, one of the forty-some stones he swapped in and out.

"Don't listen to Eddy," Evelyn said. "I'm the one who understands fiction. Semi-autobiographical suits you. This is because, while you're a decent writer, you don't know how to think."

"Gosh, Evelyn," Nancy said. "Why is it that every conversation with you leaves me feeling as though I've just survived an air raid?"

"Evelyn Waugh is *not* the expert on literature," Hellbags said. "His books are a chore to read. I'd rather do almost anything else, including Johnny, and that's saying something!" She paused and tapped her chin. "On the other hand, Evelyn's novels are miles better than his personality, so there's that."

"Evelyn," Nancy said. "I appreciate your feedback, but a *Wigs* reprisal is not in the cards. The book didn't sell, and it widened the rift in my family. All these years later, Diana is barely speaking to me, and Unity won't talk to me at all, unless she temporarily forgets who I am."

"Unity has never been pleasant to converse with," Eddy said. "So you can't be that upset."

"Diana is delightful company, though," Jim said. "I adore the woman."

"You and the rest of the world," Nancy said.

"I'm confounded," Jim said. "That you mind not getting along with Diana. I find her wonderful, of course, but if she's in prison, doesn't that make her an enemy in your view? How did you girls phrase it, when distinguishing the good people from the bad?"

"Hons and Counter-Hons," Nancy said. She smiled wistfully, her mind transported to those sunnier days. "I'm surprised you don't remember, since you acted like such the horrible Counter-Hon when Tom brought you home for school holiday."

While Tom had warned his friend about the six sisters, he failed to accurately describe the extent of their pranks, not to mention all the shrieking, crying, and training of retrievers to find dead rabbits in the couch. In the end, Jim's maiden visit would be his last, because of the unwieldy sisters, and a small fracas with Lord Redesdale. Nancy couldn't recall the topic— something about the Germans—but tensions escalated quickly, and Jim was the sort to dig in his heels. Before long, all six Mitford girls, ages six to twenty-one, broke out into song.

We don't want to lose you, but we think you ought to go!

Jim fled the next morning, and they'd not spoken of it since.

"How could Diana *not see Wigs* as a parody?" Evelyn said. "She is very sharp."

"Nazis and Fascists don't have the winningest senses of humor," Nancy said. "Shocking, I know. Nonetheless, I'll come up with *something* to write, something more serious than I have done before." Though Nancy spoke with conviction, this was really more hope than a vow.

"What about your spying?" Hellbags chirped.

"Are we back to that nonsense?" Evelyn said.

"It's not nonsense," Nancy sniffed.

"It's not spying if you were blabbing about it constantly."

"Why don't you write a novel based on your clandestine adventures?" Hellbags said. "Everyone would read that!"

Evelyn shuddered. "Spy novels are so démodé," he said.

Nancy closed her eyes to stop from crying, or shooting daggers at each of them. If her so-called friends had read *Pigeon Pie*, they would've known she'd already written a spy novel, and it was a hideous flop.

"I have to agree with Evelyn," Nancy said. "Spy novels are very 1940. Mollie! Mollie, what are you doing? You've been cowering behind that column for the past five minutes. Do you need something?"

"Uh…er…" Mollie stuttered, looking frightened and wan.

"Come on, spit it out."

"There is a man here, in a gray coat." She audibly gulped. "I tried to make him leave but he said that, if I didn't fetch you right away, we'd both be arrested for subversive activities."

Monday Afternoon

G. Heywood Hill Ltd.

"We've been over this," Felix says as Katie lurks outside the red selling room, beneath gold letters announcing RARE BOOKS. "Mister Dunne is on holiday. You are welcome to leave a note, or try again in a week."

"I can't wait that long, mate," a man says. "I've read that the Duke is currently in London. Do you think you could ring him, send him a note, perhaps?"

"I'm sorry, but no. I will not be bothering the Duke of Devonshire."

Katie's jaw drops. She peers around the doorjamb to see what kind of person demands an audience with a duke. Immediately she catches Felix's eye.

"Katharine," he says, and she jumps back. "What are you doing?"

When his companion turns around, Katie sees it's the handsome stranger from the other day. She begins choking on her own breath.

"Are you all right?" Felix asks, forehead crinkled with concern.

"Yes, hello, fine," she croaks.

Somehow, the man is even hotter than she remembered, so

good-looking that it feels contrived. He's unnecessarily tall, for one, and his cheekbones are overly defined. His eyes are bluer than blue, his hair a rich brownish black, and the overall effect is that of someone abusing an Instagram filter.

"You look peaked," Felix notes.

Katie unwinds her scarf and unbuttons her coat. "Just a little hot," she says.

"Excuse me," Felix says as he steps around the visitor. "Katharine, your lovely hostess just rang to say you were on the way. I was seconds from stepping out, so your timing is perfect."

"You're leaving?!" Katie says.

"Only for the day. I'm off to Essex, to appraise the library of an estate." Felix holds up a pair of children's books. "Jojo had these on order. Can I pass them off to you?"

"Of course," Katie says.

Felix bows in thanks, then checks his watch. "Bloody hell!" he says. "Haven't even left and I'm already late. Thank you, again, Katharine. Okay. Cheers, thanks, goodbye!" Before Katie can respond, Felix darts off, stranding her in this bewildering space (red shelves, blue carpet) with this bewildering man. Because there's no getting out of the situation, Katie throws on one of her bubbly smiles. "Hello!" she says, stepping down into the room, arm outstretched. "Katie Cabot."

"Simon," the man responds with a nod as Katie's hand remains dangling.

"All righty," she mumbles, and lets her arm drop, thinking that this Simon character is awfully rude for someone dressed like he's about to sit for a Catholic school portrait.

"Interesting reading choices," Simon says, and gestures to the books in her hand.

Katie narrows her eyes. "They're for my goddaughter," she says.

"I love *Mr. Putterbee's Jungle*."

"Okay. Well…thanks for the information. Hope you're able to track down your Duke."

Katie slides *Wigs on the Green* from its shelf.

After studying the cover, she ticks past the dedication ("To Peter") and turns to the introduction. Published in 1935, *Wigs* was Nancy's third book, and it took direct fire at the Fascist movement and two of her sisters, Unity and Diana. Nancy famously refused to rerelease it, even once she was famous, and in need of cash.

"I was serious," a voice says.

Katie jolts, and Cordelia's books plummet to the floor. "Motherfucker!" she barks, and drops to her knees. Hovering overhead is the man from before. "These books are expensive. And you really shouldn't sneak up on people! Especially women. I don't care how good-looking you are—"

"Thank you!" he answers, grinning.

"That was not a compliment!"

"Seriously, I'm sorry. I really am. I didn't mean to startle you." He reaches out, but she refuses help.

Katie lurches to her feet. "Don't worry about it," she says. Though she's now standing, Katie must still crane to see his face. He must clear six feet by three or four inches, at least. "You're very tall," she blurts, and Simon laughs.

"Excellent observation," he says as Katie looks away.

She can already sense he's like most of his height—cocky, insufferable, unable to understand the "little guy." The world looks different from way up there, and thus it's really not his fault, but this is why Katie prefers men who are shorter, more reliably compact. Men like Armie Acosta, not that he's her "type" anymore.

"When I said *Mr. Putterbee's Jungle* is a good book," Simon says as Katie massages the cramp in her neck, "I wasn't taking the piss."

"No worries," Katie says. She returns *Wigs* and moves farther down the shelves.

"The second book," Simon says, trailing her, taking one step for her every two to three. "*Edgar Allan Crow*? I don't know it. Mind if I have a look?"

Katie pivots all the way around. "Why are you so interested?" she asks. "You must have a four-year-old who's in the market for a custom library. Quite the trend. Is the local concierge out of llamas and chinstrap penguins?"

"Not sure I follow," he says, and laughs again, this time confusedly.

"I mean, I get it. It must be difficult to find live Barbies or actors to do fake James Bond–style kidnappings."

"I'm not sure how one arrives at a kidnapping from a punny children's book, but, if it helps, I've never employed a concierge service, nor do I anticipate ever being in want of one."

"What if you needed seven albino peacocks?"

"I'd have to make do with the regular kind," he says. "Or, maybe, no peacocks at all?"

"Who would you call if you had to deflate an agitated puffer fish?"

"Depends on why it was upset. Do you work in the exotic pet trade or something?"

"Do I seem like someone who works in the exotic pet trade?" Katie asks, straightening her spine, trying to seem taller and take up more space.

"You don't appear to be covered in feathers or scratch marks." He smiles widely, using his whole face.

"Very funny." Katie loops around him, allowing a berth of six feet. She returns to the Mitfords but can feel him nearby. "To answer your question, my friend uses one of those services. I guess her needs are mostly animal related. You still haven't told me why you're so curious about *Edgar Allan Crow*. Bespoke library for your kid?"

"A far more prosaic answer, I'm afraid. I work with children."

Without warning or cause, Katie's expression sours. She

doesn't know what she was expecting, or why she's so bemused. "Children?" she says. "In what way?"

"Wow. Okay," Simon says. "It seems like I should be offended, but I can't find it in me."

"No. Sorry." Katie shakes her head. "I don't know what came over me. I guess... I dunno... I thought you'd have one of those asshole jobs."

"What is an *asshole* job?" he asks, and his smile turns into a full-blown smirk.

"You know, with money, or politicians, or suing people. Ugh! Never mind! I'm not making any sense. Jet lag!" She flips around and plucks *Don't Tell Alfred* from the shelf.

"I'm head teacher at a primary school," Simon says. "Though I suppose it's possible some people think I'm an asshole."

Katie turns back. "A head teacher?" she says. "What, is that like a principal?"

"Something like that, yeah."

She shudders. "What a horrible job."

"You are very charming." Simon smiles, and it's blinding. He's a Brit with perfect teeth, which is another thing Katie finds suspicious.

"I have a question," she says. "This is going to sound strange."

"*This* is going to sound strange? Oh, no."

"It's about the kids at your school," Katie says. "Do they wear green velvet smoking jackets?"

He blinks. "Blazers, do you mean?"

"Sure," Katie says. "I'm staying with a friend, here in Mayfair. Her kids wear these ridiculous outfits. The blazers, as I mentioned, plus polo shirts. Coordinated knee socks. Wide-brimmed boat hats. The boys wear ties. *Real* ties. Not clip-ons. My friend insists all children in London dress like they've stepped out of the pages of *Wind in the Willows*."

"Aren't the characters in *Wind in the Willows* animals?"

"Fine. Kids from Edwardian-era children's literature," Katie clarifies. "What I'm asking is, do the kids at your school wear velvet, plaid, and gondolier hats?"

"That'd be a no," Simon says with yet another laugh. "Though I work at a community school in Burwash, and it's mostly red jumpers. We are sadly lacking in velvet, as well as albino peacocks."

"Excellent! I love any opportunity to prove my friend wrong. Thank you very much," Katie says. She begins paging through *Don't Tell Alfred*.

"Are you a Nancy Mitford fan?" Simon asks. "She's why I'm here, too."

Katie looks up. "It's not for the kids at your school, is it? Aren't they a bit young?"

"I think Farve beating Germans about the head with an entrenching tool might be a tad much, yes. I've come to Heywood Hill as part of a…personal project."

"What's this project?" Katie asks, and slides *Don't Tell Alfred* back into its place.

"I'm looking for an unpublished memoir Nancy Mitford wrote while working here."

"It's you!" Katie says.

"Uh-oh. Felix told you. Sang my praises, no doubt."

"To the high heavens," Katie says. Her gaze sweeps his left hand, and she curses herself once for checking, and a second time for noticing the ring finger is bare. "Honestly, what's the big deal?" she says. "Most writers have an unpublished book or two lying around. Are you related to her or something?"

"Definitely not."

"Then what is it? Why would you—" All at once, the truth hits Katie, and the corners of her mouth lift. "Ah. You're a writer. You're trying to write a book." She taps her temple. "I get it."

"Incorrect," he says.

"I don't believe you. This is too much mental energy for a random literary mystery of no ultimate importance."

"Not sure why you find it so unusual. Here's a secret." He

leans in, and Katie can smell his shampoo—a dash of coconut, she thinks. "Sometimes people just want to know things," he says. "They have intellectual curiosities not tied to concrete outcomes."

"No shit," Katie says, for she is well versed in fruitless, drawn-out searches that go in circles for years. Otherwise known as the hundreds of books and thousands of articles she's read while researching novels that don't exist.

"I've been interested in the Mitford family for ages," Simon continues. "I read English literature at university."

"Same." Katie crosses her arms. "I even wrote my senior thesis about her. That's not why."

"Haven't you ever been taken by something, or someone, for no discernible reason?" Simon asks. "A topic, or endeavor that might be categorized as a hobby? Do you have these in America?"

"I have tons of hobbies," Katie says, though she cannot think of one now. Walking her dog might count. Plus, writing is the type of job that can feel like a hobby, too. "At the risk of sounding very American," she says, "I don't think general interest is driving your quest. You called it a 'personal project.'"

"Everything's personal, Katie," Simon says with a wink.

"But you seemed anxious when you were talking to Felix. A little too hurried for someone just exploring his hobbies. A little too desperate to meet a duke."

"Goodness. You are very argumentative," Simon says. He pushes up the sleeves of his sweater. "Never has a person been subjected to such intense interrogation whilst in a bookshop. To answer your question, I don't live in London. I am on a very brief holiday and must be back in High Weald by the weekend."

"A vacation?" Katie balks. "A few weeks before Christmas break? What do the parents at your school think?"

"Not sure I need to explain my schedule to an officious American, but I customarily visit my mum during Christmas, and, on occasion, I do enjoy taking time for myself. I'm not in a position to jet off to the Algarve or some such, so London in November will have to do."

Even as Katie hassles him, Simon remains all chuckles and toothy merriment, the very embodiment of winsome, except for the fact he's a little *too* jolly for Katie's tastes.

"Why, though?" she presses. "Why not stick with Nancy Mitford's published work?"

"I'm simply keen to learn more about the last book she wrote before she moved to France. Is that so strange? Wouldn't you want to read it?"

Katie mulls this over. An unpublished autobiography is really no different from reading letters, and she's always interested in those. The memoir could be nothing more than the wrong words and clunky sentences, like Katie's unseen work, or it might be instructive, evidence of a necessary detour on Nancy's path from fledgling author to *The Pursuit of Love.*

"Actually, yes," Katie says. "I do want to read it. And I'll help you look."

"Help?" Simon flinches and goes a little cross-eyed. "Why?"

"I dunno. My curiosity is piqued, and this feels…" Katie waves around a hand. "Preordained. I know a lot about Nancy Mitford, and I have the time."

"I can't accept your help," Simon says. "Your offer is very kind but, no, I'm sorry. You shouldn't waste your time. I don't even know that I'll be successful."

"Doesn't matter," Katie says. "I think it'd be fun."

"Why would you want to, other than it feels 'preordained'?"

Katie shrugs. "Lots of reasons. My inherent enthusiasm for Nancy Mitford, for one. Plus, my life has been a bit up and down, and I need a distraction. Also, Felix promised me access to her personal papers. So, there's that."

Simon breaks out another grin. "Now we're getting somewhere!"

"Just so you know," Katie says, raising a finger. "I'm not flirting with you."

"Absolutely no one would interpret your reaction to me as flirting." Simon gives a very trenchant smirk. "Are you sure you don't have better things to do? Why are you in London, any-how? Are you on holiday?"

"I'm staying with a friend—"

"Chinstrap penguins and gondolier hats. Yes."

"She has a writing deadline," Katie says. "So, I'm on my own during the day."

"What's the name of this mysterious writer friend?"

"Jojo Hawkins-Whitshed. I doubt it's your—"

"Brilliant!" Simon says, and yet another smile blasts across his face. "I know Jojo Hawkins-Whitshed! Not personally, but she's my ex-girlfriend's favorite author. Brain candy, she called it. Cheap and chipper!"

"That's Jojo for you."

"Ah, Katie." Simon goes to place a hand on her shoulder but pulls back. "Your offer is kind, but preposterous. You didn't come to London to act as a teacher's research assistant."

"No, I didn't, but I came on a whim, which means for no reason at all." Katie exhales and reminds herself to slow down. She has been speaking at a very brisk pace. "This seems like a good way to spend my time."

Simon tucks his hands into his pockets and studies Katie for some time. "I could probably benefit from your strangely prof-fered brand of help," he says. "And it might be fun to have a re-search partner. Listen, do you need to be anywhere right now?"

"Right now?" Katie repeats, and her heart flaps like a pack of birds. "I don't think so?"

"Excellent." Simon wields another of his deadly smiles. "Whaddya say, then? Shall we get started?"

June 1942

Baker Street

If there was one advantage to being summoned to Baker Street while in front of her friends, Nancy could finally prove to Evelyn that her prior spying wasn't "nonsense."

Alas, whatever gratification Nancy felt was brief, and extinguished the moment she stepped into the familiar boxy gray building. What was she thinking, being incommunicado for so long? One did not shake a shadowy governmental entity as if it were a bad date.

I was ill, Nancy repeated in her head as she waited in the cool, blank room.

A year had passed since Gladwyn Jebb last called Nancy to this office, to discuss the problems with the Free French, de Gaulle's government-in-exile which was now operating out of St. James's Square. The Frogs were everywhere of late, drinking, and cavorting, and spilling large sums of cash. To keep an eye on the situation, Gladwyn and his colleagues—whoever they were—needed a beautiful, French-speaking spy to infiltrate their officers' club.

"Me?" Nancy had laughed. "Are you mad?"

"You've proven yourself trustworthy," Gladwyn reminded her.

"I'm flattered," she said. "But no, thank you. I don't know the first thing about Frog society, and it would bore me to death to work in an officers' club. It'd also interfere with my nightly bath."

Gladwyn intimated—nay, declared—that Nancy had no real choice, and thus she was compelled to agree. "Fine," she'd said. "But I hope you're not expecting me to engage in any Frog assignations."

In the end, charming the Free French was a delicious occupation. They were a tremendous breed, and Nancy did have her assignation, thanks to the beautiful, consumptive Captain André Roy. The affair ended when he'd gone to Africa, and Nancy to West Wycombe but, as sweet as it'd all been, Nancy wanted to leave it in the past.

As she waited, and waited, Nancy reminded herself that she couldn't possibly be in real trouble. Although Gladwyn Jebb was a high-powered governmental muck-a-muck, the Assistant Undersecretary of this or that, she'd first known him as one of the fusty old men from her father's shooting parties.

Oh, Gladwyn, you old so-and-so, how have you been? Run into Farve lately?

At last, the doorknob turned.

"Gladwyn!" Nancy cried, and leapt to her feet. "You sure love to keep a gal waiting!"

"Pleased to see you're still among the living," Gladwyn said, and motioned for Nancy to sit. "Thank you for not bringing your dog."

"Yes. Well." Nancy tossed her eyes. "Your secretary was *very* governessy about it the last time. Anyhow, you look well!" He didn't, but this was hardly the point.

"Likewise," Gladwyn said. He consulted a small stack of papers. "I trust you've recovered from your recent hospitalization? It would've been prudent to notify the department of your intended absence."

"You knew about the hospital? I had no idea…" Nancy looked down. "I meant to send a telegram, but time got away from me. My sincerest apologies. I was rather weak, physically and emotionally."

"I understand, but you have been back for…" Gladwyn checked his papers again. "Three and a half months?"

"Yes, well." Nancy cleared her throat. "I needed a job, and you stopped paying me."

"Because you stopped working," Gladwyn said, and pushed his glasses atop his head. "First, I'd like to express my condolences regarding your sister's husband. The Crown appreciates his bravery and sacrifice."

Nancy eyeballed the man, trying to intuit which sister's husband he meant. Diana's was in prison, same as his wife, and no one at Baker Street would deem such a wanton Fascist brave. Nancy saw Pam and Debo last week, and they hadn't mentioned any calamities associated with Derek, nor Debo's new husband, Andrew. Only one remained. Decca's husband had gone missing in November.

"Esmond Romilly, you mean," Nancy said. "Thank you for the kind words. It's been dreadfully hard on Decca. Part of me thinks it might be worse when a loved one goes missing, as opposed to turning up dead. It's the difference between wild supposition and knowing the truth."

"The lack of finality can be very stressful," Gladwyn agreed, "but it'd serve your sister to come to terms with the facts."

"I know, I know." Nancy flicked a hand. "Though, in fairness, his body was never found."

"His plane went down over the ocean."

"Yes, but our very own cousin advised Decca to keep the faith," Nancy said. "According to him, downed men often show up six, nine months later in prisoner-of-war camps. Can you really blame Decca for clinging to hope?"

"Your cousin really should not have said that." Gladwyn

rubbed his weary eyes, doubtless wishing protocol didn't prevent him from taking a firmer stance. It was one thing to advise against listening to one's cousin, quite another when the cousin was Winston Churchill.

"Decca believes you're keeping him somewhere," Nancy said. "Because he's a…*Communist*, but I assured her that, here in England, Reds don't seem so bad. They hate Nazis, which is ever the winning trait. They'll probably betray us eventually, but who cares as long as they kill a few million Germans first."

"Missus Rodd!"

"What?" Nancy snapped. "Come on, you know it's true."

Groaning softly, Gladwyn leaned back. Nancy quailed, wondering if the chair could hold his full weight. "The facts are quite explicit," he said. "While returning from a bombing mission in Hamburg, Esmond Romilly's plane went down over the Red Sea, and he was never heard from again. I'm happy to provide you with the British Air Commission report."

"That's not necessary," Nancy said.

"Very well." Gladwyn returned his glasses to his face. "Let's get to it. The first item of business is André Roy. You've been tailing Captain Roy for over a year but haven't filed a report about him, or any of the Free French, in close to nine months."

"I've been somewhat out of pocket," Nancy said. "For reasons previously discussed, but no one in this or any country need worry about André Roy. He's as guileless as they come. The man is a doll, and a tad tubercular."

"Being associated with the Free French is enough to warrant suspicion," Gladwyn said. "And even sickly people can undermine democracy."

"If there's one thing I've learned in my spying career," Nancy said, "it's that your obsession with the Frogs is misplaced. It's true they let Hitler goose-step up and down the Champs-Élysées, but the worst act of treason I've witnessed is all that complaining about the theater in the West End. They hate the same things we do—Germans, the Vichy, Pétain—and, on the whole, I've found them a winning bunch. All that cheerfulness and endless flattery! And they never try to take a person down a peg, unlike the English."

As she spoke, Gladwyn removed a pen from his pocket and scribbled something in his notebook. Nancy stretched but couldn't snag a peek.

"What can you tell me about Captain Roy's visits to Weston Manor?" Gladwyn asked.

Nancy blinked. "Weston Manor?"

"Yes. Home to Lady Danette Worthington, in Buckinghamshire. I believe she's a friend of yours?"

"What possible concern could you have about Danette Worthington?" Nancy said. "I can't imagine her bothering to get mixed up in espionage or collaboration. She absolutely despises inconvenience."

"Yes, but there is the matter of her husband," Gladwyn said. "We have reason to believe Greville Worthington was working with the Nazis."

"Goodness," Nancy said. "You don't soften things around here, do you? Can't say as though I'm surprised. His countenance practically screams Nazi. It's that watery, blond appearance that's so reminiscent of a budding Hitler Youth."

Nancy shuddered, and Gladwyn gaped. "You knew about this?" he asked.

"Just a long-held suspicion," Nancy said. "Danette, on the other hand, is incapable of malice. Was Greville arrested? I noticed your use of the past tense."

"No, we had him shot," Gladwyn said.

"Shot!" Nancy yelped.

"Not on purpose. He was running off with his mistress and refused to stop when a sentry ordered him to halt."

"A mistress? Poor Danette," Nancy said. "She worshipped that man."

"Let's put aside the topic of Lady Worthington for now," Gladwyn said. "Do you have an explanation as to why Captain Roy was spotted at Weston Manor on several occasions?" He paused to stare at Nancy. "Or why you were as well?"

"Me?" Nancy said, trying to arrange her scattered thoughts. "I haven't done anything wrong." At least, not in the manner Gladwyn was insinuating. Nancy despised Nazis, and Fascists, and Greville Worthington, too, and the only reason André Roy had gone to Weston Manor was because of *her*.

"There was nothing nefarious about my visits," Nancy said, carefully. "I was actually helping the government. During the Battle of London, I hosted evacuees at my parents' house, at Rutland Gate."

Gladwyn nodded and jotted something in his little book.

"The evacuations, and eventual relocations, were disorganized," Nancy said. "Dozens of people came and went. Some were directed to our home by billeting officers, others just showed up. I saw paperwork only about half the time."

Prod brought the first refugees when Nancy was still living at Blomfield Road and plotting a relocation to her parents' house in Kensington as their own neighborhood was a prime bomb target due to its proximity to Paddington. On that morning, Nancy was in the garden, collecting the aluminum strips dropped to confuse radar, when through the back gate Prod walked, flanked by two siblings, ages three and five. The boy-girl pair belonged to one of his soldiers whose house in Brixton was "blown to bits." Their mother was dying of miscarriage, and they had nowhere to go. Nancy agreed to bring them with her to Rutland Gate.

Fifteen minutes after the children arrived, Danette Worthington rang for her usual post-raid gossip catch-up. How terrifying was it? Who'd been blown up, and where? Prod did what? *Children*, did you say? They can't stay in London! Heavens, here's an idea...

"I took the pair to Weston Manor," Nancy told Gladwyn. "The bombings worsened, and soon hordes of East End evacuees were boarding at my parents' home in Kensington. My district billeting officer was overwhelmed, and Danette Worthington accepted whomever I brought, nary a question nor complaint. She was a godsend."

Nancy would never forget hauling that first group out of the city, through flames and broken water mains, in a car borrowed from a neighbor and helmed by her housekeeper. It was Sodom and Gomorrah the whole way as Gladys kept her teeth clenched and foot pressed to the gas. Nancy cursed a blue streak as Milly shivered in her lap, and the kids trembled in the back seat beneath a pile of fur coats.

"I checked on the evacuees from time to time," Nancy went on. "And my furs. Captain Roy often accompanied me on visits. We're not in trouble for *helping*, are we? I may not have done things by the book, but there was scarcely a book to be found. Perhaps if the government had been better at organizing things..." She leveled her gaze. "André didn't... He didn't go to Weston Manor without me, did he?"

When Gladwyn shook his head, Nancy nearly crumpled in relief. Though she'd been the one spying on Roy, it would've cracked Nancy's heart to discover he'd betrayed her by having an affair with Danette, or engaging in another activity even more iniquitous.

"I must confess," Nancy continued. "That you'd question my patriotism feels like an insult, given our prior dealings. Though I never wanted to, I spied on the Frogs for you, and I gave you information about my own sister, which landed her in prison."

"The information about your sister was a formality," Gladwyn said as he ticked through several sheets of paper. "We had more reports on the Mosleys than we have prisoners at Holloway. Would you swear you knew nothing of Greville's activities, were you asked in court?"

"Court!" Nancy said, perspiring at the thought. "Yes, of course!"

"Very well. That's all I need, for now." Gladwyn slid a document across the desk. "In regard to your prior duties with the Special Operations Executive—we're asking that you cease all contact with André Roy, and other French officers. Please sign this, which acknowledges our discussion."

"I'm happy to sign," Nancy said, scribbling her name. "But you're on the wrong path. Anyway, André is in East Africa, fighting for the *Allies*." She pushed the paper back.

"We also request that you stop all contact with Danette Worthington," Gladwyn said.

"Gladwyn! That's absurd! Danette helped me through a very difficult time, and I've known her practically my entire life."

"I'm sorry, Missus Rodd," he said. "I must insist."

"But—"

"I know you Mitford girls don't like to follow orders," he said. "But you've signed the paper. Under Regulation 18B, we can arrest people we view as threatening, no charges or trial required. All that to say, Missus Rodd, I strongly suggest you don't even consider stepping out of line."

Monday Evening

The Kings Arms

The Kings Arms is the quintessential London pub with a black-and-gold façade, enormous lanterns, and a dangling coat of arms. Even at this early hour, a crowd has gathered outside, and Katie and Simon must negotiate several clusters of suited men to reach the entrance. Inside, the bar is even more tightly packed.

"Let's check upstairs," Simon says, and he leads Katie up battered steps and into a red-carpeted, red-walled dining room. They take a seat beside a window overlooking Shepherd Market Street.

"How great is this place?" Katie says as she opens her menu.

Around them, the same two Champions League matches play on a dozen screens.

"Great?" Simon gives her a look. "It's just your basic pub."

"Yes. *Exactly.*" Katie's eyes skim the fried foods and the beer. "There's something about them...the uncomplicated menu, the lack of pretension. The name!" She grins. "*The Kings Arms.* I mean, it's perfect!"

"You're weird," Simon says, and the left side of his mouth curls into a smile.

Katie's seat buzzes two, three, four times. Wincing, she sets down the menu and removes her phone from the back pocket of her jeans. "Sorry to be rude," she says. "But I should probably let Jojo know where I am."

"Please, go ahead."

As she types in her passcode, it dawns on Katie that she's drinking alcohol, alone, with a man she's just met, and in a foreign country, no less. It's a fantastically poor decision and could possibly make her the subject of a true crime podcast.

"Gosh, I'm getting old," Katie says, holding the phone away from her face, like she can't make out the screen. "Should've remembered my readers!" Katie clicks the camera, and Simon squints into the light. "Whoops. Sorry!" she squeaks.

"Next time you're trying to take a surreptitious photo of someone," Simon says, "best to turn off the flash."

"Sorry," Katie says again and, face flaming, bows to read Jojo's texts.

Is 8pm for dinner OK?

8pm Y or N?

Hey, any idea when you'll be back?
Can you respond really quick?

Hello?

Are you there?

Answer me!

OMG you always answer your texts are you dead?

Katie starts to write, "grabbing a pint," but worries it's too breezy and out of character, and Jojo might read it as a call for help.

**Sorry! Bad reception. Got caught up
w/ something at HH. Meeting one
of Felix's clients now re: Nancy M.
Don't wait! I'll figure out dinner.**

Huh?

See above ↑

So you're alive but are you OK?

**I'm great!
But, in case I go missing…**

Katie sends the picture, then reads Jojo's reply, (fire emoji), before putting the phone away.

"I didn't mean to do that," she mumbles, using the menu to cover her face. "My eyes are bad. I'll delete it. What do I want to drink?"

Ordinarily, Katie prefers wine, and though the Kings Arms' list is decent for a pub, Katie chooses Fireside Ale, plus fish-and-chips, because this is London, and why the hell not. Simon orders an IPA.

"Just a beer?" Katie says as the waitress walks off.

"It's early." Simon glances at his watch. "I'll eat after I catch up on work tonight. Yes, Katie, work. Can't have the parents thinking I slack off this close to the holidays."

"Very funny," Katie says, and looks away.

Somebody scores a goal on television, and they both feign interest. Simon smiles at Katie, and Katie smiles at Simon, and she's now more worried about holding a conversation than ending up dead. Katie makes a comment like, "That was a nice shot," and is about to excuse herself to the ladies' when, thank God, the waitress returns.

"Here you go," the woman says. As she sets down their drinks, her gaze jumps to the left and to the right. A funny expression wiggles across her face, as though she's trying to puzzle out what's happening between this strange short-tall pair. Katie gives her a look that says, *I know what you mean.*

"Well," Katie says, after the waitress swishes off. She hoists her drink. "To, uh… Nancy Mitford?"

"To her missing manuscript."

Katie touches her glass to his.

As she takes a sip, Katie feels a rush of happiness, or sentimentality, or something else she cannot name. She studies her beer, lifting it up to the light. "This is good," she says. "Really, really good."

"You are very upbeat," Simon notes.

Katie wipes a drop of foam from her lips. "I'm surprised by how much I like this. I didn't anticipate needing to choke it down or anything, but I'm not really a beer person."

"Interesting that you would order one."

"This is giving me…warm feelings?" Katie says as something begins to form in her head. "Beyond the alcohol." Suddenly, the picture locks into place. "My grandmother! That's what— *who*—I'm remembering. This beer reminds me of going to NFL games together. She was big into tailgating. Whooping it up. Talking all kinds of shit."

"Talking shit. Really."

"Loads of it," Katie says. "Have you ever noticed that older people can get away with *anything*? During one game, a Giants fan called security on us, and the only reason we didn't get bounced was because I said she's hard of hearing, and it was all a big misunderstanding. Nanny Carol was so offended, she made me Metro home and threatened to cut me out of her will. We'll see if she follows through on that."

As she yammers on, Simon ogles Katie with a slightly opened mouth.

"American football," she says, to help him out.

"Yeah. I got that. Has anyone told you that you speak very rapidly?"

"Only all the time."

"I must know which team you root for," he says. "Not the New York Football Giants, apparently. The Patriots?"

"Wow. Okay." Katie makes a sound like she's dislodging a peanut from the back of her throat. "That's pretty rude to say to someone you just met."

"The Cowboys?"

"Now you're just fucking with me."

Simon mulls this over for several seconds, tapping his foot. "The Eagles?"

"Oh my God!" Katie cries. "The Eagles? Jesus! If you wanted to call me a criminal, you should've just said the Raiders and cut to the chase."

Simon laughs. "This is very fun, but I'm out of teams. I reckon your favorite is whichever is in a rivalry with the Eagles?"

"Can it really be called a *rivalry* when one team has three Super Bowl trophies and the other only has one?" Katie says. "To be clear, it's my *grandmother's* favorite team. I don't really care, either way."

"Yes, you do seem very neutral about it."

"I live in Northern Virginia, outside DC," Katie says. "Our team is Washington. My grandfather bought season tickets over fifty ago, and Nanny Carol kept them after he died, at first only because she *enjoyed Art Monk's caboose*, but then she got into the actual football aspect of it. A little *too* into it, some might argue. I was the only one willing to go with her. It became our thing."

"That's adorable," Simon says. "I realize we've only just met, but I'd rather like to know your grandmother."

"You say that now, but it really depends on the circumstance. She's about to get kicked out of our fantasy football league for, and I'm quoting here, 'being a complete bitch.'" Simon's mouth drops, and Katie waves a hand. "It's a long story," she says. "And they're not totally wrong, but she's in her nineties, for Christ's sake. Cut the woman a break! Anyway, we had lots of good fun over the years, when I wasn't away at school, or living in New York. She gave up the tickets a few years back." Katie sighs. "After you reach a certain age, doctors don't want you day drinking, or climbing stairs, or spending five hours in direct sun."

As the server swings by with the fish-and-chips, Katie orders a second beer. The woman lifts her forehead as if to say, "Bad idea, but okay."

"Would you like a fry?" Katie says, and pushes her plate across the table. "Sorry, a chip?"

"No, thanks," Simon says. "Tell me, Katie, what do you do for a living? I don't think you've mentioned."

"Oh, not much." Katie bites into a chip and glances away. There is zero chance she's telling this Simon character about her flailing authorial aspirations.

"Not much?" he says, one brow arched. "Are you a woman of leisure? Is that why you had so many questions about personal concierge services?"

"Ha. No. Not even close. I work in the not-for-profit sector," Katie says. "Grant writing, on a contract basis. Eventually, I'd like to make my way into a leadership role."

The words tumble out, and only after she's finished does Katie cringe at her tall tale. She did work with not-for-profits at one time—though not in the past two years—and did envision titles like "Senior Vice President, Climate Change," when she worked at the World Wildlife Fund. But this was years before her first book came out, and Katie's done nothing since, other than to quit a job she liked very much.

"Admirable," Simon says, and Katie thinks she might throw up. "What clients are you working with now?"

"I'm between gigs. I'll be looking for something when I get back."

This much, at least, is true.

"Back in the shop, when you said your life was 'up and down,'" Simon says, "is this what you meant?"

"Oh. That. Yep!" Katie says, and takes a gulp of beer.

"Well, Katie Cabot," Simon says, lifting his glass again, "cheers to moving forward, and more ups than downs."

After ordering another beer, Simon reaches into the knapsack dangling from his chair. He pulls out a book marked with flags and plonks it onto the table.

Love from Nancy
THE LETTERS OF NANCY MITFORD
Edited by Charlotte Mosley

"That's so funny," Katie says. "I looked for the ebook version earlier, but it doesn't exist. I even emailed my local indie to see if they can order the paperback. All this was *before* I ran into you, so don't get excited."

"But it's so hard to contain myself," Simon says as he opens the book. "Why were *you* nosing around about Nancy Mitford?"

"Remember, she was the subject of my senior thesis," Katie says. "I've admired, idolized her for decades. Plus, you know, it's one of those things that falls into the category of general hobbies and interests."

Simon smirks. "I deserved that," he says. He stops on a page and looks up. "It's interesting you idolize Nancy Mitford. She's a phenomenal writer, but wasn't she...kind of mean?"

"Mean!?" Katie squawks. "That's outrageous! It's called a sharp and biting wit. I thought Brits were known for a dry sense of humor."

"I'm not referring to her wit," Simon says. "People were actively afraid of the woman. Her sisters complained that being beastly was her favorite sport!"

Katie flicks her hand. "Such a sisterly thing to say."

Simon chuckles. "What drew you to Nancy Mitford in the first place?" he says and, without asking, snakes one of her fries.

Katie stares, and Simon says nothing about the fry, and she is forced to consider whether she's seeing things. As he takes a bite, she understands she's not.

"Uh, um, well, her voice," Katie says, still tripping over her shock. "In my opinion, she's never gotten enough credit for her humor. I also like her spirit, the way she bucked convention."

"Is it bucking convention, though, to leave one's country, one's family, to follow a lover to Paris?"

"Was it about the lover?" Katie says. "Or Nancy having the money, and therefore the freedom, to do what she wanted? She'd been fantasizing about Paris forever. Thanks to the war ending, and the success of *The Pursuit of Love*, she finally had her chance."

It's every author's dream to write a book that'd change everything—like winning the lottery, but with more work and crying involved. Katie wonders where she'd be, and what she'd do, with *Pursuit*-level success.

"Freedom, huh? I never really thought about it that way," Simon says, though he remains visibly skeptical. "I have a confession." He slaps a hand on the open page. "This 'personal project' is more personal than I'd let on."

"I knew it!" Katie sings.

"You're quite the sleuth." Simon playfully rolls his eyes. "Are you familiar with the work Nancy Mitford did with refugees?"

Katie thinks for a moment and reaches for the book. Before the war, Nancy accompanied her husband to France, where they helped with the hundreds of thousands who'd fled the Spanish Civil War. Katie flips back a few pages from where Simon had been and finds a letter Nancy wrote to her mom in May of 1939:

If you could have a look, as I have, at some of the less agree-
able results of fascism in a country I think you would be less
anxious for the swastika to become a flag on which the sun
never sets.

"She went to Perpignan, right?" Katie asks, catching the location at the top of the page. "With Prod?"

"Yes, but the refugees I'm talking about came later, during
the Blitz. Turn to October 1940."

Katie ticks forward, pausing on a portrait of Nancy and her
sister Diana. Most of the Mitford girls were known for their
blondeness, their beauty, their piercing "Redesdale blues," a color
so remarkable servants' uniforms were dyed to match. Nancy,
on the other hand, stood apart with her dark hair and unusual
green eyes. Though Diana was deemed the prettiest sister, Katie
finds Nancy more striking.

Simon directs Katie to a letter written to Violet Hammersley,
a family friend. In a paragraph three-quarters of the way down,
Nancy declares her refugees are "being awfully good," and "no
kind of person could possibly in any way be nicer." A footnote
explains Nancy had temporarily relocated to her parents' house
in Kensington, which soon became a shelter for Whitechapel
evacuees. As the only Mitford in residence, Nancy took charge
of "not only the housekeeping for 50 people, but quantities of
other things as well."

"Another thing Nancy Mitford doesn't get credit for," Katie
says, after she finishes reading. "Being a humanitarian."

"Humanitarian might be a stretch," Simon says, and Katie gets
the sense he's not the fan he's claimed to be. "Any assistance she
gave refugees was happenstance, the by-product of something
else. The first time, in Perpignan, she followed Prod. This time,
the refugees were more or less assigned to her. They had billeting officers who oversaw these things."

Simon turns to another letter, this one dated Boxing Day

1940. One of Nancy's refugees, aged sixteen, is "in the family way," and Nancy suggested "a tremendous walk a hot bath & a great dose." Nancy teases that she might have to "wield a knitting needle & go down to fame as Mrs. Rodd the abortionist."

Katie lets out a gasp. "Surely she was joking..."

"Most likely," Simon says. He closes the book. "Lucky for me, given that sixteen-year-old was my grandmother. The baby was my mum."

"Your mom?" Katie's heart skips a step. "Are you sure?"

Simon nods. "My grandmother—her name was Lea Toporek—was evacuated to Rutland Gate after her building was bombed during a raid," he explains. "Eventually, she was transferred to the home of one of Nancy's friends in Buckinghamshire. That's where my mum was born."

"Your poor grandmother, to be pregnant and alone like that." Brow furrowed, Katie performs a quick calculation. "So, if your mom was born in early 1941, she must be..."

"Eighty years old, yes."

"How old are you?" Katie asks, and Simon spits out a laugh. "I mean, to have a mom who's..."

"Almost forty," he says. "And she was forty when I was born. She never expected or even wanted children, but I came along and properly botched her plans."

"I'll admit, this is a very cool connection." *If it's true*, she does not add. Sixteen-year-olds displaced during the Blitz must've numbered in the thousands. "Where does the manuscript fit in?"

Katie leans back and takes another swig of beer, deciding that she rather likes this pint-drinking business. Maybe it will be her "thing" when she goes out, instead of mid-priced Cabernet by the glass.

"The book is a memoir of her war years," Simon says. "In particular, Nancy's work with the refugees and at the shop. From what I've gleaned, my grandmother features prominently."

Katie scrutinizes his face for signs of subterfuge, or mental confusion. Is she letting Simon's appearance and general affability cloud her judgment? A serious memoir about evacuees does not seem very Nancy-like. This is, after all, a person who wrote a lighthearted romp about the budding Fascist movement.

"A war memoir," Katie says. "Huh. And you know this... how?"

"Nancy wrote to Lea several times between 1942 and 1945," he says. "Mostly about the book. She even sent along the odd page or two, which my grandmother kept, and my mum now has."

"Really?" Katie says, swinging from dubious back to intrigued. "Your family has personal correspondence from Nancy Mitford?"

"That we do," Simon says, and he beams.

"Maybe I will flirt with you after all." As soon as she says it, Katie looks away. She hasn't known him long enough to joke like that. "So, why did the letters stop?" she asks.

"I don't know why, exactly," Simon says. "But from what I can tell, Nancy finished *The Pursuit of Love* and received what she considered a healthy advance. The war ended, and she absconded to Paris, leaving most everything behind, including the memoir, and promises made to my grandmother."

"Promises made to your grandmother?" Katie says. "What, like money?"

"Something like that." Simon pauses and bites his lip. "But there's more to it. Lea took Nancy's disappearance personally. My mum...she, I don't know, carried on the hurt, even though she was only around five years old when Lea died."

"That's awful," Katie says. "I'm so sorry."

"Never knew the woman," Simon says brusquely, and picks up his phone. "I have a few pictures, of the letters. My mum has told me about them over the years, but I never really believed her. Emma Mutrie is not the world's most reliable narrator." Simon scrolls through several photos. After finding the right one, he rotates the screen toward Katie. "Recently, I was helping her move and stumbled across some," he says. "This is the start of their correspondence, written about two years after they met."

Katie takes the phone and expands the image once, and again, to make out the tight scrawl. As she reads, her heart gallops.

27 July 1942
Dear Lea,

By now I hope Lady Worthington has shared the news that I'm writing a book. It's about me, and you, and how we both ended up at Rutland Gate, during the Battle of London.

The tone is more serious than I customarily write, but light-hearted country manor farces don't seem to agree with me... or with the general reading population, it seems! Ha! So far, I have ten pages down. Don't laugh—this is a lot! The trick is finding the time. I pray you don't mind being included. Would you let me know, either way?

With love
NR

"I can't believe you have a letter from Nancy Mitford," Katie says, and returns the phone. "You're positive she wrote this?"

"It's signed with her initials, and the handwriting matches what I found online."

"Incredible," Katie says. "Of course, this only proves she started a book. Ten pages isn't a ton, and not completing things is basically part of the writing process. I mean, so I've heard. On podcasts." Katie tosses a fry into her mouth.

"There's another one," Simon says. "From April 1945. Nancy says the book is finished but she won't seek publication. Unfortunately, that letter seems to have gone missing. I saw it, at some point, but can't find it now. I don't really want to pester my mum about it."

"I guess that's decent evidence," Katie allows. "But—"

"Need more? All right. I appreciate a healthy skepticism." Simon winks. "In a recent interview, the Duke confirmed Nancy wrote an autobiography while working at the shop, but chose to publish *The Pursuit of Love* instead. Where else would the book be, if not in his possession?"

"It makes sense," Katie says. "But why would Felix lie, especially if the Duke has spoken about it openly?"

"That's the question, isn't it?" Simon says. "Felix has been cagey."

"Felix? But he's so nice!"

"Hmm. Maybe," Simon says. "But he's been...odd. At first, he was happy to help, but, when I came in person, he clammed up. I'm positive *somebody* is hiding something. The question is who, and what."

"Okay, maybe a manuscript did exist, at some point," Katie says as she winds a straw wrapper around her finger. "But it was a tumultuous time. They were in the middle of a war. London was repeatedly bombed."

"The shop wasn't hit," Simon reminds her. "Also, people have published full volumes of Nancy's letters, yet almost nothing is publicly available from the years she worked at Heywood Hill. Why is that?"

Katie continues pondering this, until the paper snaps. She balls it up and sets it down. "What are you looking for?" Katie asks as she meets Simon's gaze. "Specifically. It feels as though you want some kind of answer?"

Laughing, Simon shakes his head. "There are many things I want to find," he says. "Entire gaps in my family's story I'd like to fill in. This is, I realize, a lot to ask from a bunch of old paper. I'm sure you think I've lost the plot."

"Not at all," Katie says, and throws back the last of her now-warm beer. "Most people want to understand their family's story. And you definitely wouldn't be the first person to believe one book could solve everything."

July 1942

Weston Manor

"It's never locked," Nancy said as she popped open the taxi door. "Won't take but a second."

After scrabbling across the pebbles and rocks, Nancy hauled open the rusty gate and peered down the long, tree-lined drive toward Weston Manor, Danette Worthington's thirty-two-bedroom, ninety-six-acre stone estate.

"Follow this road all the way," Nancy said, when she climbed back into the car.

Nancy glanced behind them toward the main road. There didn't seem to be any other automobiles, nor any discernible tails. Gladwyn Jebb expressly forbade her from coming to Buckinghamshire—*don't even consider stepping out of line*—and Nancy was twelve kinds of nervous, but she had to warn her friend.

When they reached the main house, Nancy asked the driver to wait. "I shouldn't be long. I can't afford to be. Ha!" She slipped out of the taxi and walked shakily toward the house.

As Nancy pressed the bell, her body seized up. The door swung open and Nancy shrieked, nearly disengaging herself from her sensible shoes. "Oh, hello!" she yipped. The greeter wasn't Danette, or her butler, or any one of her seven maids. The face was familiar, but Nancy couldn't place it yet. "I'm sorry," she said, "I'm a stitch addled today. Can you help me out with your name?"

The young woman said nothing, only blinked. In this silence, Nancy found her answer. It was Lea Toporek, one of the refugees who'd come through Rutland Gate. How could Nancy have possibly forgotten? She had been drawn to the girl from the outset, compelled and repelled simultaneously. There'd been something about her that was...not quite right.

"It's you!" Nancy said. "Goodness, what a surprise! Aren't you supposed to have moved on by now?"

Lea continued on in mute determination, which was so aggravatingly in character that Nancy fought a scream. On the day they met, Nancy had just returned from soliciting extra blankets and pillows from friends to find Prod downstairs, in the kitchen, beside a waifish, black-haired girl. He smiled imploringly, and Nancy groaned. She was exhausted, and the house was bursting at the gills. Every bedroom was occupied, and twenty mattresses were spread across the ballroom floor.

"No, Peter," Nancy said. "No more of your refugees. We are out of room."

"Let's talk this through," Peter said, as he pulled Nancy into the larder for a more private conversation. "Please, I beg of you. Do me this one last favor."

"With you, one favor always turns into two or three!"

"I promise," he said. "No more after this. The girl's name is Lea Toporek, and her parents were killed in last night's raid. They refused to evacuate."

Lea had dutifully sheltered in a tube station, thus saving herself, which would be the first and last time the girl ever used a drop of sense.

"It'll be temporary," Prod swore. "She's engaged to one of my soldiers, Greenie."

"Engaged!" Nancy sniped. "Good Lord. With these East End

types, there's not a sliver of daylight between the schoolroom and marital bed."

Greenie was in hospital, Peter explained, due to have his leg amputated. He'd be released soon, at which point Lea would become his problem, instead of theirs. "Surely you can make room," he said. "Or take her to Danette's."

Nancy had agreed, same as before, which was to say, reluctantly and under duress. He made it sound so simple when, really, it was not.

"You're chatty as ever!" Nancy said as she and the girl continued to face off on Weston Manor's front steps. "If this conversation has reached its conclusion, might you tell me if Lady Worthington is home?"

Lea pointed listlessly toward the sunken garden, where Danette tiptoed across the grass. She wore only a nightdress, and bare feet, and a nurse and housemaid watched it all from a safe distance.

"Oh, dear. She misses Greville terribly, doesn't she?" Nancy said, and Lea nodded.

Danette Worthington had always loved her husband to an absurd amount, never believing she measured up physically, what with her clam-shaped face and enormous bushel of hair. Though Nancy firmly believed Greville got the better end of the deal, Danette often trotted out their wedding photographs to poke fun at herself. "Look at this handsome swain," she'd crow. "So gorgeous in his morning suit. But, good God, what is that beside him? A hobbit? A small bear?" Greville was six and a half feet tall, compared to Danette, who stood at only four feet, eight inches.

"Poor thing," Nancy said, frowning, as she watched Danette cross the lawn. "Is she always like—"

Nancy's query was interrupted by a joyful, high-pitched screech, and she looked over to see a tangle of limbs and white-blond hair hurtling in her direction. It was a child, a sprite of a thing, with big, blue eyes and white downy hair.

"Is this the baby?" Nancy said, and her heart withered, the smallest bit. "She must be over a year old by now! It seems everything turned out, didn't it? I was worried there for a second, especially when you waited so long to inform me of her impending arrival." Nancy felt a flare of irritation about how it all went down. Sighing, she glanced back toward Danette. "I should check on my friend," Nancy said, and turned to go.

"Her name is Emma," Lea said.

Nancy startled. "Emma?" she said, still facing away. "Is that right? Well, it was nice to see you both. By the by, I know you're prone to lingering around. It was practically impossible to get you out of my house! Despite what I'm sure will be your best efforts, you won't be able to stay here forever, especially not with your hostess in such a state."

⁓

When she spotted Nancy, Lady Worthington sprinted across the garden and locked her arms around her neck. She held tight, feet dangling inches off the ground.

"You don't hate me!" Danette said, snuffling against Nancy's breast.

"Who could hate you?" Nancy said. "Danette Worthington is one of the sweetest girls there's ever been. All right, down we go."

She peeled Danette's hands from her neck, and the woman dropped to the ground with all the weight of a feather.

"But haven't you heard?" Danette said. "I'm a social pariah. Greville ran off with another woman!"

"Another woman," Nancy repeated, adjusting her scarf. "Is that what you think the problem is? Darling, I hate to be the one to tell you, but a love nest is not where Greville's gone."

"I know that, Nancy! Of course I know he's dead!"

"What a relief." Nancy exhaled. "A relief that you're aware. His death is properly awful." She took Danette's hands in hers.

"I'm so sorry I haven't been out to see you. I rang several times but was told you weren't receiving calls."

"I can't bear to speak to anyone," Danette said. She leaned in, and Nancy felt the breath hot on her face. "You need to be careful, Nancy. This could happen to you."

"What could happen?" Nancy said. "Peter running off with a girl? He wouldn't have the nerve! And he's violently opposed to divorce."

"I meant the shooting."

"Darling, you should lie down," Nancy said, and stroked her friend's frizzy hair. "You're not making sense."

"Where is Peter? Do you know if he's all right?"

"Why are we talking about Prod?" Nancy said, scowling. "He's off fighting somewhere. We haven't spoken in a year! It's a bit of a tetchy subject."

Nancy assumed the war would strengthen their bond—absence makes the heart grow fonder, all that—but such hopes had long since been quashed. She never heard from him, nor he from her, and Nancy hated the idea that people like Greville were missed, while she was not. Even Unity received flowers from Hitler while she was in hospital.

"Nancy! Wake up!" Danette cried. "Don't you see? The government is shooting our own men now. Peter might be dead!"

"Don't be silly. He's in Ethiopia," Nancy said. "While I don't believe our government is shooting our men for no reason, they are up to a few things we must discuss. Inside might be best?" She peered over her shoulder toward the nurse and housemaid. Everybody was on guard these days, quick to ring the Home Office with any suspicion, large or small, and Nancy had enough problems without members of Danette's staff accusing her of treason.

"Can we finish my walk?" Danette said. "Greville wanted me to get more exercise."

"Oh, for Pete's sake. The best part of being husbandless is doing what you please. Nonetheless, if you want to walk, let's walk."

Nancy took Danette by the arm, guiding her away from curious ears. "I don't want to alarm you," she began, "but certain
folks within the government suspect Greville of collaborating
with the Nazis."

"Inconceivable!" Danette gasped. "He's the truest man I've
ever known!"

"I'm not sure about that…"

"Even if he did commit such horrors," Danette said, "what
does it matter? What does anything matter? He's dead."

"The problem is that you, my darling, are not."

As Nancy said the words, Danette's mouth formed into a perfect "O" of dismay. Though her friend took a moment to process the information, Nancy was reassured to find Danette still
capable of coherent thought. "I couldn't get in trouble, could
I?" Danette asked.

Nancy shrugged. "With Regulation 18B, anything goes. If
they decide he was involved and you knew about it, you wouldn't
even get a trial."

"No…" Danette said. "That can't be."

"They carted my sister off to Holloway when her baby was
only six weeks old," Nancy said. "You haven't publicly advo-
cated for the downfall of Britain, as far as I know, but there's
no longer a distinction between a person who is fairly and unfairly accused."

"But…" Danette jostled her head. "I didn't do anything! I
swear!"

"I'm not the one you need to convince."

"I'm tired," Danette said. "I think I need a nap."

"Brilliant. You should get as much rest as possible." Nancy
took Danette by the arm and steered her back around, slowly,
firmly, as though she were an ill-behaved horse. As they neared
the house, Nancy spotted Lea by the front door. "What is she
still doing here?" she asked.

"No one's sent for them," Danette said. "I don't think they
have anywhere to go. Why? You seem concerned."

"Just…be careful," she said. "I adored all of the refugees who came through Rutland Gate…but there was something about Lea."

"What do you mean?"

"Her general insouciance, for one," Nancy said. "I had fifty, sixty people at any one time, and everyone was anxious to help—not just me, but one another. Lea, on the other hand, was there for months, far longer than the others, and never lifted a finger. It's as though she was always waiting for something to happen. Part of me believes she wouldn't have acknowledged the baby until it came out of her wailing!"

"Well, I like having them here," Danette sniffed. "Emma is a delight, and Lea's been such help with Benjamin on the days I can't get out of bed. Honestly, I think you're letting your writerly imagination get the best of you. It's like you're turning them into a set of characters."

Nancy offered a light chuckle. "There's an idea," she said. "Maybe I should just write about them. They'd offer plenty of intrigue, to be sure." Though Nancy meant it as a tease, she felt the undeniable flicker of her own imagination, the churning of her brain. The men had their war memoirs, why not she?

"Oh, look!" Danette said, pointing, as Emma poked up from a hedge. "Isn't the little one precious?"

"So sweet," Nancy said. She looked back at Danette. "I must be off. Please, if you need anything, ring immediately. If I'm not at Blomfield Road, try Heywood Hill. I'm working there now."

"At a bookshop!?" Danette yelped, her brows shooting up into her hairline. The poor girl had almost no forehead to speak of. "Nancy! You're supposed to write books, not sell them!"

Nancy laughed. "Well, my dear," she said, "the goal is to do a little bit of both."

Tuesday Afternoon

G. Heywood Hill Ltd.

In the window next to Heywood Hill, and behind painted letters declaring, "Trumper's: A Gentlemen's Hairdresser," two men decorate a Christmas tree. Though the bookshop doesn't yet have any outward signs of the upcoming holiday, its window also casts an undeniably warm glow.

Katie steps inside, and the bell jangles its familiar tune. The floorboards groan as Katie skirts the crowded tables, which are more organized than she'd first assumed. There is some order here—perhaps by genre, or by subject—but mainly the shop feels laid out to encourage browsing, and general hanging around. When Felix's voice rings in the distance, Katie follows the sound until she finds him sifting through a cardboard box as his associate Erin stands nearby.

"Hi, all," Katie says.

Felix's face brightens. "Ah, Katharine! Hello!"

"Hi, Katie," Erin says. After telling Felix she'll follow up with a customer, she scurries off.

"Back for more?" Felix says, and rises to his feet.

"I can't help myself, apparently. How was the library from yesterday?"

"Pretty fair," Felix says with a double bounce of his head. "The family won't get what they think, but I saw some gems. The Rare Books head and I are returning Thursday afternoon." He tosses a clipboard into the box. "So, what are we on the hunt for today?"

"Thanks to you, I've reread two of Nancy Mitford's novels," Katie says. "Plus one biography. I was hoping you might let me have a look in the files you mentioned?" Katie feels herself shirk, and blush a little, too. It seems like a lot to ask.

"I love writers. Such a nosy bunch. Of course you can poke around. It's what I promised. This way." Felix motions for Katie to follow, and she trails him through a doorway. "I was just in the storage room myself," he says. "Digging around for the so-called lost manuscript."

"Find anything good?" Katie asks, and Felix shakes his head. "If you don't mind my asking, why are you still looking? It's very nice of you, but you don't seem to think it exists, and Simon isn't a paying client."

Felix freezes in his tracks and slowly turns around. "*Simon?* Goodness, Katharine. I didn't know you were on a first-name basis."

"We're not!" Katie says, her face on fire. "Not at all! I just heard you guys…squabbling…yesterday, before you left…"

Felix takes a very long beat. "I'd forgotten you were there," he says at last. "Why I'm bothering is a valid question, especially considering how much of my time he's consumed. It's about chasing a story, I suppose. If I can find something—however small—it'd feel like a victory. Doesn't take much to please us bookish types." Felix flips around and they continue down the hall. "Are you looking for anything specific?" he asks as they turn a corner and greet two passing employees.

"When it comes to Nancy Mitford, it's hard to narrow it down," Katie says. "But I'm most curious about the years she worked at the shop. She had so much going on. The war. Her job. Problems with her family. On top of all that, Prod was gone."

"Which made way for Colonel Gaston Palewski," Felix says.

"At the end of it, her crowning achievement: completing *The Pursuit of Love.*"

Felix throws open the storage room door, and Katie sets down her purse. Her gaze meanders toward the metal cabinet, and she takes in a deep breath. "I'm also intrigued by her work with the refugees," she says.

"Refugees?" Felix repeats, and Katie can almost see a question mark form over his head.

"The evacuees who stayed at Rutland Gate," she continues. "During the Blitz. Do you think there's anything in the files about them?"

"Nope," Felix says. He unlocks the cabinet drawers. "Anyhow, good luck. I'm off to make a call. I'll check on you in a bit."

After Felix leaves, Katie approaches the cabinet cautiously, and with some degree of reverence. Katie may be here for Simon, but this is sacred property because anything inside was once graced by Nancy Mitford's pen.

"Here we go," Katie whispers and, inhaling, cracks open the top drawer. She reaches in for the first set of documents.

Ten minutes pass, and thirty, and Katie finds a whole lot of not much, aside from a few notes to and from suppliers, and hasty first drafts of magazine articles, all of it typed. At the one-hour mark, Katie has gone through two drawers. She squats beside the third and yanks on the handle, but the drawer jams.

"How goes it?" Felix asks, striding into the room.

Katie peers up from her crouched position. "Okay," she says. "I haven't found much. I think you accidentally locked this drawer instead of *un*locked it. Do you have the key?"

"No, no, don't worry about that," Felix says, flapping his hands. "Nothing in there. Here, let me help you up. I hate to rush you, but Stoker is due to stop past and, delightful though you are, he wouldn't relish seeing a random American pawing through his files."

Katie is deep in Simon's book of letters when she hears a click-ing, a soft but ardent tap. She tenses and looks around her base-ment room. It's windy tonight, and the sound could be from a branch hitting a window, or a thousand other things. Just in case, Katie stands to peek out onto the street, but sees nothing.

As she goes to send Jojo a slightly hysterical text, Katie no-tices two small shadows beneath the door. "Coming!" Katie calls out, surprised to have a visitor, her shock doubled upon discovering the guest is Clive.

"Might I come in?" he asks when she opens the door. He looks serious, and uncomfortable, the overall effect that of a constipated process server.

"Yes, of course," Katie says. "May I take your coat?"

Clive declines and marches toward the bed, loosening his tie. "What are you doing?" he says. "What's all this?" He gestures to the note cards, Nancy's book of letters, and Katie's collection of multicolored sticky flags. "Mum says you should be writing a book. It appears you are not." Clive takes a few more steps and halts in his tracks. "Oh. My. Word," he says.

Katie cranes around his unusually large head. "What's wrong?" she says, praying that an innocent Google search hasn't inadvertently unlocked twenty-seven pop-up windows of porn.

"Is that your mobile?" Clive says. "An *iPhone 6S*? It's not even a Plus," he adds, miserably.

"I don't really care about technology," Katie says, and Clive stalks closer, like an animal toward its prey. "I only bought that phone when I dropped my prior one in a footbath while get-ting a pedicure."

"What, was that, like, six years ago?"

Katie shrugs, which she often does around this kid.

"At least it's an *S*." He blubbers his lips. "Can I have it?"

"My phone? Uh, no. I kind of need it. I'm on my own, in a foreign country."

"That's your *only* mobile?" Clive says with a withering look. "Miss Katie, your phone is older than all of my siblings."

"In fairness, your siblings are pretty young. Honestly, it's fine. Perfectly sufficient."

"Oh, well, that's damning praise." His eyes drift toward the bed. "How old is the laptop?"

Katie laughs. "Sorry, buddy, I need the laptop, too."

Sighing deeply, Clive reaches into his smoking jacket. "This is my card," he says. "If anything breaks, I run a tech support business. One hundred quid per hour." Clive returns to his coat. "Here's a coupon for ten percent off. It expires on Monday."

"*'JUNK TRASH CRAP'?*" Katie reads. "That's the name of your business?"

"A family joke. It's what Mum yells whenever she opens my electronics cupboard. *Where do you get all this junk trash crap!?*"

"Your mom yells?" Katie smiles. "Nice."

"If she'd let me rent a *real* warehouse, I wouldn't have to keep my clothes on the fish tank. Alas, here we are."

"While I am impressed with your entrepreneurial spirit," Katie says, "I can't afford one hundred pounds per hour."

"You get what you pay for," Clive says, and flops onto the bed. Katie looks around, wondering what she's supposed to do, and when he's going to leave.

"I have another business," he says. "I make bow ties for dogs."

"Now that sounds like something I can afford. I even have a dog."

"Yes. Mum told me about your Thai trash dog."

"Street dog, I think you mean?"

"No, she definitely said trash."

They stare at each other. As Clive tries to solve some unknowable riddle in his brain, Katie frets about whether Jojo is bad-mouthing Millicent behind her back.

"How come you're not married?" Clive asks.

Katie shakes her head. She is suddenly missing her dog. "What now?" she says.

"Shouldn't you have a husband by now? I'm not trying to pressure you, but Mum has four kids."

"I am aware." Katie clears her throat. "I was engaged, *almost* married, but it didn't work out. Millions of people don't ever wed, by choice. Nancy Mitford never married the love of her life."

Clive nods, earnestly, and Katie softens toward the boy. If she had a kid, she'd probably prefer him to be a touch strange, a mild pain in the ass.

"Do you want to be like Nancy Mitford?" he asks. "Or do you think you'll get married? I guess you need a boyfriend first." He smacks himself in the head. "Clive! Idiot! Boyfriend or girl-friend... Mum told me not to make assumptions."

"Don't be so hard on yourself!" Katie says. "I like boys, but I appreciate your sensitivity. As for future boyfriends, or mar-riages, we'll just have to see."

"What if you don't have another boyfriend?" he asks. "Like, ever? What then? Will you just live alone with your trash dog? Dogs have much shorter life spans than do humans."

"Jesus. You're really putting me through the wringer tonight. The short answer is, I don't know, about any of it. For now, it's me and the dog."

Clive lowers his eyes and seems to chew on this for a while. "Maybe people don't get you," he says. "Maybe that's why you don't have a new boyfriend."

"We didn't break up all that long ago..."

"But it's okay! They all say that about me. *It's okay, Clive, you're a great kid. People just don't get you sometimes.* I don't have a ton of friends, but eight-year-olds are dull, on the whole. Do you think it's true, though? That it's 'okay'?"

"Oh, Clive," Katie whispers, unable to say much else. "Yes. Ab-solutely. People who are 'easy to get' are boring. Who wants to be predictable? You said it yourself. Other people can be insufferable."

"Mum says you have a 'hard time with kids,' but I don't think that's true."

"She said what?"

"Anyway." Clive pops onto his feet. "I should probably get ready for bed."

"Yes. Okay," Katie says. "I'm sure it will feel good to get out of that tie."

Clive stomps toward the door. "Now that I think about it," he says, and stops, "you came to London once, with a man."

"Armie. Yes. You have an excellent memory. That was the man I was engaged to."

Clive's face drops into the deepest of frowns. "So it's all over, then?"

Katie jiggles her head, unsure what he means by "over"—her relationship with Armie, or the likelihood of experiencing something like that again? "Why are you so curious about my love life, mister?" she asks.

Clive shrugs. "I don't want you to be lonely, I guess."

With that, he struts off and Katie stands, addled, unable to move. Suddenly, she hears a ding. God love him, Clive Hawkins-Whitshed is taking an elevator to bed.

"Good night, kid," she whispers, and slowly shuts the door.

Katie closes her computer, pushes aside the book, and picks up her iPhone 6S (not Plus). It's just after nine o'clock in London, which means it's only four back home. She begins to scroll and is soon deep in her messages, hovering above Armie's sunglasses-clad face. She tells herself she's calling the dog, not the ex-fiancé, though Millie's proven herself terrible at FaceTime.

Just as Katie is about to click, her phone buzzes, and Simon's name lights up the screen. "Hello?" she says, and cringes, realizing it's possible Simon's phone rang less than one time.

"I saw your text," he says. "About the mysterious drawer. That is dodgy as hell."

"Right?! He was so quick to shoo me away," she says, though Katie is still unsure how to feel about the bottom drawer, or this adventure on the whole. Felix was dismissive, but he's under no obligation to show her anything, and the only proof of the manuscript is a letter mentioning a few pages of a book. "So, what's next?" Katie asks. "I'm not sure where to go from here."

"My mum sent over some scans I think you should see," he says. "It's a few pages from a draft of the manuscript, along with a note. I'm forwarding them right now." Simon stops and takes a breath. "I know it's last minute, but are you free for breakfast tomorrow?"

Katie grins. "Yes, of course," she says. *I thought you'd never ask.*

The day I learned Lea Toporek was pregnant, I was hosting a Christmas ball. We'd dubbed it the "Feast of Queen Esther," at the refugees' request. By then, we had more than fifty staying at Rutland Gate.

The guest list included the evacuees, and Peter's fellow Welsh Guards, and I used every drop of my ingenuity and pocketbook to procure food and decorations. We even put up a Christmas tree, which looked splendid until the Luftwaffe dropped yet another cache of bombs. The tree was toppled, the ornaments shattered, and two windows blew out nearby. It was the holiest of messes and, still, the band played on.

Midway through the festivities, Lea was nowhere to be found. Truthfully, the young lass had been a bother since arriving on my doorstep weeks before. She wouldn't eat, she barely slept, and she never helped with the chores. I'd offered to take her to Weston Manor on multiple occasions, but she refused, even though the rest of my household was desperate for the countryside. My housekeeper was so perturbed by the situation she undertook an exploratory expedition. After a "very thorough cleaning" of Lea's room, Gladys found an identity card indicating the girl was only sixteen. This didn't explain Lea's reluctance, necessarily, but maybe it did her middling social skills. And it certainly drew my attention.

As the weeks wore on, Lea's attitude did not improve and, by the time of the Christmas ball, I'd had rather enough. As my evacuees sang and danced, I charged off to the small dining room, where I found her staring gloomily through the window.

"You could at least pretend to enjoy the party after I went to all this trouble," I said. "By the by, you'll need to do something at some point.

Not even I will be staying at Rutland Gate forever, and you don't want to be here when my mother returns. If you think the Luftwaffe is frightening, wait until you meet Muv."

My mother was at that juncture throwing a fit, claiming that Farve had to sell Rutland Gate, now that so many Jews had stayed there.

"I understand the world is bleak right now," I said. "We are all shaken, weary, depressed. Everyone's lost something but, I say this with great empathy, it's time to buck up, dear."

Lea released a sob and I dropped down beside her feet. "You might as well tell me," I said, rubbing her arm. "You can't sit around crying for the rest of your life."

Lea snuffled and batted those eerie blue eyes. Meanwhile, my knees began to smart. "You don't blame yourself, do you?" I said. "For what happened to your parents? They're the ones who refused to go to the shelter. You did the safe thing."

Lea squirmed in her seat. Her lips parted, and my heart sang. Hallelujah! I'd gotten through. "That's the way..." I said, encouragingly. "Tell Missus Rodd."

Lea leaned forward, and so did I. Our heads were inches apart when she vomited directly into my lap.

"Oh," I said, quite idiotically. I rose to my feet, holding my dress taut to contain the mess. Lea Toporek was pregnant. I should have guessed.

Once we got everything cleaned up, she asked me for the name of a doctor who might "regulate a cycle." It was a shocking request. After all, I hardly kept a roster of abortionists in my address book though. I suppose she noted my childless state and simply assumed.

"You don't need all that," I told her. "You're a pretty girl. If this Greenie person doesn't pan out, just find a country rube to wed, and give birth to one of those mysteriously hardy, four-kilo premature babies."

Lea never mentioned the doctor again and, the next day, Gladys and I drove her out to Weston Manor. I asked Peter to inform Greenie of the relocation, only to discover the erstwhile fiancé had died.

According to Danette, when she relayed the grim news, Lea was unusually composed. It seemed she'd already come to terms with Greenie's absence, and written him off as dead, one way or another.

1 September 1942

You can't say I didn't warn you!

I hope you don't mind the bit about your social skills, or your medical desires. It's all true! If you wrote to me every once in a while, maybe we could shape this story to be more to your liking. It's an idea, anyhow.

Overall, the writing is not going as quickly as I'd hoped. I've been a bit distracted at the shop. I also have a friend staying with me, and my nephews are coming tomorrow. While this is sure to be a drag on my time, Jonathan and Desmond are better than most children, though they're all either prigs or gangsters, and there's no winning, either way.

On top of all this strife are the ongoing war concerns. You must know what I mean! My husband is away in East Africa, which didn't bother me until Lady Worthington got into my head. Now I'm paranoid he's been shot! I've even sent a dispatch to Captain Roy—a beloved Frog of mine—asking if he could track him down. I'd like to know that he's alive, and also why I haven't heard a peep!

Setbacks aside, I'm determined to press on. And so I return to my paper and pen.
More soon.

Love from
NR

September 1942

G. Heywood Hill Ltd.

The wartime autobiography was slow going, thanks to the war itself, the shop, and all the other obligations assaulting Nancy each day.

Nonetheless, she did her best and today was squirreled away in the storage room, scratching out as many words as her hand allowed. As she completed one page and flipped to the next, Nancy heard Anne Hill barreling through the shop. She slid the notebook into her purse.

"Nancy!" Anne screeched as she burst through the door. "What are you doing? You're supposed to be working, and your nephews are running amuck in the shop!"

"Goodness, Anne," Nancy clucked. "Don't lose your wig. For someone always prattling on about wanting to procreate, you have rock-bottom tolerance when it comes to children."

"I love children," Anne insisted. "When they're at home, where they belong. Are you going to bring them *every day*?"

"I really thought you were more charitable," Nancy said. "It's only for two weeks, and it's much easier for the boys to visit their mother while they're here, with me, in London."

"You took them to Holloway?" Anne balked, and Nancy

couldn't tell if her expression was one of surprise or excitement. The prison was wretched, but most people loved to hear about horrible things. "Is it as bad as they say?"

"I've taken them thrice," Nancy said. "And, yes, the conditions are appalling. Think puddles on the floor, a straw mattress, one bucket of water for a week's worth of hygiene." Anne gasped and Nancy nodded. "All that and piles of rotten sandbags blocking the windows," she said.

Even for a traitor, it was harsh treatment. On the other hand, Diana had no one to blame but herself, and she did seem to enjoy the pageantry of suffering. Winston arranged for her to be allowed a bath each day, but she refused.

"Well, it really is terrible about Diana," Anne said. "But I am running a commercial enterprise, not a day care."

"You have to admit, the boys are awfully nice," Nancy said, and she meant it. Jonathan could be haughty for a twelve-year-old, but he spent most of his time reading *The Peerage* in the red selling room. Eleven-year-old Desmond was handsome like his father, and shared his gentle disposition, and therefore never made a peep. Though her sister would hate to hear it, their stepmother had done a magnificent job.

"The boys are very polite," Anne allowed. "But Lady Dashwood is also here, on the loose. She's at present flirting with not one but *two* doughboys!"

"Oh, brother," Nancy said. "She does seem to attract them. Usually there's more than two, so this is an improvement." Americans were everywhere lately, running around in their perfectly pressed trousers, and shouting to one another in their obnoxiously loud voices. So prolific were these men that Mayfair was now referred to as Eisenhower Platz, and Half Moon Street was more or less an American dormitory.

Nancy didn't care for the type, but Hellbags ate them up, and in large quantity now that she'd come to the city to work at a Mosquito fighter plane factory and flirt with strange foreigners.

The idea was to provoke Johnny, but he hardly cared. British men were far more concerned with their clubs and boat races than whether other people—especially their own wives—were having sex. Nancy didn't know what Hellbags saw in the Americans. They hadn't been anything close to what was promised on-screen. Where were the cocktail-swigging millionaires and gun-toting gangsters? The ones who'd descended upon London were cocksure, and governessy, and generally hopeless.

"But they're so *good*," Hellbags insisted. "You can see it in their eyes!"

"That's only their contact lenses," Nancy explained.

"All right, dear," Nancy said to Anne, and patted her head. "I'll go check on things. It's always my pleasure to chase away Americans." She trotted off.

Sure enough, the doughboys were loitering about the front selling tables, hee-ing and haw-ing and hanging all over Hellbags. Nancy sniggered. These kids stood no chance against a sultry, early-forties brunette who always kept a few tricks up her sleeve.

"How are you gentlemen today?" Nancy said. "I see you've met our loveliest customer, but is there something I can help you with? Before you ask, we're out of *For Whom the Bell Tolls*. You might try Hanwell's." *Hemingway*, Nancy thought, shaking her head. Otherwise known as the biggest bore on earth. "We do have the latest Raymond Chandler," she added, "if that appeals. I do not recommend *Put Out More Flags* by Evelyn Waugh. Do you like French novels? *L'étranger* was just published by Camus and it's supposed to be grand. Our friend here favors Agatha Christie. Hellbags, which one do you recommend? Personally, I—"

Nancy stopped. The front door opened with a whoosh. A stocky, middle-aged man entered the shop. One of the Free Frogs, she assumed, based on his black homburg hat. Nancy flashed a smile and turned back toward the Yanks. "By the by," she said, "my name is Nancy Rodd, and I see you've met my dear friend Lady Helen Dashwood. We call her Hellbags. Perhaps, when you boys are older, you'll find out why."

Nancy winked and the men began to chuckle when, suddenly, a herd of horses—or a pair of little boys—commenced a stampede. "Aunt Nancy!" Desmond yelled. "Aunt Nancy!"

"Be quiet, snitch!"

"Jonathan tore a page from a book!" Desmond said, beet red and heaving. "He ripped out a picture of a woman's *breast*."

Brow lifted, Nancy met Jonathan's eyes. He slumped his shoulders and pivoted sheepishly toward the wall. Poor boy probably just wanted to see a nipple, and Nancy didn't have the mettle to give him the what for. "Well," she said. "While I don't approve of defacing books, I hope you got something out of the crime."

"I came to London to get away from this sort of thing," Hellbags said, and looked at her Americans. "Whaddya say, gentlemen? Who needs a drink?" Within seconds, she was parading out of the shop, one man on each arm. Nancy gave her a quiet round of applause.

"Now, boys," she said to her nephews, "why don't you tell me which book this was, and what was the cost? Your auntie isn't exactly flush, so you'll have to consider this an early Christmas present. I hope it was worth it."

The boys debated the book, nearly coming to fisticuffs over whether the title started with an "*A*" or "*The*." Just as Nancy was about to give up, the homburg-hatted man materialized and told the boys he knew where to find a higher quality of breasts.

"You do?!" Jonathan said, eyes wide as the moon. "Where?"

"Are you always so frightfully helpful?" Nancy said to the man. "Well, don't hold back now! Where is this superior example, and how do you know about it?"

"I saw it the first time I was here," he said.

"You've been in the shop before?" Nancy felt a pop of surprise. "You must've been out."

"Not likely, monsieur," Nancy said, noting that the man's

English was better than that of most Frogs. "I am in this shop twenty hours per day."

"Then it must have been hour twenty-one." The man gave a simmering look and Nancy flushed to her toes. This Frog with his slicked black hair, mustache, and badly pitted skin was ugly from far away yet somehow ten times more attractive close-up. "Young men," the Frenchman said, returning his attention to the boys, "I will tell you the location of a book, but first you must pass a quiz."

The boys eagerly wagged their heads and, just like that, were back on the same team.

"Can you name the forty kings of France?" asked the Frog.

"*What?*" Jonathan yelped.

"Impossible!" Desmond cried.

The man laughed, inwardly, as if trying to keep it contained. "Don't worry, it's not as difficult as it sounds. Eighteen are called Louis, ten are Charles, and I can barely remember the others myself. I suppose I should just tell you." He glanced over his shoulder toward Nancy. "Can I reveal the secret?" he asked.

"Oh, you must," Nancy said, crossing her arms. "I'm absolutely *eaten* with curiosity."

"It's called *The Miracle of the Human Body*," the Frog said, and the boys sprinted off. Never had a person so rapidly dispensed of two children.

"Likely not the smut they're expecting," Nancy said. "Then again, it's probably the nearest thing we have to pornography. Were you really in the shop before?"

"Yes, on Tuesday, looking for Saint-Simon's memoirs, for my boss. The owner promised to locate a copy. I'm glad to have had the chance to return."

"Nice to meet you," Nancy said, and extended a hand. "Heywood isn't here right now."

"That's not really why I'm here," he said.

The Frog wrapped both hands around hers, and Nancy let a

gasp escape. She hadn't expected his skin to feel so warm, or so soft. "We shall meet again tonight, yes?" he said. "Eight o'clock. At the Allies' Club."

"That's rather presumptuous." Nancy tried to laugh, but it came out all wrong, like somebody strangling a mouse. "I don't even know who you are."

"I'm a colonel."

"Oh, well, that explains it."

"Newly arrived in London after spending the past six months commanding the Free French Forces in East Africa."

"East Africa?" Nancy said. "As in, Ethiopia?"

"The very one. Perhaps I have some information you might want."

"Prod," Nancy whispered. Sweet André Roy had come through. Fifteen months since she'd last heard from her husband and finally she'd gotten word. "Can't you just tell me now?" she said, a bit wildly.

"Eight o'clock," the Colonel repeated, and released her hand. "At the Allies' Club."

With a wink, he spun around and strode toward the exit.

When the door clapped shut behind him, Nancy sprang into action. "Telephone!" she shouted, to no one in particular. "I need the telephone now!"

Once she wrested it from Mollie, who'd been arguing about a bill, Nancy waited approximately ten forevers for the opera-tor to place the call. *"Come on..."* she said, tapping her foot. *"Any day now..."*

Finally, there was a connection. "Gladys!" Nancy said, when her housekeeper picked up. "Thank goodness you're there! Run me a bath. I'm going out to dinner with a Frenchman."

"Oh, Lord," Gladys said. "Who is it this time?"

"Some colonel who's going to tell me about Prod, I think. It doesn't matter. Apparently, almost all of them are named Louis or Charles."

Wednesday Morning

Shepherd Market

Katie and Simon meet outside the bookshop. It's early, not quite "half seven."

"Good morning!" Simon says brightly, as Katie walks up.

She smiles with her lips closed, thinking Simon must be well versed in interacting with other humans before noon, thanks to his job. The same cannot be said for her.

"Tired, are we?" He thumps her on the back and Katie croaks out a "Hello," sounding like a toad, and possibly looking like one, too. She'd worn lip gloss and mascara that morning without considering how it might read in the harsh morning light. "Shall we?" he asks, tilting his head toward the road.

Katie nods and surreptitiously rubs her mouth on the sleeve of her coat. "Why'd we meet at a closed bookshop?" she says as they cross the street and walk toward Shepherd Market. "Afraid I'll find out where you're staying?"

"Why would I be worried, when you've made it clear you're not hitting on me?" he says. "And what a shame. In any case, Heywood Hill *is* where I'm lodging this week."

Katie stops in the street. "You're sleeping in a bookstore?" she says. "How is that possible?"

A taxi zips by and Simon yanks her out of the way. "Jesus Christ!" he yells. "You're going to get yourself killed! In London, the traffic comes from the *other* direction."

"Felix is letting you stay *in the shop*?" Katie says, still discombobulated as she stumbles back to safety.

"Good Lord, no. Felix barely tolerates me patronizing it. There are apartments upstairs, leased by a management company. Felix has no say in the matter, and lucky for me."

They slip between two buildings and walk down a covered alleyway, alongside the foggy windows of closed cafés and shops. On this early morning, Shepherd Market feels like a quaint Victorian village, a world somehow apart, especially with the fairy lights and silver baubles dangling overhead.

"This is adorable," Katie says.

Simon grins. "Precisely the reaction I'd expect," he says.

In the square, a naked fir sits beside a restaurant that sells "Traditional British Fish & Chips" and "Thai English Food." A makeshift stage has been set up in front of a pharmacy, mailbox center, and tandoori shop.

"The annual Christmas lighting is tomorrow night," Simon explains. "John Cleese is flipping the switch."

"Really? John Cleese?" Katie snickers. *"'For someone called Manuel, you're looking terribly ill…'"*

"Big Basil Fawlty fan, are you? Your British accent is…not great."

Katie gives him a light punch in the arm. "*Fawlty Towers* was my father's favorite. He loved that weird British humor."

"Some might call it smart." Simon glances over. *"Was?"* he says with a wince.

"Don't worry about it." Katie waves a hand. "He died forever ago."

"Regardless…" His eyes fall to the ground. "I'm sorry, Katie."

Katie tells him that it's fine, and it *is*, more or less, but she hates to have made Simon uncomfortable. There is no simple way to discuss a dead dad, which is one reason Katie rarely corrects anyone when they assume she's related to Charles.

"The café is up ahead," Simon says, and points to a dusky teal shop front.

Across from the café is an auction house and a French restaurant, both closed. A "Polish-Mexican bistro" is also nearby, as well as the Kings Arms.

"You should go," Simon says. "To the Christmas thing. It's good fun. Live music, carolers, mulled wine. Seems right up your alley."

Before Katie can ask what, exactly, he means by that, he jogs ahead and peers through the café door. A man sees him, hesitates, but gestures for them to come inside. Katie gets the sense they're not technically open yet.

"Sit wherever you like," a woman tells them.

They settle into their chairs and, as Katie peruses the menu, she feels Simon's gaze.

"What?" she says, looking up.

"Aren't you going to say it's cute, or charming?" he says. "It really is quite precious, and it's been nearly three minutes since you've said either word."

Katie rolls her eyes. "I was not going to say that but, now that you mention it, this café is adorable."

"Ah, Katie. You have such a zest for life."

"You don't know me at all."

The waiter brings them coffee and Simon orders an avocado and toast. Katie picks a croissant but wants something else as soon as he walks off.

"Thanks for sending the story about Lea's pregnancy," Katie says as an older couple sits two tables away. "Not everyone can claim their grandmother puked on one of the greatest writers of the twentieth century."

"Yes, it really is quite the legacy," Simon says.

He sips his coffee—straight black—as Katie dumps a distressing amount of cream into hers. Now that she is almost forty,

Katie should probably admit to herself that she likes the idea of coffee, and its smell, more than the taste. If asked to choose, she'd pick her infamous early-morning Diet Coke.

"Was that the first time you'd seen it?" Katie asks. "The excerpt?"

Simon nods. "I spoke to my mum last night," he says. "Ordinarily, I avoid the topic of Nancy Mitford, but I asked about the April 1945 letter, where she mentions finishing the book. Mum got very uptight about the whole thing and sent me that instead. I think she was trying to prove she didn't make it up."

"It was fun to read, but...you're sure she wrote that?" Katie says, eyes cast down into her light brown coffee. "I realize it came with a letter, and the writing does seem to match what I've seen online, but it doesn't really sound like the Nancy Mitford I know. Especially not the Nancy who'd already written four books."

"Reads like the right Nancy to me," Simon says. "Or the one I see, at least. The letter is a bit ungenerous, petty almost."

"In what way? Are you referring to the comment about Lea's social skills?"

"The whole thing," he says. "She wrote a thoroughly damaging character study of a sixteen-year-old girl and then *sent it to her.*"

"Mildly damaging, at most," Katie says. "I'll admit Nancy was irreverent at times, but that's her personality. She's way snarkier about her own shortcomings! Also, she mentions looking after her nephews. That's nice!"

"She called them prigs and gangsters." Simon shakes his head. "Oh, Katie. You do know that Nancy Mitford famously hated children?"

"All right, buddy," Katie says, and points at him with a coffee stirrer. "Just because a woman doesn't have children doesn't mean she's a misanthrope. The mere fact she's corresponding with her former evacuees... Whatever!" She flings the stick onto the table. "Maybe when we find the rest of the manuscript, you'll see the truth."

"That is the plan," Simon says, as the server drops off their food. "Also, not for nothing, but Nancy was probably only watching her nephews because she felt guilty her sister was in jail."

"It wasn't her fault," Katie says. "Diana was married to Oswald Mosley. He was the head of the British Union of Fascists!"

"True, but Nancy did report them to the government," he says. "She even viewed herself as a kind of spy."

"She was probably being patriotic," Katie says. "Doing the right thing. As much as I love my sister, I'd definitely report her if she were trying to overthrow the government." Her eyes slide toward the couple nearby. The woman has a cappuccino, and Katie wishes she'd ordered that instead. "Did your mom say anything else?" she asks, looking back at Simon. "About the manuscript, or Nancy, or Rutland Gate?"

"We talked about the man who got Lea pregnant," he says. "My grandfather. He went by the nickname Greenie, though Mum doesn't know much beyond that, other than they met while Lea was working at a mobile canteen. It was never formal. I get the sense they consummated their trysts in alleyways, stairwells, God knows where else."

"What do you expect?" Katie says. "They were young, and in love, and it was during a war. I'm sure everything felt rushed, very dire."

"Hey." Simon puts up both hands. "I'm not judging, just relaying information. And you're right, it was rushed. Mere weeks together before Greenie left for training at Wimbledon Common. At first, Lea made a reluctant peace with their brief affair, but then her home was bombed, and she struck out to locate the only person she had left, which was how she found herself standing before Greenie's commanding officer, Peter Rodd. Captain

Rodd took Lea to his in-laws' house, where his wife promised to look after her until Greenie recovered."

"His wife, aka Nancy Mitford."

"The very one," Simon says. "Sometime later, Lea moved out to Weston Manor."

"Did she ever reunite with Greenie?" Katie asks, and Simon shakes his head.

"Somewhere along the way, he died from a postsurgical infection," Simon explains. "Lea eventually married the local vicar, who raised my mum."

"Your grandmother went through so much," Katie says. "And during a war, no less. Was your mom close to her stepfather?"

"She never really talks about it," Simon says. "All I know is his name was Harold, and it was one of those situations that wasn't bad, but neither was it good. Neutral, which is better than a lot of people get."

Katie rips off the end of her croissant and chews, all the while eyeing the old man with his soft-boiled egg, thick slab of toast, and pile of ham. Katie is not going to last all morning on one croissant.

"I am sorry," he says.

Katie looks up. "What now?"

"About your father."

"It's fine. I don't really—"

"I can't fathom it." Simon pauses, and laughs glumly. "Though I'd probably better start."

"I don't recommend it."

"My mum has stomach cancer," he says. "She's got about three or four months left."

"Simon," Katie says. She tries to catch his gaze, but his eyes are flat, directed somewhere else. "That's horrible. I wish I knew what to say."

"There's nothing to say. You know how it is."

"Well, I do, and I don't. My dad died thirty-five years ago, in

a car accident. The other guy was drunk. It was jarring, but…"
Katie's voice trails off. The swiftness with which their lives
changed was horrible, but to lose someone after forty years together was a whole different beast. On the one hand was more
time with the person, on the other, more to miss.

"She's been sick," Simon says. "On and off for years. She decided not to fight it this time, which I can appreciate. What's
the purpose of living for brief stretches, during which you feel
mostly like shit?"

Nodding, Katie bats away the building tears. Never before
has she so keenly appreciated the word *speechless*.

"We've never had the best relationship," he says. "And though
I fully support the decision, it's still…"

"Impossible?"

"Exactly," Simon says with a long exhale. "That's why I'm
so anxious to find the manuscript. Mum always viewed herself
as alone in the world, with no one to look after her, no one to
care. I'd love to show her she's wrong, or that she was part of
a bigger story, or *something*." Simon drops his head. "God, it all
sounds so foolish when I say it out loud. Even if we happen upon
it, what will it get me? Nancy Mitford was not very empathetic."

Katie steels her jaw. "Yes, well, you're wrong," she says. "And
wanting to see it makes all the sense in the world. I'd feel the
same way. That's why we are going to find that manuscript.
We're going to find the shit out of it."

Simon cocks his head. "We're going to find *the shit out of it*?"
he says.

"Yes, and you'd better buckle the hell up because Katie Cabot
can be relentless."

"Wow. Okay. I'm glad to have Katie Cabot on my side, then.
For a while there, I thought maybe you were only in this because you didn't really believe there was a manuscript, and you
wanted to prove me wrong."

"I've had my doubts." Katie sips her now-lukewarm coffee. "But I trust you for some reason, which is strange, because you've never told me your last name. This feels like something I should know."

"You've taken my photograph without permission but haven't googled me yet?" Simon says. "I'm disappointed. The name is Simon Bailey. Pleased to meet you."

Katie takes his outstretched hand. "Katie Cabot," she says, and they shake.

"Yes. I know. You've told me, minimum, seven times."

"Very funny," Katie says, and her breath catches when she realizes that he could google *her*. Then again, maybe he has. Katie can't imagine there's much to find aside from a stalled career, a defunct wedding registry, and a dozen or so innocuous posts across two social media platforms.

"Do you know those people?" Simon asks, lowering his voice. He leans in and a shiver runs along Katie's arms. "The older couple," he says. "You keep staring at their food."

"Oh, I, uh… Those eggs look really good," Katie mumbles. "Kind of wish I'd ordered that instead."

"Well, then, you'll have to come back."

Katie nods. "Maybe tomorrow," she says. "Or the day after." Sometime before Katie returns to Washington, she'll order a cappuccino and full breakfast plate. This all seems like a very reasonable plan until Katie remembers Friday is her last full day.

"Katie? Hello?" Simon says. "Did you hear what I just said?"

"Sorry. I was thinking about my…schedule. It's Wednesday. How did that happen?" Suddenly, an idea strikes Katie. She opens her mouth, and the words tumble out in one long, ill-considered stream. "Will you go with me?" she says. "To the Christmas lighting? It sounds fun and—"

"Are you asking me out?" Simon gawps. "On a date?"

"Never mind!" Katie says, retracting the invitation, like a snake striking a mouse. "Forget it!" She covers her eyes with her hands. "I'll take Jojo, or Clive. Ugh! What am I doing?"

"This is unexpected. I don't know what to say."

"Yeah, I've noticed!"

"Katie," Simon says, and pulls her hands from her eyes. "You took me by surprise. The answer is yes, of course. I'd love to attend the Christmas lighting with you."

"Don't do me any favors, bro."

"Okay, *bro*. I'm just a bit gobsmacked, since you promised not to flirt with me."

"I'm not flirting!"

"No takebacks," Simon says. He types something into his phone. "I'm already blocking off the time. Should I pick you up at six o'clock?"

"Pick me up?" Katie says, and she feels what might be a thrill, or maybe panic.

"Unless you'd rather meet there?" he says. "It could be crowded, but…"

"No, that's fine!" Katie chirps. "Six is great! At Jojo's place. I'll have plenty of time to google you before then."

As his lips twist in preparation for some caustic remark, Katie groans from the inside out. Simon is hot, and funny, and he knows about Nancy Mitford, even if he thinks she might've been somewhat of a bitch. What if Katie googles him and Simon Bailey is not who he seems?

Worse yet, what if he *is*?

September 1942

Allies' Club

It was a warm evening at the Allies' Club, but goose bumps ran the length of Nancy's arms.

"I'm absolutely *mad* to have come," she said as the mysterious Frenchman pulled out her chair. "Do you have a name, or shall I just call you Colonel?"

"My name is Gaston Palewski," he said. "And you are Nancy. It is a pretty name, to match your pretty face."

"Thank you," Nancy said. "But please be advised that I've enjoyed one French lover and will not be taking another."

"Captain Roy. I have met him." Smiling amiably, the Colonel opened a napkin and spread it across his lap. "With me, affairs usually last five years," he said.

"Well, good luck," Nancy said. "So, you've come from Addis Ababa. You saw Peter?"

The Colonel bobbed his head. "The husband I saw. We met in East Africa, during negotiations about the Djibouti–Addis Railway. There is not much to say other than you've not touched your menu, nor ordered a drink."

"I'm not hungry," she said. "Please. Tell me more."

"You must love your husband very much."

"Not especially," Nancy said. "The problem is that it's been over a year since I've heard from him. Has he received my letters? He's not *dead*, is he? The widow's pension is very small."

The Colonel cackled. "For better or worse, he is alive," he said as he scanned the menu, wondering aloud which was the best wine.

"Peter said nothing about me, then?" Nancy asked, and her voice quivered. "Don't misunderstand. I'm not one of those overly dependent wives. I prefer everyone to mind their own business, but we've been married almost ten years and..." Nancy was unable to continue.

Despite Prod's arrogance, and fecklessness, and his ability to put an entire party to sleep, Peter was still her husband, and she his wife, and Nancy assumed war might bring out the best in them both. If nothing else, it would've been nice to have been missed.

"I am sorry I do not have more," the Colonel said. "He told me that if I was going to London, I should locate his wife and inform her that he is fine. This was the extent of our discussion. You are better off. He is not very winsome. What do you think of the muscat?"

Nancy let her hands fall into her lap. "At least he sent *some* word," she said.

"Your husband is not very smart."

"Oh, no, you're quite off on that," Nancy said. "Peter is extremely smart, a self-professed expert on all topics. I'm shocked you didn't pick up on that. Within five minutes of meeting someone, he usually tells them everything he knows. Also, he's rather handsome. On this, you must agree."

"What is handsome? You can see I am very ugly, and that hasn't hindered me at all. Perhaps Peter Rodd is learned on many academic topics, but it was not clever of him to hand me his wife."

"I don't know that he *handed* you anything," Nancy said.

"I will, obviously, sweep you off your feet." He looked at the menu again. "Are we finished speaking of your husband? Excellent. Let us dine. I will not let a meal with a pretty woman go to waste."

Nancy flung a hand. "Choose whatever you'd like. I'll eat a bite of anything."

"You are a very cheap date."

As the Colonel ordered, Nancy glanced around. The room was awash in military types, a parade of every imaginable Allied uniform. With her own utility wear, even Nancy fit into the milieu. She rather liked the red woolen dress, with its nipped waist, military-minded shoulders, and short, pleated skirt. At last there was a style to complement her gangly frame and lack of breasts.

"Tell me, Gaston," Nancy said as the waiter rushed off. "Colonel Palewski." She crossed her long, thin legs and leaned into the glimmering candlelight. "Why did you leave your position?" she asked. "I thought East Africa was the place to be."

"I was tired of the squabbling," he said. "Running a bomber squadron was one thing—glorious—but commanding petulant soldiers was not how I wanted to spend my war. I was pleased to take an appointment to work for General Charles de Gaulle."

"De Gaulle," Nancy said. "Very highbrow. And how is the new appointment so far? I've heard the QG is a hotbed of infighting and gossip."

"Knowledge gleaned courtesy of your prior French lover, no doubt," the Colonel said. "Alas, he is correct. There is much pettiness and backstabbing at Carlton Gardens, not to mention incompetence. On the plus side, I'm no longer getting shot at, and I can spend my days ogling beautiful British women."

"Please," Nancy said, and rolled her eyes. "We must seem frightfully dowdy compared to the Parisiennes."

"Very much so." The Colonel took a sip of wine and Nancy blinked, surprised to learn their food had been delivered. "That's what makes you so enigmatic," he said. "For French women, arranging themselves is full-time work. They visit the collections, try on lingerie, have their hair set. But what must British women do all day, since you do none of these things? Cast spells? Visit an army of lovers?"

Nancy couldn't help but laugh. "But, Colonel, we do all those things, too. Rather, we did, before the war, though apparently to middling effect!" The Colonel chuckled, covering his mouth with a fist, and Nancy's body flooded with warmth. Though she never drank on Tuesdays, Nancy poured herself a splash of wine. "Most people consider me quite stylish and attractive," she said.

"Well, you have your points."

Nancy laughed again. "Tell me, Colonel Palewski," she said. "How are you finding London? Aside from its dowdy women. You must think it quite dreary with its sirens, and bomb craters, and abject weather. The museums have been cleared out, and all treasures evacuated to the countryside. There's nothing pretty to look at anymore. I know the French are terribly fond of their art."

"Yes, we are cultured in that way. Even old military men like me can paint. I studied at the École du Louvre, along with the École Libre and the Sorbonne."

Nancy was a tiny bit dazzled. "Really?"

"Really," he said, and slurped down an oyster. "Tell me, Missus Rodd, you have children, yes? You were very patient with those boys in the shop."

"No children for me," she said. "And, please, call me Nancy. Rodd is more a courtesy title than anything else. If you must use a surname, Mitford will do."

"No children?" he cried. "*Mon dieu!* What is the purpose of Peter Rodd if you do not have babies?"

"Surely that's not the *only* reason to wed," Nancy said, and tried on a smile. "I did expect we'd have children, when we married, but that ship has since sailed." Nancy thought about this, hand on chin. "Come to think," she said, "that might be too peaceful a description. The ship hasn't sailed, it's wrecked. It hit an iceberg, like the *Titanic*. Ironically, my parents were supposed to be *on* the *Titanic* but changed plans at the last minute. We were all so disappointed."

Nancy chortled and the Colonel's eyes widened. For a second, he resembled a child. *"Non-cee!"* he cried. "Surely, you don't mean that!"

"I very much do. My siblings and I longed to be orphans. It sounded so romantic! Whenever our parents went to their mining camp in Canada, we'd rush to the newspapers each morning, hoping to read that their ship had gone down."

"How ruthless," the Colonel said. "This family, it sounds like quite the litter of vicious pups. How many children were there?"

"Six girls and one boy," Nancy said.

"Mon dieu! You must tell me about it." The Colonel scooted closer, his chair squeaking against the floor. "You must tell me right now. *Racontez!"*

"There's not much to say. You would've thought it all so hideously uncivilized, nothing but great shrieks of laughter and big buckets of tears."

"Were you wealthy? You seem very posh."

"Quite the opposite," Nancy said. "My father is titled, but we lived in a state of upper-class poverty out in the Cotswolds, rattling about a big, draughty house. Though it was probably Farve's title that saved us from being sent to an approved home."

"Did you have no one looking after you at all?"

"Here and there," Nancy said with a shrug. "It was a feral childhood, but sheltered, too. We didn't interact with anyone else aside from our various grooms, governesses, and gamekeepers."

"You had no friends? *Quelle tristesse!"* the Colonel said, and his eyes watered in amusement, or astonishment, Nancy couldn't decide.

"We played with the neighbor children when we were small," Nancy said. "But after I told them about sex, they were no longer allowed to visit. I was eight or nine at the time."

"Sex!?" The Colonel threw back his head and crowed. "How very avant-garde! I didn't think any Britons knew about sex, much less a child."

"Don't give me too much credit," Nancy said. "The entirety of my knowledge was from a book called *Ducks and Duck Breeding*. Ducks can only copulate in running water, by the way, and good luck to them."

The Colonel continued to laugh, and Nancy wondered if there'd ever been a lovelier sound.

"Little girls are so devilish," he said. "How did your brother survive?"

"We gave Tom such a hard time," Nancy said. "He was thrilled to go off to school. No amount of bullying or hazing could compare to what our 'Hon Society' put him through."

"*Hun?* As in, the Germans?"

"*H-O-N,*" Nancy said. "Everyone thought it was short for *Honorable*, but it comes from *hen*. We adored chickens and sold eggs in the village for pocket money. We loved all animals, really. There's not a family photograph that doesn't include a dog."

"This is ever so much fun," Gaston said with a grin. "What were the rules of your Hons? What did you do? I am imagining very horrid things."

"Our stated purpose was to enact vengeance on the horrible Counter-Hons," Nancy explained. "Tom was our first target, though we soon directed our ire toward our governesses." Nancy paused, letting her joy tumble over the words. Suddenly, she couldn't remember why she'd been so frantic to leave home.

"How does one enter this Society of Hons?" Gaston asked.

"First, you'd need an invitation, and then you'd be required to pass a rigorous initiation: frog-hopping across the tennis court, turning somersaults, and successfully answering a series of questions. We had badges and everything. I was in charge."

"Because your siblings doubtless had great sense."

"Ha!" Nancy barked. "Nobody would say that about the Mitford girls. I was in charge because I'm the oldest, and the most domineering, some might say."

"Domineering is my favorite quality in a lover."

Smiling, Nancy rolled her eyes again.

"After you, who was next in age?" the Colonel asked. "Poor Tom?"

Nancy shook her head. "Next was Pamela, but she hardly counts. She ruined my life as a cherished only child, and she's even more boring than my husband. Tom came after Pamela. Even though he was the original Counter-Hon, he's loved by all. Sweet Tuddemy is the only person in the family still on speakers with everyone else." Nancy stopped to sip her win. "Tuddemy is Tom in Boudledidge, our secret language."

"Secret languages as well?!" the Colonel said. "This is too, too much! Who came next?"

"Diana, the middle child," Nancy said. "Those were her boys in the shop. Diana was the dreamiest of us all, dazzling the world from the moment she was born. She often sat gazing out the window, as if searching for a more glittering life. Ironic, given her current circumstances." Nancy passed the Colonel a hard look. "Her married name is Diana Mosley. I'm watching her boys because their mother is incarcerated. Do you know the name?"

"Bien sûr!" the Colonel said. "Everybody knows about Fascist Mosley and his terrible Fascist wife. I can't believe someone so delightful as you could be related to somebody so villainous."

Nancy beamed, tickled to have met the one man who didn't fall all over himself at the mere mention of Diana's name.

"Is there not another traitorous sister?" the Colonel asked. "An affair with the Führer? *Un bébé*, perhaps?"

"There is no baby. That is a myth," Nancy snapped. "You're thinking of Unity, who came after Diana. Poor Bobo's always had a hard time." Thickset and goosey, Unity could never compete with her physically and intellectually gifted sisters and therefore relied on ill-advised pranks and bad jokes to stand out. She kept a live rat in her handbag and did things like eat all the strawberries before a luncheon party, and steal lav paper from Buckingham Palace.

"Unity was lover to the Führer, no?" Gaston asked. "This is what the papers said."

Nancy offered a half-hearted shrug. "Probably" was the answer, but the family never spoke of it. "I believe Unity liked the idea of Hitler, and the Nazis, more than she liked the man," Nancy said. "She only wanted to be part of something, and she's never been known for her ability to think critically."

The Colonel scowled. "Is this why she shot herself in the head?"

"That's the question, isn't it?" Nancy said. "When war broke out, my sister felt torn between what she viewed as her two countries, Germany and England. She thought ending it was her only option. It didn't work, and afterward it was chaos." The family was in hysterics, and also in the dark. For weeks, they didn't know Unity's location, much less that she was in a Munich clinic, under the care of Hitler's physicians. When she tried to commit it a second time by swallowing her swastika badge, Hitler dispatched her to neutral Switzerland, where Debo and Muv picked her up. "I'm sure you saw the newsreels," Nancy said, "and witnessed everyone boo as my father helped her out of the car."

I'm glad to be in England, her sister had told the swarm of reporters. *Even if I'm not on your side.*

"This is ever so difficult," the Colonel said, and reached for Nancy's hand. "It is impossible when people we love make decisions that seem so wrong."

Nancy sniffled, her eyes burning with tears. The Colonel squeezed her hand again and asked which sister followed Unity. "Please, *Non-cee*," he said. "Tell me more of this notorious family."

"Decca was born a few years later," Nancy said, dabbing her eyes. "You might've read about her, too. Or *red*, as in the color, our dear little Communist. She and Unity were the closest growing up. They invented Boudledidge and shared a room. Try to picture it: one half decorated with hammers, sickles, and Vladimir Lenin, the other with swastikas and Hitler." Nancy believed it was this very closeness that pushed each girl to her eventual extreme. They wouldn't have been so heels-dug-in without a foil on the other side. "Goodness," Nancy said, feeling wiped out. "Aren't you bored? There are so many beautiful women here, and you've barely glanced at any of them!"

"*Non-cee,*" the Colonel said, studying her face with great earnestness. "This is the most delightful conversation I've had in years. I've been counting and there is one sister left."

"Deborah," Nancy said. "Our parents' last chance at a boy. My mother was so upset to have another girl she didn't write the birth in her engagement book, and Farve refused to look at Debo for three months!"

"*No!* That cannot be true. It is too hateful and cruel!"

"That's Farve for you," Nancy said. "And Muv as well."

Unlike her husband, Lady Redesdale wasn't a raving lunatic, and her company was mostly pleasant, when she wasn't reciting Fascist propaganda, or browbeating everybody that windows must stay cracked all twelve months of the year. Sydney was beautiful, and intelligent, and possessed a financial sense her husband sorely lacked. She actively encouraged her daughters to pursue their interests and remain independent of men. While Farve liked to scream and shoot things, Muv's hobbies included writing to newspapers about "murdered food" and the pumping of "disgusting dead germs" into bodies, otherwise known as vaccines, as well as avoiding any activity related to home and family. Farve relished the company of his children, but Muv remained cold and remote, forever disappearing into her cloud.

"Everyone cried when Debo was born," Nancy said, and the Colonel gasped. "Nonetheless, she made the perfect baby of the family—always content, never desperate to escape like the rest of us. She loved hunting, and walking the pheasant coverts with Farve, and is the only one of us who claims a happy childhood."

"But it sounds happy to me," the Colonel said. "Or else very much fun!"

"It was. I probably didn't need to be *quite* so anxious to get away."

"I love this all so much, but how will I keep it straight?" he said. "There are so many of you!"

"It's easier than you think," Nancy said. "Just remember that I'm the oldest, and Diana's the middle. The youngest three you can recall with nicknames. I used to say that our parents were so tired of children by then, they named them Nit, Sick, and Bore. Short for Unity, Jessica, and Deborah."

"Nancy! You are wicked!"

"They loved the attention," Nancy said. "Add Tom to the pile, and Pamela, if you feel like it, and there you have it—*la famille Mitford.*"

"Garçon!" the Colonel called out, snapping his fingers. He jumped to his feet. "I would like to pay my bill! Nancy Mitford and I are going dancing!"

"Dancing? Isn't it too late?"

"This is my favorite time of night! I'm a bomber. I like the dark."

"I have to work tomorrow," Nancy said, though she was already standing, and following his lead. "I'm not a romper type." On the other hand, Nancy *was* wearing her utility dress, with its ease of movement and glow-in-the-dark buttons, which lessened the chances of getting hit by an auto while on the street. Not that uncomfortable clothing and covered headlights were the only risks Nancy faced in staying out with the Colonel.

"This night is not over," he said, and offered her his arm. "There will be more of you and me."

"Oh, what the hell," Nancy said, and looped her arm through his.

Together they walked out of the Allies' Club and into the night, with Nancy feeling giddy as a schoolgirl and the Colonel humming to himself. The tune was "September Song," one of Nancy's favorites.

And the days dwindle down.
To a precious few.
September, November.
And these few precious days.
I'd spend with you...

Wednesday Evening

South Audley Street

"That pretty much sums up the arc for the new series," Jojo says as she and Katie walk up South Audley Street, killing time during Lionel's piano lesson. "It'll be a bit more on the romantic side than usual, so fingers crossed."

"You write relationships so well," Katie says. "I can't wait to read them."

Jojo sighs. "That's the hope," she says. "Of course, I have a different book to worry about right now. I'm trying to focus, but the kids are giving me a run for my money. One kid, specifically. The first time hearing from authorities. What a milestone."

The problem, of course, is Clive.

"At least his would-be crimes aren't violent," Katie offers. Though she doesn't know the particulars, Katie understands Clive did something very technical and slick, an act that could've resulted in an indictment for wire fraud, were he not eight years old. "He's not getting into schoolyard scrapes and fights."

"Yeah, but I could probably stop that," Jojo says. "The technology stuff is beyond my pay grade. And the evil genius schtick is far less amusing when Mum's on two deadlines. See that building?" Jojo points to a small, brick church with arched windows and a mint-colored spire. "Grosvenor Chapel, the place where Keira Knightley's character got married in *Love Actually*."

"I know I'm not supposed to like that movie," Katie says. "But I can't help myself."

"Same," Jojo says.

They hook right, turning into a small cul-de-sac. To the left is Harry's Bar, sitting brightly on the corner with its pink-green-and-white-striped awning, and matching pink, green, and white Christmas baubles.

"You're not in danger of missing it, are you?" Katie says. "Your deadline?"

"I'll have eighty thousand words by the due date," Jojo says. "And that equals a book. Whether these words are decent is very much TBD, and Tansy is not doing me any favors. Clive suggested installing a tracking device on her phone, and this is beginning to seem like a good idea."

"Tansy?" Katie's ears ping. "Well, well, well," she says. "What do we have here? May I presume this is the name of your top secret client?"

"Shit!" Jojo groans. "Shit! Shit! Shit!" She stops and throws back her head. "Ugh! Yes. Okay. I'm working with TansyTM. But you cannot tell anyone."

"Not a problem," Katie says. "By the by, what the fuck is a tan-see-tee-em?"

"That's her name. Tansy, followed by *T* and *M*." Jojo writes the letters in the air. "As in, a trademark."

Katie looks at her cross-eyed. "I have literally never heard of this person," she says.

"Sure you have," Jojo insists, and they begin walking again. Through a gate flanked by two red phone booths, they enter Mount Street Gardens.

"This is incredibly disappointing," Katie says. "When your best friend is ghostwriting a celebrity memoir, you expect an actual celebrity to be involved."

"She's a famous Gen Z YouTube influencer," Jojo says. "Ask Dani and Clem. They'd know. She's twenty-one."

"As in, *years*?" Katie balks. "That's too young to write a book! Her brain isn't even developed yet! What on earth could she possibly 'influence'? Does she sell makeup or hair products or something?"

"It's really more of a lifestyle," Jojo says.

"A lifestyle?" Katie repeats. "Good grief. Well, what is it? I'm dying to know."

Up ahead the path splits, and they veer right. Along the way, signposts identify the garden's birds: robins, goldcrests, magpies, and blackbirds. The palm trees and other greens are more vibrant than Katie would've expected this time of year.

"It's hard to put into words," Jojo says. "Picture a Gen Z version of a tech bro. You know how they are with their life hacks, and bio hacks, and all that crap. It's a 'tips and tricks' situation, but her ideas are accessible. She's not advocating keto diets or micro-dosing LSD, or anything too out there."

"People do that?"

"You really need to get out more." Jojo chuckles, seemingly to herself. "Tansy's pretty clever. Turns out she was ignored a lot as a kid. She's from the States, actually—West Virginia, which is why I was chosen to write it."

"What's she doing in London?" Katie asks.

"Moved here for a musician. I'd tell you his name, but you probably wouldn't recognize that either," Jojo says.

"Har, har." Katie rolls her eyes. "Are they still together, Tansy and the musician?"

"They're separated, but not yet divorced."

"Divorced! Twenty-one and divorced!"

"Please. You cannot tell a soul," Jojo warns. "I know you don't talk to anyone, but still…keep your mouth shut."

"Sure, you bet," Katie says, and narrows her eyes. "I do consort with other humans, though. I'm not a total recluse."

"If you insist." Jojo stops to check something on her phone. "So, what's going on at Heywood Hill, with Nancy Mitford? Have any good leads on the memoir?"

"Not yet," Katie admits. "Although I did come across something that caught my interest, unrelated to the manuscript. It was in a published compilation of her correspondence."

Earlier that day, as Katie read one of the letters for the second or third time, a footnote snuck up on her, appearing out of the clear blue, and Katie halfway believed it hadn't been there before.

[1]Nancy's affair with André Roy had resulted in an ectopic pregnancy.

"Nancy had an ectopic pregnancy," Katie says. "At thirty-seven." It was the first she'd heard of it.

"Wow." Jojo blinks. "Same age as you."

"Technically, I was thirty-eight." Katie exhales. "But yeah." She is glad for what they both know but don't need to say. Had her own embryo implanted in the right location and survived, Katie would be expecting a baby, due next week.

They continue along the path. Though it's not yet five o'clock, the sun is already falling, sending beams of light between the mansions surrounding the park.

"That must've been hard to read," Jojo says.

Katie nods. "A lot of it is," she says, thinking of another letter, this one written shortly after Nancy's death.

I really think she had a FOUL life, Debo wrote to Decca. *I know she had success as a writer but what is that compared to things like proper husbands & lovers & children—think of the loneliness of all those years, so sad.*

No wonder Nancy's sisters complained about sarcasm, and her cruel wit. She probably used it to get by.

"Do you miss him?" Jojo says, and Katie looks at her. "Armie, I mean."

"We still talk, here and there," Katie says. "We text about the dog."

"You know that's not what I asked."

"Of course I do," Katie says. "He was in my life for over thirty years, and now he's not. He was my first friend, which means there's a gaping hole that can never be filled. Plus, it's hard to think about all those years I frittered away, and for what? A good deal on a house that I'll probably have to sell?"

"Geez, give the guy some credit," Jojo says. "He meant a lot to you, and you can't consider the entire relationship a waste. If nothing else, maybe you needed to go through all that to end up here. It's called personal growth."

Katie looks at her friend. "Now you're sticking up for Armie?" she says. "I thought you hated him!"

"That's not true," Jojo says. "He's a good guy, when you get down to it. I just didn't like the two of you together."

"I know, I know. The competitiveness. The one-upmanship."

"That was part of it, yes," Jojo says. "But what really got me was the way he handled the—" She lets out a long and anguished breath. "What truly incensed me about Armie was how he made everything about *him*. First, he pressured you to have kids. When things didn't go his way, he acted like it was *his* damned tragedy when *you* were the one who had to deal with everything physically."

"Yeah, but they were his losses, too," Katie says. "I'm glad he was upset. I would've been pissed if he wasn't."

"I guess," Jojo says, nibbling on her bottom lip. "It kind of applies to everything, though. Like, with your dad. You're incredibly stoic and matter-of-fact about his death. Meanwhile, this joker from next door—" she crooks a thumb "—he wells up at the mere mention of Danny Cabot. Dude never even met him!"

"I'll admit it's a little weird," Katie says. "But it's never really bothered me." She pauses to consider why not. "Armie does get overly invested in things, but that's part of his appeal. He cares because he knows it was something that impacted me. As for the pregnancy stuff, I don't need you to stick up for me, because the trying *was* harder on him than it was on me, since I was more ambivalent. Anyway, it doesn't matter now. I'm not that great with kids, and Armie will be a fantastic dad, and everything worked out for the best."

"I hate when you talk like that," Jojo says, and her jaw hardens. "It's irritating and complete bullshit. Not good with kids. What about your nieces?"

"Dani and Clem are the most likable people in the world!"

"You seem to do all right with the non-likable ones, too," Jojo says. She gives Katie a pointed look. *"If you know what I mean."*

"Clive is extremely likable, but I don't do all right. He makes me very nervous!"

"He makes most adults nervous, because he's smarter than them. Clive loves you," Jojo says, and Katie snorts. "I'm serious. Because of you, he's writing a book, and *by hand*. The last time I took away his electronics, he got his fix on my Peloton screen. That cute little aspiring white-collar criminal admires you."

"You should hear what he says about my phone."

"Oh, I have," Jojo says. "He wants us to loan you money for a new one. Believe me, you have a higher Clive tolerance than anyone I know. Not for nothing, but for someone who is always *so against* sequels, you sure do love to stick to the same damned narrative."

"That's not fair," Katie says as they exit the gardens. "I broke up with Armie, didn't I? And I came to London."

"I'll give you that," Jojo says, begrudgingly.

They cross swanky Mount Street and stop beside an art installation—a raised-edge, granite pool. Every fifteen seconds, a mist forms over the illuminated water, giving an eerie, dreamlike quality to the street.

"I'm branching out in another way, too," Katie says, looking toward the Connaught Hotel, instead of at her friend. "I have a date tomorrow night."

"A date?" Jojo says. "You have a god*damned* date tomorrow night? GET. OUT." She gives Katie a playful shove and Katie nearly topples over into the water feature. "My little minx! I like this version of Katharine Cabot. I like her very much. Would've been fun to have a peck more of her at school, but here we are. Who's the lucky fellow? The manuscript bloke? He's a teacher, right?"

"Head teacher but, yeah, that's the one."

"Well, you should probably be working on a book right now instead of shagging hot schoolteachers, but I'll give you a pass, and it does beat your prior pastime of stumping about morose. Where is this lothario taking you?"

"It's very casual," Katie says. "Barely even a date. We met for breakfast this morning, and he mentioned the Christmas lighting at Shepherd Market, and now we're going. I was the one who suggested it. It sort of…came out."

"NICE. Taking charge. I like it."

"It'll never go anywhere, but I enjoy being around him," Katie says, wondering if this feeling she's presently having might be described as "butterflies."

"What's his name again?" Jojo says, and whips out her phone.

"Simon Bailey. Are you googling him?"

"Don't pretend you haven't."

"I don't need to pretend," Katie says.

Jojo looks up, alarmed. "God, you are *really* bad at this, and that's coming from four people's middle-aged mom. What am I going to do with you? Where does he work?"

"He's a head teacher in Burwash, East Sussex," Katie says. "I don't know the name of the school. It's in High Yield or something? There are letters. OMB."

"Eastern High Weald," Jojo says as she types into the phone. "AONB stands for Area of Natural Beauty, not Office of Management and Budget. You really are a Washington creature. Oh, my! Here he is."

Lips pursed, Jojo takes approximately forever to study the screen and Katie panics, contemplating the potential horrors. Unsavory political affiliations? A wife and family? Documented beliefs in ill-founded child-trafficking conspiracy theories?

Katie cringes. "What? What is it?"

Jojo lets out a long, stretchy *daaaaaaaamn*. "Ho-lee shit," she says, and turns the phone toward Katie. "The photo you sent me did not do him justice. If this is your Simon Bailey, well done. He's super fucking hot, and the teacher bit is beyond charming."

Katie stretches to see and can't help but smile. On the school's webpage, Simon is undeniably adorable with his slightly mussed hair and perfectly made tie. He has a certain awkwardness and, damn, the butterflies are back.

"Shagging hot schoolteachers," Jojo says, and slips her phone back into her coat. "Nicely done."

"I'm not shagging anyone!" Katie cries. "I've shagged three people in my life!"

As several people turn to see what kind of adult would openly admit to this, Jojo pretends to stumble backward in shock. "Three people?" she says, clutching her chest. "You probably don't even know what good sex is."

"Could that be true?" Katie says, and she is momentarily cheered by the thought of Armie being not that great in bed.

"This is an incredibly dire situation," Jojo says. "Before you go back to the States, you must get that number up to four. You're running out of time."

"I *am* running out of time," Katie agrees. "But the manuscript is what I'm worried about. I'm afraid we're not going to find it—or *anything*—before I leave."

Jojo wrinkles her nose. "What else are you looking for?" she asks.

"Lots of things," Katie says. "I told you I'm positive Nancy Mitford started the autobiography?"

"About Simon's grandmother," Jojo says, and Katie nods.

"We've seen a few pages, but this just raises more questions," she says. "Why did Nancy write about Lea and Emma, and how far did she get? If she never finished, why did she stop? If she did finish, why didn't she publish it?"

"That is a lot," Jojo notes.

Never mind the missing book, there are a half dozen other strings that still feel loose. The only thing Katie knows for sure is that whatever she was hoping to accomplish in London, she hasn't come close.

"This is an easy problem to fix," Jojo says, and again fishes out her phone. "You will stay another week."

"Jojo! Stop!" Katie grabs her hand. "You can't! You've already done too much, and I have to go home, eventually. I can't hide out in a bookshop for the rest of my life."

"Who said anything about the rest of your life? Just another week or two."

"I can't," Katie says again. "I have stuff to do." When Jojo throws on a skeptical face, Katie adds, "There's a lunch, next Friday, with an old friend."

"Oh, sure. A lunch."

"It's true," Katie says.

Last night, after checking her bank balance, Katie emailed a former colleague from the Holocaust Museum about potential job openings, and he responded within the hour. One person is on maternity leave, and another quit, and they could really use her help.

"You can't reschedule this mysterious lunch?" Jojo says.

Katie shakes her head. "I'm afraid that, if I do, it'll never happen." She's also afraid Jojo will talk her out of it.

"Didn't know you were so into your meals," Jojo says. "How

about Wednesday? This should give you enough time for a proper shag, as well as your all-too-important lunch."

"I guess that could work?" Katie's voice sounds as unsteady as she feels. "Though I'm more interested in finding this manuscript than getting in a 'proper shag.'"

"You're boring," Jojo says.

"You have to let me pay you back," Katie says. "For change fees, at least."

"Nah, I should pay *you* for all the time you've spent with Clive. Listen, I need to pop into Marchesi," Jojo says, and nods toward a building across the street, a pink-fronted bakery with a window display that resembles some kind of Parisian winter fantasy. "Do you want to come with, or wait here?"

"I'll wait," Katie says, and sits on the edge of the pool.

As Jojo scampers across the road, Katie checks her phone and sees her updated itinerary, along with several texts from Armie—all pictures of Millie, who looks by turns fretful or passed out asleep.

Thanks for sending! Katie types. **I've extended my trip so can she stay until Wed.?** She pauses, letting her hands and the phone fall into her lap. The conversation with Jojo left Katie feeling not guilty, exactly, but stung on Armie's behalf. **Hope everything is going well**, she writes. **With you. And the new girl.** Not for all the money in the world could Katie remember her name. **Sorry if I made things more difficult**, she continues. **I wasn't the most gracious there, at the end. We had some good years, my forever friend, and even the shit I can't imagine going through with anyone else. OK, bye!**

Heart in her throat, Katie turns off her phone. She exhales, feeling both slightly better and slightly worse for having said these things.

November 1942

G. Heywood Hill Ltd.

The group trekked along Curzon Street, in the blackout dark, the only light from the occasional opening and closing of a door, or the burst of an electric torch.

It was past ten o'clock and, ordinarily, Nancy would've fallen off her perch by now, but they were buzzy from the morning's news about the Allied invasion of Algeria. Already a person had to reserve a table at most restaurants and cafés two days in advance, but tonight lines were out the door. It didn't help that there were five of them: Nancy, Hellbags, Jim, Cecil Beaton, and Lord Berners.

"I think Johnny got to them," Helen groused. "I think he's gotten to every maître d' and concierge in London and told them not to let me in."

"It's merely crowded," Jim said. "Johnny would never exert that much effort on your behalf."

"We could go to the shop," Nancy offered. The Colonel was working late, and she should get some writing done, but how often did Anglo-American troops land in French North Africa? "I have some red wine in the booksellers' room," she added, and the idea built some steam. "Perhaps a sleeve or two of biscuits."

Cecil and Hellbags thought it sounded like a perfect idea, and Jim protested, but for what reason, nobody bothered to catch. "Excellent," Lord Berners said without lifting his gaze. Even in a blackout, he tried to avoid every crack in the pavement. "A unanimous vote."

Nancy unlocked the shop and her friends filtered in, gathering in their usual spot beside the fireplace. She scampered downstairs to fetch the wine and whatever nibbles she could scare up.

"Who should we eviscerate first?" Lord Berners asked as wine was passed around.

Nancy lit two oil lamps and sat down. "Let's get to that later," she said. "I want to hear about Cecil's latest assignment. Some of us fancy ourselves writers, but his stories are the best." The beautiful, blond-haired, thick-lashed photographer had spent last year photographing the Royal Air Force and his resultant book, *Winged Squadrons*, had come out a few months before, to huge accolades, and huger sales. Recently, he'd returned to London, to take portraits of the Royal Family and the Roosevelts. "Give us the news," Nancy said. "We want to hear it all."

"To start, Missus Roosevelt is enormous," Cecil revealed. "She's elephant-colored and beyond life-sized. Her eyes never focus anywhere. The woman has no repose."

As always, Cecil adored the Queen but found the King lacking in magic. Princess Elizabeth was, in his estimation, a charming and well-raised girl.

"I'm bored of the Royal Family," Lord Berners said. "Let's discuss books. Has anyone read *Grand Canyon*? Since Eddy's not here, we can argue its merits without him threatening an overdose." Eddy's cousin, Vita Sackville-West, had just published her first novel in eight years—a dystopian story set in an Arizona resort hotel. "Where is the boy, anyhow?" Berners asked.

"He ate something that didn't agree with him," Jim said. "So he's prescribed himself a week of sitting beneath an ultraviolet lamp."

"Back to *Grand Canyon*," Lord Berners said. He looked at Nancy. "Wasn't it a Book Society recommendation?"

She nodded. "I'd never recommend it to customers, though. We're a stitch too in the middle of things to comfortably picture a world in which Germany has defeated us."

"It's meant to be a cautionary tale," Jim said. "As in, don't sign peace with a Germany that hasn't been brought to its knees. Don't try to find common ground."

"Either way, I've had my fill of worst-case scenarios," Nancy said.

"Ohhhh!" Hellbags crowed, stretching, and reaching around Cecil. "The latest Angela Thirkell! Nancy, you little monster! You told me you were out!" She gazed upon the novel with the sort of moony reverence customarily reserved for her Americans. "The woman puts out something new every year. I admire her so much!"

"Angela calls it the 'new wine in an old bottle' trick," Nancy said.

"I like wine any manner in which I can get it," Hellbags said with a snicker. "And this varietal works for me. I'm swiping this copy. You can put it on my account."

"Nancy, you seem irritated," Jim said. "Do you take issue with Angela Thirkell?"

"No!" she snapped. "Not at all. In fact, we have a number of things in common. Recently, she told the *Observer* how peaceful it is with no husbands around, and I heartily agree. Of course, that's the trick to putting out a book every twelve months."

"Hasn't it been a while since you've heard from Peter?" Lord Berners said, and Nancy shot him a look.

"Over a year," Helen clarified. When she noticed Nancy's glare had shifted to her, she shrugged and bit into a biscuit.

"I don't care for Thirkell's style," Nancy said.

"Yes. Excellent," Lord Berners said. "This is precisely the cattiness I was hoping for."

"Just because Evelyn's not here doesn't mean you should make it seem like he is," Nancy said. "As I was saying, though I don't care for Angela's work, we have the same publisher. The more Hamish Hamilton makes, the more he can pay for *my* books, and thus I wish her all the luck that's ever existed on this earth."

Not that Hamish had agreed to buy anything, and he wasn't altogether sold on the idea of a memoir. When Nancy told him about it last week, he suggested she return to fiction, using Angela Thirkell as a model.

"Why, because we're both women?" Nancy had seethed. "You sound like my father."

"You share a similar sensibility," Hamish explained. "A satirical exuberance, and a comedy-of-manners style."

"Are you aware that Thirkell considers her books so lowbrow she tells friends and family not to read them?" Nancy said.

"At least someone's buying them" was Hamish's uncharitable response. Nancy figured he'd change his mind, once the book was finished.

"You had a meeting with Hamish Hamilton?" Lord Berners said. "Is something new in the works? I hope so. This war is going to end—"

"Is it?" Jim chirped.

"You have to strike while the iron's hot."

"Yes, what are you writing, Nancy?" Cecil said. "When will we see another of your brilliant books on these shelves?"

"Don't ask," said Jim.

Nancy thwacked him in the leg with the back of her hand. "I am working on an autobiography," she said. "And it's coming along nicely, thank you for asking."

"It's coming along?" Jim furrowed his brow. "How? It seems you spend all your free time working, or bedding that Frog."

"You let me worry about my own schedule."

"Evelyn told me the few pages he's read are not up to snuff," Jim said.

"That's where the editing comes in," Nancy said, and Cecil nodded to show he was on her side.

"Once again," Hellbags said, "I'd like to remind everyone that Evelyn Waugh is not the final authority on anything, other than how to be a lousy drunk."

"Too true," Nancy said with a sigh. "Evelyn aside—"

"The best place for him to be," Helen said.

"The plan is thirty thousand words by Christmas," Nancy said.

She wasn't anywhere close, but thirty thousand felt doable, like a meaningful but not insurmountable bar. Nancy had sent some chapters to Weston Manor, but Lea was no more receptive to her efforts than Evelyn had been.

"What is it you want from the girl?" Danette had asked. "Approval? Assistance? More grist for the mill?"

Nancy didn't know, other than there was something about Lea. Maybe it was her odd silence, her secretive nature, or the fact she seemed to act in direct opposition to common sense. Whichever the case, Nancy had a notion that there was a larger story to be told, and Lea held a key part of it. Plus, the book was about the Battle of London, and the trauma inflicted upon those who stayed. Nancy could speak to her own experiences, but Lea was the only displaced person with whom she still had contact.

"Whenever it comes out," Cecil said, and sipped his wine, "I'll be the first in line to read it. This wine is superb!" He held up his glass, trying to catch the small flecks of light. "You must've gotten it from a Frenchman. They're the only ones who have anything decent these days. I wouldn't have taken Captain Roy for a cultured type."

"Wrong Frog," Lord Berners said.

"Haven't you heard?" Hellbags said, rubbing her hands together fiendishly. "Our girl Nancy is head over heels with a Free French colonel!"

"Oh, please!" Nancy batted the air. "It's not as serious as all that!"

Nancy couldn't yet claim to love Gaston Palewski, but their relationship was more than a fling. Eight weeks had passed since they met at the Allies' Club, eight weeks minus one day since he came for supper, and stayed the night, and almost every night since. The Colonel's official residence was at Eaton Terrace, in a house owned by a friend of Nancy's, but mostly he slept at Blomfield Road.

They'd developed the kind of routine that felt almost like a relationship. Each evening, Gaston went from his office at Carlton Gardens directly to Nancy's house, always arriving via taxi, and announcing himself by humming a Kurt Weill tune as he sauntered down the road. In the mornings, he rose at seven o'clock, returned to Eaton Terrace to change, and rang Nancy one last time before work. During the workday, he often buzzed down to the shop and, every once in a while, Nancy joined him for lunch at the Connaught. The nights the Colonel stayed late at the office, he'd ring Nancy three or four times, just to hear her voice.

"*Allô—allô*. Were you asleep?"

"Yes, of course. What's the time?"

"About two. Shall I come 'round and see you, my little silk-worm?" He called Nancy this because of her low stamina and perpetually cold hands and feet.

"I'm not sure," she'd demur. "It's so very late."

"I must hear another story. *La famille Mitford fait ma joie!*"

Their conversations felt endless. The Colonel spoke closely, personally, using words that seemed designed for her. He asked a million questions and, when Nancy told him her tales, he laughed to tears. "I can't get enough of you, my *Non-cee*," he'd say.

"As usual, Hellbags has embellished the situation," Nancy said, even as she understood she was morphing into the giddiest, most lovestruck little beast. "Suffice to say, the Colonel and I have enjoyed a rousing two months."

"I still don't understand what's so great about him," Jim said. "Is it because he's aces in bed?"

"If you bothered to speak with him for more than five minutes, you'd know that the Colonel is terribly educated," Nancy said. "And he used to drop bombs for the French Air Force. We gals like a man who's lived a little."

"Hear, hear," Hellbags said.

"Any woman would find him superior to a soft-bottomed Brit," Nancy added. "Some bore who's to a manor born."

"Weren't you born on a manor?" asked Lord Berners.

"It's not the same thing. I'm a woman, and we were poor."

Jim rotated toward Cecil. "The Colonel is Gaston Palewski," he said. "The legendary lothario. De Gaulle's *very* spotty right-hand man."

"Yes, of course!" Cecil said, and Nancy was grateful he did not pull any particular face. "I spent some time with Palewski in Africa, at the…let's see… Grand Hotel in Khartoum, I believe."

"Where he was absolutely destroying the ladies, no doubt," said Jim.

"I don't know about that—" Cecil tried.

"Oh, yes, you do," Jim scoffed. "Gaston Palewski can't see a pretty girl without wanting to take her to bed. He's usually successful, much to the irritation of his coworkers and friends."

"I wouldn't worry about the women working for us in Sudan," Cecil said, and his gaze darted toward Nancy. "They are famous for their high incompetence and low quality of looks."

"That's exactly what the Colonel described."

"I'm sure he manages," Lord Berners chortled. "I heard a great story about him once. Apparently, years ago, Palewski offered to drive a woman home from a party, but she refused, claiming she was too exhausted to get into his car. This is the extent to which his reputation precedes him."

"His reputation doesn't bother me," Nancy said, and this was mostly true. "It all stems from his deep appreciation of women. He finds us more interesting, intelligent, and multifaceted than men, and therefore prefers our company. Plus, the Colonel has an inherently affectionate nature. As a child, his older brother teased him about his constant need for cuddling."

"That's one way to put it," Jim said.

"All right, everyone, your time's up on the Colonel," Hellbags said. "It's somebody else's turn to get dragged through the mud."

"I'm glad all three restaurants we tried were full," Cecil said, and poured himself more wine. "This is better—it's like a vaguely bawdy midnight salon."

"Aw, Cecil," Nancy said. "Always the right thing to say, at the right time."

"I'm serious. Here we are, in the middle of the war. Everything is bleak and grim, but you've turned this hodgepodge bookshop into a very gay place."

"Please come by more often," Nancy said. "You'd balance out all the malcontents."

"Enough niceties," Lord Berners said. "Let's get back to the gossip. What are the Mitford girls up to?"

Nancy sighed, her brief high spirits now dashed. "Nothing to report," she said. "Everyone's still tilling the fields of their same old misdeeds." She thought, and not for the first time, that if Farve had bothered to set aside funds to educate his clutch of very smart girls, maybe they wouldn't have been so predisposed to extreme political views and mustachioed madmen.

"Your sister told me she's pregnant," Hellbags said, and Nancy whipped in her direction. "She seems very excited!"

"Sister?" Nancy blinked. "Which one?" Despite the dark, Nancy could discern the befuddlement on Helen's face. Debo and Decca were the two Mitfords who might qualify, but Decca was in California, which left only one. Hellbags was like an older sister to Debo, a better one than Nancy had been. She'd even put up funds for Debo's wedding dress, after Farve refused. "Debo?" Nancy said, feeling choked. "She's pregnant, again?"

"Gosh, Nancy," Hellbags said. "I didn't mean to spoil the surprise. I'm sure she would've told you, had I not guessed. Poor thing is having a helluva time. She's so sick. Plus, knowing what happened with Mark…" Helen froze. "Oh, no. Nancy, I'm so sorry."

"You don't need to keep apologizing," Nancy said.

"She lost Mark, and you…" Hellbags fanned her face "I'm so sorry! I should've been more sensitive. I know how devastating it was. You were staying at my house!"

"How devastating what was?" Cecil asked.

"Nothing! Old news!" Nancy said. "I'll pour everyone the last of the wine, but then we should lock up. It's late and I don't like to leave the Colonel waiting. You know that old wolf, he'll just find someone newer and better to 'drive home.'"

❧

Later that night, Nancy lay awake in bed, staring into the blackness. When the Colonel flipped over, she braced herself for his snuffles and snores, but the room stayed as quiet as it was dark.

Nancy wasn't startled by Debo's news. In some ways, she'd been waiting for it all along. Her sister was only twenty-two years old, and it'd been a full year since the stillbirth of her first child, a son she'd named Mark. At the time, Nancy was at West Wycombe recovering from her own tragedy. The sisters had timing in common, but their losses were different, and Debo had the chance to move on from hers.

Nancy glanced over at the Colonel. She detected the fluttering of his eyes.

"Yes, darling?" the Colonel said. "Is something wrong?"

"I cannot have a child," Nancy blurted. "I know you haven't asked me to bear you any. Imagine! But you should know I'm strictly barren, and not merely because I'm one hundred years old."

The Colonel inched closer and burrowed into her side. "You are not so old," he said.

"Well, I'm younger than you are," she said. "Which is a very low bar!"

"You are also in your thirties," he pointed out. "The same cannot be said for me. What is this about, *Non-cee*? Are you worried about the *Titanic*?"

"The *Titanic*? What?" Suddenly, Nancy remembered. "Well, yes. Figuratively speaking. This old body's hit an iceberg and is now dry docked. I had surgery a year ago," she said, fiddling with a stray ribbon from her nightdress. "I'd suffered many miscarriages before but, this time, the little bugger implanted himself into one of my tubes. A fine mess!"

Nancy squeezed her eyes shut and was at once hurtled back to that horrible day last November, when she was staying with friends in Oxfordshire. At first, she mistook the pain for indigestion—Billa Harrod was a miserable cook—but she was soon dizzy, almost blind in agony. After muttering something about appendicitis, Nancy packed her bags. She hoofed it to the bus station and, upon arriving in London, proceeded directly to University College Hospital, and into emergency surgery. Nancy begged her doctor to spare her the second tube, but he wiped her clean out.

"Muv was shocked to learn of my gynecological demise," Nancy told the Colonel. "She had no idea that two ovaries were all anyone had. She envisioned hundreds, packed in like caviar. Stands to reason, I suppose, given how many children she produced."

While Nancy was in hospital, she spoke to her mother several times on the phone, but Lady Redesdale never came to visit, not a single time. Debo was recuperating from Mark's stillbirth, and Muv thought she needed the company more. Nancy was tougher, she reasoned, and her pregnancy had not been as far along.

"Come to me instead," Hellbags said, when Nancy blubbered down the line. "I'll nurse you back to health."

West Wycombe proved the solution, in the end.

"My little silkworm," the Colonel said, when Nancy unspooled her tale. He stroked her arm. "It is awful you were punished in this way."

"A punishment. What a stunningly accurate description."

"Was your husband very sad?"

"Peter? Lord, no. He didn't ring me once while I was in hospital," Nancy said. "Or at West Wycombe, or since. The surgeon told my mother-in-law that my condition was grave, and I'd be in danger for three days, but Lady Rennell didn't bother to call or stop past, or even send a bloom!"

"Ah. So this is why you were so upset you have not heard from this tedious man."

Nancy pressed her lips together to think. "Maybe," she said. "With Prod, it's impossible to know what's *most* bothersome at any given moment. It's probably for the best. I'm sure I was carrying a boy, and two Peter Rodds in one household is unthinkable."

"Absolutely horrible," the Colonel said, and kissed Nancy's shoulder. "If a man doesn't have the decency to care for his wife, he could at a minimum muster the sympathy for his unborn child."

Nancy opened her mouth but didn't know what to say. Technically, the child was not Peter's, but Captain André Roy's. For the first time, Nancy wondered if Prod somehow knew. He was good with sums, and it would explain his long silence.

"Sympathy for his unborn child," Nancy said, and forced a laugh. "You really are a terrific Catholic."

"Enough of Peter Rodd!" the Colonel said. "Quick! I need

a story to lift my mood. Something from your childhood. I command it!"

Nancy held her breath, as if trying to suffocate the frightening recollections swimming in her head. "All right, dear Colonel," she said with a long exhale. "What will it be this time? The secret Hon Society? Our beloved Asthall, with its nursery overlooking a graveyard?"

"*Au cimetière? No!*"

"*Oui.*" Nancy grinned at the memory. "We weren't supposed to spy on the funerals but couldn't help ourselves. People seemed to be dying all the time, and I was always getting scolded for pushing my sisters into open graves."

"*Non-cee!*" the Colonel cried. "No! This is too much! Even for you!"

"They didn't mind," Nancy assured him. "It was all a big tease."

"I pray you will take me to this Asthall one day."

"Sadly, I can't," Nancy said, and shook her head. "We moved out ages ago, into woeful Swinbrook, which Farve designed and built from the ground up."

The gray, blocky manor possessed all the charm of an institution, especially compared to Asthall's weathered, lichen-covered stone. It was a pitiful decline in accommodation, and they'd been depressed to move.

"I called it *Swine*-brook," Nancy told the Colonel. "It was enormous, and cold, and no fires were allowed upstairs. Our sponges and facecloths were frozen solid, all winter long, and the Hons met in the linen cupboard because it was the only warm spot in the house. Poor Farve. He did feel terribly that we all despised the place. He sold it a while back, to pay off his debts."

"I did not know your Farve had a sympathetic side," the Colonel said. "I thought he only ever screamed and threw things."

"Farve's bark is worse than his bite," Nancy said. "He's tall and ghastly, yes, but was always ready to ride out with us, or play games. Fat chance getting that level of attention from Muv."

"Tell me, *Non*-cee, what would this barking, biting father think of me?"

Nancy snorted. "Farve would not fancy you at all. First things first, he'd jot your name in the book of people he doesn't like, alongside every other person I've ever brought into the house."

Farve loathed all of Nancy's friends, in particular the effeminate men who roared up in noisy, open sports cars and spent weekends lounging about in loud Fair Isle sweaters, stinking up the house with their violet hair cream. Farve called Nancy's friends "sewers," and Tom's were "Fat Friars," but the insults and disparaging remarks went on and on.

"Lord Redesdale believes in country, king, and guns," Nancy said. "He's patriotic and abhors foreigners, so you wouldn't stand a chance. He does view Frogs as slightly better than Wops, who are preferable to Huns, but he doesn't like anything that smacks of the abroad. Of course, he also hates bankers, aesthetes, and Roman Catholics. He cannot be satisfied."

The Colonel chuckled from deep in his belly. "I love this all so much," he said.

"Enough about Farve," Nancy said. "Enough about me. I believe it's your turn. You've hardly told me anything about your mysterious former fiancée."

"About her, I've revealed everything of importance."

"You've told me almost nothing!" Nancy said. Though she tried to remain unbothered, Nancy often found herself weighing the likelihood that the Colonel had a wife squirreled away in some Parisian flat. Then again, he'd joined the Free French openly, and under his own name. If there was a wife, or anything else in his home, the Germans would've taken it ages ago. "The only thing I know about the fiancée," Nancy said, "is that she's deceased."

"Tragic," the Colonel said. "There's not much to say. You

know my rule. Never discuss someone else with a person who's never met them."

"You really are incorrigible," Nancy said, and sighed. "One day, you'll tell me everything."

"Perhaps, my little silkworm." He kissed her head. "Perhaps."

The Colonel turned onto his back and a hush fell over the room. As his breathing grew heavy, and sleep felt near, Nancy spoke one last time. "Do you mind?" she said. "That I can't have children? Surely you must want them someday."

"Oh, *Non-cee*," he said with one of his deep, weighted sighs. "You must know I don't care about children, or my family name. You are worth far more to me than that."

Thursday Afternoon

G. Heywood Hill Ltd.

"Shoot," Katie says. "Felix told me he'd be in Essex, but I'd totally forgotten. I'm sorry for bothering you!"

"It's no bother at all," says Erin, Felix's right hand in the shop. "He and Zoë left midday. They should be back in…an hour, maybe? Is there anything I can do?"

"No, that's all right," Katie says, but quickly reconsiders. She can't afford to blow an entire afternoon. "Actually," she says, with a meek smile, "there is something, but only if you have the time! I don't want to get in the way."

"You're not in the way at all," Erin says and smiles back, though hers is brighter, infinitely more assured. "Books and customers—that's why we're here! Is this about Nancy Mitford? Felix mentioned you were writing a novel about her?"

"I'm not writing anything yet," Katie says. "But Felix was letting me dig through some of Nancy's files in the storage room? I ran out of time the other day and never made it to the bottom drawer. Think I might be able to have a peek?"

As she speaks, Katie's heart sprints, and she is shocked by her own sneakiness. Maybe all criminals start this way, with one slightly shady act. What might she get up to next?

"Not a problem," Erin says, and scrambles around the sales counter. "Let me grab the keys."

She ducks behind Andrew, the reedy bookshop manager, and Katie tells him, "Hello." He responds with a nod, and a confused and crumpled brow.

Erin reappears, rattling the keys overhead. "Ta-da!" she says, and motions for Katie to follow. "What are you going to write about?" she asks, as they make their way down the hall. "Nancy's time at the shop?"

"That's the idea," Katie says. "Though, admittedly, I'm feeling stuck. About Nancy Mitford, there's just so much to know."

"If only there was a lost manuscript to help," Erin says with a wink.

"Ha! If only!" Katie is afraid to say more, nervous about on whose toes she might tread.

"Seriously, though," Erin says. "How fit is that Simon bloke?"

"Uhhh, yeahhh… He's pretty cute."

"Pretty cute?" Erin says. "Wow. High standards. Good on you. He might be half bonkers, but I don't even mind. He's welcome to hang 'round here all he wants. Another imaginary document, you say? *Why, yes, sir, I will look for it.* I'll look all day long."

Katie blinks. "Wait. So you *don't* think there's a manuscript?"

Erin shrugs and turns on the storeroom light. "Probably not, if nobody's found it yet. Then again, I doubt every stone's been unturned, and things tend to go missing around here." She slides a key into the drawer.

"Missing?" Katie says. "What do you mean?"

"Books, mostly, by certain authors, usually the contemporaries of a certain former bookseller." Erin looks up at Katie and winks. "For instance, books by Evelyn Waugh routinely fall out of their shelves, and twice we've had Angela Thirkell novels straight disappear. Felix always chalks it up to an inventory problem, or general clumsiness, but the rest of us are convinced it's Nancy's ghost."

"Really?" Katie says, and the room temperature seems to plummet. "Well, unlike Felix, I do believe in ghosts, so please let me know if you see any around. As much as I love Nancy Mitford, I'm not sure I'd want her watching me." Katie sets down her bag.

"I dunno. Might be fun to be on the receiving end of one of her barbs." Erin yanks open the drawer. "Let's see… Yep, just as I remembered," she says, and Katie cranes to look. Erin removes a folder about three inches thick and pulls off the rubber band. "These are letters Nancy wrote to her friend Lady Dashwood. Her estate donated them to us, in honor of the nighttime salons she attended in this shop during the war."

Erin extends the folder toward Katie, whose hands are now trembling. "Lady Dashwood?" Katie repeats. It takes her a second to piece it together. "Hellbags?"

"That's our girl. Funny." Erin looks down, and Katie's gaze follows. "I thought there was more in there." The drawer is now empty save a few loose rubber bands and paper clips. "I told you things go missing," she says.

Katie opens the folder and riffles through the letters, which are not in any particular order. She pauses to read, with Erin peering over her shoulder.

22 December 1942
Dear Hellbags,

Why do you insist on spending the holidays at West Wycombe? I can't imagine Johnny is much good for Christmas cheer. How I miss you at our salons, and indeed in my home!

The shop is madness right now, and everyone is acting like a raving lunatic. Books are flying off the shelves, and customers are stomping about, accusing Heywood of hiding

books, or selling them to social enemies. More than a few
have resorted to plucking new releases from the front window, or tearing open boxes left at the door! Anne is a beast
four times over, and sometimes I dream of reporting her for
treasonous activities, just so somebody will contain her. Don't
worry—I'd never stoop to such depths!

I do wish my autobiography was shelved beside the others.
Anyone who has a book out right now is making a small
fortune. Of course, I have to finish the damned thing first!
I've been plugging and plodding—a few dozen pages so far.
Though I've hinted at it, I'm thinking of asking Lea Toporek
more directly to assist. Tell me, what do you think of this
plan?

Now for the good news: Heywood is letting me take off two
weeks after Christmas to work on my book! Hester Griffin is
here for the holiday rush, and she'll stay on until I return.
Do you know Hester? She's a friend of Anne's—ordinarily a
real mousy type, but now that she has a book due out in the
spring, she's developed one of those tiresome chipper person-
alities. It's the absolute worst. Oh, Hellbags, I am dying for
a break. The Colonel and I are talking about spending the
hol with Debo, up at The Rookery. Derbyshire is supposed to
be splendid this time of year. A perfect place to write a book.
More later.

Love from
Nancy

"Pretty cool, innit?" Erin says.

"Extremely," Katie says. She is light-headed, tipsy on the notion that Nancy's friends might have something to add.

"Wow, would you look at that," Erin says. "She references
the memoir!"

"And writing it with someone else." Katie looks back at Erin. "Do you know anything about Lea Toporek?"

Before Erin can answer, they're interrupted by a series of footsteps, followed by a throat clearing and a scowl so intense it emanates from across the room.

"What is going on in here?"

"Hi, Felix!" Erin chirps. "You're back early!"

"Erin," he says, his voice a block of ice. "I never gave you permission to open that drawer."

"Don't blame Erin," Katie says as her pulse quickens and sweat bubbles at her hairline. "I'm the one who asked, and she was only trying to help." Katie clambers to put the letter back into the folder and ends up dropping the whole thing. As Katie bends down to collect them, Felix shoves her out of the way.

"I'm really sorry," Erin says. "I didn't—"

"Not your fault," Felix says, and Erin dashes out of the room. Meanwhile, Katie is cowering, wishing she could dissolve into the floor. "Tell me, Katharine," he says, "are you in cahoots with Simon Bailey?"

"I wouldn't use the word cahoots," Katie says. "We're... friendly."

"Be careful not to get *too* friendly."

"What do you mean?"

Felix stands, and socks the folder into his chest. "Has Mister Bailey revealed to you why he's so desperate to find this alleged manuscript?" he asks.

"Simon's grandmother knew Nancy during the war," Katie says. "He has some correspondence that mentions the book and wants to tie it all together. A very small family mystery, that's all." Katie leaves out the part about Simon's mom because repeating it would feel like a betrayal.

"That's all he said, then?" Felix asks.

"What else is there?"

Felix sighs, and drops the letters back into the cabinet. "It seems to me Mister Bailey has left out a few key details," he says, and locks the drawer. "I can't go into specifics, but I say this with your best interests at heart. When it comes to Simon Bailey... better that you are wary...better that you proceed with caution."

"What the fuck is that supposed to mean?" Katie says, then slaps a hand over her mouth. "Sorry about the swearing but, really, that's all you're going to say? *Proceed with caution?*"

"I am truly sorry, Katharine. I wish I could give you more, but it wouldn't be appropriate. Now. If you're finished rummaging through our files..." Felix offers an arm. "Allow me to show you outside."

December 1942

G. Heywood Hill Ltd.

"Goodness, what happened here?" Nancy said, gaping at the Christmas cards strewn across the floor.

One of their longtime customers, Missus Falziel, simpered nearby. "I upset Anne again," she said. "It seems to be a daily occurrence. My little enemy."

"My deepest apologies," Nancy said as she began scooping up the cards. "Anne is a perfect demon lately. I do hope this baby is worth all the angst."

Anne Hill had at last gotten pregnant, and in the nick of time, as Heywood was due to ship out. He'd been called up months ago, but they'd granted him a deferral because one-third of the shop's sales occurred in December, and he was a "one-man show."

"One-man show?" Nancy balked when he delivered the news. "What am I, a ghost?"

"You are not a ghost, but you are also not a man," Heywood had replied, sounding ever like Farve.

"Anne hates everyone and everything right now," Nancy told Missus Falziel as she finished corralling the mess. "Don't take it personally. The holiday madness has frayed all of our nerves."

They were mere days from Christmas, which meant a constantly ringing phone and a line of customers snaked out the door. There was scarcely a gift left to be bought, and the shop was barren, downright bleak, without books and Victorian curiosities lying about. Nancy couldn't wait for the season to end, especially with her small Christmas miracle still ahead. Heywood promised a two-week holiday for all the hours she'd put in. Finally, a chance to focus on her book.

Between work and the Colonel, and her newly implemented blackout salons, Nancy hadn't come close to the thirty thousand words she'd hoped to have by now, but the upcoming mini holiday gave her a shot at a new goal, which was to finish before the release of any book written by Hester Griffin, or Angela Thirkell.

"Were you planning to buy these?" Nancy asked Missus Falziel, about the cards. "We only have a few packs left, and I suspect they'll be gone by closing."

"Yes!" She swiped them from Nancy's hand. "That's the whole problem! When I inquired about whether there might be a second box in the back, Anne threw these at my head."

"Luckily for everyone, she does not have the best aim."

Nor Heywood, Nancy thought, which was doubtless why it took Anne so long to get pigged.

"Thank you for stopping past." Nancy leaned in to give Missus Falziel a hug. "Hester will be happy to ring you up. Have a very merry holiday!"

"You as well. By the way, when does that handsome husband of yours come home?" she asked. "I'm sure it will be such a relief to have him around, if only for a short time!"

"Oh, I don't expect to see Peter," Nancy said, and put on a smile. "He's nowhere to be found these days! Wartime makes everything so messy and unpredictable!"

Missus Falziel cocked her head. "How odd," she said. "I presumed all men were granted Christmas leave for a day or two, at least."

"Fighting never really takes a break," Nancy said, a pleasant expression still stitched to her face. "Perhaps the powers that be deem him too valuable, or he's more expendable than others, if you catch my drift."

Missus Falziel opened her mouth, only to swallow back down whatever she'd intended to say. After wishing Nancy a hasty Noël, she bumbled off. Nancy couldn't help but chuckle. Prod might be thousands of miles away, but he was still capable of scaring a person out of a room.

As Nancy turned toward the front window and its two remaining books, a great clatter and thump erupted from somewhere in the shop. Nancy followed the sound to the red selling room, where Anne Hill lay sprawled across the floor. Heywood was crouched beside her, fanning her face.

"What happened?" Nancy said, and lowered beside him.

"Anne took a tumble," Heywood said. "Poor dear."

"It's fine, it's fine," Anne said, waving around a hand. "Please stop making a fuss. I just plumb keeled over. Pregnancy is such a beast."

"Anne, darling, what can I do?" Nancy said, stroking her clammy brow.

"You can go about your day," Heywood said. "Nothing to worry about here." His strained jaw belied his attempt to stay calm.

Nancy popped to her feet. "I'll fetch some water," she said. "Don't move a muscle!"

"If only that I could!" Anne tried to joke.

Nancy was halfway through the door when she heard Heywood declare, "That's it. There's no way I'm leaving."

"Oh, darling. The government gets very cranky when you ignore them."

"Then I'll apply for another extension."

"Impossible," Anne said, while Nancy remained frozen in place, the whoosh of her heart loud in her ears. "You leave in three days. The government takes that long to open an envelope."

"I'll advertise in the paper tomorrow," Heywood said. "For a part-time employee. I'll hire the first two people who walk through the door. I don't care who they are."

"You'd never find anyone suitable on the Labour Exchange," Anne said. "They're all too old, or too derelict, or too much of a spy. Good Lord, even I'm better than the worst of the worst. If you can go off to war, I can do this. Hester's willing to stay on for a while. We'll make do."

"I'll close the shop before I let you put yourself or our baby at risk."

Nancy sighed and, though it pained her to do so, she swiveled around and returned to her boss's side. "It seems as though everyone has forgotten about me!" she said. "I'll be here. No need to hire any spies or invalids."

"But your holiday," Heywood said.

"Who takes a holiday with a war on? Really, it's too absurd."

"Nancy, you can't—" Heywood began, before his wife cut in.

"Would you really do that for me?" she said. "Oh, Nancy, you are so wonderful! There's no way I could survive with both you and Heywood gone." Anne looked up at her husband. "I'm sorry, but it's true. I'm an absolute wreck."

"But, Nancy," Heywood said, "you were going to finish your book."

"I surely wasn't going to *finish* it!" Nancy laughed. "We'll make up for it later. What's two more weeks?"

Thursday Evening

Half Moon Street

"Hello," Katie says as she stands on Jojo's doorstep, smiling oaf-ishly, unsure whether she's supposed to hug Simon, or shake his hand, or what. Ultimately, Katie pats him on the back like he's just hit a walk-off double in a junior varsity game.

Through it all, Jojo looms behind her, and Clive huffs with some blend of impatience and outrage. Earlier, he'd been alarmed to discover Katie was bringing a strange man into his house, and thus spent the better part of the afternoon installing a video surveillance system.

"A *teacher*?!" he'd cried. "It's always the people in positions of authority who become murderers and sexual predators! Haven't you ever watched a documentary?"

"I'm sure he's been background checked," Katie said, wondering what the hell kind of programs Clive sees.

"Nice to see you again," Simon says, with a twitchy, nervous smile. "You look nice."

Katie snorts. It is forty degrees and there is nothing special about Katie's jeans and black Barbour coat. "Uh, thanks," she says. "Same to you. These are my friends." She looks back. "Jojo, Clive, this is Simon Bailey. Simon, Jojo and Clive."

"Hello, all," Simon says, and shakes Jojo's hand. He reaches toward Clive who responds with crossed arms and a bushy-browed scowl.

"What sports did you play as a child?" he asks, right off the bat. His mom palpably stiffens. "I find it's a good indication of character."

"Goodness, what an intriguing query," Simon says, and glances at Katie, who shrugs.

"You're acting awfully dodgy," Clive notes. "I'll take that as *none*."

"Good grief, Clive!" Katie says. "What do *you* play?"

"Youth tennis," he sniffs. "I'm not one for team sports."

Katie bobs her head because Clive does seem like a kid who'd have bad sportsmanship. She pictures racquets hurled, and balls kicked at other people's heads.

"Ah, tennis," Simon says. "I'm a big fan, though I'm not especially skilled. Growing up, I played football, though I wasn't very good at that either. I was technically on a team, much to everyone else's dismay."

"Football?" Clive says, and makes a face.

"Don't get him started," Jojo says. "He hates it."

"How can a sport end in nil–nil draw?" Clive wails. "It's maddening!"

"Soccer does suck, I agree," Katie says, and takes Simon's arm. "Well, we should probably head out. Bye, you two. Thanks for vetting my date."

After a stilted round of handshakes, Katie drags Simon onto the street. When the door snaps shut, she feels an instant release, as though she's escaped a major calamity by a very slim margin. "Yikes. Sorry about that. Thanks for being such a good sport, though," Katie says. "I probably should've warned you about Clive."

"Ah, he's a cute kid."

"That can't be the first adjective that comes to mind," Katie says. "Clive Hawkins-Whitshed is the world's smartest and most impertinent eight-year-old." As she begins describing his most recent internet crime, Katie veers left onto Curzon Street. She walks several yards before noticing Simon has for some reason gone right. "What are you doing?" she calls out. "Shepherd Market is the other way."

"I'm in the mood for a walkabout," he says. "It's a nice night."

"If you consider relentless drizzle nice," she mumbles, and jogs to catch up.

As they walk, Katie's nerves build, starting in her stomach and rising to her throat. *Proceed with caution*, Felix warned. Of course, his word is not exactly reliable and there was more in that drawer than takeaway menus. Everything is suddenly muddled, and the only person Katie trusts at this point is Nancy Mitford, possibly Hellbags.

"What'd you do this afternoon?" Simon asks as they turn onto Lansdowne Row, a narrow, pedestrian walkway. Small tables are set up outside, and snowflakes made of twinkling blue lights dangle overhead.

"What? Me? Nothing? Why?" Katie says, sounding defensive, even to herself.

"Uh…forget I asked," Simon mutters.

"Sorry. I didn't mean to—" Katie shakes her head. "I didn't do much, to be honest. Caught up on some emails, squabbled with my sister. They're having a seventieth birthday party for my dad this weekend, and I'm missing it. He's been dead for half of that, by the way. It's stupid." She shakes her head again, then waits a beat before admitting, "I also swung by Heywood Hill." Katie pauses. She's testing the waters, seeing if she can work up the courage to mention Lea's potential involvement with the book.

Simon looks at her. "You did?" he says, forehead lifted.

"Only for a few minutes," she adds. "Felix was out, but Erin told me about some letters they have between Nancy and Lady Helen Dashwood. It's not the memoir itself but, it made me think, maybe correspondence like this—with her friends—could explain some things."

"What sort of things?" Simon asks.

"Have you ever wondered why Nancy chose your grandmother to write about, out of the hundreds of evacuees who went through Rutland Gate?"

"I have," Simon says. "My guess is it's probably one of those things. A strong friendship coming out of nowhere. An attraction you can't explain."

"But they don't seem very chummy in the letters," Katie points out. "Also, why did she wait *two years* to start the book? Part of me thinks... I wonder... Maybe it was your mom who drew Nancy's attention?"

"A baby drew her interest?" Simon scoffs. "Nancy didn't even like children."

"So you claim," Katie says. "But if that's true, why did she put herself through so much to have a child? Between the miscarriages and the full salpingectomy—that is a very rough road."

"The full what now?" Simon asks, and Katie winces.

She goes to tuck a piece of hair behind her ear, only to find it's already pulled back. "Nancy's tubes were removed," she says. "Don't mean to get graphic. I know men are squeamish about poorly functioning lady parts."

"Um, not sure that's always true," Simon says.

"Maybe with Nancy," Katie continues as they turn onto Berkeley Street, "she was living with your pregnant grandmother and there was a bit of...not envy, really, but a haunting, an idea of what could've been."

"Do you really think Nancy Mitford wanted to be a mother?" Simon asks. "Or was it simply an expectation, a thing every woman at the time thought she should do?"

"Here we go..."

"Think about what Nancy said in her letters, describing her

nieces and nephews. Prigs and gangsters, right? And what about the way she treated children in her novels?"

"Oh, come on." Katie heavily rolls her eyes. "She kept them at a certain remove, admittedly, but—"

"If by 'remove' you mean she abandoned them, or left them for dead, I agree."

"That was a form of self-protection," Katie says. "The best way to convince yourself you never really wanted something is to decide it's actually terrible. Plus, children make awful characters in books."

"You've spent a lot of time thinking about this," Simon notes. "What's that about?"

Katie hesitates before speaking, her eyes trained on the lighted sign of the Ritz ahead. Though she can't relate to a war, or living with a pregnant evacuee, Katie understands the tendency to douse pain with jokes and mockery. She's never fictionally killed off any kids, but Katie has excised children from her books, which she hadn't realized until now.

"You're right," Katie says. "I *have* spent a lot of time thinking about it. Yesterday I read about Nancy's surgery in the book you lent me, and it struck me, probably because..." She clears her throat and tries again to fix her hair. "I, uh, experienced something similar earlier this year."

They turn at the Ritz, which is bedecked with ornaments, life-sized nutcrackers, and boughs of holly tied with big red bows. "My fiancé—*ex*-fiancé—and I were expecting," she continues, carefully doling out each word. "I also had an ectopic pregnancy. It did not end well. Then again, I'm alive, so maybe it did."

"Katie, that is horrendous."

"Yep," she says without glancing up. Around them, Piccadilly teems with people, which is fortunate because Katie can concentrate on the masses, instead of whatever horror-struck expression must be on Simon's face. It takes him a long, long time to speak again.

"The fiancé," Simon says as they walk into Shepherd Market. "Is the pregnancy why you broke up?"

Katie sighs. "We had plenty of other problems, too. Maybe it was the tipping point, who knows. Can we talk about something else?"

"Absolutely." Simon flips around to face her. "How about some beers, yeah? I'll nip into Kings Arms. Do you want the same as before?"

Katie nods. He doesn't need to ask, and she's charmed he recalls.

As she waits in the crowd, beneath lights draped like blankets over the square, Katie takes in the people hugging, and smiling, and drinking their pints. Though she'd never say it out loud, especially not in front of her mom, Katie's never been one for Christmas spirit. It's too stressful, weighted by too much expectation, but London is starting to change her mind.

A few minutes later, Simon appears over her shoulder. "Hopefully you'll find this one as non-horrible as the last," he says.

"Thank you." Katie takes a sip. "Thank you for the beer, for listening, for taking me on your Nancy Mitford adventure. It's been…" Her words fade away.

"The pleasure's all mine," he says, then studies her for a second. "You're still thinking about it, aren't you? Why Nancy wrote about Lea?"

"Yes!" Katie says, wondering if he has any idea that Nancy might've written *with* Lea, too. "I'm sure your grandmother was delightful, but it's very annoying!"

Simon laughs. "I've never met someone so interested in the motives of a writer," he says. "You have some very unusual personality quirks."

As Katie opens her mouth, as she starts to say that writers are obsessive, and she knows this because she sometimes considers herself one, Simon takes her hand. "Let's find somewhere to watch," he says.

Katie feels joggled, all mixed-up. "Oh. Okay," she stutters, and trails after him.

As Simon leads her deeper into the crowd, Katie hopes he can't feel her pulse through her palm. Is the hand-holding a romantic overture, or a by-product of her height? Katie is small like a child and could easily get lost.

"This should work," Simon says. They stop beside a tall, lighted tree and he squeezes and then releases her hand. Katie's arm drops and she stares up at him, dumbfounded.

"Are you kidding me?" she says, and Simon looks down.

"What's wrong?"

"This!" Katie says, making large circles with her hands. "You really think this is a good spot? All I can see are other people's backs!"

"No. Really?" Simon says, and squats to match her height.

Katie presses down on his head. "It's more like this," she says.

"Holy shit!" Simon gasps loud enough that three people whip around. "You can't see fuck all down here!"

"Yeah, no kidding. Literally welcome to my world."

Simon stretches back to full height and reaches over to playfully yank on her stub of a ponytail. "You're so cute," he says. "Everything about you is in miniature. Your stature, your voice, your hairdo."

Katie rolls her eyes. "It's not a hairdo," she says. "It's a ponytail." Also a way to deal with scraggly, dishwater hair that hasn't been highlighted in months.

"I'm sorry. Let's find somewhere else," he says, and again takes Katie's hand. "If all else fails, we can pop you up onto my shoulders."

"You're mean," Katie says, and they find somewhere that seems better, so long as she's willing to stand in a planter.

"By the way," Simon says, "I should be the one thanking *you*, for your help with the manuscript, and coming tonight, and, yeah, everything else." His eyes dart away. "When did you say you were going back to the States? Saturday?"

"Funny story. I mentioned missing my father's so-called birthday party?" Katie says, and takes a gulp of beer. "That's because I extended my trip. I'm staying in London until Wednesday."

A grin rips across Simon's face. "Katie! That's fantastic! The best news I've heard in ages. Uh, but why do you appear distressed? Are you sad to miss the party?"

"Sad, no," Katie says. "I hate fighting with my sister, but don't feel the need to attend. She and my mom are big into the milestone shit, not me. I find it all a little weird. Congrats, I guess, on being dead for as long as you were alive."

"It is…unconventional…" Simon frowns. "Has this happened before? These celebrations?"

"Only all the time," Katie says. "When the math is compelling. I wish they'd stop it, but I can't say anything. It's always been everyone on one side and me over here." She holds her hands apart. "When my dad died, my sister and mom hunkered down in their grief. I was a resilient child, and they sort of left me to fend for myself."

Katie feels Simon nudge closer. "Fend for yourself, how?" he asks.

"Well, let's see… For example, by age seven, I was making all my own meals. At ten, I was signing permission slips, and arranging car pools to practices and games." Katie chuckles. "I'm lucky there weren't any pervy coaches in the neighborhood at the time."

Katie was fourteen when Judy married Charles, and they all moved into Little Falls Farm. That summer, the newlyweds embarked upon a three-month European honeymoon while Britt, who was twenty, stayed in Chapel Hill to work and take classes. Katie was left alone, aside from occasional supervision by Nanny Carol, and several nights spent in Armie's guest bedroom. The summer wasn't all bad—Katie ate pizza four times per week and taught herself how to drive her stepbrother's Toyota Celica.

"Katie. That is terrible," Simon says. "You were only fourteen."

"It's not that *big* of a deal. Just a touch of benign neglect. My grandmother was around, and I, uh, stayed with an old neighbor for a good chunk of it."

"Yeah, but still. It could've ended very badly," he says. "Is that behavior even legal in the States? Couldn't your parents have been arrested?"

"Nah," Katie says. "Too rich and too white. It really wasn't as bad as it sounds. No one could've called me deprived."

"There's more than one way to have a traumatic upbringing," Simon says. "Jesus."

"Are you *trying* to make me hate my parents?" Katie jokes, playfully elbowing him in the ribs. "Then and now, I refuse to let it bother me. Okay, enough about my apparently heart-wrenching childhood. Tonight, let's forget about past injustices and have fun."

"Sounds perfect to me," Simon says. He grins and puts an arm around her as John Cleese walks onto the stage. The crowd roars and tears begin to trickle down Katie's cheeks.

"John Cleese," Katie says. "Goddamned Basil Fawlty."

Simon shifts toward her and, in a thick German accent, says, *"Hors d'oeuvres...vich must be obeyed...vithout question!"*

"Don't mention the war," she hisses in return.

"Yes, you did!" he shouts. *"You invaded Poland!"*

Katie laughs, and so do the handful of people nearby who've picked up on the joke. Simon pulls her against him as John Cleese welcomes the masses.

"I'm so glad you're staying," he whispers, and goose bumps shoot along her arms.

"Three...two..." John Cleese counts. "One!" He flips the

switch, and the lights turn on. As he pops a bottle of champagne, a trio of women in elf costumes walk onto the stage.

Sleigh bells ring, are you listening?

In the lane, snow is glistening.

Katie and Simon pivot toward each other and exchange grins. Nose tingling, Katie looks back at the stage and her eyes fill with a different brand of tear, something close to joy, or maybe relief. Life was so scary and so awful for such a long time, Katie truly doubted the world would ever be the same. Of course, this isn't her world, and exactly nothing is the same, but it feels full, and it feels whole, and that seems like a miracle.

"Katie?" Simon says. "You all right?"

"Yes." She glances over. "Just a little...emotional."

Later on, we'll conspire.

As we dream by the fire...

He nods. "I know what you mean."

Simon leans down, and Katie looks up, and their lips meet. A thrill rises and Katie thinks that, maybe, in a few key areas, life is even better than before.

January 1943

G. Heywood Hill Ltd.

"Hullo, hullo!" Nancy said, dancing into the shop with a bagful of books. "I'm back! Anne, darling, where are you?"

"Excuse me, ma'am?" said a customer as she brushed past. It was an American—no time for that today.

"Sorry, Gov," she said. "A bit busy. Maybe come back later? How's noon tomorrow, while I'm on lunch?"

Nancy knew she was doing little to help the shop's bilateral reputation—the doughboys had taken to calling it "the Ministry of Fear," but they were bringing this on themselves. How Hellbags stood them was a question for the ages.

"Anne!" Nancy called again, only to find her friend slumped in a chair beside the fireplace. "Oh, ducky, you look ever like death."

Anne Hill's pregnancy had become a full-time occupation, and Nancy did not relish the added work. The burgeoning proprietress was more scattered than ever, slapping the wrong labels on the wrong boxes and sending payments to incorrect addresses. Somewhere along the way, she'd misplaced her family allowance pay book and hid sixty pounds in the shop, but could not remember where.

"What are we going to do with you?" Nancy said, and batted Anne's foot. "You still have several months left!"

"Life has become untenable!" Anne wailed. "I literally cannot carry even a few books from one place to another and I need to get fitted for yet another maternity belt. I feel horrible!"

"You're not doing yourself any favors," Nancy pointed out. "With that thing you're wearing."

Anne glanced down at her three-quarter-sleeve, camel-hair maternity jacket.

"I bought it for a pound last week," she said. "You don't like it?"

"I might possibly vomit."

"I thought it was economical of me," Anne said with a pout.

"Economical is not always the right idea," Nancy said, and set her bag on the ground. "Perhaps the goodies I snatched up at Hodgson's will give you some cheer."

As she sat beside Anne, Nancy pulled several books from her bag. "Robert Louis Stevenson's *Not I, and Other Poems*," she said. "*Life on the Mississippi* by Samuel L. Clemens. *Symptoms of Being Amused*. Don't worry, ducky, you don't have that disease. This one I nabbed for Lady Dashwood. What do you think?" Nancy held up the book: *The Sportsman's Portfolio of American Field Sports*.

"Ugh," Anne said, about this or perhaps some other thing.

"Our Hellbags is a most sporting girl," Nancy said with a titter. "I left bids for several more. Can't wait to see if I've won. How much do we have in the account?"

"About five hundred pounds?"

"Not for long," Nancy said. "What'd I miss while I was out?"

"Nothing, everything," Anne said. "It's just effort, effort, effort, all the time. And now we're dealing with air raids again. I thought we were past all that!"

"It is frustrating," Nancy agreed. To some extent, Nancy shared Anne's mental weariness. Two weeks ago, the Luftwaffe launched its first air raid in almost two years, and hadn't let up since. Fifty casualties one day, two hundred the next, and rumors that ran amok. A large bomb was said to have killed twenty at St. John's Wood, and for days people swore Churchill was dead. After one drop, Mollie failed to report to work, sending them all into hysteria. As it turned out, she'd only been getting her hair done, but these near misses could distract a person for the whole day.

Life was back to waiting for the next bomb to drop, and now the shop was responsible for fire watch, too. Three nights per week, Nancy and Mollie tromped up to the roof of Crewe House and waited for a fire to break out on Berkeley Street, or in Shepherd Market Square. At the first sign of a flame, they scampered into the blackout laden with buckets and a stirrup pump.

Despite these infringements on Nancy's schedule, the Colonel was soon leaving for an Allied conference in Casablanca, and thus Nancy might find some space. She hated the idea of him being gone an entire week, but she'd be able to focus on her writing, maybe even kick off some kind of streak. The missed holiday had disrupted everything.

"Just remember," Nancy said, rubbing Anne's swollen leg. "We got through the last set of raids and the Christmas onslaught. We'll get through this."

"But we were younger then," Anne said. "Sprightlier and less worn down. Heywood was still here at Christmas, along with Hester!"

Nancy made a face. "Hester Griffin is about as helpful as a head cold."

"What about you?" Anne said, her brown eyes choked with tears.

"What about me? I'm sitting right here."

"This is only a wartime job for you," Anne said. "You could leave at any time."

"I'm not going anywhere," Nancy said. "I need this job!

And I'm too old and decrepit for the war machine, so no worries there."

Sighing, Anne closed her eyes and leaned back into her chair. "Nancy?" she sniffled. "Do you think I've taken too much quinine for my cold? I'm worried that it might be one of those things that Doctor Saunders said not to do, like driving a hundred miles, or riding horseback."

"Surely you would've recalled if the doctor said anything about it." Nancy jumped to her feet. "Enough of this hiver-havering. I've got a brilliant idea! Let's close the shop early and catch dinner at Norway. I'm in the mood for something low-brow."

"That would be excellent," Anne said, rubbing her eyes like a sleepy child. "I do need a change of scenery."

"That's the spirit. You sit tight." Nancy dropped a blanket across her lap. "I have a few bits to sort for the shop and will be back in two shakes."

On her way to the office, Nancy popped into the lav and noticed one of Anne's letters poking out from beneath a Penguin. Anne was careless with her private correspondence, likewise sellable books that should be on the floor, and Nancy would have to speak to her about this—again.

As she lowered onto the seat, Nancy slid the paper from the book and gave it a scan. The letter was for Heywood and contained Anne's usual inventory of maladies and discontents. Nancy was about to set it down, when a paragraph drew her eyes to the page.

Jim was saying that Emerald Cunard is the only woman entertaining in all of London, but Cecil Beaton reminded him of Nancy's midnight salons, and her constant trickle of friends coming into and out of the shop. Sadly, I think our little place increasingly has the imprint of Nancy's personality and not ours.

"Oh, you little demon," Nancy murmured. The place needed some personality, didn't it? She flipped to the back and read on.

Nancy is being rather difficult, and I fear a bit bored and irritated by me, and by everything.

Nancy gasped. Her fingers slackened, and the letter fluttered to the floor. For a moment, Nancy sat frozen, pondering what to make of what she'd just read. Finally, she completed her business and collected the discarded sheets. Hands trembling, she slid them beneath the book.

In truth, Nancy *was* bored sometimes, and irritated, especially with Anne, but seeing it written down felt like treachery or, at the very least, an insult to Nancy's efforts, and her canceled December writing plans.

"Anne, darling!" Nancy called as she threw open the door. "Are you almost ready for dinner? By the by, I think you left something in the lav!"

❧ ～ ❧

"Goodness," Nancy said, heaving, as she flopped back onto the bed. She was spending the rare night at the Colonel's, which meant sleeping in her friend's bedroom, among the pink lace and frills. "Having sex with you is like getting run over by a freight train. Religious people probably feel this way sometimes."

"Religious people don't laugh half as much as you," the Colonel said, and Nancy looked at him.

"Don't all women laugh during sex?" she asked.

"With me, most of them cry," he said. "Or call out for their mothers, or beg the Lord to forgive them."

"Oh, brother," Nancy said, and rolled her eyes. "This is one of the many disadvantages to my upbringing. I never received the proper training about how to react to things."

"You are perfect to me." The Colonel rotated onto his side and dropped an arm across Nancy's waist. *"Tu te sens mieux maintenant, princesse?"*

"I feel physically better, though mentally is another matter. The gall of Anne to complain about me like that! I only wish I could bring it up, but she's already in such a foul mood. What should I do?"

"Maybe refrain from reading her private letters, to start?"

"Colonel!" Nancy said, and gave him a loving swat. "She leaves them out!"

"But you *are* bored and irritated, no? Is Anne Hill not correct?"

"No, she's right." Nancy sighed. "And things are bound to get worse. Simpkin stopped supplies! He's the chap who sells books to the trade at a discount. Now we'll have to buy directly from the publisher, which will cut into our profits, thereby sending Anne into deeper pits of despair. Meanwhile, customers are more demanding than ever, as if we can somehow make up for the austerity measures. Harry Clifton rang me at home, hoping to buy a speedboat!"

The Colonel gave one of his deep-throated laughs. "But you sell books!"

"Yes, but we are one of the few businesses still operating normally, so they think we can get anything. Col, I *must* get out of that shop." Nancy sighed again. "If there's one advantage to finding that letter, it's that Anne's given me a nice smack on the rear. Time to get moving on my book! I got down two thousand words today."

"Excellent, my love!" The Colonel kissed her on the shoulder. "You see? It turned out all right."

"For now. But Anne will have her baby soon, and the war drags on and on." It felt as though only last week Churchill was telling Decca not to give up hope, that surely her husband was missing in action and would eventually return home. Now her sister was set to marry again, this time an American lawyer who was even more of a pinko than the last. "That first summer," Nancy said, "everyone swore this would be done by the end of the year. At Christmastime we were giddy to think 1940, the most awful year to date, was over and done. Two years on, nothing's changed, and we're all accustomed to the treachery."

"This is the way of war," the Colonel said. "My sweet silkworm, this is too much speak of dreadful things. Where is my happy girl? You must cheer me up. I demand one of your stories! *Tout de suite!*"

"Surely you've heard them all twice by now."

"Then let us go a third time around," he said. "Beginning with the child hunts."

"I see." Nancy snickered. "You're in the mood to be outraged."

"It makes me outraged because it is outrageous!" the Colonel said. "A respectable father dispatching bloodhounds to chase *ses petites filles* across the Cotswolds!"

"Ah, but think of how the churchgoing weekenders must've felt," Nancy said. "When they stepped out of the morning service in time to see four hounds in full cry sprinting after a pack of little girls."

"It is truly awful!"

"But, Colonel, we *adored* the child hunts."

He slapped a hand over his face. "It is too much for me!"

"Oh, you love it," Nancy said, and she knew this to be true.

The Colonel savored any and all tales of Farve, starting with how he tramped about the estate, loud and menacing, in his corduroy breeches, canvas gaiters, and jacket filled with dead hares. Muv didn't believe in eating rabbit and so Farve stuffed the ones he shot into his pockets to pass out to villagers, most of whom hid after one glimpse of Lord Redesdale lumbering down the lane.

"More!" the Colonel said every night. *"Racontez!"*

Farve was an absolute ogre of punctuality. *"In exactly six and three-quarter minutes, the damned fella will be late!"* During church, he'd time the minister and complain if the sermon exceeded ten minutes.

Farve's rules of cleanliness were just as draconian and woe was the person who dropped a lone crumb (*"Leave this table, you filthy beast!"*). Meanwhile, there was not a single napkin in the house because Muv refused to iron, and paper was too expensive.

"Pas de serviettes!" the Colonel said, his bumpy, mottled face wide with horror. "You must have been filthy beasts, after all!"

Nancy's stories crippled the Colonel with laughter, and she loved how much he loved them. Tonight, though, Nancy was feeling less charitable about her family.

"I'm not in the mood for Farve," Nancy said. "Between his atrocious financial sense and complete disregard for education, he's half the reason I'm working in that damned bookshop. He made sure Tom was properly schooled, but my sisters and I were doomed!" Lord Redesdale saw little reason to throw money at some god-awful establishment just so a bunch of girls could learn about George III, and be made to play field hockey, and develop thick calves. All a woman really needed to learn was horseback riding and French.

"If you are very furious with your Farve," the Colonel said, "why do you not tell me more of his wickedness? Better yet, write it down, and publish it for all the world to see!"

"Wouldn't that be fun? Sadly, I vowed not to write about my family again, and it's all too depressing to put onto paper." Nancy turned toward the Colonel, her hair crinkling against the pink silk pillowcase. "Especially with Unity's problems, and Muv and Farve on the brink of divorce." Theirs had once been a strong marriage, a perfect balance of icy detachment and fiery rage, and they supported each other, follies and all. Sydney accompanied David on his fruitless Canadian mining expeditions, and he tolerated her predilection toward Christian Science. When

Diana left her perfectly nice husband for a married Fascist lunatic, the first crack formed.

From the start, Farve saw Nazis as nothing but a loathsome gang of murderous pests. Muv didn't care for the anti-Semitism business but admired their organizational skills, and how they tidied things up after the last war. Also, Hitler was very polite all three times she met him! Farve would not be moved. He forbade all family members from visiting Germany, but Muv disobeyed. Now they had a permanent reminder of their division with the incoherent, incontinent Unity lumping about, swastika badge pinned to her chest.

"I never imagined I'd see the day," Nancy said. "The war has changed everything."

"Ah, but a divorce can sometimes be an improvement," the Colonel said. "I did not think you would be so against one." He wiggled his brows.

"Ha! Yes. Sometimes it's even a goal."

The Colonel rubbed her arm. "It is very obvious to me," he said, "that even when you are angry with your father, and your sisters, memories of your family bring great joy. You could make it into a novel. You could *fictionalize*."

"I thought you hated novels."

"I prefer stories that are true, unless it's something you've made up specifically to amuse me," he said, and kissed her again.

"I've made progress on my autobiography," Nancy said. "I can't throw it all away now. Anyhow, Evelyn is always telling me to write about my childhood, and I can't take his advice. He'd never shut up about it."

"Evelyn Waugh might have one small idea, but who gave you the notebook for Christmas?" the Colonel asked. "The typewriter?"

"You, my darling man," Nancy said. "It was the most thoughtful gift I've ever received. Meanwhile, Prod sent flowers I'm allergic to."

"This is what I mean by a good divorce."

Nancy shivered and pulled the blanket up to her chin. She snuggled closer to the Colonel, and closer still. It was draughty in that room, and in that world.

"Mon coeur, tu as froid?" The Colonel wrapped his arms more tightly around her. "You really are my little silkworm."

"I'm so lucky you stumbled into my life," she said. "I've never loved anyone half as much as I love you."

"I know."

"I wish you'd say something more reassuring, like that you're lucky, too."

"You're lucky, too."

Nancy elbowed him in the ribs. "You're such a monster," she said.

"I do try."

"Oh, Colonel. I don't know how I'm going to survive this war. I don't know how I'm going to survive you."

Friday Morning

Half Moon Street

Simon stands in the doorway with a tray of coffee.

"Long time no see," Katie says.

He holds up a bag. "I brought food."

Blushing, and smiling like a dope, Katie steps out of the way and motions for him to come inside.

Since he texted an hour ago to ask if she wanted to discuss the manuscript, Katie's stomach has been a mess of lifts and drops. They've kissed, and something has irrevocably changed, and Katie is proud of herself for resisting sleeping with the guy. Granted, sex wasn't explicitly offered, but there was an undeniable hitch as they passed Heywood Hill on the way home.

"Is the Green Drawing Room okay?" Katie asks, struggling to swallow because her mouth is so dry.

"I do prefer my drawing rooms in blue," Simon says. "But I suppose it'll suffice."

"I know—it's all too fancy, but Jojo's kids are in the kitchen getting ready for school. There are four of them. Better to avoid the chaos."

"And the one bloke's imperious gaze," Simon adds.

"Clive would have a lot of questions," Katie agrees. "About

last night, about your phone, the list doesn't end." She flicks on the drawing room light. "Let's go over there."

Simon drops his laptop case on a cherrywood coffee table, and they sit in the pair of unexpectedly schlubby chairs facing the fireplace.

"That was fun last night," Katie says as she tucks herself into a cross-legged position.

"Sure was," Simon says, so casually it borders on rude. Without making eye contact, he pulls out his laptop and powers it on.

Katie reaches for her coffee, but her hands are too quivery to hold her drink, and her heart is thumping so wildly she might break a rib. It's possible she's making too much of a kiss.

Jesus, act like you've done this before.

Then again, *has* she done this before? In some ways, the answer is no. Katie hasn't kissed a semi-stranger since college, and jitters don't really factor in when you've known someone for thirty years, when you've seen him in Aquaman Underoos, or know how many times he contracted pinworms from his backyard "mud Jacuzzis."

"I brought you cream," Simon says, nodding toward the bag, and Katie blinks.

"Uh, thank you," she says. This is not how Katie expected this to go. She expected some warmth, a sly acknowledgment of what happened last night.

"And plenty of it," he adds. "I know you prefer your coffee more beige than black."

Katie might be flattered if he wasn't acting so frosty.

"I was thinking about what we talked about last night," Simon says, pulling up a document on his computer.

Katie stares, feeling blank. They discussed many things last night, none of which she can remember now. This all feels very businesslike, and office etiquette is yet another thing at which Katie is an amateur.

"Mostly, your question about why Nancy was interested in

my grandmother." He turns toward Katie, and they lock eyes. "I sense there's more to the question."

Katie struggles to think. "I told you about my ectopic pregnancy…" she says.

"No. Not that." Simon shakes his head and, for a second, he softens. "Is there anything else you're not telling me? A salient piece of information you're holding back?"

Suddenly, it dawns on Katie that he must've gone to Heywood Hill after she left. He's staying directly above the bookshop, and Erin would've probably taken any opportunity to assist him.

"Oh!" Katie chirps. "Actually, yes! Those letters I mentioned? Between Nancy and Lady Dashwood? Well, I only had the chance to read one, but Nancy specifically named your grandmother, and implied that Lea might've helped write the memoir." Katie pauses to catch her breath. She smiles, and Simon looks at her entirely without expression. "So, uh, I was hoping to go back, snap a few pictures, if I'm not banned from the premises. Felix pretty much escorted me out of the shop. He did NOT want me seeing those letters, that's for damned sure, but I'm hoping to change his mind." Katie exhales and begins fiddling with her hair.

"That's it, then?" Simon says. "That's all you have to share?"

"What else would there be? You're being kind of—" Katie freezes. She drops the lock of hair. "Why? Do *you* have something to share?" she says. "Some reason I'd need to *proceed with caution*?"

"Nope." Simon pulls a pastry from the bag and leans back in the chair.

"You're really not the morning person I thought you were," Katie mutters, and he shrugs and bites into an almond croissant.

After last night, Katie decided to trust Simon and ignore Felix's warnings. He was, after all, the only one who seemed to be hiding things. Now, though, Simon's behaving so erratically, so unlike the person she thought he was, Katie doesn't know who or what to believe.

"Do you think Lea helped Nancy write the memoir?" Katie asks, and chooses a chocolate croissant from the bag. "Has your mom said anything about that before?"

Simon shakes his head.

"If she did help," Katie continues, "no wonder Lea was so hurt when Nancy ghosted. A book is such a personal thing, especially a memoir."

"Is it, Katie? Is a book *such* a personal thing, like a secret, almost?"

Katie's face flames. She feels like she's done something wrong but can't figure out what. "Not sure why you're being so salty," she says. "I just mean, if your grandmother cowrote this memoir, I can understand why she'd be upset Nancy bailed and moved to Paris to live happily-ever-after with the Colonel."

Simon eyes her, chewing slowly. "That's how you believe it ended, huh? Nancy Mitford scrapped the bad parts of her life. She put the war behind her to live out her dreams."

"She always said her best years were in Paris," Katie reminds him. "And, in *Pursuit*, it's clear that France was her endgame. I know it's a novel, but the parallels are obvious."

"The childhood parts, yes."

"The whole thing!" Katie says, tossing her hands, nearly flinging her croissant across the room. "Think about it. Linda Radlett has two marriages, first to an attractive, wealthy 'good catch' type. A stand-in for Nancy's former fiancé, Hamish St. Clair-Erskine, as well as Sir Hugh Smiley, who proposed to Nancy three times. Then Linda jettisons Tony for Christian, the hot-blooded idealist. Finally, a man who gets riled up about things!"

"I must've missed the years when Nancy was in love with a Communist," Simon says. "You have an unusually active imagination."

"Christian is obviously Prod," Katie says. "It's not about the

Communism, but his obsession with causes—in Prod's case, the refugees. When Linda leaves Christian for her beloved Frenchman, she breaks free from society's shackles—and her own—and finally experiences true happiness."

"True happiness?" Simon snorts. "I'm starting to think you haven't actually read the book."

Katie gasps. "Are you kidding me right now?" she says. "For the record, I've read *Pursuit* twice this week, and probably fifty times before that. But please, mansplain Nancy Mitford to me. I'm all ears."

"I'm not trying to explain anything," he says. "We just have very different ideas about what it means to flourish."

"Linda got rid of Tony and Christian, who were both douchebags!" Katie says. "She met Fabrice and found true love. Isn't that all any of us want?"

"You don't *know* that she and Fabrice would've been happy—"

"It's right there, at the end of the book."

"Katie," Simon says, his face like stone. "At the end of the book, Linda is dead."

"Spoiler alert!"

"And Fabrice is captured by the Gestapo and shot."

"They were happy before all that!" Katie says. She flops back into her chair. "Agree to disagree, I guess."

As she polishes off the rest of her croissant, Simon tosses his laptop onto the coffee table. "How long were you with him?" he asks. "The fiancé. You said it was a long relationship?"

"My conclusions about Nancy have nothing to do with my personal situation," Katie says, and wipes her mouth.

"Of course they do. We're human. That's how we work."

"I've known Armie since we were five," she says. "We were together, on and off, for about fifteen years."

"Holy shit." Simon's eyes bug. "That's practically a lifetime."

"If you're fifteen years old, sure."

"A decade and a half," Simon says, and then whistles. "Do

you live in a small town or something? And you're the only two people in it? How could it possibly take you that long to figure out you weren't right for each other?"

"Wow. Okay. You're really coming in hot today," Katie says. "How nice that you are able to so deftly navigate complicated relationships. To tell you the truth, Simon…" She starts to make a joke about not wanting to leave Armie's medical plan, but doesn't want to seem flip. Plus, Simon probably wouldn't understand that affordable health care is a decent reason to marry someone in the States. "It's hard to boil down," Katie says. "But you might say we had *different ideas about what it means to flourish.*"

Simon's mouth twitches as he tries to contain a smile. He's working hard at being a grump today, like it's his full-time job. "The fiancé didn't agree that happily-ever-after included death?" he says. "That is surprising."

"Oh, Simon. We all die at the end." Katie balls up her napkin and chucks it into the Pret bag, raising her arms overhead when it lands cleanly. "All net! Suck it, Jojo. You're not the only one with skillzzz."

"Am I supposed to be impressed?" Simon asks.

"Guess you didn't properly internalize Clive's lecture about team sports." Katie slumps back into her seat. "If I went through all the little problems, Armie's and mine, we'd be here all week. The short answer is that we've been best friends for over thirty years. Most couples grow apart. We were too close. Like siblings, almost."

"Too close? I doubt that was your problem," Simon says.

"Are you a couple's counselor now?" Katie says. "The fact is, we were together for so long, and are similar in so many ways, that sometimes it was hard to tell who wanted what. Like, did I really want kids, or had I just absorbed his dreams? It's your basic can't-see-the-forest-for-the-trees situation."

"I'm sorry, Katie." Simon sighs deeply. "I didn't mean to stir anything up. I don't know what the hell I'm talking about."

"It's fine. Has anyone ever told you that you apologize up to a dozen times in one conversation? It's kind of annoying. No offense."

Simon flashes a grin, and the mood in the room lightens by five to ten percent. "I'm a Brit, so that checks out," he says. "I'm sorry. *Again.* Apparently, I really hate talking about this ex-boyfriend of yours."

"He's a nice guy. You'd like him. Everybody does."

"I doubt that." Simon stands and crams his computer back into its bag. "I should go."

"All right," Katie says, though she feels there is something left between them, a stickiness unresolved.

"So, what's next?" he asks.

"I'll try to push on Felix more," Katie says. "See the rest of the Hellbags file."

"Okay." Simon zips his bag. "For the record, you'll never convince me that *The Pursuit of Love* has a happy ending."

"Dying in childbirth, the Gestapo, I know," Katie says.

"I'm not talking about that. Those last few lines…" Simon says, and lays a hand on his chest. "They're gutting, Katie."

Katie nods and tears spring to her eyes. The ending always gets her, too, and she'd know the sentences by heart, even if she hadn't just read the book twice. As the narrator laments Linda Radlett's death, her mother suggests that maybe it's for the best, given Linda's track record with men. Fanny insists her mother is wrong.

"He was the great love of her life, you know."

"Oh, dulling. One always thinks that. Every, every time."

May 1943

G. Heywood Hill Ltd.

"I cannot handle one more bill," Nancy said, and smacked an invoice onto Mollie's desk. "I have *ceased*."

Mollie rose cautiously as Nancy ranted on. "I'm beginning to hope that I *do* get called up," she said. "Probably can't drive for the ARP again, seeing as how I wrecked one of their cars within minutes of taking it from the leasing garage, but maybe I can join the Women's Land Army and hoe some field."

"I'll take care of the invoice," Mollie said, and Nancy somewhat wanted to smack her for being so damned nice.

Of course, the real problem wasn't Mollie's generosity, but Nancy's state of mind, and the fact she'd taken on the nervous, tetchy energy of the Free French. Absolutely everybody at the QG was on edge as they waited for Generals Giraud and de Gaulle to decide whether Algiers was to be their political headquarters or a military high command. That de Gaulle hadn't immediately succumbed to Giraud's directive confounded the world, what with de Gaulle's mere two stars, compared to Giraud's five. Nancy, on the other hand, was not the least surprised. She knew from the Colonel this arrogance was very much in line with de Gaulle's personality.

Although the overall situation was complicated, for Nancy, it was simple. Whatever the decision, de Gaulle would soon leave for Algiers, and with him the Colonel. It was not unlike the latest round of Luftwaffe raids. Nancy didn't know when or where this bomb would hit, only that it would, and the effects would be devastating.

"Thank you, Mollie," Nancy said. "I do appreciate you taking up the paperwork, and I apologize for my sour mood."

"Happy to assist. Don't forget, though, we have fire watch soon."

"If only I could forget," Nancy said, and checked the clock. "It's probably about time to kick out my friends and the other stragglers. Yelling at people will cheer me up, if nothing else."

On her way to the front of the shop, Nancy poked her head into the red selling room, where Jim and Hellbags continued their hour-long row. With the National Trust recently returned to its offices at Buckingham Palace Gardens, Hellbags thought she'd ridded herself of Jim, only to discover he'd become even more invested in the fight.

"Hey, kids," Nancy said. "Reckon you might wrap up in the next five minutes? We're about to close. Also, would you mind terribly keeping it down? We've received several complaints."

"How can I keep it down when he's impossible!?" Hellbags said, flapping her arms like she was trying to take flight. "Absolutely relentless! I don't know why he's so desperate to get his hands on it. The place is a dump!"

"The estate is glorious," said Jim. "Which is why it should be owned by someone who appreciates it."

"Oh, just go ahead and take it already!"

"You've only got three and a half minutes left," Nancy warned.

She went to find Evelyn, who was in his spot by the fire, same as he'd been every day for the past three weeks. Having openly questioned the intelligence of several officers, Evelyn was now on unplanned furlough from the Royal Marines and subjected to daily meetings at the Combined Operations HQ.

"Nancy, you have a problem," Evelyn announced. "There are some suspicious characters roaming the shop. Do you see those three men by the antiquarian books?"

Nancy shrugged. "Daily occurrence," she said.

"It's a daily occurrence for eight-foot-tall majors from the Foot Guards to search for books about sixteenth-century mystics?" Evelyn said.

"Yes," Nancy said, squatting beside a box. "Do you mind helping me take this to the back? It's too heavy to carry on my own."

Evelyn stood to assist but teetered, and immediately sat back down. He reeked of whisky, and brilliantine from his trim at Trumper's next door. Nancy felt a headache coming on. "Thanks ever so much," she said. "You are extremely useful."

"What's in there?" He opened the box with his foot. "Books? These are new. Why are you taking them to the back?"

"It's *Long Division*," Nancy said. "Hester Griffin's novel. I'm returning them to Seckler because these are precisely the type of books I despise."

"Why do you have so many?"

"You really think I ordered all of these? It was Anne, and I'm furious." Nancy began pushing the box along the rug. "I can't imagine we'd be able to sell more than one copy."

"I thought you could sell any book," Evelyn said. "You're always bragging about it."

"Now you sound just like her."

Nancy stood and informed a customer that they were about to close. After a very perturbed sigh, the woman plodded off. "Some of us have wartime duties," Nancy muttered.

"Is it just me?" Evelyn said. "Or are all Londoners ugly now? Everyone's plain and messy and gray, even my own wife. Before you wield that famous umbrage of yours, know that she quite agrees!"

"One day I'll convince Laura to take a French lover," Nancy said. "What you're seeing, dear Evelyn, is the cumulative effects of stress, exhaustion, and three years without a holiday. Jim!" Nancy called out. "Yoo-hoo! Jim! I could really use your help!"

As Nancy resumed shoving the box through the shop, Evelyn stood to follow, though not to assist. "When are you going to show me your memoir?" he asked. "Have you spoken to your publisher? What does he say?"

"Hamish thinks an autobiography sounds grand," Nancy said, stretching the truth. She wasn't about to tell Evelyn that Hamish's reaction was more along the lines of dubious. "I just need a bit more on the page before showing it to him. Also, I can't decide whether to start at the beginning of the Phoney War or during the Blitz."

"Forget the Phoney War," Evelyn said. "A wretched time. The rumors, the constant bracing for disaster, all those children evacuated before it was necessary. Our biggest accomplishment was dropping pamphlets on Germany, which served only to supply our enemy with a war's worth of lav paper." He snorted and shook his head. "An utter cock-up. You asked that Lea person to help, did you not? What did she have to say about it?"

"I haven't asked yet," Nancy admitted. "I've been sending her chapters, hoping she'll strike up an interest, but am trying to drum up the nerve to ask directly. I keep thinking, what incentive does she have, really? She's tucked away with her daughter at Weston Manor, benefiting from Danette's largesse, and I've yet to prove my books are worth getting excited about. They always flop, and the world forgets about them three seconds after publication."

"Never mind the uneducated masses," Evelyn said, "I am available to offer my opinion. When would you like my critique? I'm free tomorrow afternoon. Tomorrow morning, too. Not tonight. I'm already drunk."

"I appreciate the offer but, as I said, there are a few bits to work out first." Sometimes it felt like Nancy was writing in circles, as though ten pages of work produced only a sentence or two.

"I hope you're not letting a love affair interfere with your career. This is why women rarely make good writers. They're too easily distracted."

"I'm so lucky to have you on my side. You really are a monstrous cheerleader." Nancy paused and stood upright. "Jim!" she screeched, again. "Can you stop badgering Lady Dashwood and make yourself useful for once?"

"Don't pretend it's an insult," Evelyn said, still following Nancy, nipping at her heels. "I know you agree. You turned down a very wealthy and respectable Sir Hugh Smiley *three* times because you hadn't accomplished anything yet."

"Also, I didn't want children who were blond and stupid," Nancy said. "JIM! I know you're accustomed to being yelled at, but this is getting ridiculous!"

At last he exited the red selling room, sweaty and worse for the wear, with Hellbags hot on his tail. "She slapped me three times," Jim said. "What do you need?"

"Help me with this box?" Nancy said. "Evelyn's not up to the task."

Jim saluted and took one end.

"How was last night?" Nancy asked as they completed the journey of Hester's awful books. "Didn't you attend Emerald Cunard's matchmaking party at the Dorch?"

"I did, and she sat me beside my future bride," he said. "Though I'm not convinced. She had a brown, greasy face and a furry, slip-away chin."

"That does not sound very prospective," Nancy said.

"On the other hand, I am thirty-four, and she is very rich. I could pretend to be thirty-three for a tad longer?" Jim mused.

"There's an idea. Let's set the box over there," Nancy said, and they shuffled toward the corner, where a pile of post waited, ready to go out.

"Danette Worthington was there," Jim said as the box thudded onto the ground.

"She was at a matchmaking party?" Nancy said, and crossed her arms. "Gosh, I don't know how to feel about that. It's nice to know she's starting to move on, but is it too soon?"

"Danette Worthington is not ready to move on," Jim said, and his brow darkened. "She spent the entire party alternating between pie-in-the-sky laughter and sobbing despair. It was a spectacle. People will be talking about it for weeks."

"Poor Danette," Nancy clucked. "Did she happen to mention her houseguests—"

Whatever answer Jim had was interrupted by the arrival of Anne Hill, bobbling into the room like a delirious, obese duck. "Nancy! Have you forgotten?" she squawked. "You have fire watch tonight!"

"Yes, darling, I'm aware. Please, calm yourself, or you're liable to pop out that child."

"Must be soon, eh?" Jim said with a face of deep longing. "You are luminous."

Nancy rolled her eyes. Only Jim would find a nine-months-pregnant Anne sexually appealing.

"Soon. Yes. Thank you," Anne said. "Nancy, if you don't report, we could be fined five hundred pounds. Any infraction will come directly out of your paycheck!"

"You only pay me three pounds per week," Nancy said. "We'd be onto a whole new war by then. Darling—" she put a hand on Anne's shoulder "—fire watch starts in seven minutes."

"Mollie's left already!"

"Lovely! That means I have fifteen minutes to spare."

"Nancy! Why do you hate me?" Anne cried. After an abrupt and terrifying explosion of tears, she extracted a piece of paper from her dress and waved it overhead. "I should never have filled this out!"

"What is it?" Nancy said, trying to read the words.

"The form that would allow you to stay at the shop, until August, possibly longer. Very generous of me, but now I have to ask, what's the point?"

"Oh, gosh, don't worry about me," Nancy said as her stomach fell. It was a nice thought, but she didn't like to picture herself working in the shop that many months into the future. "Don't make special accommodations."

Anne closed her eyes and sighed. Within seconds, her face returned to normal, her tears whisked away. "I don't mind," she said. "I should've done it by now. Heywood told me it was *most* urgent to complete the paperwork. They're getting very quick to call people up. All they seem to require is a pulse."

"Somewhat more than a pulse," Jim grumbled, bitter to have been permanently excluded from service due to his leg spasms and frequent blackouts. Like every other man on earth, Jim viewed himself as a hero-in-wait, capable of valiantly killing someone, if it was needed to save the world.

Anne snuffled and rubbed her nose with the back of her hand. "I've stunned you into silence, I see! No need to get shell-shocked about it, Nancy. A simple thank you will suffice."

⁂

When Nancy arrived at Crewe House, her tin hat and gas mask were laid out on the camp bed. Mollie was marching along the easternmost rim of the roof, scanning the streets for incendiary fires.

"I apologize for my tardiness," Nancy said. "Waylaid by Anne."

"It's fine. So far, everything seems quiet tonight."

"That's good," Nancy said, and rested against the chimney. "Then again, I never know whether to hope for 'quiet' or action. Either we're running around in a frenzy, lugging stirrup pumps and splashing pails of water, or we're stuck with too much space to think."

"That's the straight truth," Mollie said. "At least, during the Blitz, everything was such nonstop turmoil you didn't have time to get bored."

"Not a second to catch your breath from one air raid siren to the next," Nancy said.

"All of us constantly scrambling into shelters," Mollie said. "Quivering for hours in some damp basement, waiting for the all clear."

"Coming out only to get buzzed by low-flying planes, swastikas and iron crosses visible on the tails and wings." Nancy tightened her coat and shivered, though she was not cold. "It's amazing how easily we get used to terrible things."

Nancy turned and gazed out across the rooftops, and tried to imagine what the Colonel was doing at that moment, and what he'd be doing if the war ended tomorrow. They'd spoken of living in Paris, but would Nancy really follow the Colonel to France? She thought about all the decisions she'd made in her life—marrying Peter, her books, working at the shop—and wondered whether she was too old, or too far down the path, to backtrack now.

"What did Anne want?" Mollie asked. "You said she held you up?"

"Right." Nancy chortled. "She completed the paperwork to keep me on at the shop, until August. Hurrah! What I really need to do is figure out the brand of war work people like Cyril Connolly have managed."

"Oh, geez, what did Connolly finagle? He's a bit of a snake."

"He started a magazine," Nancy said with a hefty roll of the eyes. "Then hired all his grubby bohemian friends to write for him. The government approved this as proper war work. Men get all the breaks."

"On the bright side, you won't be conscripted," Mollie said. "Working at a bookshop has to be better than most jobs they let us have, especially since you can't drive."

"I can drive," Nancy said. "Just not very well, which is a description that can be applied to so many things." She thought back to all the war work she'd done so far. "What else might I do? Everyone absolutely despised me at the Frog canteen in White City, and I was miserable rolling bandages for First Aid. I enjoyed giving broadcast talks about firefighting, but that didn't last two weeks."

"Why'd you stop?"

"Got sacked. Nobody could abide my voice, apparently. One fella wrote in to say that he wanted to put *me* on the fire!"

Mollie threw back her head and gave a long, full-throated laugh. "Nancy!" she howled. "You're such a tease!"

"Oh, I wasn't joking."

"You see? This is why I'm always cackling hours after I've left the shop."

Nancy eyed her curiously. "Is that true?" she said. Though Mollie Frieze-Green had been friendlier of late, Nancy never fancied it was to this extent. She only ever seemed to get jolly at Nancy's expense, like when she was struggling with a pump, or running directly into a fire.

"I can't believe you have to ask," Mollie said, astonished. "Of course it's true! I don't want to get too sentimental about it." She paused and bit down on her lip. "But, Nancy Mitford, you've absolutely made my war."

❦

Nancy returned from fire watch in the predawn, walking alone along the quiet city streets, past rows of buildings whose power had been out for weeks, and others not long ago bombed. It was an endless winter in London and Nancy was aching for sunshine.

She turned onto Blomfield Road. The wind rustled the branches, and, in the distance, someone sang. Nancy squinted through the fog, trying to make out the squat figure leaning against an unlit lamp.

And someone's...

Sneakin' 'round the corner...

Could that someone...

Be Mack the Knife?

"Colonel!" Nancy shouted, and sprinted toward him. "I can't believe you're here!" She hurled herself into his body and wrapped her arms around his neck. "Shouldn't you be getting ready for work?" Nancy let go and stepped back. As they met eyes, her heart dove to her feet. There was something wrong about the timing of his visit, and the sadness of his gaze. The Colonel was never woebegone. "Why don't you come inside?" Nancy said quickly, as if she could stamp away what she already sensed. "Gladys will make breakfast. We are absolutely crawling with eggs. I also have plenty of tea, if you can believe it!"

The Colonel flicked his cigarette to the ground. "My love," he said. "I've not come for breakfast, but to say goodbye."

Nancy whimpered, though she'd known this was coming for months.

"My love, we talked about this," he said. "You knew that, once we regained power in North Africa and fixed the problems with Giraud, the seat of the Free French would move to Algiers."

"Doesn't de Gaulle need a man on the ground?" Nancy said. "Someone to monitor relations with the Brits? People don't trust the Frogs. Surely your government should keep in residence an attaché, or ambassador?"

"Your government does view us as *grenouilles suspicieux*, which is another fact of which you're well apprised." The Colonel winked. "How fortunate they've had you to watch after us all this time. Alas, your *mission d'espionnage* now comes to its end."

"Spy mission?" Nancy said. "What are you talking about?"

"Non-cee," he said. "Do not play these games with me. We all know about the French-speaking peeress dispatched to keep an eye on us."

Nancy groaned and covered her face. "Fine," she said. "I confess. The government did ask me to spy on the Free Frogs." She dropped her hands. "For the record, I never reported on you, or much of anything. Just one suspicious couple—the Selliers—and the Green Park ticket taker. Regardless, I was finished with 'spying' by the time I met you. Remember, you're the one who came into *my* shop."

"Either way," the Colonel said, and pulled her in for a kiss. "It does not matter, because you make a very bad spy."

Nancy gave him a little shove. "According to who?" she snapped.

"You are too pretty for *l'espionnage. Tu es trop charmante, trop aimante…*"

"I'm 'much too much'?" Nancy said, and put a hand to her hip. "What is that supposed to mean?"

"You are a person who is better to stand out." He tried to pinch her side, but Nancy jumped away. "My little silkworm," the Colonel said. "I hate to leave, but it has to be this way."

"The problem with falling in love with a famous diplomat," Nancy said. "You're always busy trying to save the world. How much time do we have left?"

"I leave at daybreak."

"Daybreak! That's practically now!" Nancy said. "I was thinking weeks, days at least. We've had so little time together."

"We have this moment," the Colonel said, and took her hand. "Plus eight months of perfect happiness."

"Eight and a half!" Nancy said. "I want more! I want happily-ever-after!"

"Nobody gets a fairy tale," he said. "Don't fret, *Non-cee*. There are some advantages to my departure. *Regarde les choses du côté positif.*"

"The bright side?" Nancy huffed. "And what is that?"

"You'll have so many hours to write. I was a big distraction, you see."

Nancy glowered. Like a cold she couldn't shake, she heard Evelyn's voice in her head. *I hope you're not letting a love affair interfere with your career.* "I'll be too depressed to write," she said.

"Then you'll have to find some new excuse."

The Colonel brought her into his chest, and Nancy buried her face against his coat, taking in the scent of his cigarettes, and lavender cologne. "I hate this life," she said.

"It will end, eventually. For now, you must hold on to what is good."

Nancy pulled away. "What's left to hold on to?" she said. "You're leaving. So many of my friends and family are off fighting—getting shot, captured even. My parents aren't on speakers, Diana's in jail, and Decca's practically American now. God, they're all such Fascists over there. I do not understand the appeal." Nancy stopped to sigh. "Though, I suppose it would be nice to see *Gone with the Wind*."

The Colonel chuckled. "You see? There is always a laugh to be found."

"There's nothing funny about Unity," Nancy said. "Debo remains hopelessly blithe, and Pamela can't help but be the worst. Oh, God. Everything is such a bloody mess."

"Non-cee," the Colonel said, his dark eyes glistening in the low light. "Please, don't be sad. You are breaking my heart. Whenever you feel blue, close your eyes instead and think of me."

"That'll only make me more upset. All I want to do from now until forever is to lie in bed and trade stories with you."

"Then this is what you should do," the Colonel said. "Only, you will need to write them down because I will not be there to listen. Do this, for me." He kissed the top of her head. *"La famille Mitford fait ma joie."*

"I'll try," Nancy said. "Do you think we'll ever see each other again?"

"Bien sûr, *mon amie.* When this war is over, you will come to Paris, where we will live until I am ninety, at least. Is this 'happily-ever-after' enough for you?"

"It could be, if I believed it," Nancy said.

"I have a very faithful nature."

Nancy coughed. "I've heard you described many ways," she said, "but faithful is not one of them."

"Those other people are not you." He kissed her again, on the lips. "We will one day be together in Paris. Forever is a very long time, much longer than a war. Until then, write your stories and send them to me. If you do this, we'll never be far apart."

"You'll be in Africa!"

"Don't worry, my love," the Colonel said, and brushed a wisp of hair from her watery green eyes. "You'll be always on my mind, and I on yours. When you least expect it, the telephone will ring, and there I'll be, just as I promised I would."

Allô! Are you up?

Alors, racontez!

Tell me everything!

Saturday Afternoon

G. Heywood Hill Ltd.

Katie runs into Felix as he's unlocking the shop. It's perfect timing, though Katie has increased her odds by hanging around Curzon Street for most of the day.

"Hello!" she says, popping up behind him.

"Katharine," Felix says with an exaggerated, almost jaunty roll of the eyes. "I thought I told you we were closed on weekends."

"You did, but I was doing a little Christmas shopping and happened to be walking by the shop. Voilà, here you are!" Katie knows she is speaking very quickly and can only hope he's keeping up. "I wanted to apologize, again, for sneaking into your files, and also ask a few more questions, if you don't mind? I promise not to take too much time!"

Smirking, Felix bends to retrieve a box that'd been left by the door.

"If you're too busy," Katie prattles on, "and want me to scram, just say the word. I'll oblige, no questions asked!"

"I find that hard to believe." Felix kicks open the door and leaves it ajar, which Katie takes as invitation.

She trails him inside. "I'm glad you're not mad at me," Katie says as Felix heaves the box onto a table and tears it open with a key. "I did love seeing the letters to Hellbags. Do you think—"

"Mind giving me a second?" Felix says. "Before you start in with the badgering?"

"Yes! Sure! No problem!" Katie chirps. As Felix sifts through the box, she wanders toward the shelves and, almost immediately, something snags her attention. There is a gap where her book used to be. *"A Paris Affair!"* Katie yells, and spins around. "It's gone! Did you force someone to buy it?"

"I wasn't here when it sold," Felix says. "Somebody purchased it of their own free will."

"Impossible," Katie says, envisioning some very British type reading it with a mild-to-moderate sneer. Feeling giddy but also slightly nauseated, Katie drifts toward one of her longtime favorites, Jesmyn Ward, but this shelf also seems out of sorts. It takes her a second to notice an upside-down copy of *Brideshead Revisited by Evelyn Waugh.* Smiling, Katie looks at Felix, and back to the book. She wouldn't dare mess with Nancy Mitford's wishes, and so she leaves Evelyn alone. "You know, the letter I saw to Hellbags was written in late 1942," she says, "and Nancy mentions writing about—"

"Katharine..." Felix answers, sternly.

"Never mind!" she says "Carry on! We'll talk when you're done."

Sheepish and starting to perspire, Katie takes out her phone and opens a text sent by Simon yesterday afternoon. **Maybe you were onto something,** he'd written, and attached a photograph. **From my mum.**

17 May 1943
Dear Lea,

I'm accustomed to prison censors, but I don't know what sort of censor you have in Danette. I can only pray this will land directly in your hands, sans intervention.

In short, I've heard from an incredibly reliable but very dull source that our Lady Worthington is in a state. My heart breaks for my friend, but it's not healthy for you or Emma to endure the ups and downs of her personality. There is a room available for the two of you, in my house, in Maida Vale.

It makes heaps of sense. I have the space, and a housekeeper, and my overnight guest has departed for Algiers. My boss Anne Hill has given birth to baby Harriet—"a huge, hearty hockey-playing Roedean girl" (her words)—and I'll be work-ing a million hours at the shop. All that to say, you'd be prac-tically living alone! When I am home, perhaps you might assist with the autobiography? I won't ask too much—I swear on my life! Just some input, here and there. I promise to make it worth your while. Maybe we'll both become famous, what do you think?

Let me know by post.
Love from
NR

Maybe you were onto something. These words were the first and last thing Simon said to Katie since yesterday's tense breakfast. Twenty-four hours is not a long time in general but, for them, it's practically a month. Katie is convinced this is about the kiss, and though she didn't anticipate winning any awards, she hadn't expected to be shunned.

"Are you aware of any houseguests Nancy had later in the war?" Katie asks, and Felix looks up. "I know she hosted evacu-ees at her parents' house during the Blitz, but is it possible some folks who'd gone out to Buckinghamshire came back to the city and stayed with Nancy?"

Felix tilts his head. "What are you really asking, Katharine?" he says.

"Well, you see," Katie says, twisting a lock of hair around her finger, "in her published letters, Nancy wrote about a pregnant sixteen-year-old who came through Rutland Gate. It seems they had an ongoing correspondence."

"These are questions about Simon Bailey," he says.

"No. Well, yes and no." Katie exhales. "This started with Simon, but now I want to know, for myself."

"If you're asking whether the sixteen-year-old from Nancy's letter ever came to live at Blomfield Road," Felix says, "the answer is no. There is undue fixation on this person. Too much is being made of the connection."

"Nancy was writing a book about her!" Katie cries. "I saw it in Hellbags's letter, and I find it very peculiar you won't let me read the others."

"Why am I obligated to show you the rest?" he asks.

"Well, you're not, but I mean..."

Felix closes the box and sighs. "A book was started," he says.

"I knew it!" Katie says, and marches back to Felix's side. "Why was that so difficult to admit?"

"This is to protect you, Katharine. The less time you spend entertaining Simon Bailey's claptrap, the better."

"I'm trying to be open-minded," Katie says, "but you're making it hard. All these warnings about Simon yet you're the most suspicious person around. I don't mean to be insulting, but facts are facts."

To Katie's great fortune, Felix finds this amusing, and he lets a smile escape. "I'll allow you this very small point," he says. Hands on hips, he examines Katie for two, three beats. "I certainly don't want you to be wary of me... Perhaps I have a document that might clear things up. Wait here."

He flips around and begins striding across the room, Katie on his heels. "You're not allowed to follow me!" he barks, thrusting a finger in her face. "I will abide no more of your shenanigans."

After issuing a final blistering look, Felix hurries off and

Katie is left to stand around pretending to read book jackets while she waits.

"Here's a copy," Felix says, when he returns. "It's very short, but also quite telling. Once you read it, you'll understand my misgivings about your new chum."

"Thank you," Katie says, snatching the paper from his hand. "I take back what I said about you being suspicious. Simon can be a little squirrelly, too." She recognizes Nancy's scrawl the second her eyes hit the page.

12 Blomfield Road, W9
20 August 1944

Dear Lea,
Lord knows if I'll summon the nerve to send this letter, or if it's better to discuss face-to-face. I need to know, was there ever a "Greenie," or was this Greenie really Prod?

Nancy

"You think Simon wants the manuscript because…" Katie says, heart sprinting. She performs a mental calculation and checks her math. "Because Prod was his grandfather?"

Felix nods. "We believe this is a strong possibility. As far as we can tell," he says, "the letter was never sent. We do know that, around this time, Nancy stopped writing her autobiography and soon thereafter came up with the idea for *The Pursuit of Love*. A year later, she left for Paris."

"But Simon said she stopped writing the memoir the following April," Katie insists. "After *The Pursuit of Love* was done."

Felix arches a brow. "How lovely that he said this, but have you seen the proof?"

"Well, no. He can't find the letter."

"Mmm-hmm," Felix says with a very self-satisfied nod. "I would not take Simon Bailey at face value."

"Why would he lie?"

"There are many reasons," Felix says. "Most likely, he's seeking compensation."

Head pulsing, Katie lowers onto the nearest available chair. "That can't be," she says. "Simon hasn't mentioned anything about money." Then again, there was a mention, a small one, but it was more about his grandmother than it was about him.

Promises made to your grandmother? What, like money?

Something like that...

"Shysters don't customarily preannounce themselves," Felix says.

"Shaking down a bookstore doesn't seem like something he would do." On the other hand, Katie's been in London for one week, and all she knows of Simon is what he's chosen to show. They have no friends in common, and she can't even ask around.

"I'm sorry to disappoint you," Felix says. His face shifts and for a moment he seems sad. "I'm not in the habit of spreading unfounded gossip. Unfortunately, in this case, the motives are quite evident."

"But..." Katie starts.

"Once you digest the information, you'll see why it's the only explanation that makes sense." Again, he frowns. "I hate that it has to be this way. I'm the last person who'd want to kill a budding romance."

⁂

Katie rushes out of the store, nearly crashing into a postbox, several lampposts, and two or three groups of tourists. *Felix has an active imagination*, Katie tells herself, sounding ever like Judy Cabot-Swift. *He's reading too much into things.* Despite these assurances, Katie still feels like she's going to throw up.

Turning onto Half Moon Street, Katie spots a tall, lanky figure standing on the front steps. She freezes and considers turning around.

"Katharine Cabot," Simon says. "Just the person I wanted to
see. A few questions have been weighing on me. Perhaps you
might be kind enough to entertain them."

"What a coincidence," Katie says, wishing she had another
minute to think this through. But Simon is here now, and it's
too late to run away. "I have several questions myself."

"This should be a lively conversation," Simon says, and Katie
wonders why he seems so pissed. "I'll go first. I'm going to ask
one more time: Why are you so interested in my family's story?
What's the real reason you offered to help?"

"Me?" She balks. "How can you be suspicious of me? You're
the one who—" Katie stops. Her gaze falls, and her breath fal-
ters when she sees what Simon has in his hand. "Fuck," she says,
and looks up. "I can explain."

"I'm not sure that you can."

Well, now she knows. It wasn't a random customer who
bought the last copy of *A Paris Affair*. It was Simon Bailey.

October 1943

G. Heywood Hill Ltd.

Nancy studied the sheet, as though one page might morph into two or three or four. A few paragraphs was better than nothing, albeit not by much. It'd been five months since the Colonel left, and she'd written approximately one-quarter of a not-very-good book.

"Why is it taking so long?" Evelyn said.

"I don't want to hear squat from a person who turned a military reprimand into government-ordered writing leave," Nancy snapped.

Ah, to be male and so incompetent and foul tempered nobody wanted you around. What a life.

Although the Colonel was gone, and Anne was no longer monitoring her every move, Nancy was almost more distracted by the yawning gap of emptiness than she'd been when her days were filled. As for why it was taking so long, Nancy hadn't yet heard from Lea, one way or another, and whenever she called out to Weston Manor, the phone rang and rang.

"Page two," Nancy said aloud.

She put her pen to paper just as Mollie peeped through the storage room door.

"Sorry to interrupt," she said. "I know you're technically on a break right now. But there's a man here to see you? One of those gray governmental types. Should I tell him to leave? He didn't threaten to arrest me this time."

"Governmental type?" Nancy's heart gave a thump. What did they want with her now? "I'll see what this is about," she said, shoving her manuscript into a drawer. "I hope nobody's been killed."

When Nancy hustled onto the shop floor, she was astonished to find a familiar if not slightly bloated face. "Gladwyn, my goodness!" she said, and kissed him on each cheek. "How are you? It's been a while!" Nancy hadn't thought of him in months, almost a year and a half, and she couldn't fathom what he wanted at this late date. Greville was long dead, and Danette half-mad, and surely the coast was clear by now. "Is this a social visit?" Nancy glanced around. There wasn't much doing in the shop, aside from a few browsers, and Mollie lingering in the back. "Or do we need privacy?"

Gladwyn removed a pad of paper from his coat pocket. "My visit is a courtesy," he said. "I've been transferred to the Foreign Office but, given our prior history, the old bureau asked me to stop past to discuss the Worthington situation."

"Honestly, Gladwyn," Nancy said, and blew a piece of hair from her eyes. "Maybe you all should start worrying about the real enemies, what do you think? Danette can barely keep her hat on straight."

"Have you heard from Lady Worthington?" he asked. "Do you have any idea where she might've gone?"

"Gone?" Nancy shook her head, to clear some space. "Is she not at Weston Manor?"

"She is not." Gladwyn paused, pen poised over pad. "You seem surprised."

"Of course I'm surprised!" Nancy said, her pitch sending two browsers scrambling out of the shop. "Jim Lees-Milne saw her back in May, and I've rung a dozen times since, but no one's picked up. I keep meaning to go out, but I don't have a car, and time keeps getting away from me. Plus, fuel shortages and all."

Sighing, Gladwyn returned the notepad to his coat pocket. "Well, then," he said. "If you truly don't know, I have some unfortunate news. Lady Worthington's been reported missing."

"Missing!? Why? Since when?"

"Three days ago, she left letters for her children," Gladwyn said. "She referenced embarking upon a 'long journey,' and no one's heard from her since."

"Dear God," Nancy said. "You don't think she'd commit it, do you?"

Gladwyn leaned one ear in her direction. "Excuse me?" he said.

"You know, suicide," Nancy whispered. "Danette has been unwell."

"That's what we've been told," Gladwyn said. "Are you certain you don't have any information? Something you might be holding back? What about the East End evacuee living at Weston Manor? I understand the two of you have an interesting connection."

"Lea Toporek?" Nancy said, and tossed her eyes. "There's nothing suspicious about her, aside from the mystery of what happened to her personality. I've tried to contact her as well, to no avail. I understand she's shy, but enough's enough."

"You've tried to contact her? Would you care to elaborate?"

"There's nothing to say. I've gone out of my way with the girl, but…" Nancy flubbered her lips. "She doesn't know how to accept charity."

"What do you mean by charity?" Gladwyn said, and fumbled about his jacket for his paper and pen.

"If you must know, I invited Lea and her daughter to live with me," Nancy said. "Here in London. There's nothing nefarious about the offer. Did she thank me, though, or respond? No. It's all quite galling. I'm only trying to do a good deed."

"You invited her to live with you? Now, that is something." Gladwyn stared down at his pad, seemingly mystified and unable to write.

"Why is it something?" Nancy said. "You think I don't care for the downtrodden, is that it? Peter is not the only person in the Rodd household with a heart for the displaced."

"A heart for the displaced," Gladwyn repeated, stumbling over the words. "That is one way to put it. I'm curious, Missus Rodd."

"Nancy. Please."

"Nancy. Is there a reason you've kept in contact with Lea Toporek, and invited her, and the child, to live in your house?"

"There are several reasons," Nancy said. "None of which concern you."

"Goodness," Gladwyn said, adjusting his glasses. "I was told you were likely informed of the situation, but didn't believe it until now. You are a very magnanimous and forgiving woman, Nancy. You deserve a medal, a ribbon at least."

"Don't make me sound like a saint!" Nancy trilled, though she didn't mind the compliment. "It's what any woman would do. Why are you cackling?"

"You're just so, so gracious," Gladwyn said. "I'll tell you this much, if I had a mistress, and a love child, there is zero chance Missus Jebb would invite them into our home."

～⁂～

Nancy didn't know why she was in Buckinghamshire, standing in Weston Manor's long shadow, especially when Danette Worthington was missing, and Nancy hadn't arrived at any conclusion regarding Peter. Like most men, Prod had his foibles, but the notion of a teenage paramour was too sickening to comprehend. On the other hand, it would explain Lea's odd reserve, and why Nancy intuited she had more to say.

"Just get it over with, you stupid cow," Nancy muttered, her breath making small clouds in the air. She hadn't taken the afternoon off from work, borrowed Hellbags's car, or run over three chickens, only to give up and go home. It was now or never and, because never was an awfully long time, Nancy took in a drink of air and pressed the bell.

She waited. The house felt quiet, haunted almost, and Nancy wished she'd brought Milly for moral support. She rang again and, as she began to leave, the door swung open. Nancy jumped back. "Oh! Hello!" she said, staring down into a pair of big saucer eyes. "Are toddlers working as butlers now? Start 'em young, I always say. Aren't you an adorable creature. Emma, is it?"

Nancy inhaled and took her in with one pass. Emma did share Peter's blue eyes and light hair, but so did a great many tots. Was she tall for her age? Slightly dull? Gladwyn's accusation seemed no truer, yet no less false, after seeing Emma firsthand. "I am Missus Rodd," Nancy said. "We've met before, but you probably don't remember. Is your mum at home?" Nancy peered down the long, empty hallway. There was no sign of Lea, or anyone else, and Nancy wondered about Danette's family. Had her older children returned from school, and what about Benjamin, only eight years old? Were they on tenterhooks, waiting for news, or were they marching on?

"I see you have your mother's sparkling personality," Nancy said to the girl. "Maybe you'll end up like your father, and find yourself prattling nonstop about all manner of the arcane. Although, who's prattling now, I ask you? Gosh, I wish I'd brought you a present. I work in a famous bookshop. Are you able to read? I don't know when children start these sorts of things. This morning, I boxed up some Peter Rabbits for my niece in America." Nancy made a face. "*California*. Isn't it dreadful? I should've set some aside for you. Next time, perhaps."

"I like books," the girl said, quietly. "Mum reads them to me, or sometimes Benjamin."

Nancy's heart soared. "That is something I love to hear," she said. "A person can never get lonely with a book around. You have a very lovely voice, Miss Emma." It was light and sing-song, not a monotone, like Prod's. "I hope you don't mind me saying so."

The girl smiled, bearing all of her tiny, adorable teeth.

"Speaking of books," Nancy said. "I'm writing one myself—an autobiography. Your mum will be in it, and you as well! I'm hoping she might even participate. It'd be a wonderful opportunity for everyone. After all, books are just about the only thing a person can glut themself on lately, and they're selling like mad. We can't let Evelyn Waugh and Hester Griffin have all the fun, or the cash! Especially when we're starting to see a light at the end of this extremely long and dark tunnel. Who knows when it might be over?"

Last month, Mussolini surrendered, and although Roosevelt warned the time had not yet come for celebration, it was a sign that Fascism was on the wane. People were beginning to feel optimism again, and using words like *after*.

"It's getting ever so hard to find reliably crazed dictators these days," Nancy said with a quick laugh. "Never mind. You probably don't stay up on politics. Anyhow. Back to my book. You wouldn't happen to know if...?"

"What do you want?" Lea said as she materialized behind her daughter.

"Miss Toporek! Hello!" Nancy said. "Goodness! A full sentence from you! It is my lucky day. I was just chatting with your engaging little girl. I see she hasn't inherited her father's personality. Phew!" She gave a knowing wink. "I was so sorry to hear about Lady Worthington. What do you think happened? I fear she..." Nancy went to make a telling gesture but thought better of it. "I don't suspect Danette will be back," she said instead. "That really affects things, doesn't it? Did you read my letter? About staying at Blomfield Road, and assisting me with the book?"

Lea nodded.

"Good. Well. The offer stands. I'm sure Lady Worthington has been generous. That is her nature! But you must consider what you'll do if she doesn't return. Nothing lasts forever, not even in a manor built in the thirteenth century."

Nancy waited for a response. It took Lea several minutes of great concentration to affect a very half-hearted shrug.

"A real planner type, I see," Nancy said. She removed a stack of papers from her handbag. "Here are several chapters from my manuscript. What I ask is very little—simply read my work and tell me if I've missed anything, if there's a salient detail I should add."

Lea remained silent, not a twitch on her face.

"You have nothing to lose," Nancy continued. "If the book is a failure, it's more egg on my face. I'm used to it by now! If successful, we can...split the proceeds."

"Really?" Lea said, and she suddenly perked up.

"Well, yes..." Nancy stammered, cursing her mouth for getting ahead of her brain. She was in no position to go halfsies with anyone, much less the mother of Prod's possible illegitimate child. Alas, the horse was out of the barn, and it was gratifying to help them in a tangible way, more tangible than Prod had ever done with his refugees. "Provided you are reasonably contributive," Nancy added, hastily. "I'd rather split it with you than my husband."

As Nancy babbled on, Lea's gaze tightened on the chapters in her hand. Through it all, Emma hung like a primate from her mother's left side.

"Yes," Lea said, and took the pages Nancy offered. "I'll help with the book."

Nancy clapped. "This is wonderful news!" she cried. "I've

been muddling along, writing at a snail's pace, but you'll be the jolt of inspiration I need. Oh, Lea, I see grand things ahead—not only financially, but because it'll be so cathartic to get the truth on paper. I'm bubbling over with joy!"

"I will help," Lea said again, "but I'm not leaving here."

"Fine, fine," Nancy said, and flapped a hand. "You can let me know when you change your mind. The chapters you're holding cover our first few weeks together, and the manner in which you came to me. It was before I knew about Emma. Why don't you go ahead and take a look…"

Nancy watched Lea read the first page, and the second.

"Shall we discuss this 'Greenie' person?" Nancy said, and Lea's eyes shot up. "How would you like me to portray him in the book? If there is a different—" she glanced at Emma "—a different father figure you wish to mention, I am amenable to any change. I am accustomed to wayward men, and all I want is honesty."

"I'll let you know," Lea snapped.

"Very well," Nancy said, sliding her handbag onto her shoulder. She adjusted her scarf, shivering as the brisk wind stirred her coat. "I'll let you absorb the information and will check back in a week, maybe two? You're welcome to ring, or drop a letter, anytime."

"Thank you," Lea said.

As Nancy crouched to say farewell to Emma, the door slammed in her face.

Nancy swiveled around, weighing what just transpired, and wondering why she didn't feel more triumphant. Was this the very breakthrough of which she'd dreamed? Or was it but one victory in what would prove a long and tiresome campaign?

Saturday Evening

Curzon Street

Of course Simon found out. He had access to the internet, after all, and the ability to type. As Nancy Mitford might say: "It is really too idiotic."

"I'm sorry," Katie says as they push through the holiday bustle on Curzon Street. "I don't know what I was thinking. Mostly, I *wasn't* thinking. It's like I'd forgotten that part of myself."

"Ridiculous," Simon grumbles. "You had to assume it would come up."

Katie ponders this. "Yes and no," she says. "It occurred to me briefly, but I guess I was relying on my lackluster career. My boring name. The fact you wouldn't go to all that effort."

"Yes, yes, googling is very arduous. None of this makes sense."

Katie smiles weakly but does not explain that, deep down, she believed the search would reveal what she's come to accept: though Katie was a writer at one time, she wasn't anymore.

"It's hard to explain," she says. "Katharine Cabot feels like a different persona. Some character I made up. I'm at an inflection point in my career. Calling myself a writer feels…" Katie mulls this over. "It feels like a lie, or a jinx, at the very least. Writers write, but I'm not writing a damned thing."

"Because you were looking for inspiration, maybe? Then you met me, saw a bigger story, and jumped on it."

"Okay, your family is not that exciting," Katie says, but Simon is not cracking at her ill-timed joke. "My interest in the manuscript is genuine." As is her interest in him, she does not add. "You know I've been into Nancy Mitford since college. I love research, and rabbit holes, and needed a distraction from my spiraling life. Sure, I had the vague notion that there might be a story in there somewhere, but the idea was more about the shop, and the war. I'd never write about your family. That's not what was driving me."

"I understand career insecurities," Simon says. "But I still can't fathom how it didn't come up. We had some fairly intimate conversations. Never mind the fact I straight asked what you did for a living."

"Ah, see, writing novels is not something I do for a *living*."

"Hilarious."

"And we haven't known each other *that* long," she says.

They walk another minute or two without talking, the only sound the roar of cars and motorbikes. Because of Simon's long stride, Katie is soon outpaced. She scrambles a few steps, then hiccups to a stop, and waits for him to notice.

Donning an almost cartoonish scowl, Simon stomps back in her direction. "Here's what I don't understand," he says. "You've gone through some tough shit in your life. I know you're not weak. Why are you letting yourself get derailed so easily?"

A guy walking by slaps Simon on the back. "Give her a break, mate," he says.

"Not everyone gets to decide how long they stay in a job," Katie says. "That's why the NFL doesn't have forty-year-old running backs. I swear, I wasn't trying to hide anything."

"Forget it," Simon says, so sharply that it stings. "You're right. We only met a week ago. Who am I to you, anyhow?"

Katie's bottom lip quivers. She's never felt this miserable after someone's told her she was right. "Here's the thing," she starts. Katie inhales and closes her eyes, pretending she's about to step into the batter's box. Though she's no longer twelve years old, it seems appropriate given she's going to take a huge swing on what feels like a full count. "It's true we basically just met," she says, speaking as slowly as she can. "But it doesn't seem that way. Everything I've said these past few days is one hundred percent authentic."

"Career secrets notwithstanding."

"Please." Katie puts up a hand. "Let me finish. I didn't even think of myself as a 'writer' this week. I was just Katie, just *me*, and I haven't been able to say that for a very long time." Simon takes a step closer, and Katie glances down at the book in his hands. "It's pretty aggravating," she says. "If I was going to get in trouble for being an author, I wish you'd read a different book."

"It was the only one in stock."

"Story of my life." Katie shakes her head. "How far did you get? Probably not very."

"I read the whole thing," he says.

"Oh, God!" Katie groans. "Ugh! You really didn't have to do that. You *shouldn't* have done that. Well, I appreciate the effort, but let's nottalkaboutiteveragainokaythanks."

Simon laughs, the first spark of cheer she's seen from him today. "I figured I'd like it well enough," he says. "But I did not expect to love it."

"Come on!" Katie says as her face reddens and her heart flies. "You're full of shit!"

"I tried to read it objectively," he says. "I really did. And it should've been easy, given how miffed I've been. Unfortunately, I liked every page."

"But *why*? What did you like about it?"

"Why does a person like any book? It strikes the right note, at the right time." Simon thinks. "The story seemed personal, like you were trying to work something out. I couldn't help but study the protagonist, and wonder how much of her is you."

"Absolutely none!" Katie says. "Not one bit! And I wasn't working anything out. My books are not that deep. I just write. Also, by the way, many readers consider June Clemente an extremely prickly character."

"June makes a lot of mistakes," Simon allows. "But stories need imperfect characters. Otherwise, how does anyone relate? Anyway, June is in a tough position, caught between two worlds—not only Paris and New York, but the way she's trying to move forward while clinging frantically to the past."

"That is a very...thorough analysis," Katie says, unable to look him in the face.

"Personally, I adored June. Of course, I'm predisposed to women with sharp wits and the tendency to blush."

"Oh, God, just stop."

"Let's talk about the ending," Simon says, and Katie eyes him, wary of a trap. "After the affair, June returns to her husband. She's learned a lot but picks the safe over the new. Why'd she go home? Why didn't she stay in Paris?"

"Ah. You're team Étienne."

"Not really," he says. "I can't even choose a side. Neither Étienne nor the husband seems like the obvious answer. It's a very compelling gray area."

"I purposefully end my books like that," Katie says. "In a gray area, no neat bows."

Simon grins. "So you don't just write. I knew it."

"You are very smug," Katie says, blushing again, and deeply regretful of having saddled June with this trait.

She is about to protest, to insist her novels aren't that complex, and no one's ever used one to "figure something out." Then Katie thinks of the emails she's received over the years, people who said her books improved a relationship, or made them see marriage in a new light. Some readers were inspired to travel, or reunite with a parent. Others started an antiques shop, or wrote their own books. It got people through hospital stays, and illnesses, and divorces. The books, and the emails, have gotten Katie through a few things, too.

"I don't know why June went back to New York," Katie says. "That must sound strange, since I wrote the thing. Originally, she stayed in Paris, but that didn't feel right, and so I went back and changed it."

"She probably stuck with the old," Simon says, "because you were sticking with the old, at the time."

"If you're referring to my ex-fiancé, don't even go there."

"No, really? I can't?" He affects a pout.

"Don't even get *near* it," she says.

Simon slings an arm around her shoulders and pulls her into his chest. "Katie Cabot, things are not so bad," he says, his voice echoing against her head. "I know this isn't the end for you. Every writer struggles, even the late, great Nancy Mitford."

"Please, tell me how her career went nowhere for fifteen years. I never tire of that old yarn."

"Nowhere is just a stop to someplace else. Count yourself lucky. This is not a big problem to have."

Katie looks up. "It's not my only problem!" she says, and Simon laughs.

"Do you have time for a coffee?" he asks. "Or a pint? Handy that it gets dark so early this time of year. Makes a bloke feel like less of an alcoholic."

"Either is great," Katie says, and he takes her hand.

As they walk down Curzon Street, Heywood Hill dead ahead, the questions she'd shoved down minutes before start to bubble up. How does Prod fit into Lea's story, and how much does Simon know? Katie hesitates to ask because she doesn't want another argument or, worse, to discover Simon's intentions are not what he claims.

"I hate that you're going back to Burwash tomorrow night," she says instead.

"Bloody work," Simon says. "Alas, can you imagine if the head teacher *extended* his pre-Christmas holiday? I shudder to think."

"Hey, I apologized for that!" Katie says, and lightly thwacks his arm. "Even though you're very mean, I'm sad our literary adventure has come to an end. Not sure how many more times I can go to the shop before Felix files a restraining order. Speaking of…" She swallows and prepares for another at bat. "I was there earlier today, and he seems to think you—"

Katie's sentence is cut short by a figure darting into their path. She yelps in surprise and stumbles to get out of his way. The man seizes, and Katie realizes she's staring at a familiar head. "Felix!" she says, and he remains frozen, as though stillness is the same as an invisibility cloak. "What are you doing? I can see you!"

After several full-bodied sighs, Felix pivots around. "Goodness, Katharine," he says. "You are very adroit at randomly encountering people outside their workplaces."

"This must seem very shady," she says. "And, yes, earlier I was hanging around, hoping to run into you. But this is pure coincidence, I swear!"

"Did you ask him?" he says, and dabs his head toward Simon. "What did he say?"

"Ask me what?"

"Oh, I, uh, haven't—" Katie stammers.

"Let me be clear," Felix says, gaze lasered on Simon. "Being related to Peter Rodd is worth nothing. It offers no benefits, financial or otherwise, and whatever you envision gaining, you best put it out of your head."

"Who's related to Peter Rodd?" Simon says. He whips to face Katie. "You? Jesus Christ. How many more secrets do you have?"

"What? Me? No!" Katie says. "Simon, he's referring to you!"

March 1944

The London Library

Nancy and Jim picked through the debris of what was once the London Library. There were dozens of volunteers on-site, searching for anything salvageable among the twenty thousand volumes lost.

"The world can do without theology," Jim said, and chucked one such offender into the rubbish. "Mostly, I'm concerned about saving the classics and biographies."

"I don't think we're meant to be curating," Nancy said.

"Why not donate my knowledge, as well as my time? It's a winning proposition for all involved."

Nancy rolled her eyes. Jim was more insufferable than ever, now that West Wycombe had officially been transferred to the National Trust. He'd even convinced Johnny to kick in an endowment for its upkeep. Hellbags was furious, of course, and Nancy was boggled by the whole affair. She never would've taken Jim for such a tricky devil.

"Here's another," Jim said, and passed Nancy a coverless book—*Frankenstein*—with the first ten pages burnt.

She tossed it into a keep bucket. Most of *Frankenstein* was better than no *Frankenstein* at all, and Nancy couldn't bear to throw it out.

"I think I see something over here!" Evelyn called, offering his help from a safe and clean distance, now that his hands were critical wartime machinery. Evelyn was supposed to have shipped out following the expiration of his military reprimand, but made a case for himself to the Secretary of State for War. Entertainment was now a legitimate contribution to the war effort, he argued, and whatever he wrote would be a salve to the troops. It really was the best place for him, given his impertinence and lack of physical agility.

Regardless of his head start, Nancy remained committed to beating Evelyn to the punch and was making progress on the memoir, by and by. Lea was helpful, in her desultory way, and even responded to letters and queries, every now and again. *The offer stands*, Nancy wrote, just last week. *I love the idea of a little one running around the house. We have the room, and you'll need to leave Bucks, eventually.*

Weston Manor was up for auction now that Lady and Lord Worthington were both dead. Two weeks after she went missing, Danette's coat was found on the bank of the Ouse, her handkerchief floating some miles away. Her body washed up several days later, confirming what they all knew. It was a devastating end, though at least she would never be unfairly accused of treason.

"Evelyn, what were you pointing at?" Jim asked as he lifted a chunk of plaster with his foot. "We've been through this pile. I think we're done for the day."

Nancy nodded and handed her bucket to another worker. "What time is it?" she said, wiping the dirt from her watch.

"Time for a cocktail," Evelyn said.

"Not for me," Nancy said. "I took the entire day off from the shop and need to get some writing in before I go back for fire watch."

"Look at you!" Evelyn said. "An industrious little bee. I've logged three thousand words this morning, so I'm free to get drunk. As much as I hate to say it, I think the halibut oil from Eddy's helped. I've been writing like a man on fire."

"How lovely for you," Nancy mumbled, wishing just one more bomb would fall, in a very specific, Evelyn-shaped place.

"What about you, Jimmy?" he said. "Join me for a whisky?"

"Not in the mood," Jim answered as he batted the dust from his corduroy trousers. "The thought of a cocktail is depressing. What would we even discuss? Everything is so damned terrible."

"Gosh, Jim," Nancy said. "I thought you'd be all smiles with West Wycombe in your clutches."

"You'd think, but no," he said. "It's all so grim. Even parties aren't festive anymore. Nothing to drink, and everyone's always tense. I'd rather be helping, doing something productive."

After Jim gave the wrecked library a final, mournful gaze, the three began marching across the detritus toward Piccadilly.

"I'm pleased to hear you're working on your book," Evelyn said. "I had my doubts, as you know, but only the writer himself can ascertain if a project is coming together. Only he can feel the magic, the chill, the undeniable whisper of the muse."

"Mmm-hmm," Nancy said, anxious about when her magic might set in. The book still felt like a jumble of words and, though Lea added something to the story, her cooperation was hardly the golden ticket Nancy had hoped. In letters and phone calls, they danced around Prod's involvement in their lives, but whenever Nancy inched closer, Lea pulled away. Certain questions were probably best addressed face-to-face, but with food and fuel shortages, Nancy was hesitant to waste petrol on a social call, especially as she had no faith Lea would willingly provide the answers she sought.

"Back tomorrow?" Jim said as they crossed Piccadilly.

Nancy shook her head. "There are plenty of helping hands," she said. "And I can't keep ignoring the shop. Anne and Heywood aren't returning to London until an armistice is signed, and everything's left up to Mollie and me."

"PUT THEM BACK!" a voice shouted.

"Is that what I think it is?" Evelyn said, and Nancy looked up to see a group of protestors chanting and waving their all-too-familiar signs.

"PUT THEM BACK!"

"Everyone!" Evelyn pretended to call out. "It's Nancy Mitford, right over here."

She gave him a good slap.

"I can't believe they're still at it," Jim said.

"No kidding," Nancy agreed. "I'd expected protests when they were first let out, but five months on? It's not as though Diana and Mosley are *free*. They're still under house arrest!"

When news hit London that the Mosleys were released, the press swarmed the shop and hectored Nancy for a week straight. She told them only what she knew: her sister and brother-in-law had been transferred to home custody because of Oswald's phlebitis and Diana's weak pulse. Britons took to the streets in protest, and a large demonstration was held in Trafalgar Square. One march turned into two, and they'd been yelling ever since.

"PUT THEM BACK!"

Nancy glared at the rabble-rousers. "I cannot wait to leave this city," she said. "As soon as this damned war is over, I'm board-ing the next train to France."

"This nonsense again," Evelyn said with a sigh. "I'll give you this. Never in a million years could I have predicted the two of you would still be in contact."

"Maybe it is love, after all," Jim said as they crossed another street.

"Sure feels like it," Nancy said. "I'm practically dying to be together again, and I live for the post, for the sight of an enve-lope from Carlton Gardens marked with the General's stamp."

Although the Colonel promised he'd call—*when you least ex-*

pect it, the telephone will ring, and there I'll be—they hadn't spoken in almost a year. He wrote often, and Nancy understood Algiers to London was some hard cheese, but she missed the sound of his voice. *Racontez!*

To quell her despair, Nancy wrote to the Colonel in every spare moment, starting usually with a tale of childhood adventure. In some ways, these letters were easier to get down than the book, and at times it felt like the one thing holding them together.

"Have you informed your husband of your move to France?" Evelyn asked as they walked down Half Moon Street, a neighborhood once haven to aristocratic bachelors. Now every other house was boarded up, a note pinned to the door instructing what to do with the post. "Feels as though he should be aware."

"Oh, please," Nancy said as they veered onto Curzon Street. "Peter never cared what I did. In fact, he never bothered with me at all."

"You always refer to him in the past tense," Jim said.

Evelyn nodded. "I've noticed that, too."

"What do you expect?" Nancy said. "I haven't heard from him in three years!"

They paused at the entrance to the shop, dusting themselves off best they could. When Nancy threw open the door, Mollie stood blocking the entrance, gawping and pale and severely out of sorts.

"Mollie! Goodness! What's wrong with you now? You are positively horror-struck!" Nancy said. She glanced down at her arms, and saw they were still covered in a fine layer of soot. "Oh, ducky! I'm sorry! We're a *mess*. Let me grab my things, and I'll be out of your hair. I'll be back by eight o'clock, though! I swear on my life!"

"It's not the... It's... I'm... This came for you," Mollie said, and extended a quaking hand. "A telegram."

Nancy's heart jumped, and her mind ticked through all the people who might be hurt. Tom. One of her sisters. The Colonel, of course. "I can't look," she said, squinting, and holding the paper at arm's length.

"I'll read it for you," Evelyn said. He reached for the paper, but Nancy was too quick.

"Moll, give it to me straight," Nancy said. "Who died?"

"No one's dead, but…" Mollie said. "Well, you should probably just read…"

Nancy exhaled. She bowed her head and skimmed the page. Nancy's first thought: *Thank God*. Her second: *Please, almost anything but this.*

```
1944.25.03

Nancy—

I am coming home. Build up a supply of cigarettes
whisky and other delicacies there is a kind wife.

-Prod
```

Saturday Evening

Curzon Street

"Why are we talking about Peter Rodd?" Simon says, his gaze swinging back and forth between Katie and Felix. "What does he have to do with anything?"

"Mister Bailey, you may drop the pretense," Felix says. "His Grace will not entertain any shakedowns or frivolous lawsuits."

"Lawsuits?" Simon says. "What the fuck are you talking about?"

"See? He has no idea!" Katie says to Felix, then looks at Simon. She puts the back of her hand to her forehead like an offended Victorian spinster. "Phew! Problem solved!"

"What is happening?"

"Folks, I really must go," Felix says. "Can we do this another time?"

Katie grabs Felix's arm. "We can settle this matter quickly, and then you can go," she says. "Simon. Do you think Peter Rodd is your grandfather?"

"Peter Rodd?" Simon wrinkles his brow. "Who told you that?"

"He did!" Katie says as Felix jerks out of her hold. "See, Felix? He's not trying to trick you, or anybody else."

Simon rattles his head, as if trying to knock something loose. He opens his mouth once, twice before speaking. "Where is this coming from?" he says. "And what the fuck does Peter Rodd have to do with anything?"

"That's what you're here for, is it not?" Felix says.

"What? No. What I want is what I've told you all along. I believe there is a missing manuscript and would like to see it for myself."

"But *why*?" Felix presses. "You've been very focused on your grandmother's relationship to Nancy Mitford, and her potential involvement with the unpublished autobiography. If not money, or an authorial claim to the book, what other assumption could we make?"

"Hell if I know. All I want is to show the manuscript to my mum. I don't even need the original copy! Just lend it to me. She'll be dead soon, and I'll bring it right back."

"Dead?" Felix says, and his expression slackens.

"Late-stage stomach cancer," Simon says. "I'd love to give her this one last thing, before she goes. I think it'd be cool for her to see. That's all there is to it."

Felix sighs. "Jesus. Well, I feel like an arse," he says. "I'm sorry."

"Apology unnecessary," Simon says. "But I still don't understand. Why would I associate Peter Rodd with any of this?"

"Because Nancy did," Katie pipes in. "She thought he might've fathered your mom. She even wrote a letter to your grandmother asking whether 'Greenie' was actually Prod."

"She did?" Simon says, jiggling his head again.

"Felix doesn't think she sent it, though." Katie looks back over and directly into Felix's cutting stare. "Either way, my guess is Nancy found her answer and stopped writing because everything became too messy."

"Incorrect," Felix says. "Nancy did briefly entertain the notion of a Peter-Lea connection, but it was based on little more than paranoia, and conjecture. Peter was absent a long time, and never faithful to begin with."

"She was just...speculating?" Katie asks, and Felix nods.

"Nancy let her suspicions get the best of her," he says, "but realized she was wrong. She stopped writing because, in mid-1944, Peter returned from Africa, and Nancy decided to focus on their relationship."

"Their relationship?" Katie makes a face. "Why would Nancy give two shits about Prod? She was already intent on moving to France by then!" She sneaks a glance at Simon, who still seems puzzled, as if trying to work out a problem no one else can see.

"Deep down, Nancy Mitford was a traditionalist," Felix says. "Bred to believe that marriage was the ultimate achievement."

"Okay..." Katie says. There is a niggling, a thread she cannot grab. "If Nancy was such a traditionalist, why'd she beg Peter for a divorce, and why'd she go on to stay with the Colonel for thirty years? Sorry, but I don't buy it. She didn't even seem to enjoy Prod as...like...a person."

"Huh. Well." Felix smirks. "Apparently, your snooping didn't uncover the *right* Lady Helen Dashwood letter."

"I wasn't snooping!" Katie cries. "Erin let me in!"

Felix chuckles and Katie's glad to discover he doesn't hate her entirely. "The letter I'm thinking of was written in—" he taps his chin "—the summer of 1944. Were you to read it, you'd find it full of accolades for Peter."

"What a grand idea!" Katie says with what she hopes is a winsome smile. "I'd be happy to see for myself."

Felix snorts and shakes his head. "If you come in early next week—*when we are open*—Erin or I might let you have a peek." He pauses to check the time on his phone. "While I've enjoyed our conversation, I'm due at a wedding tonight, so I must go. Again, sorry for the mix-up, mate," he says to the still-dumbfounded Simon. "No hard feelings, yeah?"

"It's fine," Simon says, dismissively.

"Simon. Katharine." Felix bobs his head at each of them. "Enjoy your night."

"Thanks, Felix! I'll stop by on Monday!" Katie shouts to his retreating back.

Felix laughs but doesn't turn around. "Of course you will," he says. "I'd expect nothing less."

～◦∞◦～

23 June 1944
Dear Hellbags,

How are you getting on at West Wycombe, now that the National Trust is your landlord? You are welcome to return to Blomfield Road, at any time. I miss you greatly.

Evelyn asked me to be godmother to his new baby. Can't you just?! With so many kids, they've probably run through all the religious maniacs they know. He's finished the first draft of his new book (damn him!) and is now "editing his magnum opus madly," as he puts it.

Well, onto the big news. Prod has reappeared! After three years gone, he walked into the shop one day, looking bronzed and tough and well, his arms laden with cheeses and brandy and ham. When I first laid eyes upon him, I nearly fainted dead. Seeing him was something like a miracle.

We are getting along famously, if you can believe it, though you can imagine there has been some wonderful toll-gating. He is toll-gating round the place & is completely bliss- ful & he's been made a colonel if you can stand it. You must admit it's a scream.
More later.

Love from
Nancy

June 1944

The Dorchester

"How did Dickie get his hands on all this food?" Nancy said. "Is he playing in the black market? I haven't seen a spread like this in years."

Nancy, Jim, and Evelyn were at the Dorchester for Dickie Girouard's wedding reception. They'd feasted on chicken mousse and tongue, with chocolate and cocktails to follow. Everyone was in spectacularly high spirits despite the bombings and ordinary wartime fatigue. The mood was so good it was almost disconcerting.

"Do you ever get the feeling," Jim said, "that some folks think this war will only harm *other* people, and the rest of us can dance and dine, more or less untouched?"

"Oh, ducky, that is not a feeling," Nancy said, and sipped her cider. "It's straight fact. Emerald Cunard swears that no one is ever killed in air raids. It's just noise and propaganda."

"Some folks in the East End might disagree," Jim noted.

"It's so sad. We were all in this together for a week or two and then—poof!—it's back to the usual way of things. There are extravagant weddings." Nancy swept a hand. "And people like Debo swanning around in diamonds and fur coats, impersonating exiled Russian grand duchesses. *Lilliput* asked me to write an article on slimming. During rations! It's utterly daft!"

"You do need the money," Jim said.

"Yes, but I declined," Nancy said. "Slenderizing? At this point in the war? I wouldn't dare. Peter and I had a good laugh about it, though."

"Anytime you can get a laugh out of Prod is a win, I suppose."

Nancy nodded and her eyes wandered the room until they found Evelyn, who was at the moment engaged in a verbal altercation, with each man shouting, "You, sir, are no gentleman," at escalating volumes.

Evelyn was making the most of his final days of leave with his book at the publisher's, and Nancy loathed him for his success. She'd nearly beaten the ogre, or tied him, at least, and her own book was so close to finished she could cry. What good was it now that Peter had returned, and she'd recommitted to the life of Nancy Rodd? Sure, she could dream of a more glittering life in France, of streets that weren't bombed, and people who took the right things seriously. But, at the end of the day, the dowdy women and schoolboyish men in this room represented Nancy's kind of crowd, her stock and trade. It wasn't all bad, of course. Nancy was alive, and working, and Peter was managing to be a decent spouse, when he was around, and not helping with the upcoming Allied invasion of France.

"Speaking of Peter," Jim said, and Nancy shook her head, having nearly forgotten where she was. "Is he still coming and going, talking of battles to come? No wonder you've been so gaga over him lately. The breaks must render him tolerable."

"Huh," Nancy said. "I never thought of it like that. And, yes, he swears troops are penned up behind barbed wire, waiting for the signal to charge. It all feels very imminent. I haven't seen him since last Wednesday."

"Lord Rothermere says the operation should be a walkover," Jim said. "He thinks the Germans are on their last leg."

"Never count out the Germans," Nancy warned.

When it came time to leave, they found Evelyn passed out in the cloakroom and decided to let him sleep it off. Jim walked Nancy as far as the Marble Arch, and she hoofed it the rest of the way alone, feeling sullen and melancholy on this cool spring night.

At Blomfield Road, Nancy opened the door and stepped into the brutal quiet. She called out, but the house only echoed in response. Gladys was likely working at her First Aid post and Milly no doubt slumbering somewhere.

As Nancy hung her coat, the telephone rang. She sighed and debated whether to answer. It was probably Debo, with a minor problem, or Hellbags, with a major complaint. Alas, any human was better than no human at all, and so she picked up. "The Rodds," she said with a yawn.

"Algiers wants you," the operator said. "Will you please hold the line?"

"Algiers!" Nancy said. "Yes! I'll hold!"

Algiers? It couldn't be. Her legs were now jam.

"*Allô—allô*," the Colonel said. "*Non-cee? Tu es là?*"

"It's me," Nancy said in a whisper. "I am here. Colonel! I'm a flooded wreck. I haven't heard your voice in a year!"

"I've missed you terribly! I do not have much time, but I needed to speak to you."

"Is something wrong?"

"Only that I am miserable without you," he said. "And anxious for a story. Hurry! *Alors, racontez!* I am ready."

A year! To hear the Colonel's low timbre after a year! It was a miracle, nothing short.

Nancy guessed the reason behind the call's timing because word was out: sometime in the next forty-eight hours, the Allies would land on a beach in France, and an all-out assault would commence. That Prod missed his customary weekend appearance gave credence to the rumors, and though Nancy was not the least religious, she'd been praying up a storm.

At half seven Sunday morning, Nancy was collecting eggs in the garden, with Milly basking in the sun nearby. For a minute, Nancy forgot about the problems of the world and pictured herself a child, gathering eggs with her sisters to sell in town. When Milly leapt to her paws, yipping frantically, Nancy nearly keeled over in shock. She'd grown so accustomed to the silence.

"Good Lord!" she said, and crouched beside the dog. "What did you see? Oh, Milly, you're trembling! What is it?" Hand raised to shield her face from the sun, Nancy looked up to discover an interloper in the form of a tiny French bulldog held by a stout, mustachioed Frenchman.

"Colonel!" Nancy said, and sprang from the ground. The Colonel released the puppy, and she propelled herself into his arms. "First a call and now a visit?" Nancy said, sobbing into his shirt. "You're going to spoil me beyond repair." She pulled back and gazed into his coarse, craggy face. Though there were certainly handsomer men, there wasn't one Nancy found more attractive. "What are you doing in London?" she asked as the puppy scrambled about their feet. "I thought all the important people were supposed to be in France."

"Soon, darling, soon," the Colonel said. "I've come for talks with Eisenhower and Churchill. I am de Gaulle's new *Directeur de Cabinet*, haven't you heard?"

"It's about time!" Nancy said. "That old sourpuss will surely benefit from your endless reserves of charm. Tell me you're staying for a while."

"Merely a few hours," the Colonel said. "I don't even have time for this, but I had to see your beautiful face. I had to make sure you're still waiting for me, and for Paris."

"Where is your faith? Of course I've been waiting!" Nancy

said, as if she hadn't days ago resigned herself to a long, dull life with Prod. Suddenly, she was stunned, almost paralyzed by her own betrayal, and not until that moment did Nancy understand how thoroughly she'd given up. "How could you ask that question?" she said to the Colonel. "Where would I go?"

"*Je ne sais pas.* That Peter is a slippery fellow." The Colonel held out an arm. "I have an hour. Maybe only half. Would you care to join me upstairs?"

Grinning, Nancy slipped her arm through his and up to the bedroom they went, with Milly and her new companion nipping at their heels.

Nancy lay against the Colonel's chest, his wiry hairs chafing her shoulder in that familiar, long-missed way. She glanced outside toward the crab apple branch pattering against the window. In the time the Colonel was away, she'd watched the tree go from bright white blossoms to golden brilliance, before bearing its shiny, scarlet fruit. The fruit dropped, leaving the branches bare until its pink buds sprang anew. Now the tree was nearly done flowering again, and the Colonel was back, if only for an hour.

"What are you thinking about, my darling?" he said, dragging a finger along her arm.

"I was thinking about Voltaire."

"*Mon dieu!*" he said, and Nancy felt his merriment against her cheek. "This is not very romantic. I must have done a very poor job."

"You were top-notch, as always, and Voltaire can be very romantic. I was thinking of that line: *je me suis mis à être un peu gai, parce qu'on m'a dit que cela est bon pour la santé.*"

I have begun to be somewhat merry because I have been told that that is good for one's health.

"It's as though you've come to remind me," Nancy said. "That it's possible to be happy, instead of merely plodding along. And Voltaire was correct. It is good for my health, which is important, what with my notoriously weak constitution."

The Colonel gave her a squeeze. "And what's good for my health is you."

"But you're about to leave again!" Nancy said. "Bad health all around. I really make myself sick waiting to hear from you, especially because you don't write nearly as often as you should. The last time you went three whole weeks!"

"Did you think I was dead?"

"It's not in my nature to think that way," Nancy said. "But had you been killed, it would've finished me off."

"Ah, so you would've died, too? How nice."

She slapped him playfully and the Colonel chortled and sat up.

"I must go," he said, and kissed her atop the head. "You are very beautiful, even when your hair is so unkempt."

"What do you expect? You caught me gardening! And we just made love. Several times, in fact!"

The Colonel laughed again as he wiggled into his pants. "Also, my darling, on the subject of health, you really are too thin."

"My weak constitution strikes again! What do you see in me?"

"It is quite strange. Nevertheless, there must be something." He leaned down for another kiss. "It won't be much longer, my silkworm. Despite your inability to believe my solemn vows, we will be together in Paris, very soon."

"Can you blame me?" Nancy said, pulling the blanket taut over her very small breasts. "You're not the easiest man to trust."

The Colonel gripped his chest and staggered backward, as if shot in the heart. *"Mon chérie!"* he cried. "How can you say such things? I am a faithful man!"

Nancy gave him a dubious look. "You weren't faithful to your deceased fiancée, Gabrielle," Nancy said. "Never mind her, each time your name comes up, I'm absolutely *demolished* by an avalanche of women. When we met, you told me that affairs last five years with you. If that's true, you're two hundred years old by my calculation!"

"Five years or five days," he said. "It's really all the same."

"I should count myself lucky, then."

"Ah, *Non-cee*." The Colonel kissed her one last time. "The difference is, I love you ten times more than the rest."

Saturday Evening

Curzon Street

Simon doesn't seem to care about Peter Rodd, either way. Katie cannot fathom it.

"You're not curious?" she says as they walk away from the shop. "Like, not at all?"

"Not even a little," he says.

"I don't get it." Katie shakes her head. "I would love to be related to Nancy Mitford."

"Related by *marriage*, which isn't the same."

"Still, though. His sister married Simon Elwes. You could be related to Peter Rodd *and* Westley from *The Princess Bride*."

"Sure, sure," Simon says, bobbing his head. "It'd be extremely useful to have a genealogical link to a C-list actor from an over-rated movie. Why hadn't I thought of that before?"

"Shut your mouth!" Katie says, and bats him with the back of her hand. "I'm sad you have such bad taste in films."

They cross a street. It's just after five o'clock and already dark, and they don't seem to be going anywhere, other than in the general direction of Hyde Park.

"You're not even tempted to find out?" Katie presses.

"You really cannot let this go," Simon says. "First of all, it seems highly unlikely. If my mum had any inkling, she would've mentioned it. She would've been trying to shake down the bookshop, not me. Second, even if there is a genetic link, what does that get me? Peter Rodd was a wanker."

Katie laughs. "True," she says. "But maybe you should take a DNA test, just to see."

Simon shudders. "I will not be taking one of those tests," he says. "Not now, not ever. I'm surprised you'd suggest it. Don't you find them disturbing?"

Katie gives him a sideways glance. "I wouldn't have taken you for one of those tin-foil-hat types," she says. "The government does not want your DNA. They're not going to clone you. I mean, they should. You'd be a good candidate. But that's not what's happening."

"Oh, I don't mind being cloned," Simon says. "It's more the idea of genetic testing for entertainment, and posting on the internet. It has… I don't know…a very white nationalist vibe." Simon looks at her. "Don't you find paying a hundred quid to break down one's blood into percentages is a tad…'one-drop rule'?"

"I guess," Katie mumbles, and makes a note not to admit she bought kits for her entire family last Christmas, as well as her dog.

They pass the Saudi Arabian Embassy. The large, white building was formerly Crewe House, where Nancy kept fire watch. Katie peers through the wrought iron fence, trying to get a glimpse of something, she doesn't know what. A guard glowers and she throws on a smile. He is not amused.

"You just want me to be related," Simon says, "because it'd make my family all the more compelling to write about."

"Okay, smart-ass. I am *not* writing about your family. And I only care because I'm a gossip," she says. "Peter Rodd is just about the least compelling thing about Nancy Mitford."

"Hear, hear," Simon says, and they round a corner.

Katie stutters in her step. Her mouth drops open and she points in the manner of a three-year-old gesturing at a clown. In the distance are two roller coasters and a jumble of lights.

"What is *that*?" she says, and clutches Simon's arm.

He squints. "What? Oh. Winter Wonderland. Bills itself as Europe's Largest Christmas Event, but it's just your basic carnival with holiday markets and rides."

Katie grabs his sleeve and drags him toward the Blue Gate.

"Don't tell me this sounds fun to you," Simon says.

"Of course it does! Which is why we're going!"

"I'm going to have to download an app, aren't I?"

"Yes, and get to it," she snaps. "Chop-chop."

"Fine," Simon says and, by the time he opens his phone, a security guard is rifling through Katie's purse. After everything checks out, he waves them through.

"This is amazing," Katie says, overcome by the noise, the flashing lights, the winter wonderland of it all. "Oh my God. Is that a skating rink?" She whips around to face Simon. "Let's do it!"

"Absolutely not. I'm not looking to freeze my arse off, or break any limbs."

"Fine," Katie mutters. She glances back at the ice. "I used to take my nieces when they were younger. I miss it. Or maybe I miss them being little."

They leave the rink and enter the Christmas Market, with its stalls of artisans, entertainers, and purveyors of food. To the left, a man carves a bear out of a wooden stump. On the right, signs advertise Fresh Fish & Chips and Hot Roast Pork.

"I'm going to need a bratwurst later," Katie says.

"Have you ever tried a Prego? It's a Portuguese steak sandwich, if you're into that sort of thing."

"Always," she says.

Katie scans the stalls until her eyes land on a collection of handblown glass Christmas tree ornaments. As Katie fingers a red-and-silver London phone booth, she thinks of her dad, who bought ornaments to commemorate all the places he traveled. Maui. Miami. The 1984 Summer Olympics (Los Angeles). Hot Springs, Arkansas. New Orleans. The Kennedy Space Center. Detroit. Dozens of ornaments, like a map of where'd he been, all of them now hanging on Britt's tree.

"Are you going to get that?" Simon asks.

"Nah. Just reminded me of being a kid," Katie says, letting the ornament fall back into the tree. She spins around and spots a massive green roller coaster named the Maus XXL. "Oh, let's do that!" she says.

"Good Lord. No. Hell, no."

"You're scared."

"Katharine. You are a child."

"Hmm, then why are you the one acting like a baby?" she says. "Fine. No roller coaster. But I'm not going to let you say no to everything."

"I won't say no to everything," Simon insists. "Just things that will likely make me want to vomit." He stops in front a wooden shack, which appears to be attached to three contiguous tipis. "How about a drink instead?"

In front of the shack, a sign reads Thor's in small yellow bulbs, not unlike the Ritz's lighted sign. Beside it, a chalkboard promises mulled wine, prosecco, hot cocoa, and draft ales.

"Not as fun as a roller coaster, but okay," Katie says.

They duck inside and into a twinkling winter garden illuminated by fairy lights and roaring log fires. The effect is charming, but Katie can't shake the feeling that this is problematic.

"Did Vikings have tipis?" she whispers. "I mean, is this...okay?"

Simon sighs. "Just try to enjoy yourself," he says.

They find an unoccupied fire, and Katie orders a prosecco, Simon an ale. As they nestle beneath a thick camel hair blanket, Katie tries to remember the last time she felt so warm. "I'm sorry we couldn't get your mom what she wanted," she says, swirling the prosecco in her glass. "Whatever that might be."

"Not even she knows."

"You should feel good about what you did," Katie says. "If Britt or I took a week out of our lives, if we pestered some book-shop employee endlessly and palled around with hapless for-eigners, all for our mom's benefit, she'd never shut up about it."

Simon smirks. "She probably won't shut up about it, regard-less," he says. "On any given day, Emma Mutrie might be grate-ful, or annoyed, or defensive. Scalding hot or ice-cold. Resenting me or making me the center of her world. It is a lot to navigate."

"Parents are hard," Katie says. "I don't know your mom, ob-viously, but my heart goes out to her. She probably never had a decent parental role model and she was *so* young when her mother died. That shit can really mess you up. Kids tend to blame themselves, or believe they could've prevented it."

"Really?" Simon looks at her. "You think so?"

"One hundred percent. For example, maybe my dad wouldn't have been driving home at *that* time if I hadn't called him at work."

"Did that really happen?" Simon asks, and Katie nods.

"I give Judy a lot of shit for ignoring me after he died," she says, "but she did get me into therapy immediately. Can you imagine how much *more* messed up I'd be? And I still had her around, and Britt."

Katie glances over at Simon, who is staring unblinking into the fire. "Simon?" she says.

"Lea Toporek died by suicide."

"My God." On instinct, Katie grabs Simon's hand, nearly spilling her drink on his crotch in the process.

"My mum rarely talks about it," Simon says. "But it was prop-erly devastating, and she's always been fearful about what that meant for the rest of us. That's why she never wanted children. Terminated several pregnancies before I came along."

Katie gasps, and puts a hand over her mouth, as if trying to physically prevent herself from saying the wrong thing.

"If you're wondering how I know," Simon says, and turns to meet her gaze, "my mum did not hesitate to share the details. Bit of a drinker, that one." He shakes his head. "When she was pregnant with me, she ascribed her symptoms to menopause. By the time she figured it out, it was too late."

"That is...horrific."

"It wasn't great," Simon agrees, and shrugs in the bashful way of an eight-year-old pretending to be tough. "But, in the end, I've got to give her a pass. As you said, the woman had a difficult life and was raised in precarious circumstances. She had no standard for what a parent should be. Took me about forty years to come to this place, but here we are."

"It's never too late." Katie smiles sadly. "I think most parents are doing the best they can, with whatever tools they've been given. We may want them to be some other way, but it's like asking a dog to be a cat, in which case, no, thanks."

Simon chuckles lightly and Katie scoots closer, wrapping both arms around his left arm. She places her chin on his shoulder, and he nuzzles the top of her head. "But I really need to know if you're related to Prod."

Simon laughs.

As Katie watches the flames sway and jump, she thinks about the Colonel, and Nancy, and the fact that she stayed married to Prod for twenty-five years. In some ways, it's confounding but, in others, it makes sense. Like everyone else in the world, Nancy Mitford only wanted to be loved. And maybe love is why she put the manuscript away—love for Prod, or the Colonel. Love for her family, or even herself.

"We really aren't so different, you and me," Simon says. "We both came to London for a story, and neither found what we were looking for."

Katie sighs and pulls herself more tightly against him. "I don't know," she says. "This trip isn't over, and I'm not ready to give up. Despite everything, this just doesn't feel like the end."

August 1944

Blomfield Road

"Here is the news."

Nancy sat perched beside the wireless in the sitting room, accompanied by Jim and her brother, Tom. Peter was half listening as he skimmed the newspaper.

"Paris has been liberated."

Two months before, the day after the Colonel appeared at Blomfield Road, Allied troops landed at Normandy. Though the Nazis were hobbled, they retaliated by launching their diabolical V–1s from German-occupied parts of France. Because they came from distant shores, instead of the skies, no warning sirens were possible. The rockets simply fell, leaving no craters, and causing twice the impact of bombs. *Nobody minds the bombs any more (I never did)*, Nancy wrote to Muv in early July, *but they are doing a fearful amount of damage to houses.*

But now, a new development, the biggest one to date: the Germans were at last retreating from Paris and the city was free. At that moment, one million Parisians were gathered from the Arc de Triomphe to Notre-Dame to cheer on the Allied troops.

"It's one of the most marvelous sights I've ever seen," said the reporter. *"All across Paris, people are coming out of their homes and shops.*

Flags are being hoisted on the buildings, and American tanks and fire engines clog the streets."

Because the last Nazi in Paris chose to capitulate instead of alert the Luftwaffe as instructed, the city was saved, thereby making a German officer an unlikely hero, sparing Paris the destruction London had seen. De Gaulle and the Colonel arrived at Gare Montparnasse shortly after the man's surrender and proceeded to the Hôtel de Ville, where crowds gathered to witness de Gaulle give his emotional, tear-filled speech.

"Paris! Paris outraged, Paris broken, Paris martyred, but Paris liberated!"

In the coming days, Nancy would watch newsreels, her eyes fixed on the Colonel in his dark suit and white pocket square, beaming as he marched a few steps behind de Gaulle. From the Champs-Élysées, de Gaulle and the Colonel walked a mile to the Place de la Concorde, then took a car to Notre-Dame. De Gaulle was fired upon twice—once while getting into the vehicle, a second time while entering the church—but remained confident and steadfast, wholly undeterred.

"Only a maniac could accomplish what he did," Tom said as they listened to the recounting of de Gaulle's march. "A man who identifies with Joan of Arc."

"You should hear what the Colonel says about him," Nancy said.

"I'd really rather not," said Tom, and Nancy gave him a swift kick to the shin.

Though her brother was acting like a dreadful Counter-Hon, Nancy was glad to have him around. One of the best days of the war was the afternoon Nancy stumbled upon a tall, dishy man smoking a cigarette in the shadow of the Ritz's arcade. It was Tom Mitford, back from the Mediterranean after two and a half years.

"I'll never get tired of hearing the reports," Nancy said, eyes welling. "It's so triumphant, so miraculous!"

"Don't get too stirred up," Tom said. "This war is far from done."

"Your brother has a point," Peter said from behind his paper.

"Are you both such monsters you can't take a second to celebrate?"

"If you're curious," Peter said, peering over his paper at Tom, "the reason Nance is in such a splendid mood is because she thinks she's moving to Paris now. When I returned from Africa, my wife greeted me with open arms. I went to Normandy, and now she can't stop prattling on about France. It's nearly as ridiculous as all her talk about an autobiography. As if any of us would let her air the family laundry!"

"You just don't like anyone else talking about refugees," Nancy muttered.

"Perhaps you can drill some sense into your sister," Prod said to Tom. "Nancy minds your advice far more than she does mine."

"I make it a rule never to mind either one of you," Nancy said. "And I have all the sense I need, though my choice of company suggests otherwise. The reason I'm happy is because Paris has been liberated."

"It's still not over..." Tom said.

"Yes, I know," Nancy said. "The Huns sent over one hundred doodlebugs last night as a reminder, and Hittie is sure to hang on until the bitter end. But Paris is free, and the end will come, eventually. It's a giant step forward. Regarding the biography, I suppose we'll just have to see."

Although she'd briefly set it aside, Nancy resumed her writing after the Normandy invasion. She'd completed the book a month ago, and had been hiver-havering ever since. Should she publish it now, or once she left the country? As much as Prod loathed the idea of a memoir, he'd be doubly incensed once he read the thing. There was also the matter of what Prod and Lea meant to each other, and whether the name Greenie must be replaced. So much time spent contemplating a dead man she'd never met.

"You're right about Hitler," Tom said, and Nancy glanced up. "And his troops fighting on. The Germans are strong, brave people."

"Good Lord, Mitford." Peter dropped the paper into his lap. "You must stop sympathizing with the Nazis. Putting aside the myriad atrocities they've committed, you're now backing the losing team."

Nancy smiled at her husband. Sometimes she did love the man, or admire him, if nothing else.

Tom lit a cigarette. "I'm not backing the Germans," he said. "In case you haven't noticed, I've been fighting for our side."

"Only because they let you go to the Pacific Theater," Nancy reminded him.

Tom shrugged. "Someone has to do it," he said. "I don't like the Japanese and I'd rather kill them than the Germans, who I do like."

"You still like them?" Nancy said. "After all this?"

"Listen, you two," Tom said, pointing his cigarette first at Nancy, and then at Prod. "Deny it all you want, but all the best Germans are Nazis. If I were German, I'd be one myself. You just gotta get past the anti-Semitic nonsense."

"Do you?" Nancy said, glaring. "Tuddemy, don't let your Nazi show. I'm not in the mood to despise any more of my family members."

"I'm an imperialist," Tom said, and took a drag of his cigarette. "Simple as that. What's life without power, without the ability to strike fear in other countries? Not worth living, that's what."

"Darling, you really do have the most charming siblings," Peter said, and stood. He folded his newspaper and tossed it onto the chair. "I'm off to the Savile."

"I thought the Savile was 'no women allowed'?" Tom said with a snicker.

Peter rolled his eyes and turned toward Nancy. "I'll see you later this evening. Don't worry about dinner."

"You're going now?" Nancy said, and gestured to the wireless. "In the middle of the excitement?"

"Eh." He shrugged. "I've got the gist. Brave Paris. Free Paris. All that. I've agreed to meet an old friend from the regiment. Haven't seen him in a year."

"Does this poor fella know he's meeting you?" Tom asked. "If not, somebody should warn him." Again, Tom tittered at his own gag and then mashed his cigarette into the table. It was the same old Tom—dashing but sloppy and absent of manners.

"As it happens, I'm quite beloved among the Welsh Guards," Prod said. "You're welcome to join me, Tom, and see for yourself. Although, ole Greenie absolutely hates Fascists, so be forewarned."

Nancy froze, a teacup held to her lips.

"*As General Leclerc's forces pushed their way into the city to complete the liberation of the capital,*" the BBC presenter droned on, "*far-reaching agreements were signed between Great Britain, the United States, and the French Provisional Government.*"

Nancy set down her cup. "Greenie?" she said.

"*De Gaulle was joined by Colonel Gaston Palewski, formerly the general's* directeur, *newly appointed as* chef de cabinet."

"Look who got a promotion!" Tom sang. "Your Colonel. What say you, Prod?"

"I thought Greenie was dead," Nancy said, heart beating out of her chest.

Prod's face scrunched in befuddlement. "When have we ever spoken of Greenie?" he said, and slipped one arm and then the other into his coat. "He's not dead at all. Are you confusing him with someone else?"

"That's what you told me," Nancy said. "After he got that

girl pregnant. Lea Toporek? You know who I'm talking about, Peter. The pretty refugee?"

"Gosh, Nancy, I've worked with thousands of refugees in my life," he said. "Tens of thousands, perhaps. You can't possibly expect me to remember them all."

"You brought her to Rutland Gate," Nancy said. "She was engaged to Greenie. That's what you told me."

Prod tilted his head, then smiled when the realization struck. "Oh, right," he said. "Greenie's cockney. I forgot. Why are you still thinking about them?"

"They are both in my book!"

Prod cackled. "Guess you'll have to start thinking of it as fiction," he said as Nancy's mouth hung open. So much for good tidings; she now wanted to slap the man.

"I don't know what's happening," Tom said. "But it seems we're about to venture into some interesting territory. With Peter Rodd involved, no less. A historic day on multiple accounts."

Nancy couldn't summon the mettle to put her little brother back in his place. She felt too disoriented, as though she'd been struck.

"Don't be upset, darling." Prod planted a kiss on Nancy's head. "It's all a big misunderstanding. Sorry to have shuffled the truth, but Greenie was in a fix. Faking his death seemed the best solution."

"You killed off someone for convenience's sake?" Tom said. "Why? What was in it for you?"

"What else was the bloke going to do?" Prod said. "Marry the girl? We all know it's unlikely he's the father."

"Nance, I finally see it," Tom said. "You've been telling me for years but, you're right, your husband is a completely different person when it comes to the displaced."

"You are a very despicable character," Peter said to Tom as a bolt of energy ran through Nancy's body.

She jumped to her feet. "Out!" Nancy said. "Everybody out!

I have things to do, and I need some time to think. Not to mention, you're ruining a perfectly good victory march. Both of you, out this minute!"

"I was going," Peter said as Nancy ushered them down the hall.

"Why are you mad at me?" Tom said. "Anyhow, it's just as well. There should be hordes of pretty girls around, happy to celebrate liberated Paris with a major from the King's Royal Rifle Corps."

"Hurry along," Nancy said, shoving them both outside. "Have a nice evening."

She slammed the door and rushed upstairs to her desk. Without sitting down, Nancy pulled a piece of writing paper from the drawer and dashed out a note.

12 Blomfield Road, W9
20 August 1944

Dear Lea,
Lord knows if I'll summon the nerve to send this letter, or
if it's better to discuss this face-to-face. I need to know, was
there ever a "Greenie," or was this Greenie really Prod?

Nancy

Not bothering with a once-over, Nancy crammed the letter into an envelope and sealed it shut. Hands wobbling like a drying-out drunk, she tucked it into her handbag alongside several other pieces of outgoing post.

Sunday Morning

Half Moon Street

"Now, this is interesting," Jojo says from her arms-crossed position at the top of her front steps. "What am I looking at here?"

"Uh, hi," Katie says. She checks her watch and sees it's only eight o'clock. "You're up early."

"Help a girl out. It's been decades, but is this…could it be…a proper walk of shame?"

"Can it really be considered a 'walk of shame' if you're with someone?" Katie asks.

"Hello, Jojo," Simon says. "Nice to see you again."

Jojo scrambles down the stairs. "You are a handful, missy!" she says. "It's almost as though I have a fifth child these days. One who's about their size, too!" She laughs maniacally and grabs Katie's hand. "I need a confab with my friend. Leave or wait, your choice. Won't take but a minute," Jojo says, and hauls Katie off to the side. "You cheeky devil!" She gives her friend a pinch.

"Ow!" Katie says, and rubs her side. "Why are you acting so weird?"

"Katie, Katie, Katie," Jojo clucks. "Lover of men, breaker of hearts. Where do you think you are, Paris?"

"Are you mad I stayed out all night?" Katie asks. "I'm sorry.

I tried to come back before you were up, but I forgot kids have no concept of weekends. I didn't mean to set a bad example about unwed overnight guests. I'll make sure they never know."

"The kids? Who cares about all that? The last time my brother visited, he brought a new girl to breakfast every morning, though never two at the same time, thank God." Jojo rolls her eyes. "No, Katie, I'm not mad. Just a bit discombobulated. Thrown off. Forced to make harried, half-assed decisions, left and right. Maybe, next time, a heads-up? A lineup might help."

"What are you talking about?" Katie says.

"A lineup." Jojo pretends to write. "Who's playing, and in what position. Otherwise, we might have people batting out of order! Do you like my baseball reference? Hope I didn't screw up the analogy."

"I'm so confused..."

Jojo dips her head toward where Simon stands awkwardly on the street. "He should leave. Don't get me wrong. I'm impressed. Well done, for sure. Didn't think you had it in you but, yeah, he needs to go."

The front door cracks open and Katie looks up, expecting Nigel or, more likely, Clive. A smile starts to spread across her face but stops cold when Katie sees a different but equally familiar face. It's a man, a man with two-day stubble and a tumble of floppy black hair.

Katie gasps, and Jojo flips around. "What the fuck, Armie!" Jojo shrieks. "I told you to stay inside!"

"Armie?" Simon balks and walks halfway up the stairs. "Armie?"

"I'm sorry," Armie says, approaching Katie, but from the other direction. "I couldn't wait a second longer."

"*ARMIE?*" Simon says again. He glares at Katie, but she can't speak.

"God, Katie, it's so good to see you," Armie says, and drags her into a hug. "I've been out of my mind with worry."

Katie can't help it; her body responds to his touch. Her muscles slacken, and her eyes water. Armie feels this change and tightens his hold.

"I'll be going, then," Simon says.

Katie claws her way out of Armie's embrace and shoves him, probably harder than is warranted. Jojo seizes the back of his red fleece pullover.

"I told you to stay inside," she hisses. "This is why I won't let the kids have a dog."

"I don't know why he's here," Katie says, pleading at Simon with her eyes. "I swear. Don't go. Please! Simon!" she calls out, but he's already turned away.

"I'll see you around, Katie," he says. "Thanks for your help this week. It's been fun."

Katie feels a whoosh of nerves as she sits down. She reminds herself this is Armie, and they've known each other for a thousand years. Also, she is extremely pissed off.

"Who does this?" Katie says, her gaze fixed on the green marble fireplace. "Who shows up in another country to ambush their ex-fiancée? Where is Millie, by the way? What'd you do with my dog?"

"It's always about the dog," he mumbles.

"EXCUSE ME?!" Katie rotates toward him, their eyes meeting for the first time.

"She's with your sister," he says.

"Britt knows about this? Son of a bitch. How come she didn't warn me? Or talk you out of it?"

"She didn't love the idea. Who was that guy? And why were you together so early in the morning?"

"It doesn't matter. Why are you here? Do I even want to know?" Even though the question demands asking, Katie fears his response. This is Armie, and he's more sentimental than most onward-and-upward types. He might simply say he misses her, or he might mention their baby's upcoming due date. It's not a discussion Katie's willing to have, especially not like this.

"It's going to sound ridiculous," Armie says as he picks at his nails, that old nervous trait.

"Oh, we've already eclipsed ridiculous, my friend." Katie exhales, a little relieved.

"I've been so bothered," he continues. "Tormented, almost. I can't get over how we ended things."

"You're upset about our breakup?" Katie eyeballs him, stunned. "What the hell? FYI, you always use euphemisms. You say we 'ended things' or 'called it a day.' It's as though you can't bring yourself to utter the words, We Broke Up."

"Fine. I don't like how We Broke Up."

"Our breakup was fine!" Katie says. "Cordial, even. And it's been seven months."

"Yeah, but I said some things that…weren't nice. I keep replaying it in my head."

"Which parts?" Katie says, then puts up a hand. "You know what? Don't tell me. I don't want to rehash it all. Whatever it was, I know you didn't mean it, and I don't recall anything particularly galling. Did I seem mad?"

Armie shakes his head. "You didn't seem angry, but you're hard to figure out sometimes."

"You've known me for thirty years!"

"And I know the more upset you get, the more 'fine' you act."

"Now you're making me sound like Judy," Katie notes.

"If the shoe fits…"

Katie steams. "Okay, now I *am* mad," she says. "This is a very low-performing apology, by the by. D-plus, at best."

"I don't know what to tell you," he says. "Other than it's weighed on me for months. I've been debating about whether to talk to you, but you sent me that text, and it felt like a sign."

Katie looks at him crookedly. "What text?" she says. "Did I ask about Millie too much? Believe me, that was about her, not you."

"Per usual," he says and, frowning, reaches into his pocket.

Like she might've done a year ago, Katie tears the phone out of his hand. She scans their texts until she finds a bubble that is more than a few words long.

Sorry if I made things more difficult,
I wasn't the most gracious there, at the end.
We had some good years, my forever friend,
and even the shit I can't imagine going through
with anyone else. OK, bye!

"We had some good years," Katie repeats. "That text?"

He nods.

"What's the big deal?" Katie says. "Apparently, I was feeling apologetic, which is not the same as inviting someone to get on a plane."

"It's the most you've opened up to me in a long time," he says. "Years, maybe."

"What are you talking about? I've always been honest with you. We've gotten into multiple fights because you think I'm too freewheeling with my opinions in social situations!"

"Yeah, but that's always about politics, or controversial takes on pop culture," he says. "It's never about you. Like, what's going on inside."

"There's not much to say!"

Armie snorts. "You know what's fucked-up? The months before our breakup, we were so happy. You always had a smile on your face. I thought things were better than ever and then, out of nowhere, you ended things." He clears his throat. "Sorry, you broke up with me. It made me feel like I don't know you at all."

"It wasn't out of nowhere," Katie says. "And my default has

always been smiling through the pain. Not the healthiest thing in the world, but you know this about me."

"That's what I'm trying to tell you," Armie says. "I've had to guess at you a lot over the years. That text was more than you ordinarily let on. I saw it as an opening."

"Well, you were wrong." Katie tosses the phone back. Armie misses, and it clatters to the ground. "Exactly why I hated having you in center field when I pitched," she says. "Lack of coordination. Not fast enough."

"Deflecting with a joke. Classic."

"Why do you think you started playing second base?" Katie sighs. "Seriously, Armie, you flew to London because I was nicer than usual one time? Either you're out of your mind, or I send extremely bitchy texts."

At this, Armie breaks into a grin. "Not always," he says. He tries to catch her eyes, but Katie won't have it. She's too experienced to fall for any of his dumb good guy moves. "The text made me feel guilty," he continues. "You copped to being 'difficult,' but if anyone made it harder at the end, it was me. I was a bit relentless."

"Yeah, I mean, if a different girlfriend ever has an ectopic pregnancy, definitely do not list for her the fifteen *other* ways she might parent a child, especially if she's still in the hospital. So many options available to the willing participant, aside from doing nothing at all."

"I'm sorry," Armie says, and his voice quivers. "I was trying to solve a problem. But I only created more."

"Armando Acosta, always with plans B, C, and D," Katie says. "Look. It was annoying at the time, but you don't need to apologize. Your heart was in the right place. All is forgiven."

"Yeah, but I'm still trying to forgive myself. The worst part is you never wanted kids, and I forced you into it, and it ended so horribly. You must hate me for putting you through all that."

"Maybe at first," Katie says. "But only because I wanted some-

one to blame. Admittedly, it could be hard to separate what I wanted personally from what we wanted as a couple but, by the time I was pregnant, I did want that baby. I was all in. It's one of the few things in this world I know for sure."

"You were all in," Armie says. He clasps his hands and waits before speaking again. "Then why did you refuse to pursue other avenues? Why did you immediately shut everything down?"

"Are you kidding me right now?" Katie says, and she can almost feel herself lift off the seat. "You literally just apologized for your aggressive problem-solving and now you're doing it again?"

"I'm talking about later," he says. "Hours later, days, weeks."

"The doctor said we shouldn't try again," Katie says, evenly, and her fury begins to ebb. "And we *did* discuss other avenues."

Though Katie liked the idea of adoption, she knew of two couples who went through multiyear processes that ultimately failed, and she never had the guts for that. Britt volunteered to be a surrogate, but Katie couldn't get past the idea of putting her egg and Armie's sperm into her sister's womb, which probably means she's not very evolved.

"We talked about *all* the options," Katie reminds him. "But I wasn't interested in the other paths. You wanted to be a father, and I wanted that for you, and here we are."

Katie waits, and Armie says nothing. The minutes tick by as he scowls and continues picking his nails. "I guess the apology isn't the only reason I came," he finally admits.

Katie stiffens and waits for him to mention the baby they never had. She could be raising a *child* with Armie right now, this person she's known forever but who remains in many ways a stranger. The idea is fantastical. It's a made-up story, fiction she could never write.

"You really hurt my feelings," he says.

"Your *feelings*?" Katie scoffs. "About what?"

"The other day when I picked up Millie from the house. I went into your bedroom, for the crow, and your engagement ring…it was just sitting there, on the dresser. Discarded, like an old coffee cup."

"Okay… Do you want it back or something? Remember, I tried, but you told me to keep it. I am planning to sell it, just so you know."

Armie looks up, eyes wide. "You can't sell your engagement ring!" he cries.

"It's my ring," Katie says. "And I'm broke. It's either that or the house, and the ring seems easier. Most likely, though, I'll have to do both."

"YOU'RE THINKING OF SELLING THE HOUSE?"

"There's no reason to yell," Katie says. "It's hard enough as it is."

With no new book on the horizon, and only a trickle of royalties on which to survive, Katie's understood this inevitability for months, but it's the first time she's faced it head-on. Katie hates the idea of selling off a life she once loved, but what choice does she have?

"Katie, you can't," Armie says. "The market is skyrocketing in that part of town. Never mind sentimental value, it'd be a terrible business decision."

"So is defaulting on one's mortgage," Katie says. "None of this makes me happy."

"You *have* to keep it," Armie pleads, and Katie can't recall him fighting half this hard for her. "Don't sell," he says again. "If you need the cash flow, you could easily rent it out for twice the mortgage. Several people at my office want to move into that neighborhood."

"Really?" Katie says, and performs some basic math. She could live comfortably on double the mortgage, even if she had to rent an entirely new place. "That's actually a decent idea. Thanks."

"Better yet," Armie says, "I'll pay it myself."

Katie laughs. "You'll pay my mortgage? That is a hard no,"

she says. "I don't need a benefactor. Well, I do, but I'd pick someone else."

"I still love you," he blurts, and it takes Katie a beat to make sense of his words.

"Armie, that's not true—"

"We never should've broken up. That was the biggest mistake of my life."

"I broke up with you!"

"Yeah, but you were 'doing me a favor,'" Armie says, his dark eyes swimming with tears. "Those were your exact words. You were giving me the chance to have kids, but that's not what I want. However much I'd love to be a dad, I'd rather be with you."

"Stop."

"We're perfect together," he says, and reaches for her hand. "No one understands you better than I do—not Britt, not your mom, not Jojo. Not a single person in this world."

"If that were true, you wouldn't have read into my very innocuous text," Katie says. She pulls away and stands up. "Don't you have a live-in girlfriend?"

"We don't live together," he says. "She seems to think so, but that's not the case."

"Sounds like you two are off to a great start."

"Forget about her, Katie. The reason you and I broke up doesn't exist anymore," he says. "You granted me permission to procreate, or whatever, but that's not what I want. I've taken away that obstacle. Now all of our problems are solved."

"Are they though?" Katie pauses to contemplate whether she really would've gone through with marrying him. Was the baby a pain too big to overcome, or was Katie just waiting for a legitimate excuse to leave the greatest guy in the world?

"I feel the same now as I did back then," she says, speaking as much to herself as to him. "We're better off apart. We don't want the same things anymore."

What Katie wants, she can't put into words. As Linda Radlett did in *The Pursuit of Love*, and Nancy in her own life, Katie
longs to strike a new path, to find that undefinable "other,"
not yet named. She doesn't want to tether herself to a kinder,
more charming version of Prod because of expectations, or time
served. Whatever life has in store, Armie won't be part of it.

"Of course we want the same things," he insists. "We always
have and we've built a whole life together. You can't just walk
away."

"I have to walk away," Katie says. "And so do you. Otherwise, we'll both be stuck. Armie, I'll always care about you. I
could live for a hundred years and no one would ever have as
much of an impact on my life. But I need something different now. You don't want to get back together. You just hate to
lose." Katie winks, a little bit joking, a little bit not. "I appreciate your bullheadedness, and how you've always challenged me.
I'm pretty sure our intense rivalry is the main reason I gradu-
ated high school, or went to a good college."

"Bullshit," he says. "You've always been brilliant."

"Though not always focused. Anytime I veered off-track, you
pulled me back on. Luckily, when I started to go sideways, you
were out of your fire-setting phase." Katie smiles sadly. "I've
always admired your stubborn nature, but now is not the time
to dig in. Come on, you know I'm right."

Armie exhales and, hands on knees, pushes to standing. "I
guess that's that," he says, his face showing the rare look of defeat. "Never thought it'd end like this."

"It didn't," Katie says. "It ended months ago."

Armie smirks and Katie flicks away a tear. "Thanks for being
my whole life," she says.

He opens his arms and Katie steps inside, his nearness warm-
ing her head to toe. The feeling isn't love, but something close
to tenderness, a deeply entrenched adoration. Soon enough,

Armie will realize she's done him a favor. He doesn't want to get back together any more than she does.

"Will you have a chance to sightsee while you're here?" Katie asks as they let go.

"No touristing for me," Armie says. "Gotta get back to work."

Katie nods. And life goes on.

"You'll always be the great love of my life, you know," he says.

Katie blinks, wondering if Armie knows how close he's come to the last line of *The Pursuit of Love*. Maybe he did read it one of the fifty times she foisted it upon him.

"Oh, dulling," Katie says, using Nancy's words, and a poor approximation of her accent. "Great love of your life? *One always thinks that. Every, every time.*"

September 1944

G. Heywood Hill Ltd.

Nancy slammed down the phone. She looked at Helen, who was roosting on a stool.

"What is it this time?" Hellbags asked, not lifting her gaze from Agatha Christie.

"Harry Clifton wants six hundred copies of a letter signed. How am I supposed to accomplish that? The speedboat he asked for would've been easier!"

"That's a tough one," Hellbags agreed.

"I have so much to do between sorting invoices, returning phone calls, and cliquing approximately one thousand books." Nancy gestured toward the towering pile. *The Book of Vagabonds and Beggars. The Atrocities of the Pirates. Consider the Oyster. Interview with Mussolini*, signed. "And Anne and Heywood still refuse to get near the shop without an armistice in place."

"People can be such worriers," Helen said. She licked her finger and turned the page.

"Meanwhile, they pay me absolutely nothing even though the business would collapse without my oversight." Nancy sighed. "It's all so wretched. To be in Paris, I'd give anything."

Although liberation happened only a month before, already

the victory felt like some lesser thing. The Colonel was working full-time in Paris, which should've been an improvement, but the situation was no better than when he'd been in Algiers.

"What about the Paris shop?" Hellbags said, and set down her book. "Have you asked Heywood about it yet? What'd he say?"

"He promised to take it under advisement, which means he ceased thinking about it the moment he hung up the phone. Oh, Hellbags." She shuddered. "I have to do something. I must get out of this shop."

With her fortieth birthday looming, Nancy was desperate for real life to begin. Alas, real lives required more than three pounds per week and Nancy no longer viewed her book as a sure bet. Though technically "finished," the manuscript remained in limbo, likewise her marriage, and the sealed envelope in her desk.

I need to know, was there ever a "Greenie," or was this Greenie really Prod?

Nancy hadn't summoned the nerve to send the letter, because she didn't know what answer she sought. If Peter wasn't the father, it'd be difficult to justify a divorce, and a relocation to France. If he was, her worst fears about Prod would be confirmed, and her entire book would be a lie.

Non-cee, never mind the refugees, she could hear the Colonel say. *Write a different kind of memoir—your own. Tu sais quoi faire. You know what to do.*

Nancy crouched behind the counter and slipped a folder from her purse. She pulled out two letters she'd written to the Colonel some months before. "Helen, would you mind having a peek at something?" Nancy said as her eyes swept the first page.

We were always either on a peak of happiness or drowning in black waters of despair; our emotions were on no ordi-

nary plane, we loved or we loathed, we laughed or we cried,
we lived in a world of superlatives.

Hellbags glanced up.

"Yesterday, I received a package from Paris," Nancy said, and passed the papers to Helen. "The Colonel mailed me an entire stack of my old correspondence. Don't get excited! This isn't a lovers' spat. These letters contain little vignettes about my life, and he thinks I should work them into a book. Here are two of them."

"Other people's love letters!" Hellbags said. "A dream come true! Should I read them in private? I hope they're properly steamy."

"Sorry, but they're about my childhood. Still, I'd love to know what you think."

"How disappointing," Hellbags said, and began to read.

Farve loathed clever females, but he considered that gentle-
women ought, as well as being able to ride, to know French
and play the piano.

"I doubt anyone would be interested," Nancy yammered as Hellbags flipped the page. "It's all so obscure! Mostly it's a lark, a way to entertain the Colonel, and unleash my long-held frustrations about Farve! I can really work myself into a lather thinking about how he deprived six intelligent girls of an education."

Hellbags peered up from the papers. "I'd prefer some old-fashioned smut," she said. "But these pages are magnificent."

"Really?" Nancy said, and her heart lifted. "Are you sure?" Hellbags was a tough critic, this she knew. "You don't think the antics are over-the-top? Read the part about Eddy Sackville-West. Now that the Colonel's learned everything there is to know about Farve, his new obsession is Eddy, specifically his traveling medicine chest and unrepentant indigestion and gas."

"Who doesn't love Eddy? Your Colonel is a smart man." Hellbags set the letters on the counter, atop her book. "I agree with him, about turning this into a book. Isn't that what Evelyn's been telling you to do?"

"Don't you dare," Nancy hissed, and raised a finger. "Do not inflict upon me Evelyn Waugh as a mentor."

Just then, a cheerful Mollie waltzed into the shop. "Hullo!" she called out. "The post has arrived! Nancy, aren't you the popular gal! Letters from Heywood, as well as Cyril Connolly and Evelyn Waugh."

"Speak of the demon," Nancy muttered.

After handing her the stack of mail, Mollie bent to retrieve the un-cliqued books, a huge, loopy smile slapped across her face.

"Ducky, leave those be," Nancy said. "I haven't had a chance to sort them. I'll get to it, I swear."

"Happy to take care of it myself," Mollie said. "I'll be in the office! Shout if you need anything!" She skipped off with the books, whistling as she went.

"Is she drunk?" Hellbags asked.

"Not that I'm aware," Nancy said, thumbing through the mail. "Heywood hired a new fella to do the accounts, and it's lightened her workload. I think she enjoys flirting with him, too. Oh, God." She made a face. "Cyril is sending me an early copy of *The Unquiet Grave*. No, thank you." Nancy pitched his missive onto the floor. "Let's see what Evelyn is up to," she said. "Hmm... Not altogether enjoying Croatia, it seems. The food is terrible, and Randolph Churchill is driving him mad. An advanced copy of *his* newest book is on the way. What bliss to have such prolific friends. Goodbye, Evelyn!" His letter joined Cyril's on the ground.

"What do we have here?" Nancy said. "How lovely. Correspondence from my boss. Must be serious, if he can't discuss it over the phone." She paused, her eyes dashing across the page. "Excellent! He will let me open the Paris branch, if I give him five thousand pounds first. Quickly, Hellbags, hand me my pass-book." Nancy's arms drooped, and she felt herself deflate. After skimming Heywood's letter one more time, she ripped it in half.

"Poor Nancy," Hellbags said. "I wish I could help, but I'm broke, too. It's criminal how much money goes into the upkeep of a house we don't even own. I could murder Johnny for giving everything to Jim Lees-Milne's endowment. Perhaps I will."

"All for the benefit of England," Nancy sang.

"On the plus side, you're in a situation you can get out of," Hellbags said. "Unlike myself. Have you shown the autobiography to your publisher yet?"

"It's quite possible publishing the thing will create more problems than it will solve," Nancy said. "Sometimes, I'm tempted to toss the lot of it into the fire. I probably would, too, if this book wasn't all I had."

"What about those?" Helen nodded toward the Colonel's letters. "The man is onto something, and so are you."

"Sometimes I do consider it, believe me, but just when I get the nerve, I think of *Wigs on the Green*. I can't put my sisters through that again, especially with our relations still strained."

"Your sisters? Oh, please!" Hellbags rolled her eyes. "They should be your last consideration. If any of them ever worried about what the family thought before they did something, your life would be better. Britain would be, too."

"You have a point," Nancy said, brow furrowed.

Hellbags leaned back. With both elbows propped on the counter, she gave Nancy a thorough up-and-down. "Let me ask you a question," she began.

Nancy quailed. "Uh-oh," she said.

"Do you even *want* to publish the refugee memoir?" Hellbags asked. "It seems to me you don't like it, or don't believe in it, or something."

"There are definitely elements I find unbelievable," Nancy said.

"You were so fixated on getting Lea to cooperate, but what did that solve? Sure, you managed to finish—no small feat—but now you're talking about chucking it into the fire. Perhaps that book is too—" Hellbags pulled her hands apart "—external. Outside of you. Those letters—they're pure Nancy Mitford. They have your verve, and your heart, and they remind me of why I adore you so very much."

"Aw, Hellbags," Nancy said, eyes pooling. "I hate it when you're sweet. But how can a few scribblings compete with an entire manuscript?"

"You tell me. You're the writer." Hellbags sighed. "Nancy, forget your sisters. Forget your parents, Prod, Heywood, everyone else. You have to figure out what *you* want. I never fully answered that question for myself, and it's the biggest mistake of my life."

"What do I want?" Nancy said, glancing at the letters. "A career, for one. I want the Colonel, of course. And Paris."

"Which book will get you there?"

"Shouldn't I put the money on the book that's written?"

"Or you can decide to write another one," Helen said.

"Do you have any idea how long that would take?" Nancy said. "I've been working on my autobiography for years. I have a job, and fire watch, and can only move so speedily."

"Then do what the men do," Hellbags said, shrugging, like this was the simplest act in the world. "Take a few months off."

"A writing leave? Ducky, something has gone loose in your head."

"I don't see why you can't," Helen said. "Mollie is perfectly capable of handling the shop while you're out, in particular if she stays on the cocaine."

"Mollie is not taking cocaine!"

"Either way, I just witnessed her competence firsthand," Hellbags said. "You don't have children, and the Colonel isn't around. Prod is—" she waved a hand "—doing whatever Prod does."

"Leaves are for people with money, Hellbags. And penises."

"You could do it," Helen said. "If you really wanted to."

"I wouldn't last on my savings for more than a few months. There's no way." Nancy shook her head. "Prod would never agree to it."

"Then you'd better work fast." Hellbags winked. "And get a divorce if you don't want him offering his two pence."

"An answer for everything, I see," Nancy said. She hardened her face, her entire body, refusing to let the idea take hold. "I've brought up separation a dozen times, but Peter won't hear of it. By the by, I never would've expected the wife of Johnny Dashwood to be advising *me* to get a divorce."

"I loathe Johnny," Hellbags said. "But I like being married to him."

"Even if I could get everything to line up, what would I do with the memoir? I joked about burning it but, the truth is, it kills me to think of all that effort going up in flames."

"You'll figure out a way to make use of it," Hellbags said. "Just like you'll figure out a way to pay for a leave. You're excellent at making something out of nothing, Nancy. The main thing Jim hates about you is that you're so adept at economizing."

"That's true..." Nancy said. She swallowed, feeling breathless, winded by possibility.

"Don't wait another minute," Hellbags said. "Everybody knows one minute turns into two, and two minutes turn into a month. Just like that." She snapped her fingers. "The years are gone. Do you want to be eighty years old, still scrambling around this natty old shop, hiding Angela Thirkell books? You are meant for bigger things."

"Don't you reckon it's a touch late for bigger things?" Nancy said. "I'm almost forty."

"Wrong again," Hellbags said, and wiggled her brows. "I've

got five years on you, and middle age is when the fun begins. You'd better hurry, though. Otherwise, you're apt to miss your own prime."

Monday Afternoon

Half Moon Street

Katie is a teenager again, lying with feet on the headboard, a phone pressed to her ear. Though she prefers texting, or seeing Simon in person, he's returned to Burwash, and Katie will soon be in the States. For now, a phone is all they have.

"Why are you trying to torture me?" Katie says. "No more questions! You're like every book club I've ever visited. Even if they read something else, they want to talk about *A Paris Affair*. These are mostly ladies in their fifties and sixties, by the way."

"Then I consider myself in good company," Simon says. "And it's more of an observation than a question. I'm dying to know what happened to June Clemente, when she got back to New York."

Katie glares at her phone, wishing they were on FaceTime so he could register her scowl. "You're one of those, huh?" she says. "One of those thoroughly vexing write-a-sequel types. Let me stop you right here. Although this has been suggested approximately one million times, I will never travel down that road."

"Why not, if it's something people want? You know who wrote a sequel, don't you?" he says. "You know who wrote two?"

Katie narrows her eyes. "You're not playing the Nancy Mitford card with me," she says.

"You have to admit it's interesting," Simon says. "In the nearly three decades Nancy lived in France, she wrote only one more novel that wasn't a spin-off of *The Pursuit of Love*."

"Is that true?" Katie says, and tries to visualize all of Nancy's work. For the first time, she wonders if Nancy embraced her hit in a way Katie cannot, or whether she felt compelled. "Anyway, good for Nancy," Katie says, "but I'm not a sequel kind of gal. They're fine, for other people, but not for me."

"Don't take this the wrong way," Simon says, and Katie grits her teeth. "But why are you so hesitant to revisit that story? You seem…scared."

"Scared!" Katie quacks. "Ha! No. My writing isn't so terrible that I'm actually afraid of it. A sequel does make sense, but…" She mulls this over and says the first thing that pops into her head. "Okay, let's say I do write one, and that fails, too. What happens after I've used up the very last trick in my bag?"

"I knew it," Simon says. He laughs, and Katie wishes hanging up on someone had the dramatic effect it once did. "I knew you weren't ready to give up. Otherwise, you wouldn't be protecting that one last trick."

Katie rolls her eyes. "Okay, smart guy," she says. "Maybe I'll empty the bag, one day, but for now I'm considering a different direction. You see? I have ideas. I'm not afraid."

He laughs again. "I'm pleased to be right in this manner, too. So what's this new book about?"

"I'm not sure yet," Katie says. "There's something about the way Nancy worked out different versions of her life in *The Pursuit of Love* that's made the wheels start to turn. A retelling, maybe? Don't worry! I won't exploit any of your family members."

"I remain unconvinced," he teases. "Not that you could exploit them, even if you wanted to, seeing as how we never found the book."

Katie sighs. "I know," she says. "And I'm sorry we didn't get more. I really thought we would. I guess I overestimated Felix's willingness to help, or my skills of persuasion."

Part of Katie still believes she can find that last thing, the final clue to explain what, if anything, Lea meant to Nancy, and what she meant to Prod, and why Nancy decided not to publish the manuscript. On the other hand, Katie understands that life is too messy, too complicated for one piece to ever explain everything.

"We may not have found the manuscript," Katie says, "but I maintain you gave your mom something better. All that effort is a special type of love. It's pure and uncomplicated. It doesn't keep score. What's more valuable than a person's time?"

"In fairness, I did personally benefit from my endeavors," he says, and Katie can hear him smirk through the phone. "And *pure* might not be the best word to describe my intentions."

"Now I'm blushing."

"I can see it from here," he says. "If time is a valuable currency, you must feel very flattered that a certain gentleman followed you across full oceans. That's time *and* money. Quite the statement."

"One ocean," Katie says. "And I'd much rather somebody find a rare book."

"I dunno, in terms of grand gestures, transcontinental travel is hard to beat."

"Didn't we promise to NEVER TALK ABOUT IT AGAIN?" Katie says, glad they can joke about this, and so quickly.

Last night, over Indian food, Katie rehashed her and Armie's relationship, beginning to end. Convincing Simon she wasn't swooning over Armie's "grand gesture" was easier to explain than her career. In the end, Simon trusted what he saw in Katie's face that morning on the doorstep. Never had a person appeared less pleased.

"You're right," Simon says. "I did promise, but you did almost marry the bloke, so it's a bit of a mindfuck."

"You have no idea," Katie says. It *was* a bit of a mindfuck to see the two men in one place, and Katie spent most of the night awake, head brimming with thoughts of Simon, and Armie, and the infinite ways her life might've gone. How bizarre to think she was in London, kissing Simon, when she could've married Armie years ago, or stayed at her corporate job. Katie might've tried for kids earlier, and been successful, or never pursued writing a novel. Between these and other paths, Katie has enough material for two or three versions of *The Pursuit of Love*. As the idea passes through her mind, it sticks for a moment. Goose bumps break out along her skin.

"You should stay in London," Simon says.

Katie shakes her head. "What?"

"That might sound abrupt," he says, and Katie senses him shrinking against the phone. "But writers can live anywhere. Take a leave from your life in the States. Stay here, write another book."

"I'd love to stay in London." Katie tries to rub the chill from her arms. "But I don't think they let you turn a vacation into a permanent stay. I don't want to be deported, or banned from the country."

"Get a six-month visa," he says.

"That is…an idea," Katie says, thinking it ludicrous yet not entirely out of the question. Armie said it himself—she could (and should) let the house. If Katie does this, she'll have to move somewhere. But a foreign country? This feels like a lot. Also, she can't leave Millie, and definitely not for six months. Can dogs get visas? What paperwork did Millie use to travel from Thailand?

Someone clears a throat. It's Jojo, leaning against the doorjamb. She makes one of those "hurry along" motions with her hand.

"Maybe I'll look into it," Katie tells Simon. "I should go. Jojo's just walked in, and this phone is starting to burn the side of my face."

"That is…not good."

Jojo begins to dramatically tap her foot.

"All right," Katie says. "Mom is pissed. I'll call you back later?"

"You'd better."

Katie smiles. "I promise."

"Ignoring your best friend?" Jojo says, sauntering into the room. "For a boy? Damn, that's cold. I've held your hand while you cried, and your hair while you puked. I've walked in on you hooking up with a random dude while wearing nothing but penny loafers and never told a soul."

"Yet you mention it once a year, minimum," Katie says. She flips around and sits up. "I'm not ignoring you. You were at your in-laws' all day yesterday, and I went to bed before you got home."

"Fine, but now it's time to discuss the men. There are only two, right? Or do I need a spreadsheet to keep track of these sexual escapades?"

"First of all, I did *not* invite Armie to London. You saw him leave yesterday morning, and I haven't spoken to him since."

"All right. Got it. Only the one escapade, then. No spreadsheet required."

"No escapades!"

"Really?" Jojo sours. "You didn't sleep with the extremely delicious schoolteacher? That's upsetting. Oh. Wait. Was it one of those 'everything-but' situations?"

"No!" Katie groans, and she feels a bounce as Jojo plunks onto the bed. "I slept with him, okay?"

"Geez. That bad?" Jojo says. "The hot ones will trick ya. They don't think they have to be good at it, but no one cares what your face looks like when the lights are out."

"He was good, okay?" Katie glances away. "Great, in fact. Lord knows what he'd say about me, but I didn't expire from sheer panic, like I thought I would. So, that's something."

When Simon's hand had slid between her shirt and her skin, Katie's chest tightened, and she found herself short of breath. But Simon pulled her closer, and Katie felt him hard against her, and all thinking stopped. They tumbled into bed like they'd done it a dozen times before.

"What's there to panic about?" Jojo says. "It's only sex."

"I've known him a week! And the last time I slept with someone other than Armie, the iPhone hadn't been invented yet. Also, there's the height discrepancy. I didn't know how it would work! Tell me you wouldn't be panicked in that situation."

Jojo cackles "Whoa, slow down," she says. "I hope things weren't that fast in the bedroom."

"Forgive me if I was a stitch overwhelmed!"

"So. Simon is good, apparently, but the real question is, how did he compare to Armie?" Jojo asks.

Katie screws up her face. "Wouldn't a fling almost always be better than what's happening fifteen years into a relationship?" she asks. "I'm all for monogamy, but no one gets married for the sex."

"Who knew," Jojo says with a decidedly wicked smile, and now Katie is forced to imagine whether Nigel is a tiger in bed. "Well, if you're going to get back into the swing of things, Simon's the right partner for the dance. Very nicely done. Ten out of ten. A-plus-plus." Jojo kisses her fingers, like a chef. "I wanted you to find your writing mojo, and part of me is irritated he distracted you. But if you're happy, so am I."

"Actually, I might've found some writing mojo after all," Katie says, and taps her forehead. "There might be a new story percolating."

"A new story!?" Jojo claps. "Hurrah! Erotic fiction, yes? About a hot principal? I'd read that book. I'd read it every damned day. You can name the protagonist Jojo, if you want."

"Very generous," Katie says. "And it's not erotic fiction. I'll keep my 'sexual escapes' private, thank you very much. The idea is just a tiny little germ of a thing. I thought of it this morning and immediately felt those good old writerly chills."

Jojo squeals. "The second-best feeling in the world!" she says.

"It seems so obvious," Katie says. "Too obvious. I was thinking...maybe...a modern retelling of *The Pursuit of Love*?"

"Yes! Of course!" Jojo says. "Would yours be semi-autobiographical, too?"

"I'm shocked you know that about the book," Katie says. "Whenever I mention Nancy Mitford, I assume you're only half listening."

"Oh, that's true," Jojo says. "But I finally read the thing. Between you and Nigel going on about it, I figured it was about time. Plus, he really wants to watch that dumb adaptation."

"You read *The Pursuit of Love*?" Katie slaps both hands over her heart. "This is a seminal moment. What a gift."

"Okay, calm down."

"You've made my day!" Katie springs forward and tries to tackle Jojo into a hug.

"Enough of that," Jojo says, wiggling free. "It was damned funny, I'll admit, but the book I want to talk about is yours."

"Don't jinx it by calling it a book," Katie says. "I haven't written a word, but the idea would be to play out different versions of my life, or someone's life, I'm not sure. But, realistically, not in a time-hop, *Sliding Doors* kind of way."

"Not how I read *The Pursuit of Love*, but okay," Jojo says.

"Obviously, I'd take a lot more liberties than Nancy did," Katie says. "My upbringing wasn't as entertaining, and I only had the one sister, and no screaming fathers."

"Don't sell yourself short," Jojo says. "Your childhood was

pretty wild. The outrageous lack of supervision, for one. And, really, Armie was like a sibling, before you slept with him. Maybe even after you did."

"I will not be having my protagonist sleep with her brother."

"That's a relief," Jojo says, grinning. "Well, my friend, you're supposed to write what excites you, what gets you out of bed in the morning, and this definitely qualifies. Sounds like you found something better in that shop than someone else's book."

"We'll see…"

They hear a click. The door pops open and Clive appears bearing an expression of angry-browed distress. Katie smiles nervously, hoping he didn't hear anything about sex.

"Did you change the Wi-Fi password?" he asks his mom, and with some heat.

"You can have it after you finish your schoolwork."

"I need the Wi-Fi to accomplish that," he says. "We've been over this."

Jojo throws Katie a look. "The way things are now, it's impossible to know if your kid is doing homework," she says, "or faffing about on Twitch."

Katie nods, wondering, *What the hell is a Twitch?*

"If you bothered taking five minutes to google it," Clive says, "you could easily figure out how to block certain websites. I'd show you, but…" He shrugs. "Probably best to keep that information in my back pocket."

"Go set up in your father's office," Jojo says. "Where you can be supervised. I'll be up in five minutes, with the password."

Clive sets a timer on his Apple watch. "Five minutes starts NOW!" he says.

With great flourish, he swirls around, but pauses one last time, just outside the door. "Hello, Miss Katie," he says, glancing over his shoulder. "I didn't mean to be rude. I like your sweater. Very beige."

Clive advances toward the elevator with great pomp and determination, like a miniature general.

"His mum must be a total nightmare," Jojo mutters.

"I'm sure he's not the easiest person to live with—"

"Ha! That's one way to put it!"

"But I love that kid," Katie says. "There's no one like him in the world."

"He is indeed one of a kind. Brilliant and exhausting." Jojo closes her eyes and touches her temples, as if she feels a headache coming on. "Eventually, Clive is going to realize he's smarter than his parents, and then we're truly fucked." She opens her eyes again. "It's probably happened already and he's toying with us, like a cat with an injured mouse."

"His schemes seem more practical, or financial in nature," Katie says. "As opposed to diabolical."

"It's a very fine line," Jojo says. "Feel free to take him home. We don't have to formalize it or anything. Happy to agree to a very flexible arrangement."

Katie laughs. "Not sure I have the capacity to take on the whole of Clive," she says. "But if you ever need to off-load him for a bit, send him to DC. I'm pretty sure I can keep him alive for a week or two."

"Careful, or I might take you up on that." Jojo freezes for a second before swiveling toward Katie. "Oh. My. God," she says, smiling so wide she's showing nearly all of her teeth. "Now, hear me out before you say no."

"Oh, no…"

She grips Katie, cutting off the circulation in her hand. "I have the best idea," Jojo says. "Not only will it solve *both* of our problems, but it just might change your life."

"I feel like I've heard that before."

"Maybe you have." Jojo grins. "The good news is I'm never, ever wrong."

March 1945

Oxfordshire

Nancy arrived at Faringdon House after the grimmest Christmas in years.

The shops were empty, the celebrations desultory, and everyone was tired, and wan. The lone bit of excitement came from next door, when Trumper expired during a trim. As he went down, he sliced off his customer's ear and the shop closed for a week.

"I wish it had been Dearest," Nancy joked to Mollie, and by "Dearest," she meant their boss. But as much as she complained, Nancy had to give Heywood his due. He was not entirely made of denials and tyranny.

"You may take off from January through March," he'd said when, upon taking Hellbags's advice, Nancy raised the idea of a leave.

"Three months?" Nancy said, stunned he'd agreed, but worried he'd ultimately rescind this holiday, too. "Are you sure the shop can afford to be shorthanded? I do the work of two people, you know."

"So you tell me," he'd said. "Every day, it seems. I think we'll manage nonetheless."

Mollie was pleased to shoulder the extra work and Handy, their new employee, offered to help with the accounts and fire watch. Either he was very generous, or had his eye on Mollie, which seemed the more likely case.

Her last night at the shop, Nancy giddily locked up the cash, the ledgers, and her old manuscript. With a hatbox filled with letters to the Colonel, Nancy sailed out of Heywood Hill and proceeded directly to her writing sanctuary, otherwise known as Lord Berners's home in Oxfordshire.

There were a million ways to describe Faringdon House, the gray eighteenth-century home built by the father of Britain's worst poet laureate. The estate was a mixture of high and low, the serious and the absurd, starting with his collection of storks, shrimp-fed flamingos, and doves dyed pastel to resemble confetti in flight. Dogs scampered about the property in pearl necklaces that were constantly snapping and needing to be replaced.

Inside, the home was just as irrational, featuring an unholy combination of gilded furniture, antique carpets, mechanical toys, and crass joke books. Several bedrooms had Dali-designed bureaus that cocked to the side, and signs were posted throughout.

VISITORS ARE REQUESTED NOT TO LET OFF FIREARMS BETWEEN THE HOURS OF MIDNIGHT AND SIX A.M.

And:

OWING TO AN UNIDENTIFIED CORPSE IN THE CISTERN VISITORS ARE REQUESTED NOT TO DRINK THE BATH WATER

And:

MANGLING DONE HERE

Flowers were cultivated in the kitchen garden, as were melons and the most delicious peaches Nancy had tasted, which Berners claimed were "ham-fed." For supper, the chef kept a prewartime menu of caviar, foie gras, and plovers' eggs to feed an entertaining rotation of guests.

Nancy spent her days in the red bedroom, writing beside an enormous four-post bed, Milly and the puppy Rififi snoring at her feet. From her desk, Nancy could look out across the spectacular patchwork of fields, a landscape not unlike Asthall, her childhood home, renamed Alconleigh in her book. Beautiful Asthall-turned-Alconleigh, with its covered walkways and rolling hills. Alconleigh, where life was all summers, and Nancy could restore her family, if only in words.

"You are now called Lord Merlin," Nancy said to Lord Berners. They were in his green drawing room, surrounded by dark olive walls, towering piles of books, and butterflies and birds— some alive, others stuffed, or pinned under glass. "Mainly because of your warlock-inspired attire, and your home's magical effects. It's produced an entire novel, after all."

As in her letters to the Colonel, Nancy's sentences had come swiftly, and without much fuss. Three months at Faringdon, and she was nearly finished.

"Faringdon is thus named Merlinford," Nancy continued, glancing down at her paper. "I've described it as a house to live in, not a place from which to shoot animals, as opposed to the type of home Farve prefers."

"Perfection!" Lord Berners said, with a chuckle. "What else can you reveal?"

"Fanny is my narrator," Nancy said, sorting through her work. "I gave her the most delightful guardian—Aunt Emily, a kindly figure who supports a girl's right to an education. Though Fanny envies the Radletts' 'freedom from thrall and bondage,' she does feel a priggish satisfaction in not being forced to grow up unlettered."

"Did you decide on a name for the protagonist's much-derided firstborn?" Lord Berners asked, and Nancy beamed.

"Linda Radlett's daughter is called Moira," she said. "In honor of Hellbags. It's her middle name."

"I hope Lady Dashwood doesn't mind."

"That's the beautiful thing about Hellbags," Nancy said. "She never minds much."

Lord Berners giggled, and it was good to see him in such a jovial mood. Since turning sixty, he'd been through many trials, including two grave illnesses, and a visit to the eye hospital. He now had to wear dark glasses full-time, though insisted it wasn't a medical necessity but because his "kind eyes caused beggars to swarm."

"Hallo!" a voice said, and a young man's head poked through the partially opened door. "I'm escorting Pansy Lamb on a walk 'round the lake. Does anyone else need a dog taken out?"

Their visitor was Lord Berners's companion, the twenty-eight-years-younger Robert Heber-Percy, otherwise known as Mad Boy. Three years ago, Mad Boy married a woman, thereby transforming their duo into a ménage à trois. They had a daughter together, but the wife and child soon tired of the arrangement and left last year.

"If you don't mind taking Milly and Rififi, that'd be grand," Nancy said. "But if Milly puts up a fuss, leave her be. She's been a brat since Rififi's come along."

Mad Boy nodded and disappeared. A few minutes later, Nancy saw him through the French windows, near the fountain, dragging along four dogs of comically differing presentation: a retriever, a dalmatian, a pug, and a baby French bulldog.

"In the book, your dogs are whippets," Nancy told Lord Berners. "And they wear diamonds instead of pearls."

"Nancy! Diamonds would be so excessive!"

Nancy smirked. "Yes, quite different to pearls."

Lord Berners stood and smoothed the wrinkles from his green

crêpe de chine pajamas. "I think I'll join Robert by the lake," he said. "I need to get in my exercise. Are you still available for the party tonight?"

"I wouldn't miss it for anything," Nancy said.

She tried to divine the thoughts Farve—Uncle Matthew in the book—would have about the event.

"*...a lot of aesthetes, sewers from Oxford, and I wouldn't put it past him to bring some foreigners.*"

Incredible, Nancy thought, as Berners stepped out of the room. Everything was finally coming together—her book, this war, life in sum. Nancy couldn't remember the last time she felt so gay, so uplifted, so filled with a sensation she could only describe as "hope."

While dressing for dinner, Nancy thought nothing of the phone trilling downstairs. It rang several times a day and never portended bad news.

Several minutes later, there was a knock at the door, though the clock indicated the party was some ways off. With a wobble in her stomach, Nancy walked cautiously across the room. Inhaling, she opened the door. Though he never entered this part of the house, Lord Berners stood before her, his face white, his eyes watery and red.

"What happened?" Nancy said, struggling to catch her breath.

"Oh, Nancy," he whimpered. "The very worst."

As Lord Berners spoke, Nancy absorbed the information without truly hearing his words. She stared at the Bessarabian carpet, dizzying herself with its kaleidoscope of pink, red, and light blue bouquets.

"You don't have to come to dinner," Berners said, when all was laid out. "I'll have food brought up to your room."

Nancy was fuzzy, confused, entirely numbed. "I'll see you in ten minutes," she said, and closed the door.

Heart thronging, she slathered on her face. Nancy stepped into her frock and adjusted her hair. All night long, she made steady work of being bright, while Lord Berners fretted and gaped. It was all an act, of course, the last desperate gasps of her three-month halcyon. Nancy understood she'd have to return to the real world eventually. She just didn't expect her reentry to be so sudden, or so cruel.

April 1945

Rutland Gate

As they packed into the gray-and-gold drawing room at Rutland Gate, Nancy couldn't help but count what they'd lost. Beginning first and foremost with her brother, Tom.

Sweet Tom, but also stupid Tom, who volunteered for the Far East, only to get shot in the neck as a result. Though initially expected to survive the attack, he caught pneumonia in the field hospital and died on Good Friday.

The family had lost others during these past five years, among them several close cousins, Decca's husband, and Debo's brother-in-law, once married to the Kennedy girl. Nancy's beloved André Roy succumbed to his own fragility weeks ago, and there were countless more friends and acquaintances who would not live to see armistice.

On top of this were those not dead, but in some manner gone, like Unity, who was wandering Tom's funeral luncheon, airing her grievances. "I hated all our governesses!" she cried. "They were always telling me, why don't you have a nice walk, dear, it will do you good."

As Nancy observed this horror show alongside Debo and Pam, she desperately longed for the real Unity, as well as Decca, who hadn't the money to travel all the way from California. Diana was in London, but still on house arrest.

"Poor Bobo," Debo said as they watched Unity assault some new guest. "Muv always says she's improving, but that's never the case."

"Of course not, because they live on Inchkenneth," Nancy said, about the Inner Hebrides island Farve bought after he sold the family estate. "Seems to me it's the sort of place where one develops several life-threatening ailments, instead of recovers from them."

"To think of Unity living there," Debo said. "It's unconscionable! And merely getting to London—it must've been so difficult for them both."

"Here's where Unity's memory problems are to her benefit," Nancy said. "No one would willingly undergo that journey more than once."

Nancy had been on the island when the war broke out, and leaving the windswept, squelchy mound of moss was one of the most onerous exercises of all time, beginning with a rowboat taken to a desolate beach on the Isle of Mull, after which was a ten-mile ride to port, followed by a ferry-steamer to Oban. Nancy then spent twelve hours hanging about a station, waiting to board a sleeper train. Several more trains followed, and she was lucky to make it alive.

"Inchkenneth is a place best forgotten," Pamela agreed.

"Do you know how they call a doctor?" Nancy asked, and her sisters shook their heads. "Whenever Unity requires medical attention, Muv places a black disc on the garage. Every so often, some doctor on Mull uses a pair of binoculars to scan the property. If he sees the disc, he rows over, to see what's what."

"What a nightmare," Pamela said.

"We weren't allowed to have people over," Unity continued to whine nearby. "Only Nancy's and Tom's friends, who always came in hordes, shrieking and guzzling. Why, oh why, did Tom have to die?"

"She gave up so much for that horrible Hitler," Debo said. "And where is he now?"

"Probably hiding out in his Führerbunker."

"Be serious, Nancy," said Debo.

"Is everything a joke with you?" Pam asked.

"I *am* being serious!"

"How could he have done this to her?" Debo said. "How can he leave her to suffer for the rest of her life?"

Nancy raised a brow. "It's almost as though he's unmoved by human suffering," she said. "But that can't be it."

"Enough," Pam sniped.

"The papers have stopped reporting she birthed his love child, at least," Debo said.

For now, Nancy thought.

"I can't talk about her anymore," Pam said, turning away, erasing Unity from her periphery. "Let's discuss the good times, with Tom. Nancy, remember how we'd go to church together whenever he came home from school?"

"How could I forget?" Nancy said, while Debo crossed her arms and scowled.

As the youngest sister, Debo knew Tom the least and loathed being on the outside of a thousand inside jokes.

"We were positive he was living a glamorous life of sin," Nancy told the little one. "And were seething with jealousy."

"Not me!" Pamela squawked. "I was appalled." She glanced at Debo, who was now pouting mightily. "Whenever the minister reached the 'thou shall not commit adultery' bit, we'd nudge each other, and poke Tom, and make *such* a spectacle."

"Inevitably, Farve would start screaming and interrupt the service."

"Tuddemy took it like a sport, though," Pam said.

"He always did," Nancy said. "You know, I saw Tom more

during the war than ever. This past year, he was in London constantly. During Christmas…" She bit her lip, tears threatening. "He was so wonderful, and gay. I'm glad he was happy, at the end."

"Sometimes, I wish we could go back," Pam said. "Back to the carefree days at Asthall and Swinbrook. Reading in the cloisters, running across the fields. The Hons cupboard. Even Farve constantly gnashing his teeth. Never thought I'd long for his tantrums."

"Maybe we *will* go back," Debo said, and threw Nancy a grin, thrilled to be back in the middle once again. "When Nancy publishes her book!"

Pam's blue eyes flared. "You said you were writing a new book, but I didn't know it was a sure thing! Is this the autobiography?"

"It's hardly a sure thing," Nancy said. "And it's a novel, based on our childhoods. I have lunch with my publisher next week, so cross your fingers. Hopefully, by this time next year, we can holiday at Asthall once again."

"I've got such masses to tell you, Fanny, what we really need is hours and hours in the Hons cupboard."

"Heavens, should we brace ourselves?" Pam said, and feigned weakness in the knees. "Which of us will you send up this time? Whose ideologies?"

"Don't worry," Nancy said. "It's nothing like *Wigs on the Green*."

"Nancy keeps telling us not to worry," Debo said. "But after she sells it, she's moving to France. This feels an awful lot like an escape!"

"Going to France is closer to a wish," Nancy said, "than an actual plan. I'd need to make gobs of money to even consider it."

"France?" Pam said. "Oh, dear Lord. Tell me you're not following the Colonel. You must know he'll never marry you,

Nancy. Sorry if that seems harsh, but I don't want you to get your hopes up."

"Hoping for marriage?" Nancy chuckled. "Ducky, no one in her right mind would wish for that. If I go, it will be on my own."

"Maybe the book will be your ticket out," Debo said. "You can make enough to invest with Heywood, and live a glamorous life in the City of Light."

"Sure," Nancy said, thinly, and without much conviction. Five thousand pounds was some hard cheese, and she hadn't made a quarter of that in all her prior books combined.

"You're going to be famous!" Debo said in the bright and plucky way of the youngest child who was also a duchess-in-wait. "You'd better keep a room just for me. I'll be coming to Paris every August, when the new collections are out."

"Honestly, Debo," Pam said. "Now is not the time to entertain fairy tales. You know Nancy can't live with the Colonel while she's still *Missus Rodd*. It doesn't sit well."

"Goodness!" Nancy said. "You girls are absolutely showering the Colonel with attention! This isn't about him, which you'd understand if either of you bothered to listen to me at all. It's long been my dream to be a famous purveyor of highbrow Frog books. Should I manage the funds, I plan on securing a business license, and my own flat, and thus won't be living with the Colonel at all."

Debo clutched her chest. "You'll live alone?" she gasped. "Like an old, depressed spinster? Why won't the Colonel let you live with him? Oh, I don't like this. I don't like it at all."

"It's not a matter of *allowing* it," Nancy said. "In France, you can't simply move in with your lover. It's so frightfully Catholic over there! And de Gaulle is so priggish. He almost fired the Colonel after a concierge caught me sneaking into his room at the Connaught! The world has changed, my darlings. Gone are the cheerful days when French politicians were expected to die in their mistresses' arms. It's really a sad state of affairs."

As her sisters quivered and clucked, Nancy began scouring the room, noting distant relatives, close friends, and dozens of strangers. Finally, her eyes landed on Farve, who stood in a far corner, looking hunched and forlorn as he chatted with Debo's husband and Jim Lees-Milne.

"If you don't mind," Nancy said. "I should check on *Uncle Matthew.*"

"Uncle Matthew?" Pamela said, and wrinkled her nose. "Who's that?"

"With any luck, you—and the rest of the world—will soon find out."

"The best brain of our generation," Jim was saying as Nancy approached. "Beloved, handsome Tom, the most loyal and affectionate of friends. He should have married and had hosts of beautiful children."

"Couldn't agree more," said Debo's husband, Andrew, the future Duke of Devonshire. "England is missing something without his genes. Quite a lot of that going around. Ah! Look who it is! Our favorite authoress. Hello, Nancy."

"Greetings, gentlemen," Nancy said, and passed around a sad smile. "How are you holding up, Farve?" Nancy took one of his hands in hers and gave him a squeeze. Though his cheeks were jowly, and his Redesdale blues clouded by cataracts, Nancy could still see the chiseled, hawklike features of Tom. "It's lovely to see everyone, despite how much I hate the circumstance." She pivoted toward her brother-in-law. "And Andrew, in person! It's bliss having you back. I know every man dreams of heroics, of medals and parades, but you must've been somewhat comforted to return."

Andrew's face soured and Nancy understood he was not in fact pleased to be yanked from the front thanks to his family's wishes, and their pulling of strings. Now Andrew was home and safe, but miserable, proving once again that Nancy would never understand the will of men.

"I miss the action," Andrew said. "Though, it's nice not to contemplate my mortality on a daily basis."

"Tom almost made it," Farve said, his voice a toss of gravel and rocks. "He was so close."

The group gave their heavy nods, and Jim launched into a story about the last time he'd seen Tom. It was in December, and they'd enjoyed a drink at Brooks's. "The fog was thick," Jim said. "A dreary, moody night. After we parted, I walked a few blocks and bumped into a stranger, only to discover the stranger was Tom. We shared a good laugh and went to his *garçonnière*, where we ate scrambled eggs and drank red wine until dawn."

Nancy smiled at the memory and wondered what else the old friends might've gotten up to. It occurred to her that Jim had been at some point in love with every Mitford, aside from her, and Unity, of course.

"I'm so tired of the damned war," Andrew said, and slammed his drink on a nearby table. "Let's discuss something else. Nancy, Deborah tells me you've written a book."

"That's correct," Nancy said. "It's about all of us when we were little. A novel. Don't be nervous!" She laughed, sounding more than a touch nervous herself. "It's presently called *My Cousin Linda*, though I'm hopeful my publisher will come up with something better. We're meeting next week. You're featured prominently, Farve." Nancy placed a hand on his arm, and he jumped. "As portrayed by the blustery but lovable Uncle Matthew. Like you, he's full of wind and menace, and he's ground away four pairs of dentures during his fits. But he is the most winning character in the book." Nancy smiled to herself as she reminisced about Uncle Matthew's attributes.

Much as we feared, much as we disapproved of, passionately as we sometimes hated Uncle Matthew, he still remained for us a sort of crite-

rion of English manhood; there seemed something not quite right about
any man who greatly differed from him.

"The story came out so easily, more fountain than pen,"
Nancy prattled on, then stopped to consider this. The book
might've taken only three months to put down, but she'd been
writing it for years. "I pray you'll adore Uncle Matthew, too."

"Do any other Mitfords make an appearance?" Andrew asked.

"Oh, sure. Aunt Sadie is a dead ringer for Muv. There's a Tom
character—he's called Matt. The narrator is a mix of the Mitford girls but, mostly, she has Debo's sweet nature."

"Tell us, Nancy," Jim said. "Did you add Prod to the narrative? Where does he fit in?"

"You know very well—"

"Where is he this afternoon?" said Andrew as he made a show
of looking around.

Nancy shrugged, occupying herself with a loose thread on
her suit jacket. "Peter might come later," she said. "Expect him
to be in a mood if he does."

"He's always in a mood," Jim griped.

"What does he think about you moving to Paris?" Andrew
asked. As he took in Nancy's expression, his pleasant face went
south. "I'm sorry. Is that not widely available information? Deborah said something. Perhaps I misunderstood?"

"Paris?" Farve said, turning an even paler shade of gray.

"Oh, I don't know," Nancy said, and brushed a piece of hair
from her brow. "It's mostly talk right now. Hard to plan anything with a war still on. Goodness, it's warm in here. Perhaps
we can open a window or two?"

"So, you're not going?" Andrew frowned. "Or are you? I'm
confused. Deborah said—"

"I know what Debo said," Nancy snapped. "And Paris *is* the
idea, if I can drum up the money."

As Andrew again tried to interject, a commotion broke out in
the reception hall. Nancy craned to see. "Oh. My. Lord," Nancy

said, and her heart seized. She looked back at Farve in time to see all emotion slide from his face. What must it be like, she wondered, to see one's daughter for the first time in thirteen years?

"Good God," Andrew muttered.

"Diana never stopped being beautiful," said Jim.

The room was so flooded with chatter and buzz and great gaping mouths that only Nancy noticed when one more person slipped through the door. It was Prod, visibly angry but devastatingly handsome in his uniform, with his bronze skin and the gold on his jacket glistening in the chandelier light.

"Hello, everyone," Diana said, wafting in like a dream.

"Absolutely gorgeous," Jim murmured.

"Isn't this the *most* devastating thing there ever was?" She stopped to slap away her two accompanying policemen. "Can you give me a speck of space? Have some respect for my late brother!"

A hand fell to Nancy's waist. "Hello," Peter whispered, and Nancy lurched so violently she almost threw up. "How do you like that? Only Diana would bring footmen to a funeral."

Nancy resisted a laugh. It was nice not everyone was bowled over by her sister's beauty, but Nancy wasn't sure how to talk to her husband, or how much he knew by now. "Did you come from Heywood Hill?" she asked, her voice sounding strangled. She squirmed to put more distance between them.

"Yes," he said. "I did exactly as you asked. Can we go somewhere?"

"Not now!" she hissed, then glanced back. "I do appreciate you coming, though."

"Excuse me," Farve said as he splintered from the group.

"I'll go with you," Nancy said, but Farve was already off, wending through the crowd.

"What is he doing?" Andrew said. "Should we help?"

"He forgot his cane," noted Jim.

Farve walked into the reception hall, and the room held its

breath. Whimpering softly, he pulled Diana into his arms. The pair wept openly, no sign anything bad had ever passed between them.

Peter stopped Nancy near the door.

"You're not trying to leave, are you?" he said, blocking the exit.

"I am," Nancy said, hurriedly slipping on her gloves. "My nerves are frayed, and I need fresh air. It was kind of you to pay your respects. Thank you for coming."

"Why are you thanking me? It was my duty." Prod took a step closer. "I'm not letting you go."

Nancy squinted at her husband, wondering whether he meant in this moment or in general. Her eyes flickered toward the door and she sighed, understanding there was no getting out of it now. "Did you read the manuscript?" Nancy asked.

"Yes, I read the manuscript," he said. "What choice did I have after receiving such a peculiar missive from my wife?"

Nancy nodded, picturing the words she'd written and rewritten a dozen times.

Prod—
I have finished my new book, which makes two completed in the past twelve months. Before I come home, I need you to see the first. Mollie has it at the shop. You may read it there, under her supervision.
Talk soon.
-NR

"I won't ask if you enjoyed it," she said.

"Of course I didn't. It's utter bullshit," Prod said.

"Really." Nancy eyed her husband, unsure what she hoped to glean from the situation she'd provoked.

"Whose idea was it?" he asked. "This Lea person?"

"The idea was mine," Nancy said. "But Lea did help, if you can call it that."

"You didn't give her any money, I hope."

"I promised her a share of royalties, if it was a success. That's neither here nor there, as I doubt I'll end up publish—"

"Royalties!" Prod roared. "Are you mad? That woman scammed you!"

"How could she have scammed me?" Nancy said. "When it was *my* autobiography, *my* version of the war? I haven't given her a pound, and I likely never will. Really, Peter, you know how poor I am. I'm the last person anyone should bother extorting!"

"She doesn't know that. I'm sure she saw this house, with its ballrooms and chandeliers." Prod waved his arms overhead. "She heard your posh accent and sensed your kind soul—"

"That is sweet."

"Nancy!" he shouted. "Don't be stupid! I'm not complimenting you! There's no other explanation for her involvement because I did not father that child. Honestly. Do you think I'd be attracted to a teenage cockney? Give me some credit."

"Well, your romantic tastes *are* very perplexing," Nancy said.

"This is absurd!" He pitched forward, trying to tower over Nancy, as if he'd forgotten how tall she was. In fairness, his girl-friends were always on the miniature side. "What did she say, specifically? About me and this baby?"

"Well, she wasn't *specific*," Nancy said. "I told her I wasn't angry about whatever happened between the two of you, and she thanked me repeatedly but never seemed keen to discuss it in any great detail."

"Goddammit, Nancy!" he shouted. "So *you're* the one who made it up?"

"She was not my only source of information," Nancy said as

a departing couple shuffled into the hall. She paused, offering a somber farewell as they fetched their coats.

"What was this source?" Prod asked, after they left.

"A man I've known my entire life. He's very high up in the government."

"Let me guess." Peter rolled his eyes. "Gladwyn Jebb. I presume he came up with this yarn while getting drunk and shooting things with Lord Redesdale?"

"This has nothing to do with Farve."

Peter exhaled, both hands on his hips. "It's odd," he said. "I'm not terribly upset. More so, I'm concerned about your mental state. A resting cure might do you some good, bring you back to your senses. Switzerland, perhaps? Shall I call Mummy's doctor?"

"You're precisely as awful as everyone thinks you are," Nancy seethed.

"Darling, the suggestion comes from a place of great care," Prod said. "You've been through a lot over the years. Your sisters' antics, your parents' separation, Tom's death. With your family, nothing's ever easy, and my sympathies run deep."

"That's a fine statement, coming from you," Nancy said. Living among the Mitfords could send almost anyone to the sanitorium, but the Rodds were no picnic themselves. At least Nancy's family liked her, as opposed to Peter's, who excluded him from most major holidays. "What I find deeply intriguing," Nancy said, "is how anxious you are about a book you've described as utter bullshit."

"I'm anxious because people will think it's true!" Prod said. "Never mind the implication that I'd impregnate a child, I come off as a heartless prick. You described me as...what was it?" He twisted his face, trying to recollect. "Something about a ship in a lonely ocean, crashing into people onshore."

"You don't *realize* there are people onshore."

"Readers will think I don't care for you at all. It's just...not true." Prod's chin trembled. His shoulders slumped, and his skin seemed to lose most of his tan.

Nancy shook her head. Speaking of maritime metaphors, she was suddenly at sea.

"What else would I think?" she said, after several minutes passed. "You went to war for *three* years. You wrote me twice, sent flowers once, and visited not a single time. Everyone thought I was such a dope, insisting the Guards never gave you enough leave to come home. Of course, they all knew the truth, including me."

"You didn't want me here! You were too busy with your Frogs!"

"I needed some company!"

"Another thank you to Gladwyn Jebb," Peter groused. "If I were a paranoid sort, I'd think he was actively trying to ruin my life. You're not really going to publish it, are you? This so-called autobiography?"

Nancy closed her eyes and let Hellbags's words run through her head. *Nancy, forget your sisters. Forget your parents, Prod, Heywood, everyone else. You have to figure out what* you *want.*

What Nancy wanted was to live in Paris, with the Colonel, and introduce the Radletts to the world. The autobiography didn't seem important now, and Nancy didn't feel the same as she had back when she told Hellbags she couldn't stomach it all going up in flames.

You'll figure out a way to make use of it, Hellbags had declared in her strident, raspy voice. Now, as Nancy stood in the entryway, facing off against Prod, she was struck by an idea. Maybe the memoir *was* the answer, albeit not in the way she'd envisioned.

"I won't publish it," Nancy said, leveling her gaze on Prod's.

"Oh, thank God!" Peter shouted toward the ceiling, as if the good Lord himself granted this wish. "I may not have married the prettiest Mitford, but I did get the one who is least deranged."

"You might want to hear me out first," Nancy said. "I won't publish the book, but you won't stop me from moving to Paris."

"Paris!?" Prod's prior exaltation came crashing down. "No. Absolutely not."

"Then I'll have to publish the book, I suppose."

"I'll never agree to a divorce," he said. "No matter how many threats you make."

Nancy shrugged. "I don't need a divorce," she said. "I only want to leave. Heywood is letting me open a shop on the Seine."

"In exchange for five thousand pounds," Prod said. "Where will you get the money if you don't publish the memoir?"

"I wrote two books, remember?" Nancy said, starting to smile.

"Your second book." Prod snickered, and the hairs on Nancy's arms rose. "You're very amusing, darling. Very droll. But people don't want to read about a bunch of bratty aristocrats tumbling around in some broken-down manse. Be realistic. It's time to forget Paris, and silly books. It's time to restart our lives as husband and wife. You really can't afford to do anything else."

"How perfectly Prod," Nancy said, and she had half a mind to laugh. "Who needs romance when you can have grim practicality? There are exactly two choices, my darling. Agree to my conditions or don't."

"It's not going to happen like this," Prod said as a jagged vein bulged on the left side of his head. "You are not publishing that book, and I'll never agree to a divorce."

"I don't need a divorce," Nancy reminded him. "I only want Paris."

"I'll countenance no more of this conversation," Peter said, and put on his hat. "Poor Tom. He'd be so disappointed to see you like this."

"Tom couldn't stand you!" Nancy screamed as Peter stormed out the front door. She had to admit, the red satin lining of his coat really enhanced the drama of his exit.

"Absolute bastard," somebody said, and Nancy whipped around.

At the writing desk, in the alcove beneath the stairs, a lonely figure sat. A cane was propped up on the wall next to him.

"Farve!" Nancy said, and rushed to his side. "Don't startle me like that! I have a delicate pulse! Gosh, I hope you didn't see that little squabble. It was just Peter being Peter. You know how he is. Such a Counter-Hon."

"Koko—"

"Forget all that," Nancy said. "You were absolutely wonderful with Diana, especially after all she's put this family through. It was beautiful to witness. The living embodiment of unconditional love."

"Thanks," he muttered, reaching into his desk. "On the topic of wayward daughters, I have something for you." Farve extended an envelope toward Nancy, and she stepped back. "Due to my myriad financial follies, and your profligate spouse, you've had to cobble together a life without any assistance."

"And without a proper education," Nancy said, because she couldn't help herself.

"Too true," Farve said. "And I know you despise me for it. This won't make up for all you've not had—" he flapped the envelope "—but it's five thousand pounds. Enough for your investment in the shop."

"Five thousand!" Nancy cried. "You can't possibly have that much to spare!"

"I'm an old man," Farve said, "with not many years left."

"FARVE!"

"I've always regretted not being able to do more for my first-born, my favorite child."

Nancy snuffled, knowing she was only his favorite now that Tom was gone.

"Of all my children," he said, "I've always enjoyed your company the most."

"That's because we share the same offensive temperament, according to Evelyn Waugh."

"That man is a damned sewer," Farve snapped. He scowled briefly before his face softened again. "My little Koko, my blob-nose. If you want to go to Paris, don't wait around. Use this money and become Heywood's partner, instead of his employee."

"You really wouldn't be upset if I moved to France?"

"Of course I'd be upset," he said. "I loathe Frogs of every shape and stripe, but London is in shambles. It's hollowed out, a wreck of a place. Our family, I'm afraid, is much the same."

Farve's unparalleled generosity bewildered Nancy. It rendered her mute, and she worried she might not ever be able to speak without sobbing. Finally, Nancy closed her eyes and accepted the envelope.

"Start a new life, Nancy. Go to your—" Farve made a face like he might throw up "—Colonel. Go and...be happy."

Nancy studied the man, the brutish "Uncle Matthew," bludgeoner of Germans and scolder of little girls. "We probably won't marry," she said. "The Colonel and me. Peter will never agree to a divorce, and the French are very uptight about mistresses, and wives, and living arrangements."

"Everyone in France is terrible, and I'd prefer not to attend another wedding in my lifetime, so that suits me just fine. Go, Nancy. Enjoy your life."

"Farve. I can't..." Nancy said.

She tried to return the gift, but he swatted it away. "You can, and you must," he said. "If you give a shilling of it to Peter Rodd, however, I'll never speak to you again."

"I wouldn't dream of it," Nancy said, and put a hand to her heart.

"Paris." Farve grunted. "I don't know what you see in the goddamned place. It's filled with aesthetes and Catholics and other unsavory types. But you've always had your own mind. If you want to go to Paris, now is the time. There aren't many chances in life, and you have to take them where you can."

Tuesday Afternoon

G. Heywood Hill Ltd.

Katie arrives carrying a tin of home-baked cookies, like a soccer mom or an officious lady from church.

"I leave tomorrow night," she says to Felix, proffering her gift. "This is a small thanks for all you've done."

Felix peeks inside. "Christmas biscuits! Excellent."

"In full disclosure," Katie says, "the Hawkins-Whitsheds' concierge made them, but only after Jojo found me pawing through her cabinets for ingredients. I did supervise, though. The guy thought he was going to make some sage-and-onion shortbread bullshit, but I stepped in."

Chuckling, Felix takes a stained-glass cookie. As he chews, he studies Katie with one brow perfectly raised.

"What?" she says. "What are you looking at?"

"This gift is a surprise," Felix says after swallowing. He extends the tin in her direction. "I was certain you still thought I was holding back."

Katie chooses a ginger biscuit dipped in white chocolate, the one she'd been eyeing all day. "Not at all," she says. "You'd have no reason to lie, especially now that we both know I was right about Simon."

"You love to win arguments, don't you?"

"Who doesn't?" Katie says. "Plus, you helped with a whole lot more than a manuscript. You, this shop, it's given me direction in a way I never could've imagined."

"That's very kind of you," Felix says.

As he sets the tin on the counter, Katie pulls a small stack of stickers from her tote. They bear her signature and the Antilles Press logo. "These are also for you," she says. "Bookplates. I signed them in case you ever stock my novels again. No pressure, though! I won't check or anything!"

"I will gladly take these," Felix says, and swipes the bookplates from her hand. "And they'll go to terrific use. I've ordered multiple copies of all three of your novels from the publisher. They should arrive any day."

"Now I feel like I should've brought more cookies," Katie says, blushing hard.

Felix laughs again. "The real question is whether there'll be a new Katharine Cabot book soon," he says. "After my customers read the others, they'll be clamoring for a fourth."

"Actually, I wanted to talk to you about that," Katie says, offering a feeble smile.

"Oh, dear, not a new odyssey, is it?" he says. "Should I sit down? Fetch the keys to the storage room?"

"No. Not yet, anyway. You see, I'm working on a new idea," she says, speaking rapidly and without taking a breath. "It's sort of a retelling of *The Pursuit of Love*. I've written three thousand words, which doesn't sound like a lot, but it's only been a day. What do you think?"

"A modern retelling of *The Pursuit of Love* is brilliant," Felix says, "and I'd love to read your version of it."

Katie puts her hands together as if praying. She releases a long exhale, and practically everything else she's been holding in for a week. "I'm so relieved you approve," she says. "Thank you."

"You must return to London for a signing," Felix says. "I

recognize it's a long trip, but I hope you'll make an exception, just for Heywood Hill."

He winks, and Katie's phone buzzes in her hand. "I'll do whatever I can to come back," she says, her eyes skimming the screen.

The incoming text is from Simon. It's a picture accompanied by a message—something about "one final puzzle piece...even if a thousand more remain lost."

"Anyhow," Katie says, slipping the phone into her bag. "I can't thank you enough. Heywood Hill feels like a turning point. Jojo was right; the shop is pure magic."

"Even though you didn't find Simon Bailey's manuscript?"

"Yes, even so," Katie says.

"Well, Katharine Cabot, it's been delightful getting to know you," Felix says. "And if I happen upon anything else you might need, I'll contact you immediately."

Katie smiles, amazed to feel tears pricking her eyes. As they say goodbye, Felix does the last thing Katie would've expected. He throws open his arms and welcomes her into a hug.

25 April 1945
Dear Lea,

First, my apologies for the long silence. I hope you didn't think I'd fallen off my perch!

I wanted to let you know I've decided not to publish my autobiography, after all. The timing doesn't seem right, nor the subject, and the entire world has changed since I began. In fact, I plan to publish an entirely different book. Enclosed is a small thanks for your contribution, even if I had to drag it out of you.

You're welcome to keep the parts of the manuscript you have. Who knows, maybe my novel will be such a hit those pages will one day be worth something. A girl can dream!

On the topic of exciting news, Charles Worthington (Danette's eldest) tells me you're engaged! And to a vicar—how very countrified! I send all my best wishes, and my best to Emma, too. Everything has worked out for you, and I'm thrilled.

One last thing. Whatever mistakes you've made, whatever secrets you've kept, or lies or truths you've told, don't let these drag you down. When it comes to you and me, all is forgiven.

Love from
Nancy

August 1945

G. Heywood Hill Ltd.

Nancy bounced into the shop wearing sunglasses and an oversized hat. She was in a gay mood, even with Eddy, Evelyn, Hellbags, and Jim flanked around the fireplace looking like a klatch of malcontents waiting for an overdue train.

"Hello, friends!" Nancy called out. "Can you believe this terrible weather? It's so windy and dry. It's as though London never wants anyone to be comfortable for more than a minute or two."

"What is happening here?" Eddy said as he studied Nancy, his top lip curled. "Are you wearing a disguise?"

"It's called *fashion*, darling," Nancy said. She popped off her sunglasses and brand-new hat—a straw affair with immense velvet bows—and tossed them as well as her handbag onto a nearby chair.

"I'm glad we arrived ONE HOUR AGO," Jim grouched. "I thought this was supposed to be a farewell party, yet the guest of honor was on the lam."

Mollie peered around the corner. "We've all been terrifically concerned," she said.

"Goodness, Mollie, you, too? I told you I had some bits of last-minute business, though it's ever so nice to be missed!"

Nancy turned back toward her friends. "I do extend my *greatest* apologies. A delay could not be avoided. I was at Drummonds, seeing about my passport and exit papers. Apparently, they were trying to be as inefficient as possible, and to wild success. One more stamp from the Foreign Office, and it's off to France!"

Nancy's dreams, out of reach for so long, were on the brink of coming true. Within weeks she'd be in Paris, and *The Pursuit of Love* would publish at the end of the year. Nancy had the money to do what she wanted, thanks to Farve, and a two-hundred-fifty-pound book advance, which she considered enormous. She'd mailed half to Lea, since she didn't anticipate ever putting out their war memoir.

Thanks also went to Peter, who relented to Nancy's plan under three conditions: Nancy never demanded a divorce, the memoir would remain locked up, and he could stay on at Blomfield Road. Peter probably got the better end of the stick but, when it came to Paris, Nancy would give anything.

It wasn't merely Nancy's life that was falling into place, but the world at large. Hitler was dead, her friends were coming home, and last week peace was officially declared. While Evelyn had celebrated by being drunk from eight o'clock in the morning until midnight, Nancy and Hellbags swarmed with the masses outside Buckingham Palace, chanting for hours for the King and Queen to appear. The royal couple came out soon after midnight and treated everyone to ninety seconds of listless hand-waving before slipping back inside.

"The best night of my life!" Helen declared.

Nancy wouldn't have figured her for packing in among the hoi polloi, but Hellbags relished the bonhomie.

Jim and Eddy had been less enthused by the day's events. The relentless drizzle, crowded streets, and lack of buses vexed Jimmy, and Eddy's stomach had gone into full revolt after he ate an éclair.

"How has everyone been enjoying the peace?" Nancy said,

and sat on the arm of Evelyn's chair. "Isn't it incredible? Some mornings I wake up and can't believe the thing is done."

"Nothing is over," Jim said. "The world has been left a victim of chaos and heinous turpitude. The treachery will go on and on."

"That's my sunshine," Nancy said with a grin.

"And people like Nancy aren't helping things," Evelyn said.

"Oh, really? What have I done now?"

Evelyn snatched Nancy's handbag from the chair. "What's yours is now mine," Evelyn said. "It's official. Labour has begun."

"I see," Nancy said. "Socialism, all that. I was fearfully pleased with the election results. It's time for this country to move forward."

"I hate to agree with Evelyn," Hellbags said. "The only reason you can be so blithe is because you're leaving."

"Ten thousand votes against Churchill in his own constituency," Evelyn griped, "for a man who's a lunatic. The British citizens have demonstrated new levels of stupidity. Another tithing for me!" Evelyn swiped Nancy's hat and plopped it atop his head. Between the ribbons and his jowls, he rather resembled a Victorian spinster. "Jim agrees with me, don't you, old chap?" Evelyn said. "About the results?"

Jim shrugged but also shook his head. "My delight in Churchill's defeat is equaled only by my despair that the Socialists have won."

"That's our Jimmy," Hellbags said. "Able to view anything from multiple bad sides."

"You do realize," Evelyn said to Nancy, "that this book you're planning to release puts on a pedestal the old guard, the landowning gentry. When you voted Socialist, you voted against your own self-interest."

"I'm not concerned," Nancy said. "The Radletts are hardly old guard and, if anything, people will relish their struggles. So, who brought the champagne?"

"I did!" Hellbags chirped. "And a lot of it. Cleaned Johnny out of his best collection. He's going to be furious." She was positively lit from within.

"And the memoir?" Evelyn said as he tried to swat the dangling bows from his periphery. "That's well and truly done?"

Nancy nodded. "I've moved on," she said. She'd debated sending the manuscript to Lea, but the girl was married and likely didn't want to get dragged back to the past. For now, it remained locked in the storage room, a bit of insurance, should Nancy need it. "I've come to realize," she said, "not every book should be published, and the autobiography did have its use. It got me writing again, which paved the way for my Radletts, and for Paris."

"I've never met anyone so excited to leave civilization," Jim said.

"There are things I'll miss," Nancy said. "My friends most of all. I'll also miss our customers, and Mollie, and the midnight salons. Of course, I'll have to ring Evelyn regularly, just to hear him complain about his children and brag about his sales."

"*Brideshead Revisited* is doing tremendously well," Evelyn said, in case they hadn't caught the news any of the prior thirty-seven times he'd brought it up. "I've become a literary star!"

"I still don't understand," Eddy said. "How can you leave your home, a place you've lived forty years, to be with a man you were only involved with for a few months?"

"Our 'involvement,' as you call it, has lasted three years and counting," Nancy said. "Mollie! Yoo-hoo! Would you mind getting everyone champagne? There are coupes in the storage room."

After passing Nancy a slightly winnowed look, Mollie hurried off.

"Though I don't agree with your decision to leave," Evelyn said, "the Radletts are something to celebrate. Writing half of a good book is harder than most people assume. Well done!" He lifted an imaginary glass.

"God, Evelyn, you're the worst," Helen said.

"What? I just said parts of it are good."

Nancy tittered. "When I move to Paris," she said, "I really need to befriend one of those jolly drunks people are always going on about. What must that be like?"

"I think you have to go to Ireland for that," Hellbags offered.

"I was complimenting you!" Evelyn snapped. "The book is actually quite strong in places, albeit planless, hasty, and flat in others. It's probably too late for edits to this edition, but maybe before the Penguins come out?"

"I've told you," Nancy said. "I won't be doing that."

"The chief difference between a journalist and a real writer is that a writer cares to go on improving."

"Call me a journalist, then. There are worse things."

"I give up!" Evelyn said. He tossed up his hands, knocking Nancy's hat from his head. "I've done all I can! You say I'm your mentor—"

"No, I do not."

"Yet you never take my advice! I came up with the title, didn't I?"

"Yes." Nancy smiled. "And I appreciate it."

"*My Cousin Linda*. God-awful." Evelyn sighed. "Why won't you listen to me on the rest? *Brideshead* has sold twenty thousand copies and everyone loves it, here and abroad."

"I doubt everyone loves it," Eddy said.

"Perhaps not people who are embittered by class resentment, but they don't count."

"Do you ever just *shut up*?" Hellbags said.

"It's as though you are trying to sabotage your career," Evelyn went on. "First, you refuse to make the appropriate edits."

"I thought you were 'giving up,'" Jim pointed out.

"Second, this Paris nonsense," he said. "Only you would leave England after telling everyone it was their obligation to stay during the war. Only you would leave after voting Socialist, and rendering it uninhabitable for the rest of us."

"Goodness, Evelyn, I didn't know you'd miss me so much," Nancy said, and Hellbags snorted. "I'm rather tingly at the thought."

"I'm warning you," Evelyn said as Mollie and Handy approached with the champagne. "If you move to France, you'll never write a decent novel again. You are radically English, and even the most bookish minds decay in exile."

"I wouldn't say radically."

"You *are* England," Evelyn insisted. "And England is you. That's what your entire book is about! If you want to write another masterpiece, you cannot change your environment."

"Masterpiece? The last I heard, I'd written only half of a good book."

"You know I think it's genius," he mumbled, and for a moment Nancy thawed.

"Thank you, Evelyn," she said, quietly. "That means a great deal."

"What does Prod have to say about all this?" he asked.

"Don't worry about old Prod," Nancy said. "We've come to an arrangement and, anyway, he's off to Spain. He's hoping for a revolution, which would mean loads of refugees for him to save. A real dream scenario."

"Brilliant." Evelyn grunted. "Laura and I are going to Spain next month. Do you think you could ask him to postpone his invasion?"

"I'll try, but he is very hard to reason with."

"Don't go," Evelyn said, pleading. "You can't. This country has nourished you. It's turned you into the writer you've become. If you want to survive, you must maintain an English diet."

"An English diet?" Nancy said, laughing, as Mollie passed around the champagne. "Don't be silly. Everybody knows that if a girl wants nourishment, Paris is the place to feast."

Wednesday Afternoon

London Heathrow Airport

As they follow the signs marked "Departures," Katie's heart sits in her throat. She's trying to think of a clever way to say farewell, but keeps drawing a blank. Nothing too jokey, nothing too meaningful. It's an impossible note to hit.

"That must've been their last contact," Simon says.

It takes Katie a second to remember what they're talking about. "Oh. Right," she says, and clears her froggy throat. "The April letter. I can see why your grandmother was put off by it. Nancy was a little dismissive, then she bailed for Paris."

"I suppose it was a bit curt," Simon agrees as he pulls alongside the curb. "Though, to be fair, Nancy was going through a lot at the time. Her brother died. She was waiting to hear about the book, and figuring out a way to get to Paris."

"Look who's defending Nancy now." Katie smiles slyly and hops out of the car. As Simon pulls her bag from the "boot," she tries not to think about the fact that he left work early, drove ninety minutes from Burwash, and another thirty to the airport. How is she going to end this? Kissing someone at an airport feels like a lot, but she can't tell him to "take care" like he's a Lyft driver she just met. "Next I'm going to change your beliefs about happy endings," Katie says, peering into her laptop bag to check for her passport again.

"Not likely," Simon says, and her suitcase thumps onto the ground. "Hey. I have something for you."

Katie glances up as he reaches into his pocket.

"It's nothing big," he says. "A trinket to commemorate your trip."

In Simon's outstretched palm sits a small, rectangular object that's red, and silver, and glittery. Katie stares a beat, trying to make sense of it. "Are you serious?" she says, starting to tear. "A Christmas ornament?"

"The phone box you were eyeing at that terrible carnival."

"I didn't see you buy it!"

"I went back," he says.

Sniffling, Katie takes the ornament from his hand. "This is one of the nicest presents I've ever been given," she says.

"You need to get new friends," he says, blushing, looking away.

Katie wraps her fingers around the ornament, holding it against her heart before laying it gently in her bag.

"Any idea when you'll be back?" Simon asks. "Or is that an obnoxious question to ask when you're literally still here?"

"I'm not sure." Katie smiles through the still-bubbling tears. "Soon, hopefully. Jojo's hatching all kinds of plans."

In truth, Jojo has only one plan and it is fairly well mapped out: Katie will let her house, obtain a visa, and stay six months in Jojo's guest suite. Her monthly rent will be in the exact amount of "helping with Clive."

"This is a horrible deal for you!" Katie had balked when Jojo brought it up. "I don't know the first thing about kids, and there's no way I can help with homework."

"Clive does *not* need help in school," Jojo said. "All I'm asking is that you entertain him, and partially bear the brunt of his monologues about Minecraft and organizing iPhone components."

"I'm not sure..."

"Why not? It's what you've been doing for the past ten days," Jojo said. "He's attached to you, and I'm clearly struggling to give him the attention he needs. My patience—" she pinched her fingers together "—razor thin. If anything, you'd be doing *me* a favor, instead of the other way around."

"I guess I can see about renting out the house..." Katie said, her pulse racing as she said the words.

"What a genius idea!" her agent said, when Katie called to float the concept. "I love it! Especially if you write the book while you are in London. It'll be great backstory when it comes time to promote."

Katie hasn't mentioned any of this to Simon yet. She is happier, more clearheaded than she's ever been, and though Katie's not afraid of the future anymore, she's not looking for any jinxes, or ways to tempt fate. She'll tell Simon later, after a few more ducks are lined up.

"So, this book you're writing," Simon says, scanning the area for any security guards who might tell him to move on. "Does it have a theme?"

Katie thinks about this. "It'd be similar to one of the main themes in *The Pursuit of Love*, I guess. Something can have meaning, even if you have little to show for it. In other words, a road can go nowhere and still be worth the trip."

"A good theme for a book, and for life."

"Also," Katie says, and gives him a pointed look, "a departure or ending can still qualify as happily-ever-after."

Simon smirks. "Don't mince words, Cabot. Just say death. You really are dark up there," he says, and pats her head. "Linda Radlett did not have a happy ending, but at least Nancy Mitford got hers."

"As far as we know," Katie says. "I do think it was the *right* ending, for her."

"And how will *your* book end?" Simon asks. "Which plotline will work out? Pray nothing that involves the Gestapo, or the expiration of all main characters."

"Not *everybody* dies. Not Fanny, or Uncle Matthew."

"Thank God for small mercies."

"I have no idea how it will end," Katie says. "This time, I'll figure it out as I go. As for the perfect ending…" She inhales and throws on a smile. "I'll know it when I see it."

It's all she has, but it's enough, for now.

April 1946

The British Embassy, Paris

It was a delicious spring evening at one of the most magnificent homes in Paris: 39 rue du Faubourg Saint-Honoré, otherwise known as the British Embassy.

Nancy's close friends Duff and Diana Cooper had moved in after liberation, when Duff was appointed ambassador, and the Embassy had become one of Nancy's favorite haunts. Tonight, the festivities were bright as ever, thanks to the company of an old friend.

"I'm honored you made time to stop on your way back from Nuremberg," Nancy said. "I know how much you hate Paris."

"It's not the place," Evelyn said. "It's the people. The French have been destroying Europe for the past two hundred years." He glanced around at the Louis XV architecture, the Borghese decorations. "Though, I must admit, this is a beautiful home. How is it the Germans never wrecked it?"

"They were probably preserving it for some evil-doing Fascist to keep as his weekend pied-à-terre," Nancy said. "Apparently, the place was a disaster when Duff and Diana arrived. No water, no electricity, and filled to the rafters with furniture left by fleeing Nazis—pianos, hat stands, bath mats, boxing gloves, much of it stolen or looted, no doubt."

Because Diana was Diana, the Coopers were hosting garden parties and nightly free-for-all drinks within weeks of moving in. The aim—Franco-English relations, much strained due to the animosity between Churchill and de Gaulle. It was the only situation in which Evelyn made for an easier date than the Colonel, who usually spent the evening pointing out collaborators, while Nancy spent it avoiding confrontations.

"Is that Philippe de Rothschild?" Evelyn said. "I have a few opinions for him, about what constitutes good wine. Oh, my! It's the Windsors." He made a face. "David looks like a balloon, and Wallis like the remains of a small bird."

"Drat!" Nancy said, ducking behind his left shoulder. "Don't let them see me."

"What do you have against the Windsors?"

"The Colonel *loathes* them," Nancy hissed. "They're such Nazis and are always ordering us to get married. 'Look at us,' they say. 'It's the only means to happiness!' Meanwhile, they're practically ravaged by misery."

"Didn't they give your Radletts to friends and family for Christmas?" he asked.

"Yes. Lowbrow circles, to be sure," Nancy said as she stepped out from behind him.

Evelyn eyed her. "This is how you spend your time in Paris?" he said. "Hiding from acquaintances?"

"Sometimes." Nancy adjusted her skirt. "I also attend cocktail parties, meet friends for lunch, and shop."

Evelyn chortled. "Shopping. Yes. Hopefully not always to the extent you did today."

"I didn't buy that much," Nancy said. "Only three day dresses, one evening dress, and a coat. Oh, yes, and that wonderful printed suit. It's heaven to have the money to accompany my taste for spending it. No more staring glumly at hundred-pound dresses at Lelong."

"I must hand it to you," Evelyn said, craning, searching for a waiter with more champagne. "I knew your Radletts would do well, but I did not expect them to soar."

"Even Farve loved it," Nancy said. "That he read it is a miracle. You know how he brags about never touching a book. Naturally, he did offer a few critiques and areas for improvement."

"He wished to be portrayed as a peck less monstrous?"

"Oh, he didn't mind." Nancy flicked a hand. "His problems were more along the lines of he didn't buy his stock whips in Canada, they were a gift, things like that. See, Evelyn? I didn't need to make your silly edits. People adore *The Pursuit of Love* as is."

Most people, though not everyone. Some cow at the *Spectator* described the novel as "not great literature or great wit but otherwise all right," and the *New Statesman* deemed it rewardingly funny in places, though this was "the last, and indeed the most, one can say of it." The Hons cupboard made Cyril Connolly and his Bloomsbury group "want to vomit" and even the Colonel had a few gripes, chief among them the book's dedication, and how it drew the notice of the press.

HITLER'S MISTRESS'S SISTER DEDICATES DARING BOOK TO M. PALEWSKI

Historically, the Colonel had taken most of the punches thrown at de Gaulle. The press already loved to mock him, calling him *l'empereur*, or *la lavande*, due to his lavender cologne, and the timing of the headline was not ideal. It came out right as de Gaulle and the Colonel were stepping down.

"How could you do this to me?" the Colonel wailed.

Nancy made a show of sympathy, but didn't feel too badly,

in the end. Never had anyone been so ruffled to have a book named in their honor.

The Colonel's bruised feelings aside, Nancy didn't concern herself with criticisms or complaints. The proof was in the numbers, and the numbers were huge. More than two hundred thousand copies sold to date, and Nancy was currently negotiating film rights.

"Take no less than two thousand," Evelyn advised. "Five is the absolute most to expect. If you weren't such a Socialist, I'd tell you to split it over two payments, but I know how you love giving money to the government."

Brideshead Revisited had sold five hundred thousand copies, so Evelyn was still the one to beat, but he had a seven-month head start and Nancy was catching up.

"How does it feel?" Evelyn asked. "How does it feel to have everything you ever wanted?"

"As though every day is my birthday," Nancy said. "It's intoxicating, a whirl of triumph! Life with the Colonel is grand, the success is thrilling, and I live in the most charming flat. All this, and I spend my days in Paris. Can't you just?! Please, no pontificating about how much you hate it here. It's so much better than London, which was like living in the bottom of a well."

Evelyn rolled his eyes. "I've resigned myself to the truth. Your obsession with Paris is a pathological condition."

"You have to admit it's cheerier here," Nancy said. "London is doom and gloom, while Paris is bubbles and light. And the food! The glorious food! Everything cooked in butter and meat that's never seen a Frigidaire. It makes the Dorch and Ritz seem silly."

"I hate that you're so happy," Evelyn said, and his entire body sighed. "Heywood Hill is dull without you. I can't even go anymore, and I spend my days drunk, languishing in hotels and clubs. I've been praying you'd have second thoughts, and return home."

"You're some friend!"

"Can you blame me? Anyhow, it happened before."

"That was a different situation," Nancy said. "A different world."

When she'd come to Paris last September, Nancy was astonished to find a city that was poor, humiliated, pared to the bone. Because she wasn't French, or rich, Nancy couldn't get a ration card, or a reliable place to live. For weeks she was a vagabond, moving between borrowed rooms and dodgy hotels like the sort Oscar Wilde might've died in. The final straw came while Nancy was renting a flat inside a gray building that could've been mistaken for military barracks, had it more charm. One morning, Nancy went to heat a pannikin of water, only to discover a single egg sitting on the kitchen counter. She shrieked and whipped around to find a short, fat, bald man in his underclothes. He claimed to live there, too.

"Monsieur de Seyres is the lessee," the landlady said, when she came to sort it out. "I am sorry. There are no flats or hotels available in Paris, unless you are very rich."

At the time, Nancy wasn't even a little bit rich, having spent her advance on food and maintaining Prod at Blomfield full blast. Though she was supposed to be running Heywood Hill's Paris operations, no one in the London branch seemed to care. Heywood never answered her letters, and Mollie complained that Nancy's only achievement was to increase *her* workload. The five-thousand-pound investment felt like a farce, which just went to prove Farve's money always had a way of wasting itself. When all of these things came to a head, the Colonel was in Brussels, and due in Rhineland the next week, and Nancy had no choice but to sheepishly return home.

Claiming she was in London for the publication of *The Pursuit of Love*, Nancy went back to stocking books at Curzon Street and hanging about with Evelyn. Every once in a while, Nancy thumbed through the autobiography, pondering whether she'd have the nerve to publish it, should she need the money.

At the end of January, Nancy received the first piece of good news—royalties for the first three weeks of *Pursuit* were seven-hundred-fifty pounds, which was more than she'd earned on her four previous books combined. When Hamish announced a second printing, and a third, Nancy locked up the memoir for the last time and went to Paris for good.

After five published novels, Nancy finally figured it out. Thanks to the Colonel, she now knew to write from the heart. She knew to write her own story, instead of somebody else's.

"You don't really want me in London," Nancy said as they plucked glasses from a passing tray of champagne. "Imagine! Every day you'd be screaming at me that I can't be a shopgirl for the rest of my life."

"I suppose that's true." Evelyn paused and screwed up his mouth. "Well, what are you going to write now that you're a smash hit? You realize you've used up your two main plots in one book: Farve and Fabrice."

"I have more plots than that!" Nancy said, praying it was true. Half the problem with being a writer was that even once-in-a-lifetime success could feel like a failure, if enough time passed. "For now, I want to bask in the excitement. Don't worry, I won't let my mind decay in exile."

"Your mind is tops," Evelyn said, to Nancy's surprise. "You've proven me wrong and, regrettably, I have faith in you now."

"Aw, Evelyn, you're going to make me cry," Nancy said, and raised her glass. "Shall we cheer? To friendship, and love."

"To selling a million copies." Evelyn clinked her glass. "And writing enough books to keep you forever in charming flats and fashionable suits."

"Yes, cheers to all that! *Vive la France! Vive la littérature!*"

Thursday Morning

G. Heywood Hill Ltd.

As he stares at the stack on his desk, Felix assures himself he made the right call. Though he's no longer concerned about dodgy head teachers pulling grifts, showing Katharine Cabot this manuscript might've been a different strain of disaster. She is on the right track and needs to complete the story she's begun. Everybody knows writers are easily distracted, especially excitable ones like Katharine. More importantly, Felix can't go against the Duke's wishes, or the Duke's promises to Nancy. He can't break a generations-long vow to keep the manuscript secret.

Felix slides a rubber band around the pile. He hears footsteps as he rises to his feet.

"Felix!" Erin calls out. "Are you back there?"

He freezes, heart pattering. It's not quite panic, but something close. Felix glances at the manuscript once more, then scrambles to find a place for it in his desk.

"Yes, I'm here!" he says as the lock clicks.

Felix strides toward the door, confident that some stories are best left untold.

Dearest Hen
Nancy died in her sleep at 1:30PM yesterday.
The Colonel had been to see her in the morning & thought she recognised him.
Thank goodness it is over, she really had the most awful time any one can ever have had.

—Letter from Debo to Decca
1 July 1973

So many things come flooding to mind about her, such as Muv saying 'Nancy is a very curious character,' too true. The great regret being that she hadn't the strength to do the Memoirs, where said curiosity of character wld. have come out full force, don't you agree? But she did leave far more behind than most people, such as her smashing books & the general memorableness of her.

—Letter from Decca to Debo
2 July 1973

ACKNOWLEDGMENTS

As I write these acknowledgments in February 2021, exactly one year has passed since the idea for *The Bookseller's Secret* first sparked, which means this book was sold, written, edited, and re-edited (several times over) during a raging pandemic and non-stop political turmoil. It was a haul, one of the most grueling things I've ever done, and I hope to never again be able to say, "glad I turned in my edits this morning, before the insurrection."

I gave everything to this book, but could not have done it without serious heavy-lifting from others, first and foremost Barbara Poelle, my agent of over thirteen years. Cheerleader, truth-teller, idea-generator, sounding board—there are a thousand reasons this book is dedicated to her.

Enormous thanks to my incredibly diligent editor Melanie Fried, who put her full heart and mind into every comment. Thank you for your tireless effort, lack of sleep, and for making my day (my month, my year) one Friday in late March, when the world seemed to be falling apart. I'm so happy to be working together again after all these years! Thanks also to my brilliant copy editor, Bonnie Lo, and to Justine Sha, Pamela Osti, and Susan Swinwood for their enthusiasm and bright ideas. I'm grateful to be part of the Graydon House team (and how about this gorgeous cover?!? Thank you, Kathleen Oudit and Elita Sidiropoulou.). A million thanks must also go to my wonderful friend and Graydon House sister, Brenda Janowitz.

Big buckets of love to my writerly support system, especially Liz Fenton. The early-in-pandemic Zoom calls with Liz, Lisa

Steinke, Sue Meissner, Kate Quinn, and Kristina McMorris, got me through. Shout out also to my other San Diego sisters Shilpi Gowda and Tatjana Soli and, as always, Tammy Greenwood-Stewart.

What would I do without Lisa Kanetake, who is some combination of friend, sister, and co-parent? Most of the best memories from the past decade star Lisa and her family (hello to Audrey, Emily, and Charles Bergan!). Make no mistake, Lisa, your generosity and friendship helped write this book, and all the ones before it.

Thank you to Karen Landers and Lauren Gist, who've been propping me up since middle school. I also want to give a special mention to our fantasy football league, "Pretty in Pigskin," led by the incomparable Renn Plsek. Kira Haley—I hope you don't mind me using your very clever team name. Thank you also to Erin Holl, excellent tennis partner and even better friend. Could you picture yourself working at Heywood Hill?

My hilarious and brilliant nephew Will Wheatley inspired Clive Hawkins-Whitshed's better traits, including his technology acumen and entrepreneurial spirit. His mom, my sister Lisa Wheatley, is the original inventor of "Junk Trash Crap." Because of her, I love writing about sisterly relationships. Though we're not as colorful as the Mitford girls, we do have a shining favorite boy around thanks to our brother, Brian Gable. I'm so grateful for you both, and also our parents Tom and Laura Gable, who are always supportive and gave us the best possible start in life.

To my favorite pair of sisters… Paige and Georgia Bilski. What can I say, other than you two make mothering and pandemic-surviving almost easy? Thank you for being the models for the near-perfect Dani and Clem (with their near-perfect hair), and for all the Gen Z expressions. Poggers! Paige, thank you for helping with French. Georgia, it's because of you Jojo has such dedication to her sport. Your tenacity blows me away. Thank you to my comfort animal, my very own "Thai trash dog," Winnie, otherwise known as my favorite child (kidding, girls!).

Dennis, we're on book number five and I still can't think of a way to adequately thank you for everything you've done—for me, for them, for us. This has been a hard year, and living with a writer on a tight deadline is like walking into a different climate every day. I did not make things easy for you, but you somehow made things easy for me, despite your own very big job.

Finally, I must thank the readers, who've kept me going, even when I wanted to give up. To everyone who's dropped me a note, or asked when the next book comes out, thank you for reminding me I am a writer, after all.

AUTHOR'S NOTE

My interest in Nancy Mitford began twenty years ago, when I read *The Sisters: The Saga of the Mitford Family* by Mary S. Lovell. How could I not be compelled by that band of girls? As my fictional Nancy says, "a Nazi, a Communist, and several Fascists in one family tree."

The Sisters drew me into the Mitfords' incredible world and soon I was reading everything I could about them. Of all the books I picked up, *The Pursuit of Love* was far and away my favorite. I felt an immediate kinship with the way Nancy wrote and thought about things. The book feels so thoroughly modern, it's hard to believe it was written over seventy-five years ago.

Most biographies don't explore Nancy's years at the bookshop in great detail, making it a juicy area to mine for fiction. This part of her life is such a unique blend of the unimaginable (staying in London during the Blitz) and the relatable (Nancy doubting herself and her career), and shows Nancy Mitford at the precipice of stardom. When *The Pursuit of Love* was published in December 1945, it was every bit the success she dreamed, even though, or maybe because, the novel centered on a world that was disappearing.

In 1949, Nancy published the sequel, *Love in a Cold Climate*, in which Cousin Fanny narrates another family's story. Next came *The Blessing* (1951), which many view as an attempt to explain Nancy's enduring love affair with the Colonel. Five more books followed, including four biographies and one more novel—*Don't Tell Alfred* (1960), the final book in the Radlett trilogy.

Although Nancy Mitford wrote over eight thousand letters in her lifetime, there are yearlong gaps in the correspondence that has been made publicly available, including while she worked at Heywood Hill. It's in these gaps that I let my imagination run. Nancy did host refugees at Rutland Gate, including a pregnant sixteen-year-old, and some of these refugees went to her friend Lady Diana Worthington's home (renamed "Danette" in the novel), Weston Manor. Though Lady Worthington and her husband died in the ways described in the book, I don't know whether Nancy stayed in contact with the sixteen-year-old, or any other refugee. Lea and Emma are entirely fictional.

Nancy spoke often of writing her memoirs, but there's no evidence of a "missing manuscript" (though, as a fan, I'd like to imagine one exists). Throughout the book, I used snippets from Nancy's many letters to mimic her language and verve, though mostly I had her speak the words instead of writing them.

This is not a biography, and the point of a novel is to reflect the inherent truth of a situation, and not merely recite a list of facts. While the Nancy in my book does many things the real Nancy Mitford did not, I hope this novel is a reflection of the spectacular personality and wit of one of the most underrated authors of the twentieth century.

Below are real-life epilogues for several key characters.

NANCY (1904–1973)

When Nancy returned to Paris for the second time, the move would prove permanent. With money in the bank, Nancy settled in a flat on rue Bonaparte and, later, rue Monsieur. She would cite these as the happiest years of her life. In 1967, Nancy moved to Versailles, where she resided until her death.

In France, Nancy had a wide circle of friends, including intellectuals, artists, French nobility, and fellow English transplants. She relished her newfound fame and success, but this also made it more difficult to get rid of Prod. He refused a formal separation, and Nancy went on supporting him until 1957, when he finally agreed to a divorce.

One year before her death, the French government awarded Nancy with the Légion d'Honneur and the British government appointed her a Commander of the Order of the British Empire (CBE). Evelyn had been offered a CBE at one time but considered it a grave insult and turned it down.

Nancy experienced the first signs of cancer in 1968, though her doctors and sisters hid the diagnosis until the end. Around the time Nancy began feeling ill, the Colonel married Helen-Violette de Talleyrand-Périgord, thereby ending their nearly three-decade long relationship. Nancy would go on to battle cancer for many years, finally succumbing in 1973, at sixty-eight years old, a young age for a Mitford. Tom and Unity predeceased Nancy, but the remaining Hons outlived her by twenty to forty years. Nancy's tombstone reads "Nancy Mitford, Authoress, wife of Peter Rodd."

THE COLONEL (1901–1984)

Born into a Polish-Jewish family that settled in France, Gaston Palewski was educated at the École du Louvre, École Libre des Sciences Politiques, and the Sorbonne, with postgraduate studies at Oxford. His Air Force career proved his worth as a military man.

As in the book, the Colonel became General de Gaulle's *chef de cabinet* before ultimately resigning in January 1946, when de Gaulle stepped down as head of the French Provisional Government. The Colonel would go on to hold many positions of importance, both elected and appointed, including vice president of the National Assembly, ambassador to Italy, and several posts within Prime Minister Georges Pompidou's cabinet.

The Colonel was awarded many French decorations in his lifetime, including the Légion d'Honneur. He married Helen-Violette de Talleyrand-Périgord, duchesse de Sagan, in 1969, and visited Nancy on the last day of her life.

Gaston Palewski died of leukemia in 1984, at the age of eighty-three.

PETER RODD (1904–1968)

After Nancy moved to France, she still supported Prod, and he continued his longtime affair with Nancy's cousin, Adelaide Lubbock. Though he and Nancy were divorced for over ten years when he died, Peter's body was found in Malta with one of Nancy's letters clutched in his hand.

LADY HELEN DASHWOOD "HELLBAGS" (1899–1989)

Despite my best efforts, I couldn't dig up much on Lady Helen Dashwood, otherwise known as "Hellbags." The details in the book, including her orgies, her nickname, and her reputation as "the most beautiful brunette in London," are true to what I uncovered about the spirited, fiercely intelligent woman. Lady Montdore in *Love in a Cold Climate* is based on Hellbags.

JIM LEES-MILNE (1908–1997)

James Lees-Milne was instrumental in the transfer of country houses from private ownership to the National Trust, including Hellbags's West Wycombe. Dubbed by some as "the man who saved England," Jim was a prolific diarist and would go on to publish his journals along with many other books.

In 1951, Jim married Alvilde, Viscountess Chaplin, a prominent gardening and landscape expert. Both Jim and Alvilde were bisexual and she was said to have had affairs with many prominent women, including Eddy's cousin Vita Sackville-West. Jim and Alvilde remained married until her death in 1994. Jim passed away several years later, at the age of eighty-nine.

EVELYN WAUGH (1903–1966)

There is much to say about Nancy's rival, mentor, and favorite correspondent. Waugh was a social climber. He was drunken, snobbish, and rude. He hated his own children and feared the end of aristocracy.

A late-in-life Catholic convert, the ever-grumpy Waugh became a literary star when his book *Brideshead Revisited* was published in 1945. He wrote nearly twenty novels in his lifetime.

Evelyn married twice, first to the Hon. Evelyn Gardner, otherwise known as She-Evelyn, the model for the "Bolter" character in *The Pursuit of Love*. He married Laura Herbert in 1937, and together they had seven children, six of whom survived infancy.

Like most, Nancy found Evelyn vexing, but it's clear there was a deep love and respect between the two. When Nancy heard news of his passing on the French wireless, she was distraught. "Yes I'm in despair about Evelyn," she wrote to Decca, "he was such a close friend & I suppose knew more about me than anybody."

She added: "I'm burying my head in the sand & have bought a house in Versailles in which to moulder until I fall down dead as Debo's children confidently expect me to at any minute."

EDDY SACKVILLE-WEST (1901–1965)

Edward Charles Sackville-West, 5th Baron Sackville, lived a life of angst. Though he understood he should be grateful for the privilege he was born into, he felt incapable of true joy on account of his delicate constitution and generally poor disposition. A devotee of the occult, Eddy was every bit the hypochondriac as portrayed by his alter ego, Uncle Davey, in *The Pursuit of Love*.

Eddy was a novelist, music critic, and member of the House of Lords. He also served on the board of the Royal Opera House. At the age of sixty-three, Eddy died suddenly of asthma-induced cardiac failure at his house in Ireland. Along with Evelyn, Eddy was one of the few people in Nancy's circle whom she outlived.

HEYWOOD HILL EMPLOYEES

After a brief engagement to Jim Lees-Milne, Lady Anne Gathorne-Hardy married Heywood Hill in 1938. They would go on to have a second daughter in addition to Harriet, who was born during the war.

In the early nineties, Anne and Heywood sold their bookshop to Debo's husband, Andrew Cavendish, 11th Duke of Devonshire. Upon his death in 2004, his ownership passed to his son, Peregrine Andrew Morny Cavendish, 12th Duke of Devonshire, known as "Stoker." Heywood died in 1986, after a long battle with Parkinson's, and Anne lived on another twenty years, passing away in 2006 at the age of ninety-five.

Heywood hired Mollie Frieze-Green (or Friese-Green, the spelling varies) a bit later than my novel suggests. Though Mollie was single when hired, she'd eventually marry Handy, the new employee they took on at the end of the war.

THE MITFORDS

The bits I read made me think once again how ghastly all Mitfords *sound*, though of course in real life ha-ha they are ideal.
—Diana to Deborah, 11 August 1975

LORD (1878–1958) AND LADY (1880–1963) REDESDALE

Though Muv and Farve never repaired their relationship, they also never formally divorced. Following Tom's death, Lord Redesdale retreated to Inchkenneth, before ultimately moving to Redesdale in Northumberland, the family's ancestral home. Having never fully recovered from Tom's death, Farve died a recluse at the age of eighty.

Lady Redesdale cared for her injured daughter until Unity's death in 1948 and resided at Inchkenneth after Farve left. In early 1963, Nancy, Debo, Diana, and Pamela gathered on the wretched island to care for their eighty-three-year-old mum in her final days. In true Sydney fashion, she was furious with her daughters for "dragging her back from the grave."

Nancy would famously say that, although she respected Muv, she did not love her, for the simple fact Sydney never loved her in return. About this, Nancy claimed no ill will and believed it was well within a woman's right to like or dislike her children.

PAMELA (1907–1994)

Described as "relaxed and ordinary," Pamela was the rural Mitford, the sister who loved cooking, gardening, and animal husbandry. After the war, she and her husband, Derek Jackson, heir to the *News of the World* fortune, moved to Ireland as tax exiles. They divorced in 1951, after fifteen years of marriage, and Pamela became instantly wealthy. Derek would marry a total of six times.

Following their divorce, Pamela began a longtime affair with an Italian horsewoman, Giuditta Tommasi. Decca described this as Pamela becoming a "you-know-what-bian." Pamela died at the age of eighty-six due to a blood clot after a fall.

TOM (1909–1945)

As in the book, Tom Mitford died after being shot in Burma and contracting pneumonia in a field hospital. He'd chosen fighting in the Pacific Theater because he had so many German friends.

By all accounts, Tom was smart, talented, and charming. Sheilah Graham called him "one of the handsomest men I had ever seen." Tom was the ultimate "Hon," polite and courteous, and utterly comfortable in a house filled with girls. Despite this bright and sparkling façade, Tom had a dark side and endured many bouts of depression. It was said that nobody knew quite how he felt about anything.

DIANA (1910–2003)

After Nancy's death, Diana learned that her sister had reported her Fascist activities to the MI5 and Home Office at the war's onset. This was a stunning revelation but later documents revealed Diana's ex-father-in-law, Lord Moyne, also reported her "extremely dangerous character."

Following the war, Diana and Oswald Mosley maintained homes in Ireland, London, and Paris. Though known for entertaining, they were banned from all functions at the British Embassy and denied passports until 1949. In France, they held a second marriage ceremony because Hitler had their original marriage license.

Diana published four books, including three that might be described as "memoir" and one biography about Wallis Simpson, the Duchess of Windsor, a close friend. Diana died at age ninety-three, following a stroke. A diamond swastika was found among her personal effects.

UNITY (1914–1948)

Unity was conceived at her parents' gold prospecting claim in (ironically) Swastika, Ontario. Unity's health never improved after her attempted suicide, and she remained incontinent and childlike until her death from pneumococcal meningitis at thirty-three. As the writer Jan Dalley said, "Unity found life in her big family very difficult because she came after these cleverer, prettier, more accomplished sisters."

JESSICA (1917–1996)

The hunger marches of the 1930s put young Decca on a path toward activism, and her raison d'être became to defeat Fascism at any cost.

Decca emigrated to the United States with her first husband in 1939, starting in Washington, DC, before ultimately moving to Oakland, California, where, as a young widow, she involved herself in left-wing politics. Decca trained people to organize at the California Labor School and was fiercely passionate about civil rights, which is how she met her second husband, attorney

Robert Treuhaft. Treuhaft ran a "radical" law firm that would one day employ an intern named Hillary Rodham.

Decca left the American Communist Party in 1958. In 1963, she published her hit exposé *The American Way of Death* and would go on to write many other books. She became a minor celebrity and was close friends with Maya Angelou.

Decca was the only sister who drank heavily and smoked, and she succumbed to lung cancer in 1996. True to her beliefs, she had a plain, low-cost funeral and a burial at sea. Ten years later, the writer J.K. Rowling would cite Jessica Mitford as "my most influential writer, without a doubt."

DEBORAH (1920–2014)

Debo's husband became heir to the Duke of Devonshire when his older brother, who was married to Kick Kennedy, died in combat. Debo's father-in-law passed in 1950, and her husband ascended to the dukedom, making Debo the Duchess of Devonshire. In their roles, she and Andrew received all the best invitations, from President Kennedy's inauguration to the wedding of Charles and Diana.

Debo gave birth to seven children, only three of whom survived infancy. Her third-born child, Peregrine, inherited the Duke of Devonshire title and is the owner of the Heywood Hill bookshop.

Like many of her sisters, Debo wrote several books, and she helped turn Chatsworth House into one of Britain's most successful stately homes. In 1999, she was appointed a Dame Commander of the Royal Victorian Order (DCVO) by Queen Elizabeth II, for her service to the Royal Collection Trust.

Debo died in 2014, at the age of ninety-four. It's believed she was the last living Briton to have met Hitler.

SELECTED LIST OF SOURCES

Acton, Harold. *Nancy Mitford: A Memoir.*

Beaton, Cecil Walter Hardy, Sir. *Memoirs of the 40's.*

Bloch, Michael. *James Lees-Milne: The Life.*

Cooper, Diana and Viscount John Julius Norwich. *Darling Monster: The Letters of Lady Diana Cooper to her Son John Julius Norwich 1939-1952.*

Dashwood, Francis, Sir, editor. *The Dashwoods of West Wycombe.*

De-la-Noy, Michael. *Eddy: The Life of Edward Sackville-West.*

Devonshire, Deborah Vivien Freeman–Mitford Cavendish. *Wait for Me!: Memoirs.*

Guinness, Jonathan and Catherine. *The House of Mitford.*

Hastings, Selina. *Evelyn Waugh.*

———. *Nancy Mitford.*

Henrey, Robert. *The Incredible City.*

———. *The Siege of London.*

Hill, Heywood. *A Bookseller's War.*

Hilton, Lisa. *The Horror of Love: Nancy Mitford and Gaston Palewski in Paris and London.*

Hutton, Mike. *Life in 1940s London.*

Lees-Milne, James. *Ancestral Voices.*

———. Diaries, 1942–1954.

Lovell, Mary S. *The Sisters: The Saga of the Mitford Family.*

Mitford, Jessica. *Decca: Hons and Rebels.*

Mitford, Nancy. *The Blessing.*

———. *The Bookshop at 10 Curzon Street: Letters Between Nancy Mitford and Heywood Hill.*

———. *Don't Tell Alfred.*

———. *Highland Fling.*

———. *Love from Nancy: The Letters of Nancy Mitford.*

———. *Love in a Cold Climate.*

———. *The Pursuit of Love.*

———. *Wigs on the Green.*

Mosley, Charlotte, editor. *The Letters of Nancy Mitford & Evelyn Waugh.*

———. *The Mitfords: Letters Between Six Sisters.*

Mosley, Diana. *A Life of Contrasts.*

———. *The Pursuit of Laughter.*

Sweet, Matthew. *The West End Front: The Wartime Secrets of London's Grand Hotels.*

Taylor, D.J. *The Lost Girls: Love and Literature in Wartime London.*

Thompson, Laura. *Love in a Cold Climate: Nancy Mitford, the Biography.*

————. *The Six: The Lives of the Mitford Sisters.*

Waugh, Evelyn. *The Diaries of Evelyn Waugh.*

READING GROUP GUIDE

1. Discuss the similarities between Katie's and Nancy's stories. How have society's expectations for women changed or not changed over the decades?

2. Which of Nancy's friends did you enjoy most? Why?

3. How much did you know about Nancy Mitford before reading the novel? Did you learn anything new or surprising about her or her family? Which Mitford family anecdote was your favorite?

4. For Katie, the Heywood Hill bookshop is the perfect escape from her troubles. If you could escape to anywhere in the world, where would you go?

5. Did you understand why Katie withheld her profession from Simon? Have you ever struggled to reconcile your personal and professional lives? Is it possible to keep them separate these days?

6. Discuss Nancy's decision to drop the memoir project in favor of what would become *The Pursuit of Love*. Did you think this was a wise choice given her family's notoriety? Should family stories remain private?

7. Did you agree with Felix's action at the end of the novel to protect Nancy's privacy? What role should famous

figures play after their deaths? Should their secrets stay secrets?

8. If you haven't already, will you be reading any of Nancy Mitford's novels in the future?